Sarah Julku

About the Author

JAMES L. NELSON has served as a seaman, rigger, boatswain, and officer on a number of sailing vessels. He is the author of *By Force of Arms*, *The Maddest Idea*, *The Continental Risque*, *Lords of the Ocean*, and *All the Brave Fellows*—the five books of his Revolution at Sea saga, as well as *The Guardship*, *The Blackbirder*, and *The Pirate Round*—the books of the Brethren of the Coast trilogy. He is also the author of the nonfiction book *Reign of Iron: The Story of the First Battling Ironclads*, the Monitor *and the* Merrimack. He lives with his wife and children in Harpswell, Maine. His website is found at www.jameslnelson.com.

GLORY IN THE NAME

A Novel of the Confederate Navy

James L. Nelson

Perennial

An Imprint of HarperCollinsPublishers

A hardcover edition of this book was published in 2003 by William Morrow, an imprint of HarperCollins Publishers.

HarperCollins books may be purchased for educational, business, or sales promotional use. For information please write: Special Markets Department, HarperCollins Publishers Inc., 10 East 53rd Street, New York, NY 10022.

First Perennial edition published 2004.

Designed by Bernard Klein

The Library of Congress has catalogued the hardcover edition as follows:

Nelson, James L.
Glory in the name : a novel of the Confederate Navy / James L. Nelson.
p. cm.
ISBN 0-06-019969-5
1. United States—History—Civil War, 1861–1865—Naval operations—Fiction.
2. Confederate States of America—History, Naval—Fiction. 3. Confederate States of America. Navy—Fiction. I. Title.

PS3564.E4646 G58 2003
813'.54—dc21   2002029568

ISBN 0-06-095905-3 (pbk.)

04 05 06 07 08 ❖/RRD 10 9 8 7 6 5 4 3 2 1

To Ed Donohoe—engineer, mariner, raconteur—in grateful
appreciation of your help and friendship

Acknowledgments

My deepest appreciation to Ed Donohoe, for sharing with me the accumulated knowledge of his many decades at sea, and his all-encompassing understanding of the ways of steam. Thanks to David Nelson for help with the music. My thanks to David Grene for all of his support from the beginning. I am grateful, and continue to be grateful, for all the support from David Semanki and Hugh Van Dusen at HarperCollins. And, as always, my thanks to Nat Sobel and all the kind people with him.

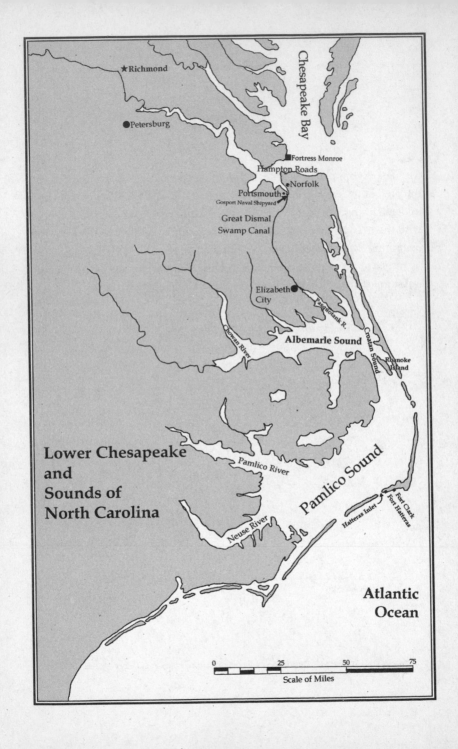

Richmond

Petersburg

Chesapeake Bay

Fortress Monroe

Hampton Roads

Portsmouth • Norfolk
Gosport Naval Shipyard

Great Dismal
Swamp Canal

Elizabeth
City

Pasquotank R.

Chowan River

Albemarle Sound

Croatan Sound

Roanoke
Island

Lower Chesapeake
and
Sounds of
North Carolina

Pamlico River

Pamlico Sound

Neuse River

Hatteras Inlet

Fort Clark
Fort Hatteras

Atlantic
Ocean

0   25   50   75

Scale of Miles

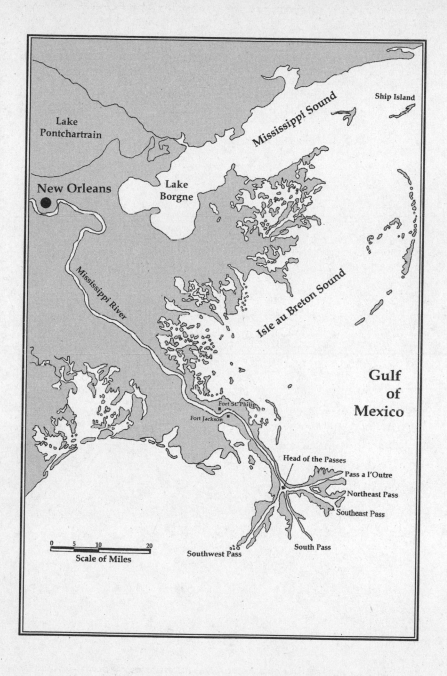

Lake Pontchartrain

New Orleans

Lake Borgne

Mississippi Sound

Ship Island

Mississippi River

Isle au Breton Sound

Gulf of Mexico

Fort St. Philip
Fort Jackson

Head of the Passes
Pass a l'Outre
Northeast Pass
Southeast Pass
South Pass
Southwest Pass

0   5   10   20
Scale of Miles

Then call us Rebels if you will
We glory in the name,
For bending under unjust laws
And swearing faith to an unjust cause,
We count as greater shame.

—*Richmond Daily Dispatch*, May 12, 1862

Book One

A THIMBLEFUL OF BLOOD

1

. . . [A]t twenty-five minutes past four o'clock A.M., the circle of batteries with which the grim fortress of Fort Sumter is beleaguered opened fire.

—Report of the *Charleston Press*

Oil on canvas, in his signature fine brushstroke, Samuel Bowater painted the opening shot of the War for Southern Independence.

He stood on a small, grassy rise at White Point Gardens at the very tip of Charleston, where the Cooper and Ashley rivers met. From there he looked out over the dark water of Charleston Harbor, six miles to the open ocean and the weak gray band of light in the east.

It was a cool morning, early April, and the damp found its way through his frock coat and the white linen shirt he wore under it. Civilian clothing, not nearly as warm as the uniform he was used to. A cloak coat was draped over his shoulders. He pulled it snug, rubbed his arms together, hunched his shoulders as he waited for the light to come up. The air smelled heavily of salt marsh and the smoke from early-morning fires wafting from chimneys. What sounds there were were muted and distant—birds and crickets, the lap of waves, the creaking of ships at the wharves.

Charleston was holding its breath. It had been for some time, since Anderson left Fort Moultrie for Sumter, and it could not continue to do so much longer.

In front of him, still lost in the predawn dark, the twenty-by-twenty-four-inch canvas on which he had been working for the past five mornings.

Samuel stared out past the black humps of land which were just becoming visible in the morning light, out toward the sea, where the growing dawn was beginning to bleach out the stars and the night sky.

He wanted to be ready for that moment when night yielded to dawn, when the daylight asserted itself and the tenor of everything changed. It was a moment he had witnessed a thousand times at sea, and now he wanted to re-create it on the canvas.

And then, right in front of him and four miles off, a sharp muzzle flash of red and orange, and lifting up from that flash, a long, hair-thin arc of light where the burning fuse of the shell tracked against the dark sky. Samuel Bowater swallowed, closed his eyes as the familiar flat *pow* of the distant artillery caught up with him.

It was followed immediately by another, and then the twin explosion of the shells.

So it shall be war . . .

It was a resolution, at least. For months Bowater had been knocked about by the crosscurrent of speculation and rumor; the likelihood of peace, then the near certainty of war, then back again. Now, with the single jerk of a cannon's lanyard, the question was decided.

Morris Island, he thought. The shot had come from Morris Island. Stevens's Iron Battery.

Samuel Bowater, thirty-three years of age, lieutenant, United States Navy, on extended leave, had been kicking around his hometown of Charleston for months with little to do. He had come to know the harbor defenses well.

It would be days before he learned that the honor of firing that first shot had been offered to Congressman Roger Pryor of Virginia. That Pryor, understanding as Bowater did the enormity of the act, could not bring himself to pull the lanyard.

It would be a long four years before he read that the man who did finally discharge that shot, Edmund Ruffin, put a gun to his head rather than suffer the unbearable burden of a lost cause.

But that was in the future.

Samuel opened his eyes.

From all around Charleston Harbor, from Fort Moultrie and Stevens's Iron Battery, the Floating Battery, and the Dahlgren Battery, the Enfilade Battery and Major Trapier's Battery and Fort Johnson, the guns opened up on the sixty-eight Union troops huddled in Fort Sumter. The dark harbor was ringed with flashes of light, the bombardment so insistent that in some places it looked as if the shore had taken fire, and the bright trails crisscrossed the sky.

It was an awesome sight, beautiful and terrible at the same time. But in his mind Samuel Bowater saw only that first flash, that first arch of light.

The sky was growing rapidly brighter, and Samuel picked up his thinnest brush. He angled his paint kit toward the east, found the tube of cadmium yellow, squeezed a pea-sized drop on his palette. He stood back, but it was not yet light enough for him to see the canvas. He picked up the easel, turned it so the gray dawn light fell on the painting.

He took one last look at the harbor, the flames from the guns' muzzles, the streaks through the air like a hundred falling stars, and now the bright flash and deep rumble of shells that found Fort Sumter and exploded against its twelve-foot-thick walls.

Samuel turned back to the canvas. He dabbed the brush in the yellow paint, sighed, touched the sharp pointed bristles to the canvas right at Morris Island, and made a little slash of light, up and off to the left.

He squeezed yellow ocher onto the palette, augmented the yellow on the canvas, and then added red, blending the colors until he had the subtle multihues of a muzzle flash, as he himself had seen it that morning and so many times before.

He stood back, dabbed the cadmium yellow again, took a deep breath. One stroke to paint the trail of the shell's fuse, but it had to be perfect. He moved his hand over the canvas, the brush less than an inch from the surface, practicing the trajectory.

The dull sounds of the ceaseless bombardment surrounded him like a soft gray blanket of noise. And below that sound he heard another—cheering, shouting from the rooftops and along the harbor walls and from the ships tied up to their docks—but like the gunfire he was hardly aware of it. He was no longer in that scene, he was completely in his canvas. The painting was his world and he was aware of no other.

Slash, slash, and then the tip of the brush came down on the canvas and a long, arching yellow streak cut across the oil sky, reaching its apex and dropping toward the small hump that was Fort Sumter.

Samuel Bowater stepped back, let out his breath, took in the canvas as a whole.

Perfect. It was just as he had seen it. Now, regardless of what happened next, of what he saw in the years to come, of how his memory of that morning was polluted by the dubious influences to which memory is susceptible, regardless, that moment was captured forever in oil.

He pulled his eyes at last from his canvas. A dozen people had joined him on his grassy rise, pointing toward the batteries and whooping and shouting and carrying on without the least shred of dignity, and more were hurrying toward them.

They had come to gawk, while Bowater had come to paint. He frowned at the intrusion, disapproved of the sentiment that made those civilians come running as if this act of war was a burlesque. Under his own strict code, he would not consider indulging his curiosity in so crass a way.

Samuel turned back to the action in the harbor.

The sun was up, dull yellow behind the veil of thin clouds, and the muzzle flashes and the streaks from the flying shells were not nearly so bright. But the sound was a continuous rumble now, and the gray clouds of smoke hung like morning mist over the batteries.

The smell of gun smoke reached the city at last. Samuel took a deep breath, and with that smell a thousand memories came back. Until he had taken leave of the navy five months before, there was rarely a day that passed that he did not smell it.

He shook his head as he watched the barrage that was being released on Fort Sumter. Those walls might well have collapsed by now, he thought, if they had been built by anyone other than the government of the United States. Bowater had not seen anything like it, not for fourteen years, not since the Mexican War, when, as an ensign fresh out of the Naval School at Annapolis, he had participated in the shelling of Veracruz.

For some long time he watched in silence and tried to fathom what this meant for him, but it was so very complicated and the gunfire was so murderous and the shouts of the people on the rise so distracting that he could not think.

Sumter has not fired back. He wondered if they had surrendered. The rumor was that they were nearly out of provisions, that bombardment or no they could not remain long on that little island.

Samuel picked up his haversack and stuck his hand inside, felt the cool brass of his telescope. He pulled it out, let the haversack fall. He snapped it out full length, brought it up to his eye, fixed Fort Sumter in the lens.

There it was, undulating in the light offshore breeze. The Stars and Stripes.

Oh, say can you see . . . Samuel thought of the words to that popular song. A circumstance just like this, when it was written, but then at least the flag stood against a foreign enemy, all of the United States battling their common foe.

He took the glass from his eye, snapped it shut. *Always hated that song, mawkish, overwrought sentimentality.* . . .

The bombardment had settled into a steady monotony. Samuel stared at his canvas, crossed his arms, rested his chin in one hand, stroked his perfectly groomed mustache and goatee, and considered what he had done.

Over the past five days he had worked on the sky and the distant land, filling the canvas with rich purples and greens and oranges, creating a lush early-morning scene.

Talk about mawkish, overwrought sentimentality,. . . .

He had been trying to eschew the silly romanticism of the Hudson River School, of Washington Allston—revered in South Carolina—of Thomas Cole and that lot. He had failed.

Samuel scowled at the canvas, squeezed a bit of blue and black on his palette, swirled it together. *Get rid of some of this purple . . .* he thought.

With delicate strokes, like fingers on a lover's cheek, he applied the paint to the top of the canvas, recreating the dark fringes of the western morning sky. He lost himself in the work, and the morning hours and the drama before him faded away as he got inside the painting, becoming part of its reality and dabbing away in an effort to make it reflect the reality he saw and felt.

After some time he heard footsteps behind him, on the soft grass. He felt his stiletto-sharp concentration waver, and he cursed under his breath. He waited for the stranger to come up, look over his shoulder, make some comment. Every passing philistine felt welcome, almost obliged, to look and comment.

Sometimes they would make a noncommittal grunt, sometimes say a word or two. Sometimes they would praise his work, which was the worst. Bowater could not tolerate praise coming from someone unqualified to give it, which was just about everybody.

The footsteps stopped. Samuel could feel the presence of someone behind. He braced. A woman's hand reached past his arm, pointed to the American flag, a tiny spot of red, white, and blue he had painted over Sumter.

"May as well paint that right out," his sister said.

"Are you a secessionist, now, Elizabeth?"

"I always have been, brother. Sitting on a fence is unladylike. But more to the point, has this gunfire knocked you off? And if so, on which side have you fallen?"

Samuel had joined the navy, entered as midshipman at the Naval School—now the Academy—at seventeen, driven by his father's urging and a love for the sea with which he was born, as much as he was born with arms and legs and brown eyes.

With the one exception of the Mexican War at the very beginning of his career, Samuel Bowater's time in the navy had been largely uneventful. For the past decade everyone's career in the somnambulant United States Navy had been largely uneventful. But that was over. And service in the United States Navy was over for him.

"In any event, Colonel Chesnut says not a thimbleful of blood will be shed in this war," Elizabeth said.

"Indeed."

The garrison at Fort Sumter was firing back now, stabs of flame just visible as they shot out from the gray walls of the fort. Heroic, futile defiance. Not the sort of action that would lead to a bloodless revolution.

Samuel Bowater had not thought much about any of the questions that were tearing the nation apart, questions of sovereignty and the permanence of Union, questions of slavery. He was of the navy, half of the past fourteen years he had spent in foreign service, where his only connection to his home was his fellow officers, most of whom were Yankees, and the Stars and Stripes flying at the gaff.

Samuel Bowater was a man of the sea and he did not give a damn what happened in Kansas or Nebraska or Missouri. It was all very abstract to him, very theoretical, like a discussion of the latest elections in England or the uprisings in Germany. The United States Navy was what he knew and loved. And now he would have to reject it, and fight against it.

Samuel had joined the navy, but he had been born to South Carolina, and in the end he knew where his loyalty lay. He knew that he did not care for the Yankees deciding any question that related to his beloved state. But he could not hate the Yankees as so many of his fellow Southerners did. He had messed with too many of them.

The gunfire continued without letup. It was nearing noon and the barrage had not slackened in the least since that first shot at four-thirty. Bowater was terribly hungry.

"I think perhaps it is time to go home," Samuel said. He cleaned his brushes and carefully packed his paint kit. He treated it with such care that it looked exactly as it had the day he bought it. Other painters wore special smocks to protect their clothes, which always seemed foolish to Samuel. If you were careful, you did not need a smock. There was no excuse for splattering paint on your clothes.

He took the canvas off the easel and leaned it against his haversack and folded the easel up.

He looked up, and his eye caught a cluster of dark shapes on the horizon. Ships, though a less experienced eye might not have recognized them as such, or might not have seen them at all.

Samuel fished his telescope out again, trained it on the distant vessels. Men-of-war, Union ships. They were just outside the harbor entrance, a good five miles off, but he thought that he recognized the profile of the twin-screw steamer USS *Pawnee*. She was less than a year old, but he had seen her often enough for her profile to be familiar.

In company with her he recognized the *Harriet Lane* and a steamer that he did not know. An expeditionary force, no doubt sent for the relief of Fort Sumter. He shook his head. "Too damned late," he said. "The war has started without you."

2

*The streets of Charleston present some such aspect as those of Paris in the last
revolution. Crowds of armed men singing and promenading through the streets,
the battle blood running through their veins . . .*

—William Russell, London *Times*

$\mathcal{S}$ amuel and Elizabeth Bowater left White Point Gardens and
walked through a Charleston that Samuel had never seen, a jubilant, ec-
static, self-congratulatory Charleston. There was a universal joy and
goodwill; it was Christmas and Easter and the Fourth of July, and many
times more than that.

Sumter was fired upon. The waiting was over, the war had commenced. South Carolina, leader in secession, was the leader in the
fight. Now that powder was burning, those states of the upper South—
sister North Carolina, Virginia, Maryland, Kentucky, Tennessee,
Arkansas, and Missouri—had to secede and then join in with the Confederacy. Now there was only to lick the Yankees and the South would
be free.

Samuel was not immune to this mood, not entirely, though he found
the crowd's enthusiasm cheap and facile. Still, there was a new liveliness
to his step, and he returned enthusiastic waves of greeting with a smile
and a broad gesture, whereas just the day before he would have frowned
and given a halfhearted shake of his hand.

"I don't recall ever seeing you so enthusiastic, brother," Elizabeth said.

"I am not made of stone, my dear," Samuel said. He thought of their father. There was a man made of stone. He was not like that. "At least I am not treating the event like a circus come to town."

"No? I could swear I caught you down at the Gardens, gawking like one of the mob."

"I was painting, I was most certainly not gawking," Samuel replied, but his sister's implication rattled him. She was good at rattling him, always had been.

They walked on, and Samuel's thoughts returned to the firing on Sumter, and with that thought his good mood returned. The waiting was over, the torment of indecision. He was not happy about war, had not wanted it. The United States Navy was his life. He had sworn an oath. No event short of his beloved South Carolina's taking up arms against the United States could have moved him to break that oath. So he had waited, and suffered the suspicions of both sides.

They walked down King Street, shouldering through the crowds. All of Charleston was in the streets, and Samuel caught snatches of conversation as he passed, men bragging on what they would do in the upcoming fight, women adding to their bravado, or speaking in fearful tones, or gushing about the strength of Southern arms. He heard the word "honor" punctuating conversations like an exclamation point, and "Yankee" and "Black Republican"; it all swirled together in a patriotic gumbo.

They came at last to the Bowater house, three stories of brick walls and white-painted window frames and green ivy, standing shoulder to shoulder with the other fine homes on Tradd Street. A sign over a side door proclaimed, "William Bowater, Esq., Attorney at Law."

It was the only home that Samuel had ever known, the only place he had ever lived besides the dormitories of the Naval School and the wardrooms of various ships. It was the place where Samuel had grown to manhood under his father's seemingly omniscient eye, his unwavering rule.

It was where Samuel had learned to be a gentleman, and, more to the point, a Southern gentleman. Courteous to the last. Studied, urbane. Personally disciplined—a gentleman, he was taught, did not show womanly weakness of any sort. Passionately loyal to his country and his state. Unwilling to suffer even the hint of insult. Tolerant of the lower classes, appreciative, even, of their labor, but always aware of their place, and his. Kind to slaves. These were the things that made the Southern man, and the instruction was so thorough that those traits became a part of Samuel Bowater as much as his height and the color of his eyes.

They climbed the stairs, brother and sister, and crossed the porch, and Samuel pushed open the big front door. It opened onto an expansive foyer, at the far end of which was the wide staircase to the second floor.

The floor was tiled, white-and-black checkerboard. A deep brown, ornately carved Venezuelan ironwood table sat to the right of the door. Samuel had brought it back from Caracas following a cruise in South America.

Samuel had not yet closed the door when Isaac appeared, his dark face—nearly the color of the ironwood table—showing no hint of interest in the commotion going on in the streets.

"Here, Isaac." Samuel handed the black man his haversack and easel and paint kit.

"How da paintin' go today, Misser Samuel?" Isaac asked. Samuel held up the canvas for the servant to inspect.

"Ain't dat somethin'?" Isaac said. It was what he always said. Samuel considered it one of the more insightful comments he received.

"Samuel?" His mother's voice came from the sitting room off to the right, a lovely, strong voice with just a hint of her native Ireland. There was a rustle of crinoline and silk, the tap of shoes on the marble floor, and the heavier footfalls of his father.

"Samuel!" His mother, Rachel, raced out into the foyer, his father right behind. "Oh, Samuel, have you been down to the harbor?"

His mother, at fifty-four, was still a beauty, with her once black hair now showing signs of gray, her strong features emboldened with tiny lines around her eyes and mouth. She came up to him, put her hands on his arms. "You are all right?"

"It was a near thing, Mother. I almost stabbed myself in the eye with my paintbrush. But my dear sister was there to see I came to no grief."

"Our Michelangelo was well out of the way of the flying metal, Mother."

Over his mother's shoulder Samuel met his father's eyes. He wore a vest and bow tie, as he did every day of his life, as far as Samuel could recall, and his white hair and beard were as perfectly groomed as Samuel's dark brown hair and goatee. "What news, son?"

"Stevens's Iron Battery at Morris Island opened up just at dawn, and the rest right after that. The firing has been continuous since. There was a relief squadron in the offing. *Pawnee* and *Harriet Lane*, looked like, but they'll never dare come in now."

"Sumter still stands?"

"For the time being. Not for much longer."

William Bowater nodded.

"You are only people in all Charleston not in the streets, I reckon," Samuel observed. He knew that his father, like himself, thought the gawking crowd unseemly.

"Let us retire from here," William suggested, and the party moved *en masse* from the foyer to the big, open drawing room. Through the tall windows they could see throngs in the streets. The jubilation seemed to reach through the glass, to sweep the elegant room and its occupants along with it. The excitement was like the odor of spent gunpowder that drifted over the city, ubiquitous, invading every space, wrapping itself around every person.

"Isaac, coffee," William called as he sat in the big wing chair, the patriarch chair, and turned to Samuel. "I would say this is war, son. What will you do now?"

Samuel let out a breath. He had no notion of what his father, a staunch secessionist, thought of his long resistance to joining the Confederate forces. His father was a lawyer—his feelings were not easily read—and he was a gentleman, so he did not impose those feelings on others. He and Samuel talked at length about politics. They did not talk about emotions.

"I had hoped it would not come to this, I won't pretend differently," Samuel said. "I swore an oath to the United States, once. But it is war, as you say, and now my duty is clear."

Isaac came in with the silver tray. He poured the coffee, added sugar and cream to each individual preference, and handed out the bone china cups.

William Bowater balanced his cup and saucer on his knee. "You are resolved, then, to fight for the Confederacy?"

"It is my duty. Honor demands it. But it was not an easy thing, Father, not at all."

It was not an easy thing.

Samuel Bowater viewed South Carolina as the hub of all that was civilized and proper in America. When he thought of the Yankees coming, of the low, dirty mechanics and foreign-born plug-uglies, the dried-up abolitionists in their black clothing, the fast-talking, haughty New Yorkers running unchecked through his beloved Charleston, lording over his fellow Southrons, it made him angry in a way that surprised him.

They were the unwashed, battering down the gate to his shining city, the Persians coming to topple his perfect Athens. It was silly, of course. He knew plenty of Yankees, had been shipmates with them, and they were fine men. But somehow those men with whom he had sailed were not the same as the infidels who were coming to destroy his cherished South Carolina.

"No," William Bowater said, "I should think it is not an easy thing at all. For thoughtful men it cannot be an easy decision," and for the first time Samuel believed he heard a note of approval in his father's voice. "Will you apply to the navy?"

"The navy is all I know. But there are plenty of naval officers who have not been sitting on the fence, and I fear the available berths have gone to them. There can't be but a dozen or so ships in the whole Confederate Navy."

Samuel was being generous, and he knew it, referring to the ragtag collection of tugs and paddle wheelers and sundry craft as "ships." If there was no navy, he did not know what he would do. Join the army, perhaps, but what good could he be to an army?

"Perhaps it is too late, perhaps not," William Bowater said. "I think your action in the Mexican War has not been forgotten."

Samuel tried to wave the comment away. A stupid, rash move, a burst of youthful enthusiasm, more than a dozen years ago. By some miracle he managed to rescue a few dozen sailors when by all rights they should have been dead, along with himself and his crew. It had been a foolish act, but since he lived it was viewed as heroism.

"What is more," William added, "Stephen Mallory and I are acquaintances, I might venture to say friends."

"I had no idea," said Samuel. Stephen Mallory was a former senator from Florida, former chairman of the United States Senate's Committee on Naval Affairs, and, as of February, Secretary of the Navy of the Confederate States.

"We had occasion to work together on a matter concerning a merchantman belonging to a client of mine wrecked on Key West," William said. "We only met twice, but have kept up our correspondence, even to this day. If you like I will write you a letter of introduction."

"Yes, if you think it proper."

"I will do no more than attest to your character. The rest is between you and Mallory."

"I would expect no more." Samuel felt his mood buoyed by the promise of action. Not combat—he was a long way from that—but something, anything beyond the purgatory of indecision to which he had condemned himself.

After more than a decade in the United States Navy, where action and promotion were equally unlikely, where discipline and protocol were maintained out of habit and not out of any pressing need, the idea of an upstart navy was refreshing. Better to play at David, with blood pumping in his veins, than be a sleepwalking Goliath. He was eager to be at it.

"I will leave tomorrow for Montgomery," Samuel announced, even as he reached the decision himself. "Isaac, fetch Jacob."

Jacob stepped into the room. He was the son of Isaac and Isabella, the Bowaters' cook, had been Samuel's servant for the past seventeen years, since Samuel had turned sixteen. Aboard the *Pensacola* he had acted as Samuel's cabin steward, and had handled rammer and swab on the starboard midships thirty-two-pounder while at quarters.

"Jacob, I'll be off to Montgomery in the morning. Pray pack my bag. I imagine I shall be away a week or so."

"Yes, Misser Samuel. I's goin' with you?"

"No, I think not."

"Yessuh," he said and was gone.

"Dear Lord, but I am famished!" Samuel announced. "Is dinner not yet served?" He had not felt so sharp an appetite for months.

3

I shall never forget that beautiful day, and how elated I was, marching down the street while the band played "The Bonnie Blue Flag" and "Dixie." Thousands were on the sidewalks, cheering and waving handkerchiefs. Some were crying, and of course it never occurred to me that many of us would never see those dear friends and neighbors again.

—Private George Gibbs, 18th Mississippi Infantry

The late-afternoon light was muted and soft and the breeze had died away and the warm ground gave off its smell of early spring. The Yazoo River moved slowly down to its rendezvous with the Mississippi, where together they would flow to the sea. But all of the earth's somnambulant pace could not smother the excitement that rang through the halls and fields of Paine Plantation.

Robley Paine, owner of the plantation, patriarch of the family, stood on the wide porch, under the roof painted light blue on the underside to mimic the summer sky. One hand on the brilliant white porch rail, he stared out at the vast green lawn which rolled down to the Yazoo River, the grass as smooth and flat as the water, with only the one old oak to break the straight run from porch to river.

Paine Plantation, all nine hundred acres of it, was just south of Drumgould's Bluff, on one of the rare straight stretches of the twisty Yazoo. From northeast to southwest the river ran like a great corridor though the green, fertile country of western Mississippi, past countless fields of cotton, cotton, cotton, the currency of the South.

Cotton was to the Southern man what the buffalo was to the Plains Indian, and Robley figured that if cotton could migrate, then the Southerners would pick up and follow after it.

A shout from inside the house, and Robley was pulled from his thoughts by the commanding voice of his oldest boy, Robley Paine, Jr., ordering, "You give me back that gun, now!"

Robley Junior was a venerable twenty-two and took his leadership and manhood seriously.

"Yassa, General, suh!" the higher-pitched voice of Jonathan Paine, third and youngest son, eighteen years old. Paine smiled and shook his head. How ever would those three boys manage under the real discipline of army life? They had lived their wild, rambunctious, and carefree youths there on that plantation, on the banks of that river. They had grown to manhood under Robley's eye, Robley's none-to-firm hand.

He would not crush the joy from them, as his father had done to him, just for the sake of making them strong. Robley was strong, and he reckoned he would have been strong even without the sermons, the beatings. Stronger, most likely. He probably would not have the brittle feeling inside him, as if his soul was a skim of ice on a water trough in early winter.

Robley Paine had let his boys run their heedless way, let them suck the joy out of every moment of their youth. Despite the disapproval of his fellow planters, all the head-shaking and tongue-clicking over the subject of his easy parenting, he gave them little by way of discipline. Just his quiet instruction and his love, and that he gave unstintingly.

And for all the predictions of worthlessness and profligacy, his boys, Robley, Nathaniel, and Jonathan, had grown to fine and honorable young men.

Robley Paine, Jr., was talking again, in his officer's voice. "Git your goddamn gear on, and be quick about it!"

He was now, informally, Lieutenant Robley Paine, Mississippi Infantry. The young men of Mississippi were responding to their state's call to arms. From Ocean Springs and Amite and Covington and Pike, from Marshall County and Carrol County and Clark County and from Yazoo, from every town and county in the state, young men were becoming young soldiers.

In Yazoo they were signing on under the captaincy of Clarence F. Hamer, who, until just weeks before, had been a lawyer in Yazoo City. Though there was nothing yet official, Robley had been appointed to the rank of lieutenant. That rank was the result not of family influence or money, but rather of the acclamation of his fellow soldiers.

Unfortunately for him, his younger brothers did not appreciate, as he did, his importance and position.

"Y'all wanna miss the whole damned war?"

Robley Senior frowned and shook his head. *Such language.* The boy thought it made him sound more like a soldier and a man.

Under the oak tree the two dozen other young men assembled there looked up at the sound of Robley Junior's voice. Like the three Paine boys, they were the sons of the planters that lived pressed against the Yazoo River. Like all the sons of the wealthy plantation owners, who had grown up to understand that they must serve honor as faithfully as they would serve God, they had flocked to join the new-formed Confederate Army of Mississippi.

Like his boys, Robley reckoned, they all had fathers both proud and sick with fear.

The boys had been gathering all day under the big oak at the Paine plantation. Now they were all there, twenty-four young men, and soon Lieutenant Paine would lead them up to Yazoo City, where they would join the rest of their regiment. From Yazoo City they would travel by steamer to Vicksburg, then by train to Jackson, where they would begin to learn the art of soldiering.

Robley smiled. To listen to them and their pontificating you might think they were already veterans of years of bloody fighting. They dis cussed war the way they discussed the young ladies: high talk and great bravado based on an absolute dearth of practical experience.

He heard shoes in the hallway and turned, and the door opened and his boys joined him on the porch. His heart lifted to see them; tall and strong, handsome, smiling boys. Jonathan and Nathaniel wore identical gray shell jackets, Robley Junior a gray frock coat with a single second lieutenant's stripe on the collar. They wore gray trousers and kepis tilted back at a jaunty angle—save for Lieutenant Paine, who wore his perfectly horizontal.

Each jacket sported a single row of brass buttons with a star in the middle and the word "Mississippi" surrounding it. The buttons ran down the front of their jackets and held them snug against their strong, lean forms. They had slung over their shoulders cartridge boxes and canteens and haversacks, and they carried knapsacks on their backs. They clutched their shiny new .58-caliber Mississippi rifles. They smiled as if setting off for a great camping trip.

Robley Paine ran his eyes over each grinning boy and he smiled as well. They looked like window displays for a shop selling soldiering gear. "I'm proud of you boys," he said.

"Thank you, Father, thank you," they mumbled, embarrassed, trying to be weighty and sincere. They were too young to understand the depths of a father's love, so he let it go at that.

Robley Paine, Sr., was a passionate secessionist, what the papers liked to call a fire-eater. As a senator in Jackson he had been calling for Southern independence since long before it became the fashion to do so.

Paine loved his nation, his new nation, the Confederate States of America. There was nothing, save for his boys, that he loved more. And now the one love was demanding the sacrifice of the other. It was Abraham and Isaac, to the third power.

"Y'all write your mother, you hear?"

"Yes, Father . . ." The boys were glancing over at their comrades, who were standing and adjusting themselves for the march. The Paine boys were eager to be at it. They were afraid their father would do something embarrassing, such as hug them. Robley understood that, and desperate as he was to embrace each of his boys, to never let go of them, instead he thrust out his hand and gave each a manly shake.

"Very well, then. Off with you," he said and managed something of a smile.

Robley Junior, Nathaniel, and Jonathan clumped down the stairs to the lawn and over to where their fellows were clustered in the shade under the big oak. It was a massive tree, hundreds of years old and easily seven feet wide at the base. Twelve feet up the trunk, two huge limbs thrust out at right angles. From the river, looking back at the house, the tree seemed to be welcoming with arms spread, ready to embrace anyone tramping up the lawn toward the Paine home. Robley loved the tree and its insinuation of hospitality.

"All right, y'all, form up, now," Lieutenant Paine was saying, and Robley was happy to see that the boys were obeying, after a fashion. His son had a lot to learn about command, but Paine did not want to see the boy's authority questioned now, at the very outset of his military career.

The door opened again and Katherine Paine, his wife, the boys' mother, joined him, and he put his arm around her. Her eyes were red and her eyelids swollen. He had thought she would not join him, did not think she could stand to see her boys, her only children, marching off to war.

The young soldiers formed up, and with Lieutenant Paine in the lead began to walk off toward Yazoo City. They made a lovely sight in the warm sunlight of the late afternoon. Jonathan turned and in a very unsoldierlike manner grinned and waved, and Robley and Katherine waved back and a little sob came up from Katherine's throat.

All these young men . . . Robley thought. *The finest of all of us are marched off to die.*

The boys' feet raised little clouds of dust as they moved off the lawn and onto the dirt path that would meet with the road that ran from Vicksburg to Yazoo City and on which the Paine plantation was situated.

We don't send our best horses to become food for dogs, we don't feed the best of our crops to the pigs . . . why do we send the best of our future off to fight?

It was not an original thought, Paine understood that, but that did not make it any less true. *We should send broken old men like me to the fight, and leave the young and the strong to rebuild when we are done.* It all seemed very backward to him. But Robley Paine, Sr., had taken a bullet in the leg during the Mexican War, and that made marching even to Yazoo City out of the question, and so he could do no more than outfit his progeny and send them off.

The gray-clad, well-equipped troops marched out of sight. Katherine buried her face against his arm, and he could feel her body shake as she tried to subdue her sorrow. It was the duty of a Southern woman to send her boys off to defend their nation, but she was a mother first, a Southern woman second.

Robley squeezed her tight. It was hardest for the mothers, he knew. Fathers understood in their guts why their sons could not remain safe at home while others fought. Young men took up arms and young ladies were flush with romantic talk of soldiers, and full of scorn for those not in uniform.

But for the mothers, there was nothing, save anxiety and grief.

He pressed his cheek into Katherine's hair and looked out past the massive oak, down to the Yazoo River. He had always thought of that river as a moat, as a watery defensive line that kept his home and his beloved family safe from whatever was out there. He loved that river.

And now as he stared at it he allowed himself to wish that it really was a moat, some impassable barrier which the filthy Yankee hordes could not cross. They would stand on the other side and howl and wave their arms and throw stones, but Robley and his family and his new nation would be safe on this side, and they could go about their business unmolested until the Yankees tired of their fruitless effort and went home.

But the Yazoo was too far south to protect all of his nation, and it was not a moat in any event. And now his boys, his Robley, his Nathaniel, his Jonathan, were marching away, leaving the safety of the river, the welcoming arms of the big oak.

This war will not last, Robley thought, not for the first time. *Be over before those boys reach the lines. Going to war is not the same as being sentenced to death. Odds are they'll come back without a scratch.* That thought had brought him comfort once, but it did little for him now.

His boys were going where he could not protect them anymore. It made him sad and filled him with dread, and he felt the tears coming too.

4

The Charleston Mercury

BOMBARDMENT
OF
FORT SUMTER!

Splendid Pyrotechnic Exhibition

FORT MOULTRIE
IMPREGNABLE

THE FLOATING BATTERY
AND
Stevens' Battery a Success,

"Nobody Hurt" on Our Side.
ETC., ETC., ETC.

We stated yesterday, that on Thursday, at three o'clock p.m., General Beauregard had made a demand upon Major Anderson for the evacuation of Fort Sumter through his aides, Colonel Chesnut, Captain Lee and Colonel Chisholm . . .

Bowater read the newspaper account, but he did not witness the final act.

Even as General Pierre G.T. Beauregard was issuing the conditions for the surrender of Fort Sumter, Samuel stood on the platform above the tracks at the central depot of the Charleston railroad. He stood with carpet bag in one hand, the folded *Charleston Mercury* in the other, trying to read as the swarming crowd jostled him, knocked into him, excused itself as it brushed past.

All of Charleston was in a hurry. For no rational reason that Samuel could divine, the tempo of the whole city had changed. It was like the sensation of a ship building momentum, the massive vessel gaining speed, becoming more unstoppable, after one has called down to the engine room for more steam. Did the firing on Sumter mean for all these people what it meant for him? He could not imagine.

. . . and that Major Anderson had regretfully declined, under the circumstances of his position, Samuel read, and then a handsome gentleman in the gray coat of a Confederate officer, stripes and swirls of gold on his cuffs, slammed into him so hard that he dropped the paper.

"My apologies, sir," the officer said, stooped, retrieved the paper, handed it to Samuel, and disappeared into the crowd.

Samuel sighed, muttered under his breath. He looked down at the paper. The right-hand side of the front page consisted of three columns of advertisements for Haviland's Compound Fluid Extract of Buchu, Compound Fluid Extract of Sarsaparilla, Hembold's Genuine Preparation for the Bladder, Moffat's Life Pills. Here, the most momentous event in half a century, and the quackery and charlatanism went on and on. It shared the headlines with the first shots of civil war, as many thought they might prove to be.

Samuel shook his head, smoothed his black frock coat, resettled the tall silk hat.

He had considered wearing his uniform, wondered at the appropriateness, even the common sense, of appearing in public in the uniform of a lieutenant of the United States Navy. Probably not a very good idea, but still he was torn. It did not seem right to go on this official business in civilian dress.

He had laid the blue uniform coat out on his bed and spent some long time looking at it; running his eyes over the gold stripes and star on the cuff, the double row of brass buttons with their eagle design. For all the moral certainty he felt about joining with the Confederacy, he could not deny the sadness as he hung the blue broadcloth up in his wardrobe and removed the black frock coat he wore now.

There was something clean and precise about the navy, stolid and predictable. Going aboard a strange vessel, you knew beforehand exactly what your greeting would be, because the protocol was written in hundreds of years of naval tradition and spelled out plain in the Articles of War. You knew that the ship would be in perfect order, clean and tidy, the men respectful. There was an orderliness to the navy that any other life could not hope to achieve, and Samuel Bowater liked it.

He called to Jacob to have the frock coat pressed, then sat down and addressed a letter of resignation to Gideon Welles, Lincoln's Secretary of the Navy.

The distant chugging of the steam locomotive grew louder, and the platform beneath his feet began to vibrate and the train appeared down the track. Four hundred miles to Montgomery over the rough and unreliable rails of the South, and Samuel Bowater was not looking forward to the trip.

The train came to a huffing stop at the platform. The cars were nearly empty. Charleston was the point of origin for the westbound train, which would call in at Atlanta, where Samuel would change to another bound for the Confederate capital. He doubted he would enjoy the luxury of near-empty cars for long. They would be half filled by the people on that platform alone.

He pushed his way through the crowd, bag in hand, made his way, step by step, aboard the nearest car. He stowed the bag and pulled his handkerchief from his breast pocket and deftly wiped the seat before sitting.

There was little he hated more than idle talk foisted on him by some cretinous stranger, so he tried to make himself look as inhospitable as he could, to discourage anyone from sitting beside him. He was successful, and twenty minutes later the train lurched away from the station with Samuel Bowater happily alone on the nearly straight-backed benchlike seat.

The miles passed by. Samuel rattled and shook and stared out the window as the train rolled through the western country of South Carolina. They rumbled through the tidewater region, wheezed and hissed up into the Piedmont, screeched and lurched across the state line into Georgia. With each stop the car grew more crowded as the train picked up more and more people, like a snowball rolling toward Atlanta.

It was a mixed crowd; workingmen and men in frock coats and silk hats, women in sensible traveling attire, people whose wealth was obvious, and people who tried to make their wealth obvious, rough-looking men in fine clothing, who had made their fortunes in the slave trade or supplying the western regions.

There were pious-looking men and men who drank and cursed and spit tobacco and played cards at the small tables scattered around the car.

There were women who looked to their men to protect their virtue and women who looked to offer their virtue for sale.

And there were soldiers. Most of the military men still wore the uniform of their local militia, and since there had never been any sort of standard, the car looked like a convention of armed forces from the world over. The air was thick with opinions.

Samuel listened in silence and stared out the window and later tried to lose himself in Alexis de Tocqueville's *Democracy in America*, until he decided that the man was insufferable in the way that only the French can be. He tossed the book back into his carpet bag.

It was late evening when he arrived at Atlanta and carried his bag across the depot to the train bound for Montgomery.

He was not greeted by a near-empty car this time. Montgomery was the seat of Southern government, and every office-seeker and aspirant to military command and every other Southron who felt he had something of importance to add to the Southern cause was descending on that formerly inauspicious town. Their name was legion and they were, by Samuel's estimate, all jammed onto the train that he was trying to board.

He managed at last to push his way onto the penultimate car. He was bumped hard as he pulled his handkerchief but still managed to wipe a seat and settle himself, and soon the train was underway. The smell of close-packed men, all in low conversation, the sound of chewing and spitting tobacco, the rhythmic motion of the car, the smell of coal smoke drifting in through the windows—it was all like being back aboard a man-of-war, though considerably less pleasant.

Samuel slept and woke and stood and stretched and sat and fumed all through the rocking, jerking, loud, uncomfortable night. It was well past dawn when the train came to a ragged halt at the main depot in Montgomery and Bowater secured a black porter with ragged trousers and an old wide-awake on his head to carry his bag in a barrow.

They walked down the wide, sandy main street. Samuel had been to Montgomery only once before, a decade ago, and it was more built-up and crowded than he recalled. Trees and buildings of various height and description lined the street, and in the distance the Alabama River moved slowly between its brown banks. The huge capitol building loomed over all, like a magnificent Greek temple on a hill, Alabama's own Parthenon.

Bowater arrived at last at the Exchange Hotel, where he intended to stay, on his father's recommendation, and with the use of his father's name he was able to secure a room, despite the mass of people crowding the place, and, indeed, crowding all of Montgomery.

Once in his room, Samuel unpacked, then washed up in the basin standing in a corner. The water was tepid but it felt utterly refreshing, splashed on his face and run through his hair. He was exhausted from the trip, but far too excited to sleep. He stepped out into the hot, dusty late morning, made his way to the capitol building.

It was an enormous edifice, three stories tall and fronted with six grand columns that rose forty feet to support a heavy portico over the grand entrance, and a clock, itself fifteen feet high, on top of that. Rising up behind the clock, a magnificent dome capped the building proper.

Beside the clock, standing straight and bold, as if being purposely defiant, a flagpole, and hanging listlessly from the pole the flag of the Confederate States of America: a blue field in the canton with a circle of white stars, reminiscent of the flag of the Revolutionary forefathers, a wide red stripe, a white stripe, and a red stripe.

It was not as original as Samuel might have wished, and he wondered how well it would be distinguished from the United States flag at a distance.

Bowater made his way into the grand foyer and found the offices of the Navy Department, shunted away in a far corner of the building. It was Sunday, but the building was still crowded with men. Things were happening too fast, and there was too much to do, for officials of the Confederate government to enjoy the luxury of keeping the Sabbath holy.

He left his name, determined the hours that Secretary Mallory would be seeing people on the morrow, then returned to the hotel, where he dined on an excellent wild duck and rice and then retired to his room.

Samuel pulled a chair over to the window, sat with stocking feet up on the sill, sketched the scene laid out before him with pencil and charcoal; Montgomery, Alabama, capital of a new nation.

He thought of all the hard lessons learned by the founding fathers—three different capitals, the faltering start with the Articles of Confederation, the long uncertainty regarding strength and place of the military. The Confederacy had already benefited from those lessons, taken the best, discarded the mistakes, set up fresh and decades ahead of where the United States had been at its birth.

He sketched and pondered and soon he could hear snoring coming through the wall from his neighbor's room and he was reminded of how tired he was. He packed the sketch pad and pencil and charcoal away and crawled wearily into bed.

Samuel Bowater woke the next morning and dressed with care. He was surprised by the nervous agitation in his stomach, the slight tremor of his fingers as he anticipated the morning's interview. *I have been too damned comfortable for too damned long*, he thought as he looked himself in the mirror and brushed his hair and mustache and goatee. He relished the fear. It meant he was not dead.

He arrived at the capitol building well before the naval office opened. When at last the clerk opened the door, Bowater found a seat, addressed it with his handkerchief, and waited for his appointment to be called in the order it was made.

He sat, undisturbed, for six hours.

His eyelids were growing heavy with the stuffy heat of the office when the clerk called, "Samuel Bowater?"

Samuel stood, smoothed out his frock coat, took up his bundle of papers, and stepped through the door.

The first he saw of Stephen Mallory was the top of the Secretary's head and his unruly mop of hair. Mallory was seated, his elbows planted on his desktop, his head, which he was slowly shaking, sunk in his hands.

Bowater stood for a moment at something near parade rest, waiting for Mallory to recover.

At last the Secretary gave a loud sigh. He straightened, leaned back in his chair, eyed Samuel with an expression that seemed to say, *Now what?* Apparently he was not having a good day.

Samuel Bowater had a preconceived idea of what a navy man should look like, and Stephen Mallory was not it. His hair, which looked unruly from the top, looked worse from the front. It seemed as if no amount of brushing or cutting would contain it.

Mallory's face was round and fleshy. He wore a beard that skirted the perimeter of his face like a chin strap and made him look like a Quaker or Amish or some member of one of those severe Northern sects. But his eyes were dark and penetrating and he did not look like a low-level, lickspittle pencil-pusher.

"I am here to request a commission in the Confederate States Navy, sir."

"Indeed?" Mallory's enthusiasm was not excessive. "What is your naval experience?"

"I am a graduate of the Naval School in '47. Saw some action in the Mexican War. I have been commissioned lieutenant in the United States Navy since. I last sailed as second officer aboard USS *Pensacola*."

At that Mallory smiled and shook his head, and Bowater bristled. "The *Pensacola* was a good and fine ship, sir. Just because I find myself in opposition now to the United States does not change that fact."

"No, no, Lieutenant. It's not that. I am well aware of how fine a ship the *Pensacola* is. She was one of mine."

"Sir?"

"I was the one who shepherded her construction, back when I was chairman of the Committee of Naval Affairs in the United States Senate. A fine ship, and now my handiwork comes back to bite me in the ass. Do you see the irony of that, Lieutenant?"

Samuel nodded. "I do, sir."

"So tell me, you are just resigned from the United States Navy?"

"Yes, sir."

"I have had officers coming south for half a year now. You are a bit tardy, sir, in deciding where your loyalties lie."

Bowater stiffened. Mallory's remarks were coming very close to insinuation, and he would not stand for it.

"Mr. Secretary," he began, and his voice carried an enforced calm, "I swore an oath to the government of the United States, and I take my oaths seriously. A man of honor could do no less, nor would I expect you to look for less in your own officers. Now that I have seen where my duty lies, you can expect me to display the same loyalty to the Confederate States."

Samuel waited for a reply, wondered if his words sounded as pompous to Mallory as they did to himself. Still, he would stand for only so much where his honor was concerned. It was a hanging offense to challenge a superior officer to a duel. What about a cabinet member? Of course, Samuel realized, he was not an officer in the Confederate Navy. He was still a civilian. And after that exchange likely to remain one.

"From what state do you hail, Mr. Bowater?"

"South Carolina. Charleston."

Mallory's eyebrows went up. "Indeed? Such reticence from a Charleston man. I had thought you were all a bunch of fire-eaters. Well, no matter. I think men of sense do not rush into these things. I myself have been accused of being too lukewarm to the cause, even treasonous, if you can believe it. My own state of Florida did not support my nomination to this post, did you know that?"

"No, sir, I did not."

" 'Bowater' . . . are you by any chance related to William Bowater, the attorney?"

"Yes, sir. He is my father."

"Ah!" Mallory's expression brightened.

"If I may, sir, my father has given me a letter of introduction." Samuel flipped through the papers neatly arranged in his folder and handed his father's letter to the Secretary.

Mallory took it, ran his eyes over it, smiled. "I see he speaks highly of your character but no more. He does not go so far as to ask I favor you with a commission. That is the William Bowater I know."

Mallory set the letter aside, looked up at Samuel. "You are holding out on me, sir. Now I recall. You were responsible for some great feat during the Mexican War. I recall reading some small account of it in the papers. And your father wrote about it in great detail to me. He was very proud."

This was news to Samuel. His father had never said a word to him in that regard, beyond a single "Well done, Samuel."

"It was no more than luck, sir. I foolishly risked my life and those of my men in my youthful exuberance."

Mallory smiled. "You are your father's son, I see. That does much to recommend you. In any event, I hope the years and the United States Navy have not worn all of the exuberance out of you. We will need it. Let us hope it can take the place of ships. What sort of position were you seeking?"

"I should be happy to take up at my former rank in the U.S. Navy." Bowater handed Mallory his commission and sundry other relevant papers. "Wherever I might be of use."

Mallory leafed through the papers. "Our cause has much in common with the War for Independence fought by our forefathers," Mallory said without looking up. He finished with Samuel's papers, set them aside, met Samuel's eyes. "One of the similarities I find, in the naval line, is that we have plenty of men who wish to be officers and damned few who wish to sail before the mast. What if I were to tell you that the only position I can offer you is able-bodied seaman?"

Samuel pressed his lips together, waded through this unexpected development. The thought of living in the uncouth, half-civilized world of the lower deck was abhorrent to him. But honor demanded that he serve where he was needed, and honor would be satisfied before any concern for his personal comfort.

"If that is the only position available to me, then I would be grateful to accept it, sir."

Mallory nodded his head, and Samuel had the idea that his declaration had not come out as sincere as he had hoped.

"Well, sir, as it happens, I believe I can offer you something better. Not in terms of rank, I'm afraid. You'll have to remain a lieutenant. But I can offer you a command of your own. Then you would be a captain by courtesy. How would you like that?"

"There is nothing I should like better, sir." Samuel felt a bit dizzy, and the room took on a vaguely dreamlike air. It was hard to keep his mental footing as Mallory jerked his thoughts first one way and then another. Could he have heard right? A command of his own? After a dozen years as a lieutenant he had resigned himself to never having his own ship.

Did he say a command of my own?

Mallory was shuffling around his desk, flipping through piles of documents, some preprinted forms, some letters, some official-looking reports. "Here she is . . ." he said, pulling a couple papers free from a stack. "She is the CSS *Cape Fear*. Eighty feet in length, eighteen feet on the beam, draws seven feet aft. Screw propulsion. She is, in fact, a tugboat. Current armament . . . none. What say you, sir?"

Bowater could not help but smile. He was aware that there were plenty of very senior captains from the old navy who were commanding vessels not much better than this. Men who had owned the quarterdeck of some of the most powerful steam warships in the world were now scrambling to command converted riverboats and steam packets.

"I would be honored, sir, to command this vessel."

"Well, you are in luck. She was already given to another, but he seems to have come down with some sort of fever, no doubt brought on by the terrific reduction in the size of his command. I haven't time to root out another captain."

"However it comes about, I am pleased to have her, Mr. Secretary." Samuel Bowater had found even the midshipman's berth on his first ship to be a nearly intolerable den of barbarous behavior. For one who just a moment before was facing the possibility of life on the lower deck, the thought of command, any command, was welcome indeed.

"Good, good . . ." Mallory was hunting around for yet another document. His tone suggested that the interview was over, but Samuel did not know if he should take his leave.

"The *Cape Fear* is in Wilmington, North Carolina, as you might have guessed. Crew is all in place . . ." Mallory looked up. "Where are you staying, sir?"

"The Exchange," Bowater said.

"Very well. I'll have your commission and orders drawn up. Come by here tomorrow afternoon to fetch them and then you must make the best of your way to Wilmington. No time to lose."

Mallory stood for the first time since the interview began and stuck out his hand. "I congratulate you, Lieu . . . Captain Bowater. I have faith that you will do honor to our nation."

"Thank you, sir." The genuine sentiment of the moment took Samuel aback, and he did not know what to say. "Thank you, sir," he said again, then he turned and left.

Samuel wandered through the high halls, through the crowds of harried men, through the big doors under the portico. *My own command. . . .* He was having a hard time coming to grips with the idea. *My own command. . . .*

He stepped out from under the portico and the sun seemed very bright and he was not sure of which way to go.

5

Events of recent occurrence, and the threatening attitude of affairs in some parts of our country, call for the exercise of great vigilance and energy at Norfolk.

—Gideon Welles, Secretary of the United States Navy,
to Commodore G. J. Pendergrast

Engineer in Chief of the United States Navy Benjamin Franklin Isherwood sat down on a wooden tool crate at the forward end of the engine room and rested his head against the softest thing available, which was a ten-inch-by-ten-inch oak stanchion supporting the deck above. He closed his eyes and sleep washed over him, warm and lovely, and he did not possess the power to stave it off. He did not move—could not, with the weight of his arms and his legs—and soon his thoughts, which were generally honed to exact tolerances, began to dissolve into so many soft and discordant impressions.

It was not a particularly quiet place to sleep. The hot space was filled with a hundred different sounds, the hiss of building steam, the tapping and clanking of pipes coming to life, the drip of water in condensers and hot wells, the crunch of shovels in coal, the clang and bang of iron doors and dampers opened and shut. And under it all the low rumble of the boilers as they got up steam.

But those noises were as much a part of Isherwood's existence as the rattle of cart wheels to a teamster or cannon fire to an artilleryman. Isherwood could not have counted the number of times he had taken a caulk in some dark corner of an engine room, oblivious to the cacophony of the machinery.

So once again he drifted off to the sounds of a steam engine at work, as familiar as the house in which he grew up. But this time he could not rest. Something was bothering him, tugged at him, and he forced himself to open his eyes.

He looked around him, dull and uncertain. He was in the cavernous engine room of the steam frigate *Merrimack*, staring at the round faces of the five tubular, Martin's-type boilers. Thoughtlessly his eyes traced the maze of pipe rising up from their steam domes and off to two massive engines—double-piston-rod, horizontal, back-acting, condensing engines— and the seventy-two-inch-diameter cylinders housing the pistons that would turn the great screw somewhere beyond the confines of the hull.

There were lanterns hanging everywhere, and tools and parts and debris scattered over the deck and stacked on benches against the outboard sides of the engine room. It looked like a disaster, but it still looked better than it had three days before.

Isherwood listened to the thump, the twenty seconds of silence, the thump again of the pistons and realized that that was what had waked him. The thumping, the heartbeat of the ship. Slow, just three revolutions per minute, dockside, but there it was. *Merrimack* was alive.

On the day that Fort Sumter had surrendered, on the day that Samuel Bowater had boarded the train to Montgomery, Benjamin Isherwood had taken the Bay Line steamer from Washington, D.C., to the Gosport Naval Shipyard in Portsmouth on a secret mission.

He stepped off the little steamer and onto the docks of Portsmouth and was greeted with the sensation that his secret orders were now none too secret. There were ugly glances thrown his way, fingers pointed with no attempt at discretion, conversations interrupted and immediately resumed in hushed tones as he hurried by, head down, eyes front.

The Gosport Naval Shipyard was surrounded by a brick wall, ten feet high and eighteen inches thick. In terms of real defense it was meaningless, but it gave Isherwood some sense of relief as he passed through the iron gate. He had seen no overt signs of hostility or preparations by the Rebels to storm the naval yard, but he could sense it was coming, and he was not alone in that thought.

The yard's commander, Commodore Charles S. McCauley, had looked displeased to see him, and he probably was. He looked a bit drunk, and he probably was that as well.

"Ah, Isherwood, yes. Got Welles's note just today, said you were coming . . ." The old man—he was sixty-eight—searched his desk as if he was looking for something, then sat back, looked at Isherwood, said, "Ah . . ."

"Sir, as the Secretary related to you, it is his desire to see the *Merrimack* is brought to Philadelphia. He has asked that I personally oversee the refit of her engines."

"Ah, yes, *Merrimack*. She is in dreadful shape, Mr. Isherwood, you will find. Her engines were nothing to crow about in her best days."

"So I understand, sir." Isherwood was not overly interested in Mc-Cauley's opinion. McCauley had told the yard's chief engineer, Robert Danby, that it would take a month to get *Merrimack* underway, which was absurd. But most of the officers at the yard were Southerners, and they were influencing McCauley, and the old man was neither strong-willed enough nor sober enough to make up his own mind.

"Very well, Mr. Isherwood, do what you will . . ."

And so he had. He and Danby, working around the clock, twelve-hour shifts, supervising whatever men they could scrape up to swing a hammer or turn a wrench.

The machinery was in a bad way. The braces had been pulled out of the boilers, the engines torn apart, air pumps disabled, their components scattered around the machine shops and blacksmith shops that crowded the huge shipyard.

Night and day for four days they labored, and now he heard the giant's heartbeat, the steady thump of the pistons. The ship was stirring. In order to get to sea now, they needed only permission.

Isherwood stood with a groan and tried to shake the kinks out of his legs. "What do you say to that, Chief?"

Isherwood turned. Danby was there, his face smeared with grease, his hands black, a filthy bandage with a dark spot of dried blood tied around one finger. "Don't she sound fine?"

"She sounds like hell, Mr. Danby, but she'll do. Let me go talk to the old man."

They had gone to visit McCauley the day before, he and Danby, and reported the machinery ready in all respects. They had hoped for the order to fire her up and go. But McCauley had hesitated, told them they would be in season the next morning to get up steam.

Now it was next morning. The fires had been lit around midnight, and sometime around daybreak the water in the huge boilers began to pro-duce steam. Now the engines turned slowly, and the only things keeping *Merrimack* in Norfolk were the chain and rope fasts holding her to the dock, and McCauley's orders.

Wearily, like soldiers in the aftermath of battle, Isherwood and Danby climbed the ladder from the engine room, emerging into the blessed cool-ness of the tween decks, then climbed up the scuttle and onto the main deck.

It was nine o'clock and the sun was brilliant in the spring sky, and Isherwood was a little disoriented. It had been full night when he had gone down into the bowels of the *Merrimack*.

He paused and took a moment to look around and realign himself. *Merrimack* was an awesome vessel, 275 feet long and thirty-eight feet on the beam. She normally carried forty guns: fourteen eight-inch guns, two ten-inch, and twenty-four nine-inch, a powerful battery. The guns were off her now, making her deck seem even more expansive.

She was too much ship to let her fall into the hands of the Rebels rumored to be massing outside the walls and setting up batteries across the river. With *Merrimack* alone, the Confederates could cause real trouble for the Union navy. Time to get her out of there.

Isherwood and Danby walked down the brow from the *Merrimack*'s deck to the shore and across the big shipyard, their shoes loud on the cobblestones in the quiet morning. It should not have been quiet—the yard should have been in full production at that hour, with hammers falling and forges and heavy machinery and capstans and draft animals all filling the air with noise—but it was not. Most of the civilian workers were gone, either unwilling to work for the old government or unwilling to let their neighbors see them doing so. Those still reporting to work spent the day lolling around their work stations or doing desultory chores. They all seemed to be waiting. Waiting for orders, waiting to see who it was who would be giving orders come the end of the day.

The engineers walked past the looming twin ship houses with their odd A-frame shape, a third one under construction, past the foundries, machine shops, boiler shops, sail lofts, timber sheds, burnetizing house, riggers' lofts, and ropewalk.

It was no wonder that the Rebels were starting to gather like vultures, ready to fall on that place. Gosport was the most extensive and valuable shipyard in the country.

Isherwood and Danby walked past the huge granite dry dock, and Isherwood thought, *The secessionists would dearly love to have hold of that.* . . . There were only two in the country, and no real navy could be without one.

They arrived at last at McCauley's office. There was no one in the outer office. McCauley's door was open. Isherwood stepped across the room, rapped lightly on the doorframe.

"Commodore?"

"Ah, Isherwood, come in come in . . . damned secretary is gone, a damnable Democrat, took off with the secesh trash . . . ever since Lincoln called up them men, every damned one reckons it's war . . . like rats, sir, rats from a sinking ship, if you'll pardon the old saw . . .

Isherwood and Danby exchanged glances. The commodore was not doing so well. His frock coat was tossed over the back of his chair, his hair was wild. There were stains on his shirt, from what, Isherwood could not tell. From the doorjamb he could smell the booze.

"Commodore, I am here to report that the machinery aboard *Merrimack* is ready. We have steam up and the engines are turning now."

" 'Turning now,' eh? Good, good. Good show. Haven't quite made up my mind about sending her away. . . ."

Isherwood and Danby exchanged glances. "Pardon, sir?" Isherwood asked.

"Haven't quite decided whether or not I'll send her away. It is a damned complicated situation, Mr. Isherwood, far more than just a matter of working engines."

Isherwood straightened and made an effort to contain his surprise and mounting dismay.

He has been talking to some of these Southern gentlemen, I suspect. Or they have been talking to him.

"Sir, might I remind you that the orders which I delivered to you were peremptory, that Secretary Welles was quite unequivocal about wanting *Merrimack* moved to Philadelphia. He does not generally dispatch the engineer in chief of the navy to fix a broken engine if it is not important."

"Yes, sir, I am aware of that." McCauley was annoyed and he did not try to hide it, but he also looked uncertain and even fearful. "But it ain't that simple. The Rebels have put obstructions in the river."

"The *Merrimack* can easily pass through them, Murray determined that, but if we wait another day they may sink more, and then the ship will be stuck."

McCauley shook his head. "We send the *Merrimack* out of here and the Rebels say it's war and attack! And then we don't have her battery for defense. We leave her and put her ordnance aboard and they say we are turning the naval yard into an armed camp, and *that* is an act of war! One damned officer tells me one thing, another something else. Damn it, man, it is not that damned simple!"

McCauley slumped back exhausted, and he had a hungry look in his eyes, hungry for a drink. Isherwood felt pity for the old man. He had been fifty-two years in the navy. He may have been something as a young man, but now he was played out.

"It is complicated, sir," Isherwood said. "But the orders from Secretary Welles are clear."

"Clear, clear, yes, yes . . ." McCauley straightened himself out somewhat. "I shall make my decision later in the day, sir. Right now we will leave things as they are . . . not so pressing now. . . ."

Isherwood tried to think of a reply, but he could see that any would be pointless. He was a stranger there, whereas the officers whispering in the commodore's ear, those with South-leaning sympathies, were old and trusted colleagues.

"Very well, sir," said Isherwood crisply. "I shall wait your orders." He turned and stamped out of the office, feeling like a petulant child, but he could not help it. Behind him, wordless, Danby followed.

They stepped out of the granite building in which the commodore had his office and right into the path of Commander James Alden, who had been sent by Welles to take command of *Merrimack*.

"Mr. Isherwood, good morning. Mr. Danby. I was just on my way to see the commodore."

Isherwood waved his hand, as if waving a mosquito from his face. "The commodore is drunk with indecision, and other things, I suspect. It's no use talking to him. Come."

Isherwood walked off, and the other two men followed behind. They stepped quickly over the cobblestones, men with serious business to attend to. It was something new for Benjamin Isherwood.

His time in the navy had been exciting, challenging, after a scientific fashion. But now, in some small way, a part of the fight for Union hung on his ability to transform a boiler full of water into the force necessary to turn a massive screw propeller and drive 3,200 tons of wooden frigate into open water.

They made their way to the *Merrimack* and stamped up the brow and onto the deck, then down the scuttle to the tween decks and down again to the engine room, where the heat and noise were bad, but not nearly what they would be with the ship running at flank speed. The firemen and coal heavers looked up, their eyes white through black grime, expecting orders, but they would be disappointed.

"Danby, you had best see the fires banked," Isherwood said, then turned to Alden. "As you can see, Commander, the engineers and firemen are aboard. Men enough to get you to Newport News or Fortress Monroe. Out of danger in any event. The engines are operational. As far as the engineer department is concerned, the vessel is ready to go. My orders are fulfilled."

"Ah, yes, Mr. Isherwood. The machinery seems in fine shape. . . ."

Isherwood sighed. "See here, Alden," he began again, in a softer tone. "I tell you this by way of letting you know there is nothing keeping *Merrimack* here. Nothing but McCauley, and what he will do I do not know. The time may come, soon, when you must simply act. Do you follow me?"

"Yes, sir, I do."

"Good." Isherwood looked around the engine room, at his beloved pumps and boilers and piping and valves and gauges. "The barbarians are at the gate, Mr. Alden. They will be breaking it down soon, I do believe."

6

Then the navy men came under discussion. There is an awful pull in their divided hearts. Faith in the U.S. Navy was their creed and their religion. And now they must fight it—and worse than all, wish it ill luck.

—Mary Boykin Chesnut

The Confederate States Ship *Cape Fear*.

She was somewhere around eighty feet long, perhaps twenty on the beam. One hundred tons or thereabouts. A nearly plumb bow and a bit of counter at the stern. Her hull was black, the dull, flat black of coal-tar paint, a workboat finish. One strake, painted white and running the length of the vessel about four feet below the rail, was her only bit of trim.

Most of her deck fore and aft was occupied by a big deckhouse, painted a brilliant white and interrupted at various intervals by doors and windows. At the forward end of the deckhouse and on top of it sat the wheelhouse, which rose another level above the rest of the superstructure.

Abaft the wheelhouse, supported by wires fore and aft, the stack rose straight up, twice again as high as the deckhouse.

Wonder how the fireboxes would draw with that shot away. . . . Flying metal had not been a consideration in the tug's original design.

There was no smoke coming out of the stack, not the smallest tendril. Her fires were dead.

At the very stern, on the ensign staff, the flag of the Confederate States, its blue canton and three stripes just visible whenever the soft breeze disturbed it.

She had formerly been the screw tug *Atlas*, but now she would officially be known as the screw steamer CSS *Cape Fear*. That was all that Samuel Bowater knew about his ship, and most of it was only what he could observe, standing anonymously at the top of the low hill that ran down to the riverfront of Wilmington, North Carolina.

It had been a wild ride so far, with the events in the life of the new nation moving as fast and unpredictably as Samuel Bowater's own.

On the day that Samuel, in Montgomery, Alabama, was commissioned an officer of the Confederate States Navy, Abraham Lincoln in Washington had ordered 75,000 troops called up to suppress the insurrection. It was not a declaration of war, but near enough for most. North Carolina and Kentucky refused to send men. The fire-eaters were howling.

Lincoln called for a three-month enlistment, reckoned, apparently, that that was all it would take. An insult, heaped on top of great injury.

As Samuel was boarding the train to take him back to Charleston, outrage over the firing on and capturing of Sumter was sweeping the North. A nation that had seemed half inclined to let the Southern states go their way and be damned with them was now fervent about stopping secession immediately and for good.

On the day that Samuel Bowater arrived back at his home in Charleston and directed Jacob to pack his trunks for sea service, and Jacob's own things as well, the state of Virginia, in secret session, voted to secede from the Union rather than bear arms against her fellow Southrons. All of Lincoln's attempts to coddle the state were for naught. She would not fight for the Union.

It was the following day, Thursday, the 18th of April, 1861, that Samuel returned to the train station in Charleston, accompanied by his father and mother and his sister. He dispatched a telegraph to the ship, giving warning of his coming. He said his goodbyes to his family and boarded the train to Wilmington, North Carolina, while Jacob stowed his bags away and found a seat in whatever part of the train that Negroes rode.

On that same day, Colonel Robert E. Lee declined President Lincoln's offer of command of all Union forces.

Around the time that Samuel Bowater stepped off the train in Wilmington, Major Robert Anderson and the garrison that had defended Fort Sumter were stepping ashore in New York, the great heroes of the Union.

All of that history was swirling around him, but Samuel Bowater disengaged himself from it, there at the top of the road that ran down to the river, a quiet place where he could look down on his first command. Jacob waited patiently behind, their bags and trunks piled on a wheelbarrow.

What would greet him when he stepped aboard? He had long envisioned this moment—assuming command of his own ship. But it had been different before. Before he had behind him nearly one hundred years of United States Navy tradition, and that based on hundreds more years of Royal Navy tradition. There was never any question then as to how he would be received by officers, warrants, men.

But this was something new, a renegade service. He would not be part of a grand tradition, stepping aboard his ship, but rather he would be setting the protocol in place.

Perhaps in one hundred years' time, a young captain would come aboard a ship of the Confederate States Navy, confident of his part because it was a part that had been set for a century, stretching back in a great unbroken line to the year 1861. But not for Samuel Bowater. He did not have that foundation; for him it was shifting sand.

Bowater's eyes moved beyond the former tug and took in the Cape Fear River, which ran like a rippling highway past the town. The banks were low and green and brown, and without thinking on it Samuel began to mix paint in his head, green on the palette with a touch of black, a hint of yellow to bring out the early spring colors.

He shook his head. The most important moment of his first command was upon him, and he was thinking about painting. That would not do. He had to think about first impressions, about establishing in the minds of all aboard his absolute authority over them. He was setting precedent, for his own first command, and for all the first commands of the Confederate Navy to come after. He headed down the hill, and behind him he heard the squeak of the wheelbarrow, the slap of Jacob's bare feet.

Sailors are sailors, he thought. Even if the history of the Confederate States Navy could be measured in months, there was still the custom and usage of the sea. There were always traditions to which they could look for guidance. Samuel Bowater had no doubt that the dignity and command presence that was part of being a Southern gentleman would see him through any awkwardness.

Still, it had annoyed him to find no one at the station to meet him. He had expected a few bluejackets at the very least, to carry his gear. A decent first officer should have seen to that.

Samuel and Jacob walked past the brick stores and the white clapboard houses of the lovely town of Wilmington, and a part of Samuel's mind took it in, but his eyes were still on the CSS *Cape Fear*, his world now. There were people on her afterdeck, he could see, just smudges of gray cloth and white skin and, back a ways, nearer the deckhouse, black skin as well.

Closer, and Samuel Bowater could hear music, just the faintest strains, and he was curious, and as he grew closer still he could see that the fellow sitting on the after rail was playing a violin.

He paused again to listen. Bowater had no talent for music, but that did not quash his passion for it. He went regularly to the Charleston Symphony Orchestra and had sought out performances in every port where he had found himself for any length of time.

The strains of the violin came to him now, and he listened. The tune was familiar. Not classical, something else, but not displeasing. As a rule he despised folksy, crude ditties, such aberrations as "Dixie" and "Turkey in the Straw" and "Roll the Chariot Along." But this was something different. The tune moved through him, clear and melodic.

And then he realized it was "Shenandoah," the capstan chanty he had heard so often. It was one of those songs enjoyed by the lower deck, but he had a grudging affection for it as well.

And then a deep bass voice, clear and full, twined itself around the notes of the violin.

Oh, Shenandoah, she's a lovely river . . .

And then, soft but all together, the rest of them,

Aaaway, you rolling river!

Then the single bass voice again.

And I shall ne'er forget you, never . . .

Then together,

Away, I'm bound away, 'cross the wide Missouri. . . .

Samuel turned and smiled at Jacob, and Jacob smiled back. "Sweet as sugar, ain't it, Massa Samuel?"

"Lovely." The crew was gathered there on the *Cape Fear*'s afterdeck, singing as one, and Samuel Bowater was standing alone, watching. But he was captain, and that was how it would always be. He continued on, moved faster, anxious now to be aboard.

Hieronymus M. Taylor closed his eyes and let the bow move over the violin's strings, let the fingers of his left hand fall easily on the fingerboard of the instrument, let the graceful melody of "Shenandoah" flow from the hollow place inside the instrument. He had a notion that every beautiful tune in the world was stowed down inside there, that his finger placement and strokes of the bow were not so much creating the sound as releasing it.

The violin smelled of coal dust and oil and smoke and soot, but there was nothing for it. It had been with Taylor for years, through his time as fireman and oiler, third assistant engineer, second assistant, and now on his third berth with the rating of first assistant engineer. Everything he had smelled that way, his clothes, his books, his bedding. Hieronymus Taylor himself smelled of those things, and even the most conscientious scrubbing could not rid him of the smell entirely.

He moved through the first refrain, and then the merest pause, and then as the violin sounded again, so Moses Jones's voice rose with it, soft at first and then building in strength like the note that Hieronymus was coaxing from the instrument. It was as if the voice and the note were coming from the same place, as if they had been born joined in that way.

Oh, Shenandoah, she's a lovely river . . .

Then the rest joined in, soft, and there were enough of them that the cumulative effect was good.

Aaaway, you rolling river . . .

And I shall ne'er forget you, never . . . Moses came in on the last dying note of the chorus, bold and strong, and Hieronymus felt the hairs on the back of his neck stand up.

Damn me, but that darkie can sing, he thought.

Three weeks the ship had been there, tied to the dock, waiting on a captain, any captain. Hieronymus, at sundown, his third day aboard, came aft and sat on the stern rail, sawed away on his fiddle, as was his habit and had been since he first put to sea. Moses had drifted over after a while, started singing soft to the tunes that the chief played, and just for fun Hieronymus stuck to song melodies, tested the breadth of Moses's repertoire, which turned out to be extensive.

And Moses, fireman, unofficial chief of the coal heavers, caught on to the game, sang more boldly each day. He was a freeman, unlike most of the coal heavers, who were slaves and hired on to the navy by a master somewhere—somewhere safe, Taylor imagined. Moses had, for some reason, volunteered for the navy. Like any Southern black man, he knew how to move through the white man's world without giving offense.

And so, each afternoon, the crew of the CSS *Cape Fear* began to drift aft, and soon they were all coming around and sitting on the deck and listening to the music and Moses's lovely bass voice and joining in on the chorus.

The "luff," the first lieutenant, was a moon-faced young man of twenty-eight perhaps, an unassuming officer with what Hieronymus Taylor considered the command presence of a greased pig at a county fair. But he was agreeable, and Taylor liked him well enough. His name was Thadeous Harwell and he had graduated from the Naval Academy eight years before, but Taylor still liked him.

It had been a busy three weeks. Harwell had been issued orders to get the tug in shape for combat, and for the arrival of the new captain. And

Harwell, an Academy graduate and an eager young officer indoctrinated into the ancient traditions of the navy, had very definite ideas of what a man-of-war was, and the *Atlas* was not it.

The deckhouse, for one, had been laid out and maintained to the standards of the tugboat's small and none too demanding crew. The cabins were filthy and stuffed to the overhead with all manner of junk: old coils of rope, fenders, rusting machinery, lumber of all sizes, stacks of newspapers. It did not appear to have ever been cleaned.

Harwell turned to the work with a will, and did an admirable job of driving the others. They cleared out each of the cabins, scraped the decks, painted the bulkheads. They tore out the berthing for four crew in the forecastle and installed berthing for ten, plus additional berthing for the Negroes aft and storage amidships. They gutted the master's cabin and turned it into a place fit for a naval officer, and the same with the luff's and the chief's cabins.

They scraped, scrubbed, and painted the galley until it no longer made a man nauseous to look at the walls or the deck.

Hieronymus had his own problems. Despite the title of first assistant engineer he was in fact the officer in charge of the *Cape Fear*'s machinery, the former tug being too small to warrant an officer with the rank of chief engineer. With the fires drawn and no coal to heave, he set the black gang to scraping and painting the engine room, draining and cleaning out boilers, taking on and shifting stores of coal.

He and his firemen first class, the Scot Burgess and the Irishman O'-Malley, had their own work to do. They had mapped and scraped the bearings, balanced out the high- and low-pressure cylinders, rebuilt the boiler stops, reconditioned the air pumps, replaced fire tubes. The engine had not been in bad shape to begin with, and by the end of three weeks' constant work it was as perfect as it was going to get.

The Cape Fears spent their days toiling to turn their little floating world into something that could be a part of the coming fight, while the newspapers told them of all of the extraordinary events spooling out across the nation, history of which they longed to be a part. And then in the evenings, their sing-along.

Burgess was sitting on the deck, leaning against the bulwark, smoking his pipe in silence. O'Malley was leaning on the ladder that led from the afterdeck to the roof of the deckhouse. He began every evening by ostentatiously refusing to sing, because he would not sing with Negroes, and certainly not if Moses Jones was left to sing the lead parts. That generally lasted about twenty minutes, and then he was adding his clear tenor to the mix—an Irishman could not remain silent at a sing-along forever.

The luff was sitting on an overturned bucket now, singing the chorus of "Shenandoah" in his alto voice, having finally abandoned any hope of putting a stop to the music. It was clear that Lieutenant Harwell thought perhaps he should not allow the crew to congregate as they did, officers, men, slaves, all together. He spent a week of afternoons floating about and fidgeting and looking as if he wanted to say something. But Taylor just chewed on the stub of his cigar, looked the luff hard in the eyes, and any objections died a quick death and the men had their little time.

Hieronymus Taylor came to the part of "Shenandoah" where he improvised on the reprise. He had been working on it, changing it around in subtle ways, for the past week, and he was coming to love what he had. He felt the music lift out of the violin, and then, just as he was coming to the high point, the part that near moved him to tears, just as his bow drew out that quivering note, a voice shouted from the dock, saying, "Ahoy, da boat!"

Taylor clamped his teeth down on the unlit stub of his cigar, drew the note out, but the mood was shattered.

"Ahoy da boat!" There was always some idiot coming by. It was the disadvantage of being dockside and not at an anchor.

This darkie son of a whore better have a damned good reason. . . .

"Who goes there?" Lieutenant Harwell called out, and a voice, someone who was definitely not a darkie, and probably not a son of a whore, answered, "*Cape Fear.*"

Cape Fear? Ah, shit. . . . Their captain, come at last. Just when Hieronymus Taylor had Harwell trained up right, now there would be another damned officer for him to teach. He lowered his bow and violin, opened his eyes to a scene of confusion. Half the peckerwoods on board clearly did not know that only the captain referred to himself by the name of the ship, and they were staring wide-eyed at the others, who were scrambling to get up and stand at some kind of military readiness.

"Fall in there, men, fall in, fall in. Dress it up," Harwell was saying in a stage whisper as he inched backward toward the brow.

Taylor smiled, set his violin and bow down. He considered pulling on his frock coat, which was draped over the rail, and decided against it. "Moses, get them darkies in some kinda order. Captain's comin aboard."

Moses began to maneuver the coal heavers into line, and then Lieutenant Harwell was back, practically genuflecting to the man who followed behind.

"If we had had any idea, sir, that you were arriving today . . ." the luff stammered.

"You did not get my telegram?"

"Telegram? No, sir . . . telegram?" Harwell looked around as if hoping for more intelligence regarding a telegram, but none was forthcoming.

Taylor grinned around his cigar. No telegram. This meeting would not have been half as much fun if he had given the lieutenant the telegram announcing the old man's arrival.

The chief ran his eyes over the new captain. Thirties, nice uniform frock coat. Mustache and goatee trimmed and groomed to an absurd perfection. The accent was Charleston, and it wasn't peckerwood. Charleston elite. Naval Academy. Regal bearing.

This one got a ramrod right up his ass, he thought. Taylor stepped across the deck, brushed past Lieutenant Harwell, thrust out his hand. "Captain . . . ?"

"Samuel Bowater." He took Taylor's hand, matched the strength of his grip, looked him in the eyes with no hint of expression. If he was angry or afraid or disgusted or pleased, Hieronymus Taylor could not tell. "And you are?"

"First Assistant Engineer Hieronymus M. Taylor, sir. This here's my engineering division. Them there's the black gang. Coal heavers is black as coal, as you can see."

"Hmm, indeed." Captain Bowater released his grip. His eyes flicked up and down Taylor's clothing. His patrician expression did not change any more than that of a statue would change, but still Taylor felt the disdain radiate from the man. It was a particular trick that these *gentlemen* had.

"What is the state of the engine, Chief?"

"Ready for fire. Coal boxes are full. Soft coal, not so bad. Shit, we been sittin here for three weeks with our thumbs up our collective asses. Managed to get some damned things done."

Bowater just nodded and his eyes did not leave Taylor's, and the chief thought, *Damn, he got some fire in his belly*. This Captain Samuel Bowater would not be so easily cowed. Hieronymus Taylor wondered if they might get deep into the monkey show after all. Maybe do some real fighting, put a shell through a Yankee or two. He felt a spark of hope, even through the immediate and thorough dislike he was harboring.

"When can you have steam up?" Bowater asked.

"Don't you want to have a look 'round the ship first, Cap'n?"

"I am looking at the ship now, Chief. I want to know when you can have steam up."

This ain't goin so good. "Five hours."

"Good. Make it so." Bowater turned away, done with Hieronymus Taylor. The chief felt like an overseer being dismissed, sent back to the cotton fields.

"Lieutenant," Bowater said to Harwell, "please have some hands help my servant with my things. You may show me the master's cabin, if you will, then muster the hands aft for inspection. Then I will inspect the ship."

"Aye, aye, sir. McKeown, Williams, bear a hand with the captain's things! Please, this way, sir." With that, Harwell and Bowater walked off down the side deck and disappeared around the corner of the deckhouse.

"Well, damn me," Taylor said. He pulled his soggy cigar stub from his mouth, spit out the flecks of tobacco on his tongue. He scratched at his chin and the usual three days' growth of beard there. He was never certain if he was growing a beard or not, it was a day-by-day decision. Finally he returned his violin to his case and snapped it shut. "Moses, get them darkies down t'the engine room and start buildin' the fires. Y'all heard what Captain Samuel Bowater said."

7

I reached Norfolk on the morning of the 19th instant and found the city in a state of great excitement. . . .

—Major General William B. Taliaferro, Virginia Provisional Army,
to John Letcher, Governor of Virginia

There was panic in the air. Commander James Alden thought he could smell it, like a whiff of smoke from a far-off fire. Far off, but closing.

The Gosport naval yard seemed wrapped in an intangible strangeness, as if all the people there—and there were not so many anymore—were mesmerized. They seemed to wander about, unsure what to do, not knowing who was in charge.

Alden paused at the *Merrimack's* brow, looked around, unsure himself. The yard seemed bathed in a weird light. The colors were different. Brighter. Everything seemed more intense.

He shook his head, cursed himself silently. He would not be caught up in this nonsense.

That is not my affair . . . . Alden clambered down the brow, stepped quickly across the yard, making once again for the commodore's office.

The rumors had been filtering in: militia and Confederate Army troops massing in the city, thousands arriving by train, batteries going up on Craney Island and all the points that commanded the shipyard and the anchorage.

Those stories had been circulating since before he and Isherwood had arrived, but now they had a new momentum, and every hour brought fresh and more alarming news. Rumor built upon rumor until the people found themselves glancing up at the brick wall that surrounded the yard and half expecting to see Rebels pouring over it.

Head down, Alden paced off the steps across the cobbled shipyard. *I'll wear a path in these stones before I am free of this place. . . .*

The shipyard was McCauley's concern. The *Merrimack* was his. His only thought was to get the frigate under the guns of Fortress Monroe at Old Point Comfort.

He stepped into the building that housed the commodore's office. It was Thursday, the 18th of April, but it might as well have been a Sunday evening for all the activity there. Gone were the officers and warrants hustling in and out of the various offices, pleading for this or that, gone were the civilian engineers and shop stewards and correspondence secretaries and enlisted men. Gone was almost everyone, and more leaving by the hour.

Of those who were left, Alden was not sure whom he could trust. He hoped to soon be one of the gone himself.

McCauley's office was open, and Alden entered without knocking. The old man had his frock coat on and was wearing sword and pistol. He was not alone.

Commodore Pendergrast, commander of the Home Squadron, was there. The Home Squadron had found itself at Norfolk when the trouble first began to simmer and had been ordered by Gideon Welles to remain and lend its weight of iron to the defense of the shipyard. Along with Pendergrast was Captain Marston, captain of the 1,708-ton sloop-of-war *Cumberland,* flagship of the squadron.

"Commander Alden, good you are here . . . should be part of this . . ." McCauley said, and his voice sounded even less promising than it had that morning. "Just discussing the strategic situation here . . . last report I heard, must be two thousand of these damned Rebels massing . . ."

"It would seem so, sir. Commodore, *Merrimack* has her head up steam. I've men enough to get her to Fortress Monroe, at least. I beg of you, sir, give me leave to go."

McCauley threw a hopeful look at the other officers. "Pendergrast, what do you think?"

"Welles says to move the ship. It ain't going to get any easier. Best do it now."

Alden wanted to cross the room and hug the man. How clear and straightforward was his perception of the situation!

"Well . . ." McCauley sputtered. "You have men enough for this, Alden?"

"There are men enough in the engine room. If I can beg of Captain Marston thirty men from *Cumberland*—I'll send them right back, soon as we're under Monroe's guns—then I have enough."

Marston frowned, and the expression brought out a hundred more lines in an already craggy face, but he nodded his big head. "I can spare you thirty men, Commander, if you sent 'em right back."

All eyes turned back to McCauley. The commodore breathed deep. Alden tensed. *This is a lot of work just to get the old bastard to let me do what the Secretary of the Navy ordered me to,* he thought, and then McCauley nodded as well.

"Very good, Commander. Take *Merrimack* out of here before these Rebels can get their damned hands on her."

Alden straightened, and he felt inches taller. "Aye, aye, sir," he said.

Marston stood up from the desk on which he had been leaning. "I'll arrange for those men, Alden, march 'em over to *Merrimack*," and with no more ceremony he left McCauley's office.

"Thank you, sir. Oh, and sir?" Alden turned back to McCauley. He felt he was pushing his luck, as if inching farther out on ice of dubious thickness. "Sir, the ordnance is all out of the ship. If I could have a couple of field pieces, something we could bring right up the brow, that should serve as battery enough for now."

"Yes, yes, very well," said McCauley. Now that the decision was made, he seemed to not want to hear more about it. "Go see Tucker about it."

"Aye, aye, sir. And sir . . . you have done the right thing, if I may be so bold . . ."

"Yes, yes, yes, dismissed, Commander." McCauley waved him away, did not meet his eye.

Alden fairly ran out of the commodore's office, raced back to *Merrimack* and up the brow. Lieutenant Murray, first officer of the *Cumberland*, who had volunteered to help with *Merrimack*, was on deck. He was in discussion with Chief Isherwood.

"Mr. Isherwood, Murray, praise God, we have orders to get the ship out of here!"

"Most high miracle," Isherwood said dryly. "God alone could have moved that man to make a decision."

"God and Commodore Pendergrast, reminding him of his duties. Where is Lieutenant Poindexter?" Poindexter was the *Merrimack*'s first officer. Alden would have expected to find him on deck as well.

"I haven't seen him," said Murray.

"No matter, I'll find him. Mr. Isherwood, if I might impose upon you to see the engines ready to get us underway?"

Isherwood nodded.

"And Mr. Murray, we need a pilot. Do you know of a pilot who will take us out of here?"

"Ahh," Murray equivocated in a way that Alden did not like to hear. "That won't be easy. Since Virginia went secesh, none of the pilots'll work a government ship. They're all afraid of being hanged, apparently, by the damned Rebels."

"Well, find one. Offer a thousand dollars to the man who will get *Merrimack* to Fortress Monroe. Wait . . . offer twice that if he can get the *Germantown* there, too. We'll tow her out. And offer a place for life in the navy, as well."

Murray smiled. "He'll need that. Damned sure won't be going back home anytime soon."

"Good. Go."

"Aye, aye!" Murray hurried off, and Alden was glad he did not ask if he, Commander Alden, had the authority to make such offers. *To hell with it. We'll sort it out when the ships are safe.*

"I must see to getting us a few guns, Mr. Isherwood," Alden said next.

"I will see the fires stoked up, Mr. Alden," Isherwood said. He looked pleased. That was a change from the seemingly permanent dour look that the frustrations of the past week had stamped on his face.

Alden raced back down the brow and back across the yard to the ordnance shed. It was a grand warehouse of artillery, and where it met the water's edge, a great set of shears rose up overhead, used for lifting the heavy guns and setting them down on ships warped alongside. He would have liked to put those to use, to have *Merrimack*'s twenty-four nine-inch guns back in place, but there was no time. If he could get a couple of three-inch ordnance rifles he would be happy.

He stepped out of the sunshine and into the gloom of the cavernous ordnance building. On the far side of the big shed door was the office of Commander J. R. Tucker, ordnance officer for the naval yard. One of the few officers who had not resigned.

Alden crossed over to Tucker's office, knocked, and entered. Tucker was at his desk, his frock coat unbuttoned, his feet up, heels resting on the edge of the desktop. He made no move to assume a more businesslike position.

"Commander Alden! What can I do for you, this fine spring day?"

Alden stiffened. Tucker's informality would have been objectionable in the normal course of affairs. In the current crisis it was near insufferable. "I need guns, Mr. Tucker. For . . ."

"No, no, no. That ain't gonna happen, Mr. Alden. I don't have men to work the shears, or . . ."

"Damn the shears. I need two field pieces, that's all. Howitzers, three-inch rifles, whatever you have, just something I can defend the *Merrimack* with."

Tucker smiled, shook his head. "It's all these damned disloyal workers, all gone over to the Rebs, now Virginia is out."

"Never mind the workers. Marston's giving me thirty men out of *Cumberland*. Give me a pair of guns on field carriages and we'll get them up the brow."

Once more Tucker shook his head. "It ain't just men I'm wanting for, Alden. I haven't got the requisition forms I need to issue guns, don't know where in hell I would get them."

Alden made to speak again, but Tucker talked right over his protest. "And even if I had them, who would approve them? The damned office is deserted, old McCauley's too drunk, I'll bet. I'm sorry, Mr. Alden, I sure as hell would like to help you, but there is just nothing I can do." He shrugged, smiled, and then Alden realized what was what.

The commander straightened, looked down on Tucker, hoped that the disgust he felt was evident. He could see what Tucker was, now. Traitor, secesh. It was like discovering that a friend and shipmate is in fact an escaped criminal. He tried to think of something to say, something proportionately scathing, but nothing would come.

"Good day," he said, and turned and stamped out. Through the open door he could hear Tucker call, "And good day to you, Commander! Good luck with them guns!" The humor in his voice was like a knife to Alden.

He crossed back, making once again for the commodore's office. Having ordered *Merrimack* away, perhaps McCauley would have the guts now to stand up to Tucker. He saw Lieutenant Poindexter across the yard.

"Lieutenant! Lieutenant!" Alden shouted, and Poindexter stopped and waved. Alden hurried over to him. "Lieutenant, we've received orders to go. Isherwood is stoking the boilers up. I need you to single up the fasts and have the ship winded. We've no time to lose."

"Single up the fasts . . . ?"

"Yes, Lieutenant. It is customary when leaving a dock. What in hell is the matter with you?"

"It's just . . . well, sir, I reckon you need to get permission from Commander Robb."

"Robb?" Commander Robert Robb was the executive officer of the shipyard. "I have orders from Commodore McCauley!"

"Well, pardon, sir, it's just, I think we need Commander Robb's permission to do that. . . ."

Alden looked at Poindexter, and where before he had seen a handsome young lieutenant of the United States Navy, he now saw a loathsome, ugly thing. Like Tucker. A man whose loyalties were not where Alden had thought.

Involuntarily he glanced to his right and left. It was like a dream, as if he suddenly realized that he was not in the place he thought he was, that the people he took to be friends and comrades were really people he did not know.

Without a word he abandoned Poindexter to his halfhearted protestations and headed back to McCauley's office, his pace just short of a run.

"Whoa, there, Commander!"

Alden looked up. Standing in his way was Commander Robb. Had Robb not spoken, Alden would have run him down like a ship in a fog.

"See here, Robb . . . what's the meaning of Poindexter telling me we need your permission to get *Merrimack* underway? I've orders from McCauley, and I don't reckon I need any others . . ."

"Hold up, there, Mr. Alden!" Robb held up his hands in mock defense. "No one is saying that Commodore McCauley isn't in charge here. But I am the executive officer, as you well know, and these things must come from me."

Alden drew a breath. "Very well, then, may I have permission to single fasts and wind the ship?"

"No."

"No?"

"I'm sorry, Commander. You may not have the ship."

Alden just shook his head. He had no words.

"Commodore McCauley has changed his mind. We need to keep the *Merrimack* here. If we try to move her now it will only infuriate the thousands of troops mustered in town."

Alden glared at Robb through narrowed eyes. Robb's soft voice, the accent of northern Virginia, sounded to Alden like the strident shriek of a traitor, howling out his perfidy. "Damn you . . ."

"Yes, yes. Now please go and draw your fires."

"To hell with you, sir. I will not take orders from a traitor." Alden pushed past Robb, made a point of physically pushing him out of the way, and stamped into McCauley's office.

"Sir!" Alden shouted. McCauley looked up, his eyes bleary and rimmed with red, his face gray and sagging. He looked much worse than he had even that morning, and Alden, who had intended to shout at him, softened his approach.

"Sir, I have just spoken with Commander Robb, whose loyalties I frankly question. He could not have told me the truth."

"I've spoken with Robb. We both agree *Merrimack* should remain. You may draw the fires and stand down to an engine watch."

"Sir . . ."

McCauley slammed the flat of his hand down on the desk, a more energetic move than Alden would have thought him capable of, and Alden started. "Goddamn it!" McCauley shouted. "Do you think I have not examined this from all angles? Goddamn it! Fifty-two years I have been in this navy, was a captain while you were still at your mother's tit, sir, and I will not have you in here questioning my every order!"

Alden straightened, came to attention. McCauley was no traitor, but traitors had his ear and they had swayed him and he would not be swayed back. He had made the last decision that he had the energy to make, Alden could see that, and that decision would stand.

"Aye, aye, sir. I will go and see the fires are drawn." He turned and left the office, and he knew he would not return.

A cable length from the *Merrimack* he stopped and ran his eyes over her. She was a grand and solid thing, with her high black sides and the single white band running from gunport to gunport. She had none of the elegant sweep of the ships of an earlier era—her sheer was perfectly straight—but what that lost her in grace it added in giving her a formidable, martial look. If she was the descendant of the great high-pooped, gilded men-of-war of centuries past, then she had evolved into something leaner, more efficient, more deadly, the naval equivalent of Mr. Darwin's theory.

She did not look so magnificent now, with her masts and yards all gone, down to the lower masts, and not a bit of standing rigging to support those. Smoke was rolling out of her funnel, midway between the fore and main masts, a thick black smoke, and Alden knew that down in the belly of the ship Isherwood was pushing the men to get the fires up and the boilers churning and the steam pumping through the pipes.

Isherwood. Alden did not think he had the strength to tell him.

The *Merrimack* had been in commission less than six years. She had cost the United States nearly $700,000 to build. She had had her problems, sure, and she was not much to look at now, dockside and stripped of her rig. But she was in her heart a magnificent ship.

I should just damn well take her anyway, Alden thought. *Just cast off, let her drift out into the stream . . . Murray at the helm, one of the firemen at forward lookout . . .* He felt a tremor of excitement as the idea built in his head. Just take the *Merrimack* anyway, and damn McCauley and his orders.

But he could not and he knew it, and the fantasy faded away. He was a naval officer, had been for all of his adult life, and the habit of obeying orders was far too deeply ingrained for him to ignore it now. Like a peddler's horse that has tramped the same route every day of its life, and knows no other, so Commander James Alden could not alter the route along which his sense of duty and respect for rank led him.

He felt sick, down deep in his stomach, as he stepped up the brow. He crossed the deck to the scuttle and climbed slowly down to the engine room, where he would tell Benjamin Isherwood to draw the fires and let the beast die.

8

[U]nder the orders of Flag Officer Paulding, was inaugurated and in part consummated one of the most cowardly and disgraceful acts which has ever disgraced the Government of a civilized people.

—Major General William B. Taliaferro, Virginia Provisional Army, to John Letcher, Governor of Virginia

It took the Confederate States Ship *Cape Fear* a little over fifty hours' steaming, Cape Fear to Cape Henry.

From Wilmington, it was three miles downriver, feeling their way in the moonlight, to the point where the Cape Fear River opened wide and Bowater could feel the tension ease as the muddy banks and their hidden snags receded from view. They passed Orton's Point and finally, with Smith's Island looming, turned southeast, leaving Zeek's Island to starboard. Fifteen miles from the dock at Wilmington they steamed through New Inlet and met the long rollers of the Atlantic Ocean.

Then it was northeast and forty miles off the low, treacherous shore of North Carolina, the Outer Banks. Once Samuel had determined that tricky Diamond Shoals were well astern, dead reckoning with the chart spread on the table in his cabin, it was a near-ninety-degree course change to northwest and the entrance to the Chesapeake Bay.

That was pretty much how Captain Samuel Bowater had figured it. Fifty hours, Wilmington to Cape Henry, and that had them steaming into the bay in full darkness, and running past Fortress Monroe and the naval installations at Newport News and Norfolk in the dead hours, the least watchful hours. They could anchor once they were well up the James River, once they were safely in the bosom of Virginia.

Three hours and ten minutes after he had stepped aboard, they had slipped the fasts and worked their way out into the stream. The chief engineer, Hieronymus M. Taylor—Bowater smiled as he recalled the name—had said five hours to get head up steam, but that was the sort of thing engineers always said. Made them look particularly efficient when they had steam up in half that time.

Engineers . . .

In the days of sail, an officer learned it all. He could navigate, sure, and work his ship in a harbor or in a storm. But he could also knot and splice, he could lay aloft to stow sail, he could stand a trick at the helm, and had done so. He could set up standing rigging and send spars down to the deck and act as gun captain or sailing master or mast captain. There was no part of any job on board that the captain had not, at some point, done himself.

But with the advent of the steam engine, that all changed. Now there was someone aboard his ship who knew more about its most vital part than he. It was a relationship that Samuel Bowater was still struggling to define.

Goddamned engineers . . .

He had begun defining it for his present circumstance the second he stepped aboard. It had not been his intention to get underway immediately—first light in the morning would have been sufficient—but one look at Hieronymus Taylor and Bowater knew that the first conversation he had with that man had better end with an order, and an unequivocal one. The relationship of superior to inferior had to be established immediately and forcefully. Bowater knew men like Taylor—rough, uneducated, surly—and knew they had to be handled in the same way one handled a bad-tempered servant.

So he ordered steam up, turned his back on the engineer, ordered the luff to show him the master's cabin.

Harwell turned to the tasks with a will, overseeing every aspect of carrying the trunks and bags aboard and maneuvering them down the port side deck that ran the length of the deckhouse, fifty feet, to a ladder that ran from the front of the deckhouse to the wheelhouse above.

Harwell gestured for Bowater to go first. "The captain's cabin, sir, is in the wheelhouse, just behind the wheelhouse. I hope you will find that convenient."

Bowater stepped through the wheelhouse with its big varnished wheel and bell lanyard for communicating with the engine room, and through the open door into the cabin beyond. The walls of the cabin were also painted white, gleaming and spotless, and the deck was covered in the tra-

ditional black-and-white-checkered canvas. The overhead was white as
well, with varnished deck beams at regular intervals. There were windows
with curtains on three sides, and even in the evening sun the cabin was
wonderfully lit.

On one wall was a built-in bunk, against another a washstand. A generous table was lashed down against the forward bulkhead. In all it was a
very agreeable space, light and airy as a deckhouse.

The disadvantage, of course, was that this cabin and everything in it
would likely be reduced to kindling when the iron started to fly.

"Very good, Lieutenant. Jacob, stow my gear away. Mr. Harwell, let us
see if the men are assembled."

Bowater led the way aft. They came around the corner of the deckhouse and found the ship's company, all twenty of them, standing at attention by division and department. After years aboard USS *Pensacola*,
with her crew of more than five hundred, it was not an inspiring sight.

The Cape Fears' uniforms were generally clean and in good repair.
Most of the men wore the pullover bibbed wool shirt, loose-tied necker-
chief, and flat cloth cap that were the standard dress of sailors the world
over. They wore trousers that were tight at the waist and flared out at the
feet to pool on the deck in a wide bunch of cloth, the descendants of the
slop trousers worn by sailors of the last age. Half of the men had shoes.

The loose-fitting clothing gave the seamen a rangy, casual look, a look
that was both military and subtly insubordinate, all at the same time. The
clothes seemed to imply a relaxed discipline and at the same time something
much more important: professionalism, dedication to the mariners' arts.
The clothes were the unconscious reflection of the sailors' mind; they said
the men who wore them would take their sailoring, their ship, and their fellow seamen seriously, and all and anyone else could go to the devil. It was a
look and an attitude that Samuel had come to respect.

If their style of dress was similar, the colors were not. Some were out-
fitted in cadet gray, some in blue, uniforms they took with them from the
old United States Navy when they went south. Some had black, some had
combinations of all three.

Some—the landsmen—looked as if they had just left the farm.

"Mr. Harwell, please show me your master's division," Samuel said with
military formality.

"Aye, aye, sir!" Harwell led the way, six feet to where the ten men of the
master's division were formed up. They were the seamen, the ones who
worked the ship when underway. They were nominally under the charge
of the master, though the tiny *Cape Fear* was without such a warrant.

"Captain, this is Eustis Babcock, boatswain." Babcock stiffened, said,

"Suh." Faded blue uniform, with dark patches where Federal insignia once were sewn, salt-and-pepper beard, face tanned and lined, he looked every inch the old salt.

"Babcock," Bowater said. "Are you old navy?"

"Oh, aye, sir. Twenty-six years. Boatswain aboard *Merrimack* for the last ten, when all this present goings-on begun, sir. Bid adieu to them Yankees and come south when dear Alabama left the Union."

Bowater nodded. "I was second lieutenant aboard USS *Pensacola*. Reckon we've both taken a step down in our accommodations."

"I reckon, sir. But I sure do admire having some damn thing worth fighting for."

Samuel smiled. He was pleased to have men like Babcock under his command, men who formed the backbone of any real navy. "I agree, Boatswain. I look forward to serving with you."

"Suh."

They moved down the line, but Harwell did not bother introducing the other sailors and landsmen. There would be time later for names and assessment of each man's ability.

They came at last to the single black man in the master's division. He was wearing gray pants with a jaunty black stripe down each leg, a frock coat which, if old, was still in fine shape, a bow tie, and a derby.

"This here is Johnny St. Laurent. Cook," Harwell said. The luff's tone was odd, part exasperation, part resignation.

"Good day, *mon capitaine*," St. Laurent said, and his accent was an odd mix of Southern black and Parisian French.

"*Bonjour*. Where are you from?"

"New Orleans, sir."

"Were you a cook in New Orleans?"

"No, sir, I was a chef. A chef at the Château Dupré Hotel."

"How did you get here?"

"I come with Monsieur Taylor, sir."

Bowater glanced over at Hieronymus Taylor. The engineer was standing at something like attention, staring out over the water, his now-lit cigar waggling as he chewed on the end and puffed smoke like a steam engine. There was a story there, he imagined, but too much curiosity about the men was not a proper trait for a captain.

"I consider a clean galley to be of the highest priority, St. Laurent. I expect you to keep it thus. If you need help, speak to Mr. Harwell and he will see you get it."

"*Merci*, sir. Chief Taylor, he allow me some of ze engine-room niggers, when I need help, sir."

Bowater nodded. "Very good."

That was the end of the master's division, so Bowater took two steps down the deck until he was standing in front of First Assistant Engineer Taylor. "Very well, Mr. Taylor, you may report."

"Well, suh, this here's the engineering division. The firemen first class are Mr. Ian O'Malley from Belfast. He is of Hibernian descent," Taylor added in a loud whisper. "Mr. James Burgess of Aberdeen, who ain't been known to speak three words consecutive. The Negroes is the coal heavers. They have the singular advantage of not appearing dirty, though devil take me if I can find 'em when they're hiding in the coal bunkers."

Bowater held Taylor's eyes, did not acknowledge his attempt at humor. He shifted his gaze, looked over the engineering division. They were the same men he had seen in every engine room aboard every ship he had sailed. "Very well. Carry on."

Fifty hours. . . .

Hieronymus Taylor slumped on his stool and leaned against the forward bulkhead of the engine room, disassembling a recalcitrant gauge with a small screwdriver. He pictured in his mind the chart, Cape Fear to Cape Charles. They had been steaming fifty hours now. That should put them into the Chesapeake Bay.

Now, from his place on the stool, Taylor could feel the motion of the ship change, the slow roll of the ocean swells give way to a shorter, faster pitch, and he guessed that they were finally inside the Capes.

"Missa Taylor?"

Hieronymus looked up. Moses was leaning on his coal shovel. "What?"

"We gots the fire going nice an hot. You wants us to clean up here, or sommin'?"

"Clean up what?"

Moses shrugged. "I dunno. Clean de deck plates, mop her up. Make her look good, fo' de new cap'n an all."

Taylor scowled, looked around. "Where the hell is O'Malley? Ain't it his watch?"

"Reckon it too hot down here for dat Irishman. I thinks he's havin a smoke, topside."

Taylor pulled his shirt away from his chest. It was intolerably hot, by most normal standards. But with the sun set and the engine running at cruising speed, the engine room was not much above one hundred degrees, and for any veteran of an engineering division, that hardly constituted hot.

"Well?" Moses asked.

" 'Well, sir.' "

"Well, suh?"

"Well what?"

"You want us to mop de deck?"

"Why?"

"Case de cap'n come down here agin."

"Devil take the captain." Bowater had made his inspection of the ship soon after muster. He had looked around the engine room, found not one thing wrong, because Hieronymus M. Taylor made sure there was nothing wrong to be found. That perfection had earned only a nod, and a "Very good. Carry on, Chief" from the Academy stiff.

"You think I need to mop the deck to impress his lordship? Ain't a goddamned thing wrong with the deck. Lookee here . . ." Taylor fished a chunk of bread from the pocket of his coat, hung beside him on a hook. "Lookee here." He dropped the bread on the deck, got down on his hands and knees, and grabbed the bread in his teeth.

"See here?" he said through the chunk of bread. "I can eat off the damned deck!"

Nat St. Clair, coal heaver, began to bray like a hound dog, and the call was taken up by the other two coal heavers on watch. Moses grinned down at Taylor. "Now you got the boys all worked up!"

"Shut yer damned gobs, dumb coons." Taylor got back to his feet. "I'll make y'all eat yer damned dinners off'n the deck."

Overhead the bell from the wheelhouse sounded, *riing, riing*. Three bells, full ahead. Taylor scowled at the polished brass irritant.

"Dat you massa calling!" Moses said.

"Shut up. Didn't I tell you to wing that fire over?"

"No, suh."

"Well, wing the rutting fire over." Taylor glared at the bell. "St. Clair, go find O'Malley, tell him to tell them stiffs in the wheelhouse that's all the steam we're going to get out of this ain't-for-shit coal."

Just spoil 'em, if I give 'em everything they ring for. Next you know they'll come to expect it. . . . He picked up his gauge and gently turned the brass screw that held the backplate in place. *Give 'em a little more steam in twenty minutes or so. That should do for them wheelhouse beats.*

The *Cape Fear* steamed on, the thrum and hiss and bang of her engine so regular and perfect that Taylor did not even hear it, not on any conscious level. Any tiny change in the sound, he knew, would have sat him bolt upright, even if he had been asleep, every sense straining to determine the cause. But there was no change.

O'Malley stumbled back into the engine room, mumbled some excuse for his absence, spoke too low to be heard over the working of the engine, the roar of the boilers, the hiss of the air pumps. Taylor considered turning in.

A draft of cool air blew over him, and he looked up to see landsman Bayard Quayle come through the door and make his way warily down the ladder to the engine room. He stopped at the bottom, turned, and looked around with the wonder and uncertainty of one not used to the heat and the noise. Then he spotted Taylor and made his careful way over.

"Chief? Capt—" The tug took a harder pitch and Quayle grabbed frantically for a workbench, as if he was afraid of being sucked into the machinery. "Captain's compliments, Chief, and . . ." He paused, trying to recall the exact wording. ". . . and things is getting a bit tight, and he would be obliged if you was to . . . ah . . . *make the coal perform to satisfaction* . . . is what he said."

"That a fact?"

"Yes, suh. . . . Oh, and he asks would you please report to the wheelhouse?"

"What for?"

"Dunno, suh. Don't see nothing out of the ordinary. But the boatswain, he says it looks to him like all damned hell is breaking loose out there."

9

The most abominable vandalism at the yard. The two lower ship houses burned, with the New York, line of battle ship, on the stocks. Also the rigging loft, sail loft, and gun-carriage depot, with all the pivot gun carriages and many others.

—George T. Sinclair to Stephen R. Mallory

Captain Bowater stood in the wheelhouse, just to the left of the helmsman. He stared out of the window at the shorelines, set off from the water by a sprinkling of lights, and at the traffic on the water, and he knew that something was wrong.

There was too much going on for so late an hour, too many vessels on the move, too many lights onshore. There was an energy in the air that should not have been there twenty minutes after midnight.

"Come left to a heading of east northeast," he said, and Pauley Mc-Keown, able-bodied seaman, eased the wheel to port and said, in the remnants of an Irish burr, "Coming left to east northeast . . . east northeast."

At the far side of the wheelhouse, the luff's pencil scratched the course change in the ship's log.

Bowater frowned to prevent himself from smiling, because smiling for no apparent reason was the sure sign of a weak-minded idiot. Still, the smile wanted to come, despite his apprehensions about the night and the traffic on the water. He was overcome with the pure joy of the thing; the vibration of the engines coming through the deck, the motion of the vessel through the water. The quiet formality of the quarterdeck.

Not a quarterdeck, of course, not the wide, open quarterdeck of the

Pensacola, but a wheelhouse. *His* wheelhouse. There was no one to whom he must report the course change, no one to whom he must try to explain the odd feeling he was having. No one to whom he need speak at all.

He looked down at the rounded bows of the *Cape Fear* as they butted their way through the small chop and he knew that they were *his* bows and he loved them.

But he allowed no inkling of this newfound passion to creep into his voice, or his demeanor. His attitude was perfect disinterest.

"Helmsman, steady as she goes," he said and stepped behind the helmsman, behind Lieutenant Harwell, and peered out the side window on the starboard side. Just forward of the starboard beam he could make out Fortress Monroe. It was about two miles off—he had been giving it a wide berth—but even from that distance he could see that it was a busy place.

He frowned again, in earnest this time, and put his field glasses to his eyes. The magnification made the activity more obvious. He could see lights moving on the water, where small boats were pulling here and there, and more lights moving onshore. He could see lights along the top of the fort's walls. Something was happening.

Bowater stepped back across the wheelhouse and out the side door, peering out into the night. It was cool. He was wearing his old U.S. Navy uniform, with the insignia removed, and the breeze made the tail of his blue frock coat flap and beat his legs. He grabbed the patent-leather visor of his cap and tugged it lower. Up in the wheelhouse, the roll and pitch of the little man-of-war was much more pronounced.

Samuel Bowater had not realized, during his long self-imposed exile in Charleston, how very much he missed this.

He felt the platform on which he stood shake and turned to see Hieronymus Taylor mounting the ladder. The chief reached the top, paused, gave something that could be construed as a salute, which Bowater returned.

Then, before the captain could speak, Taylor turned his back on him and stared out over the water, then peered through the wheelhouse windows north toward Fortress Monroe. He made Bowater wait for an audience, as if it had been Taylor who summoned the captain, and not the other way around.

When the chief was done looking around he fished a lucifer from the pocket of his frock coat, which was unbuttoned to reveal the sweat-stained cotton shirt beneath, scratched the match on the rail, and stoked his cigar to life. He coughed, spit over the side of the ship, and returned the cigar to his mouth.

All the while Samuel Bowater quietly regarded him, the unshaved face, the squinting eyes, the hands black with coal dust and oil. An occasional unfortunate turn of the breeze brought the smell of the engineer to Bowater's nose. Samuel Bowater had never cared for engineering officers generally, as a class of men—dirty, artless mechanics—but so far Hieronymus M. Taylor was in the lead for most objectionable of the lot.

At last Taylor pulled the cigar from his mouth, looked out toward Sewall's Point, just off the port bow. "They's somethin happenin out there . . ." he said at last. "Somethin ain't right . . . bad ju-ju . . . don't know what it is, but I can feel it." He turned, looked Bowater right in the eye for the first time. "You feel it?"

Bowater nodded and Taylor nodded, and for a moment they said nothing.

"Chief, we've been steaming for fifty hours now, so I imagine you have a good idea of the state of our engine and boilers. How are they?"

"Fine, fine. Ain't a damned thing wrong with either."

"And the coal? O'Malley seemed to think there was something wrong with it."

Taylor grinned at the crude verbal trap. "We got that all straightened out, Captain."

"So if we get into action tonight, I can rely on the engine?"

Taylor pulled the cigar from his mouth. "Action? What the hell we gonna do, throw biscuits at the Yankees?"

"Perhaps."

Taylor replaced the cigar, nodded, and grinned. He had an eager, hungry look that Samuel did not find altogether disagreeable, not in the given circumstances. "Well, don't you worry about the engine, Captain. Get you in and out of any damned thing you can dream up."

"Good."

The two men were quiet for a moment, looking out at the dark humps of land, the lights like fireflies on the water, wrapped in the weirdness of the night.

"Chief, if you do not mind a personal question . . . what does the 'M' in your name stand for?"

"Michael."

"You were not, perchance, named for the fifteenth-century Flemish painter Hieronymus Bosch?" The question sounded idiotic, even as it left his lips.

Taylor took his cigar from his mouth so he could grin wider. "I don't reckon, Cap'n. I don't reckon my pappy'd know a Flemish painter if one come up, kicked him in the balls. He spent his whole life humpin freight in New Orleans. Don't know where he come up with 'Hieronymus.' "

He put his cigar back in his mouth, turned his head into the breeze. "That's the damned thing about a name, ain't it? The very thing that God and man knows ya by, and you ain't got a thing to say in choosin it."

"I suppose that's so. You were not in the old navy?" Bowater asked next.

"Navy? No, that ain't for me, all that 'yassa no suh' horseshit."

"Until now."

"Well, suh, now's different, ain't it? Now we gots a chance to kill us some Yankees. Besides, if I didn't join up with the navy, some dumb ass like to put me in the army, now ain't they? Don't reckon you'd care to suffer that fate anymore'n me."

Samuel ignored the comment, which hewed pretty close to insubordination, and decided instead to wring more of Taylor's past from him. He had no personal interest in the man's history, but knowing the chief's background would help Bowater size up his reliability. The fact that he was not a navy man had already lowered him considerably in Bowater's estimation. "So you learned your trade in the merchant service?"

"Might say that. Bangin around riverboats and such. Thing of it is, Captain, I got me a natural inclination toward anything mechanical. Something a man's born with, like music or painting or such. If it's driven by steam, I know how to make it work. In my gut. Ain't no other way to explain it."

"I see." Taylor apparently equated his proficiency with a wrench and screwdriver with Beethoven's genius for music or Rembrandt's mastery of the brush and palette. It was amusing, and charming, in a rough sort of way.

"Very well, Chief," Bowater said, by way of dismissal. "Why don't you lay below and conduct your orchestra of crankshafts and valves. And I promise I will let you know if we are going to get into any action tonight."

Lieutenant Henry Wise of the United States Ship *Pawnee* sat in the stern sheets of the launch and held the boat's tiller as the twenty bluejackets pulled slow and steady at the oars. Off the starboard side, across the river, some in shadows, some not, he could make out crowds of men, restless, ready for violence. He could feel their eyes on him. He could see the gleam of rifle barrels. Virginians, now secesh. They were waiting.

Thirty-five yards away to port, the granite seawall of the Norfolk naval shipyard made a sharp black line in the starlight. Beyond that, the yard receded into darkness, a darkness which swallowed up the brick wall on the perimeter and left what might be lurking beyond it to Wise's imagination.

He pictured a growing army of militia, armed, drilled, waiting for the moment to attack. All night long they had been hearing trains pulling into the station in town, carrying, it was said, thousands of troops. Rumors were swirling around the yard, and they all pointed to an overwhelming attack, ready to break at any second. The lieutenant could practically smell the panic in the air.

Wise looked to his right again, over the dark stretch of the Elizabeth River to the lights of Norfolk. There were boats all over the water, lights moving onshore, a general noise of activity, like the growing buzz of a restless crowd waiting on some grand event.

It was all over for the naval yard; there was nothing more they could do. The *Pawnee*, under the command of Commodore Paulding, had steamed to Portsmouth to save what ships they could from the massing Rebels. They were too late. McCauley had ordered them all scuttled two hours before.

Wise had hit the dock, raced to *Merrimack*, his particular charge, and found the water already over the orlop deck. It was over.

Someone shouted, out in the night, something made a clattering noise, then the report of a rifle and the water spit up, ten feet astern of the boat.

"Son of a bitch!" Wise shouted. "Lean into it, you men," he called, but the bluejackets needed no command, and like the experienced sailors they were they picked up the speed of their stroke without missing a beat.

Another rifle went off, and another, little shoots of water coming up around the boat. A ball thudded into the bows and then the boat moved into the shadow of the sloop-of-war *Plymouth* and was lost from sight of the mob.

The USS *Plymouth*, which had been perfectly serviceable that morning, was down by the stern and sinking slowly into the mud.

"Hold your oars," Wise ordered, and the men stopped rowing, let the blades drag in the water, and the boat slowed until it was nearly stopped. From out of the night he could hear the clank of *Pawnee*'s anchor chain coming on board, the chugging of the steam tug *Yankee*, come to take the *Cumberland* in tow. She was all that they could save.

"Not long now, boys . . ." Wise said.

"Till what, sir? Till the secesh come over the wall?" one of the men asked, and got a chuckle from the others.

"No, till we blow this place to hell and the secesh with it," Wise said. "Give way, all."

Once again the sailors leaned into the oars and the boat gathered way. They glided down the long black side of the *Plymouth* and came out under her bows. He could see the mob again, in the shadows and the pools of light. They moved and swayed like a wheat field, and their shouts punctuated the night.

"Pick up the stroke," Wise said, and the bluejackets leaned into it again and the boat shot forward just as the first rifle fired at them. Here and there muzzle flashes pricked the darkness and the balls whizzed around them, but they would be no more than a dark shadow on the water and it would be a lucky shot indeed that did any damage.

Now the once mighty *Merrimack* loomed up over them, and with one pull they were behind her protective wooden walls. She reeked of the turpentine with which Wise and his men had doused her decks hours before.

"Hold your oars."

Over the noise of the *Pawnee*'s anchor chain he heard a voice, clear and loud, call, "Up and down!" *Pawnee* was nearly underway.

Wise shifted in his seat, turned to look in *Pawnee*'s direction, and as he did a rocket lifted off from her deck and streaked up into the sky. The yellow tail made a slash of light against the backdrop of the stars, and then the rocket exploded in a burst, its fragments trailing fire down to the water and hissing out.

"That's the signal, boys. Toss oars. Bowman, ease us along to the powder train."

The oars came up in two straight rows, and the man in the bow hooked onto the sagging *Merrimack* with his boat hook and pulled the boat along her black side. Ten feet above their heads the white band along her gundeck made a ghostly trail the full 275 feet of her massive hull. At regular intervals along the white band, the empty gunports gaped open, like mouths trying in vain to protest. One of the *Wabash* class, the most powerful, most valuable men-of-war in the United States Navy. She seemed too substantial to be destroyed.

"Here, sir." The bowman had reached the gunport to which they had earlier run the train of combustible material—rope, ladders, grating, hawsers—which they had laid in the form of a big letter V forward of the mainmast and then doused with turpentine.

The bowman gave a final pull of the boat hook and then checked the motion as Wise came up level with the gunport. Cotton waste and frayed rope hung out of the square hole in an unsightly fashion. Wise sighed, looked around one last time, tried to put off doing that terrible thing, but there was no delaying it.

He pulled an oilskin pouch from his pocket, fished out a match, and struck the match on the gunnel of the boat. It sputtered and flared and caught, and Wise held it to the cotton waste. The flame jumped onto the spirit-soaked cotton, consumed it, moved inboard along the flammable trail.

"All right . . . shove off, give way, all." The bowman pushed the boat off from *Merrimack*'s side and the oars came down and the boat pulled away. Wise pushed the tiller over and turned to look back at his own handiwork. His foot kicked a binnacle lantern lying in the bottom of the boat. He had saved it out of *Merrimack* earlier—why, he did not know. Because he had to save something, perhaps.

The oarsmen dipped their blades and pulled, dipped and pulled. They were twenty feet from the steam frigate when Wise turned back again to see if the flames had taken, and as he did the decks and gunports, the masts and rails seemed to explode in flame.

The shock of light and heat slammed into the boat, and Wise threw his arm up over his eyes.

He heard one of the men curse, and the confusion of an oar crabbing, oars banging on oars. Flames burst from each of the *Merrimack*'s gunports. Fire mounted up the lower masts, like the stakes in an old-time witch-burning. From over the high bulwarks they could see the flames run fore and aft along the deck, they could hear the low roar of the inferno, and now from the shoreline they could hear shouts of outrage, the sounds of the mob spurred to action, but it was too late for them.

"Well hell, sir," the bowman called. "Reckon she's afire now."

"Reckon. Very well, let's get a move on. We got more to do like her." Wise turned his back on the burning *Merrimack*. He was blind now in the dark, after staring into those wicked flames. He pushed the tiller over and headed for where he knew the *Germantown* to be.

Paulding had ordered him to see about firing the *Merrimack* and he had done it, done it damned well, and now that honorable ship, the pride of the United States Navy, was engulfed in flames. In his stomach he felt physically sick. It was the most shameful duty he had ever been ordered to perform.

Together, as if they were puppets on one string, the heads of Samuel Bowater, Thadeous Harwell, and Hieronymus Taylor all moved right to left as they traced the line of the rocket streaking up, almost directly overhead.

"Well, now, that's got to mean some damned thing . . ." Taylor observed.

Bowater pulled his eyes from the sky just as the rocket burst into flaming fragments. The three of them were standing on the roof of the deckhouse, where they could get an unobstructed view all around.

He looked to port and the town of Norfolk, and to starboard at the Gosport naval yard, two hundred yards away. If something was acting,

Bowater had guessed it would be at the naval yard, and it seemed he had guessed right.

He could hear a ship winning her anchor, he could see boats moving, men on shore, their rifles gleaming. The occasional smattering of gunfire. There was a powder-keg atmosphere, ready to blow, and Bowater was not sure where to put his ship to keep her clear of the blast.

"Look here, sir," said Harwell, and Bowater looked where he was pointing. A line of flame, a ship on fire, perhaps, it was hard to tell.

"Now, what in hell . . ." Taylor began and then suddenly the line of flame exploded into a great sheet of fire, illuminating the ship fore and aft, spilling out of the long line of gunports, climbing up the lower masts.

"Ho-ly . . ." Taylor muttered.

"That's one of the *Wabash*-class frigates," Bowater said. He could see her perfectly in the flames of her own destruction.

"I think she's *Merrimack*, sir," Harwell offered. "They've fired *Merrimack*."

For a brief instant Bowater considered coming alongside her, wondered if the *Cape Fear*'s pumps were equal to the task of saving the burning ship. He opened his mouth to speak, and then the whole world seemed to explode into flames.

10

The flag of Virginia floats over the yard.

—George T. Sinclair to Stephen R. Mallory

*B*eyond the pyre that was the frigate *Merrimack*, first one, then another, then another of the massive A-framed ship houses burst into flame, the base of each building engulfed, the fire licking its way up the curved sides. At the other end of the yard, where Samuel knew the ropewalk and sail loft and rigging loft to be, now suddenly there was only fire. In a flash the dark night was turned into a brilliant inferno.

Across the river came shouts of rage, impotent gunfire.

"They're firing the yard!" Samuel said, and even he could not keep from shouting that time.

"Who, sir?" asked Harwell.

"Got to be the damned Yankees," Taylor said. "Got to be them damned Yankees running away and burnin the yard behind 'em."

A bell rang and Bowater turned and out of the dark thrashed the steam frigate *Pawnee*, with her high sides and straight sheer and ugly, foreshortened masts. Samuel Bowater knew her well.

Black smoke poured from her funnel and the water creamed white around her bows as she gathered way. The burning ships and yard washed her in yellow light and weird dancing shadows. Samuel could see men lining her rails and imagined they were marines, ready for whatever else the night would bring.

From her after chocks, a hawser ran straight back, like a leash, and made off to the end was the USS *Cumberland*, which *Pawnee* had in tow. Unlike the squat *Pawnee*, *Cumberland* had the lofty spars, longer bowsprit, and jib boom and more elegant sheer of a pure sailing vessel. But without steam, she was helpless in the light air.

"Ahoy, the tug!" A voice came from *Pawnee*'s quarterdeck.

"Ahoy!" Bowater shouted back.

"Come up on *Cumberland*'s starboard side and make fast! Go on, get a move on!"

"Aye, aye!" he shouted, then turned to his officers. "We have to go ashore, see what we can do. Mr. Harwell, assemble a landing party. Tell off five steady hands."

"Aye, aye, sir. And sir, may I lead the party?"

"No, Luff. I'll go. I need you here."

"Aye, sir," Harwell said, and Bowater could see the genuine disappointment. But he could not send Harwell. He did not know himself what he would do once he was ashore.

"Mind if I tag along, Cap'n?" Taylor asked. He had his hands in his pockets and was leaning back some, as if loitering by the woodstove at the general store.

Bowater considered the request. He didn't like Taylor, but the engineer's perceptions that night had impressed him. Besides, Taylor had a wolflike, all but feral look in his eyes that his casual stance could not disguise. Bowater suspected the man would be good in a fight. "Very well. Arm yourself as you will."

Bowater dashed back into the wheelhouse, grabbed the pull for the engine-room bell, rang up half ahead. "I'll take this," he said to the helmsman, pushing him aside and taking up the wheel. Tight maneuvering in a small vessel—it was easier for him to do it himself than to give helm commands.

He swung the *Cape Fear*'s bow off, headed her right for the granite breakwater. The shipyard was in flames from one end to the other, and some of it was lit as if it was noon and some was in shadow. The edge of the seawall made a sharp line where the yard met the river.

Samuel spun the wheel and the *Cape Fear* heeled into the turn and he rang for engine stop. It was a heady sensation to feel the tug move under his hands, feel the strong boat respond to his hand on the wheel, his hand on the engine-room bell.

The bow swung past the seawall, and Bowater rang engines astern and with a twist of the wheel brought the eighty-foot tug against the granite pier.

One jingle, all stop, and he felt the tug settle down as the screw ceased its thrashing. He leaned out the wheelhouse door. The fire had taken over the ship houses and engulfed them, the flames already reaching hundreds of feet in the air. There was a great roaring sound, the sound of rushing air, as the fires consumed everything: wood, stone, metal, the air itself.

Eustis Babcock was ashore with the forward fast, and he was directing the others to stern and spring lines.

Samuel Bowater took a deep breath, took in smoke and the swell of burning wood and paint and the coal smoke from his own boilers. He felt the excitement rush through him. He thought of how the fire had raced over and consumed *Merrimack*. That was it exactly. He felt strong, charged, with a head up steam, alive, as he had not felt in years. He was Rip Van Winkle. He was experiencing his own personal Great Awakening.

He turned, raced down the ladder to the side deck, nearly colliding with Thadeous Harwell.

"Sir, shore party is told off and assembled on the fantail, sir," he said. Harwell could hardly contain his excitement, and it reminded Bowater to get control of his own.

"Well done, Lieutenant. Now see here, you are in command while I am gone. You are to concern yourself with the safety of the vessel above all else, even if it means casting off and leaving us, do you understand?"

"Yes, sir."

Bowater regarded the young man for a moment, saw himself with the guns of Veracruz firing in the distance. He felt sorry for him. "Your chance will come, Mr. Harwell."

"Yes, sir. Thank you, sir."

Bowater gave him a slap on the shoulder, hurried down the side deck. There on the fantail was Hieronymus Taylor. He had shed his coat and now his braces made two dark lines across his stained white shirt. He held his cigar clamped in his teeth, and on one shoulder rested a sawed-off double-barrel shotgun.

The rest of the party was assembled, with cutlasses hanging from belts and rugged sea-service carbines in their hands. And there was Jacob, who had been though this drill many times, waiting with sword belt, sword, and pistol.

Eustis Babcock was back aboard. He had his back toward Samuel, staring out over the water, and then he turned and Bowater could see tears streaming down his deep-lined cheeks.

"Mr. Babcock?"

"It's the *Merrimack*, sir. The dear old *Merrimack*. Look what them Yankee bastards done to her, sir, just look!"

Bowater nodded. Ten years as boatswain aboard that ship, Babcock would love her as much as he loved his home state. He might as well have been watching Mobile burn.

"Well, let us go and make them pay for this," Bowater said, a silly, shallow platitude that disgusted him even as he said it. But Babcock nodded and wiped his cheeks with his sleeve. Looked more like a boy in a sailor suit than the grizzled veteran that he was. The words seemed to have bolstered him.

Sailors and their damned sentimental . . . Bowater thought, and turned his attention back to the rest of the shore party.

"Listen here, men . . . . stick close by me when we're ashore . . ." He raised his arms and let Jacob wrap the belt around his waist and buckle it. "We'll . . ." He was not sure what else to say. He did not know what they were going to do. Instead he pulled his pistol from its holster, his own personal .36-caliber Navy Colt, a present from his father. It gleamed in the light of the fires onshore, and the engraved vines that twisted around the sides of the weapon stood out bold and the ivory handle glowed orange. He spun the cylinder, checked the caps, reholstered it.

"Let's go."

He turned and stepped up onto the tug's rail and jumped the five feet to the cobbled yard below. The heat was overwhelming, even from that distance, like standing in front of an oven. One by one the men dropped to the ground beside him.

He turned and counted. The shore party was all there. He marched off toward the burning ship houses, because that seemed the focal point of the growing destruction. He wondered if the yard was still in Federal hands, or if the Confederates had come over the wall. He wondered if they might be shot by their own side.

"Don't see how hell could be much diff'r'nt than this," Taylor remarked, stepping up to Bowater's side. "Reckon we'll find out, soon enough."

Hell, indeed, Bowater thought. The fire could be measured in square acres now, and the buildings were mere ghostly outlines in the center of the flames. Fire reached hundreds of feet in the air, arching over in the light breeze, dancing and swirling like yellow-and-red dragons. And under it all, a low and steady roar and the crash of structures collapsing as they burned through.

Fifty yards away, black against the flames, a knot of men moved toward them. Bowater's hand reached under the wide flap of his holster, pulled his Colt, cocked the hammer back in a motion as familiar as pulling his watch.

"Hold up!" Bowater held up his hand, and the men behind him stopped.

The approaching men grew closer, and as they drew away from the flames Bowater could see the dark blue frock coats and the sky-blue trousers of United States Marines.

"Keep your mouths shut. Don't do anything unless I tell you to."

The marines came on at the double quick, rifles held against chests, and then they noticed the band from the *Cape Fear*. Bowater saw the lieutenant redirect his men.

Brass it out . . . have to brass it out with this type . . .

"Lieutenant!" Bowater called in his best quarterdeck voice. "What are you men still doing here? Report!"

The marine lieutenant stopped, and Bowater saw his eyes move up and down his uniform, but the frock coat he wore was the same one he had worn in the Union navy, the same worn by naval officers everywhere, and it did not give Bowater's secret away.

"We were detailed to protect the men blowing the dry dock, sir."

"Good. You are the detail I was looking for. Get down to the ordnance building, there, there," Bowater pointed, "and cover the boat tied up at the seawall. We'll see to the dry dock and get the men out."

The lieutenant hesitated. He began to say something, a protest forming, but marines did not protest, it was not a part of them, so finally he said, "Yes, sir!" and led his detail away.

Bowater watched them go, watched the smoke swallow them up, then said, "Come on, men!" and led his people off at a jog.

Blowing the dry dock. That was what the man said.

Samuel knew Gosport, he had been to the naval yard often enough. The dry dock was the most valuable thing there. If the Yankees managed to burn every last inch of the yard, it would still be a godsend to the Confederate Navy if the dry dock was saved.

Blowing the dry dock. That could not be allowed to happen.

They raced along, closing with the ship houses, beside which Bowater knew the dry dock lay. Two hundred yards away, the heat seemed unbearable, but they ran on and Bowater wondered if the heat would discharge the rounds in his pistol. He shifted his holster so the barrel was pointing away from any part of himself.

The smoke from the burning building rolled over them, and they slowed their pace, coughing and staggering forward. Bowater felt as if his skin was on fire, as if it would start peeling and blistering, but they staggered on.

Thirty yards away, a gang of men hurried along, moving in the opposite direction, like specters, barely seen through the smoke, but they did not seem to notice the men from the *Cape Fear*, or if they did, they did not care who they were or what they were about.

Then, right ahead, Bowater could see gleaming in the light the long line of bollards and the small capstans that ran the length of the dry dock, and beyond them, the black pit of the empty dry dock itself.

"Taylor!" Bowater called, shouting over the roar of the flames, then paused for a fit of coughing. "Take . . . Babcock and go that way." He pointed toward the river end of the dry dock. "See if you can see if the dock is mined. McNelly, come with me! The rest of you, station your-selves here, keep a weather eye out."

Taylor hurried off and soon disappeared into the smoke, and Bowater and McNelly raced off in the opposite direction. They inched toward the edge of the dry dock and peered down. The bottom was in deep shadow; they could not see if there was anything there, powder kegs or such.

"Sir!" McNelly shouted, pounded him on the shoulder. Bowater looked up, looked in the direction that McNelly was pointing. Through the smoke, silhouetted by the burning ship houses, he could see two men, one standing, one kneeling, concentrating on some job at hand.

Bowater stepped forward, waved McNelly after him. He picked up his pace, reached under the flap of his holster, pulled the Colt free.

Then he was up with the two men in the smoke. He tightened his grip on the pistol, held it away from his body, stepped boldly forward.

One of the men, the one standing, noticed him at last. He turned until he was facing Samuel straight on, took a step forward, put a hand on his holster, paused.

Bowater stopped five feet from the man. He was framed against the wall of flame that was the ship building, and Samuel could barely look at him, could see little beyond a black shape against blinding red, yellow, and white.

The man crouching paused in what he was doing, looked up, and for a moment it was a stalemate, like the moment with the marines. And then the standing man took another step and said, "Lieutenant Bowater? Samuel Bowater?"

Bowater coughed, squinted at the man. His eyes were sore and running with tears from the smoke and he brushed them away. "John Rogers? Is that you?"

The man stepped forward, hand outstretched, and he materialized into Lieutenant John Rogers.

"Lieutenant . . . !" Bowater shook Rogers's hand, glanced at his shoul-der boards. "Forgive me, Commander!" Bowater had been fourth lieu-tenant and Rogers second aboard *Wabash* five years before.

"Good to see you, Samuel," Rogers yelled. Bowater could see the sweat streaking through the grime on his face. "Hell, I thought you'd gone secesh!"

"I'm here, aren't I?"

"Sure! What are you doing here?"

"Came to see about the dry dock!" This reunion in the smoke only added to the dreamlike, unreal quality of the night.

"She's set! See there?" Rogers pointed down at the ground. Through the smoke Bowater could see the sparking flames of a powder train, racing toward the edge of the dry dock. Lighting the powder train, that was what the kneeling fellow had been doing.

"Two thousand pounds of powder!" Rogers shouted. "Gonna blow this son of a bitch to Kingdom Come!"

"Then shouldn't we get the hell out of here?"

"It'd be a good idea. Got five minutes till it blows, maybe less!"

Bowater felt the salty sweat running down his face and burning his eyes. He wiped a sleeve over his forehead. "I have men down there!" He pointed toward the river. "I have to go get them!"

"Be quick about it!" Rogers turned to the other man. "Captain Wright! Let's go!"

"Which way?" the other shouted. Bowater looked at him for the first time. He wore the uniform of a captain of Army Engineers.

Rogers looked around, unsure. "Boat's that way!" Rogers shouted, pointing past the burning ship houses. "Don't know if we're going to make it through!"

"Best try!" Bowater shouted. "Go on, I'll follow behind!"

"All right! But get out of here, quick!"

John Rogers gave Samuel Bowater a fraternal slap on the shoulder, and Bowater saw the eyes follow the hand, saw the absence of shoulder boards register on Rogers's face.

"Let's go!" Bowater shouted to McNelly and turned away from Rogers, and Rogers let the question go. He and the other man stumbled off into the smoke and the shadows and the brilliant glare of the flames. Bowater watched them until their dark silhouettes disappeared.

"Let's get the hell out of here, sir!" McNelly shouted, but Bowater shook his head.

"We've got to put out the powder train!" he shouted and started running. At the edge of the dry dock the cobbles gave way to smooth granite stones. Bowater approached the edge of the dry dock carefully, peering through the smoke, trying to see the powder train and avoid falling over the edge.

"Sir!" McNelly whined. "It's gonna goddamned blow . . ."

"Shut up, sailor!" Bowater shouted, staring down through the smoke. He saw it at last, a bright dancing light, crawling along near the bottom of the dry dock, moving toward the unseen barrels of powder. "Go find Chief Taylor, tell him I've gone down to put the powder train out!"

He turned to see if McNelly had heard him, but the sailor was nowhere to be seen, and Bowater could do no more than hope he had run off to obey the order.

Samuel Bowater raced along the length of the dry dock, his eyes moving between the burning train and the edge of the dock. The dry dock was constructed in a series of great granite steps or ledges angling down to the bottom, like a long, narrow coliseum. Bowater took the first, three feet high, and the next, climbing fast to the bottom of the dry dock, trying not to slip or tumble on the granite ledges.

It was black in the dry dock, and many degrees cooler, as he climbed down and down, and the flames of the shipyard were now no more than an orange glow overhead, and the omnipresent roar.

Down, it seemed a terribly long way, and then his foot came down in water and he stepped down another step and another and the water rose around him. It had not occurred to him that the dry dock could be partially flooded, but if the water was over his head he would have to swim for it, and he was none too sure of his ability to do so.

Another step down and his foot hit the slick, granite floor of the dry-dock. The water was up to his waist. He pushed forward, breasting the water, which dragged at him and slowed him down as he tried to race for the distant moving flame.

The powder train, he could see, had been laid along the far side of the dry dock. He would have to push his way through the water and reach it before it reached the powder. He forced his legs to work harder.

Goddamned . . . damned . . . nightmare . . . Bowater pushed on through the blackness and the water. It was just like one of those hellish dreams, in which he would run harder and harder from some nebulous evil and get nowhere.

The spark hissed and leaped and flared and raced toward the powder as Bowater raced toward it, and it seemed as if the entire world was compacted down to that space between himself and the flames. With his mind so focused he did not hear the grating, mechanical sounds at first, did not register the rush of cool water, he just forced himself on.

"Captain! Captain Bowater!" The voice came through his fog, but far away, barely audible above the roar of the flames and his own heaving breath.

"Captain Bowater!" It sounded like Taylor, Hieronymus Taylor.

Bowater stopped long enough to suck a lungful of air and shout, "Down here, in the dry dock!" He paused and realized that the mechanical sound he had heard was getting louder now. He staggered as an eddy of water caught him in the midriff.

"We're opening the damned gates, Captain! Get the hell out of there!"

Opening the gates . . . Then Bowater understood that the mechanical, grating sound was the sound of the floodgates being cranked open, which also explained the sudden eddies of water rushing in. Taylor was flooding the dry dock.

Good, good . . . Bowater thought as a fresh surge of water knocked him off his feet. He flailed at the water, kicked with his feet, but his shoes could not find a foothold on the slick bottom.

The water rolled him over and he sucked in a mouthful and then managed to get his feet down and stand. He spit, gagged, thrashed his way toward the side of the dry dock from which he had come.

Son of a bitch . . . son of a bitch . . . He could see nothing in that black pit. He looked up and could see the edge of the dry dock, impossibly high overhead, framed against the orange, burning sky. The water swirled above his stomach, up his chest. It was cold, coming in from the Elizabeth River.

Another step and his foot was out from under him and the water tumbled him again, pushed him under and swirled him along. His arms grabbed out for something, but there was nothing but water. He kicked, reached out again, and this time his hand came up against cold granite, the side of the dry dock.

He steadied himself, tried to get his feet down, but there was no bottom anymore, the water was over his head. He tried to lie back, float, but the surge of fresh water coming in would not allow it. He slammed against the side of the dry dock, bumped and scraped down its length, completely at the mercy of the roiling river water.

And then his hand hit something, something jutting out from the wall of the dry dock, a ringbolt for tying off a fast. He grabbed it, held himself in place, climbed up one of the granite steps, then another, found another ringbolt to grab. The water swirled around and tugged at him, but he held fast to the bolt, pressed his face against the cold granite, and breathed.

"Captain? You down there?"

Bowater wanted to respond but he could not. He gave himself a moment, heaving for breath, and then when he had his wind called, "I'm here, Chief! Coming up!"

"I suggest you hurry, sir!"

The powder. With drowning imminent, he had forgotten all about the chance of being blown to hell. He swiveled around, stared across the black space toward the powder train. He could still see it, that hateful flame, creeping toward the unseen charge. Bowater gritted his teeth, hating the thing, waiting for the blast.

And then it winked and then it was gone.

The spark had drowned, and he, Samuel Bowater, had not.

He turned his face back toward the side of the dry dock, pressed his cheek against the granite, closed his eyes. The fire that had burned in him earlier was out, the head of steam that had propelled him with such fearless energy was gone. He could feel his hands trembling. His knees began to vibrate. He squeezed his eyes tighter shut, clenched his teeth.

Then he opened his eyes, looked up, said, "Oh, Lord!" then turned and vomited into the water swirling around him.

For a long moment he lay there puking, until nothing else would come. He spit out, again and again, lowered his face into the water to wash the vomit away. He could not let anyone see the shame of it.

"Captain?" Taylor's voice again.

"Coming up!" Bowater shouted back, and took the steps one at a time, his confidence and his strength returning as he climbed up out of the pit.

At last he came up over the edge, not where he had first climbed down, but near the far end of the dry dock. The inrush of water had pushed him nearly the length of the thing.

He straightened and looked around. The blast-furnace heat from the ship houses felt good on his wet clothing. Shapes moved out of the smoke, and they materialized into Hieronymus Taylor and Eustis Babcock.

"Hell, Captain . . ." Taylor said. He shook his head. He was grinning.

"Hell, indeed. Where's McNelly?"

"Ain't he with you?"

"No. He must have run off." Bowater forced McNelly out of his thoughts. "Good job, Chief, opening the gates."

"Thankee, sir. Sorry 'bout near drowning you."

Bowater shook his head. "It couldn't be helped." Now that his thoughts were settling back into place, he was feeling a bit sheepish about not having thought of the floodgates himself. "Let's get back to the ship."

Wearily they trudged off, making their way back in the direction they had come. With the bulk of the flames at their back they had an easier time of it, the shipyard before them brilliantly illuminated, the light making a million little bright spots and shadows over the rounded cobblestones. But the smoke was a dense fog, and their visibility was down to a hundred feet or so, and after a few moments Bowater found himself questioning his own sense of direction.

"Chief . . ." he began and then from behind him an explosion jarred the ground, tossed bright volcano flames high in the air. Bowater and Taylor and Babcock were flung forward, part from the shock and part from a desire to get down. For a long minute they lay there, unmoving, their hands clapped on their heads, as if that would save them from the falling granite of the dry dock.

Another explosion, and they felt the cobbles tremble under them.

Bowater rolled over, sat up, realized that lying on the ground would do them no good. He could see the fires at the ship houses had redoubled, and the wooden frame that had once been at the center of the inferno was gone.

"Reckon that was the dry dock?" Taylor asked.

"No," Bowater said. "Probably some powder stores, or such. They put two thousand pounds of powder down in the dry dock. If that had gone off we'd be under half a ton of granite right now."

He turned and looked at Taylor, who was on his belly and propped up on his elbows. Incredibly, his cigar was still in his mouth. The engineer nodded.

The three men hauled themselves to their feet, stumbled off again. The roar of the flames had dropped off a bit, as the fire consumed everything it could and began to starve.

They found the others, and together the lot of them made their way back to the *Cape Fear*. In the east, the sky was beginning to show signs of dawn, but Samuel Bowater could think of nothing but sleep.

We will anchor out . . . if it is safe . . . anchor out and let all hands sleep . . .

The tug was where they had left her, tied to the seawall, but lower with the ebbing tide. She looked like a ghost ship in the early-dawn light and the ubiquitous smoke. Samuel could see men moving about her deck.

Quite a lot of men, it seemed.

His weary mind toyed with this observation as he and his men shuffled the last hundred yards to the vessel. And then, twenty yards away, he became aware of more men, to his right and left, men closing in on them, and suddenly he was alert again, and his pistol was in his hand.

"Hold!" a voice called. Bowater turned. Men were coming at him from both sides, armed with rifles, some in uniform, most not. "Hold, sir!" the voice said again, and the man calling stepped forward, a sword in hand. He stood directly between Bowater and his tug, pointed with his sword to the pistol in his hand.

"Lay down your weapons, all of you!" he said in a commanding voice. "You are all prisoners of the Provisional Army of the State of Virginia!"

Bowater watched the officer's expression of cool command turn to anger as he holstered, rather than dropped, his expensive presentation pistol. He did not know what to say. He wanted to laugh, but he was far too tired for that.

Book Two

HAMPTON ROADS

11

𝕽𝖎𝖈𝖍𝖒𝖔𝖓𝖉 𝕯𝖎𝖘𝖕𝖆𝖙𝖈𝖍

TUESDAY MORNING. . . . . APRIL 23, 1861

BURNING OF THE NAVY YARD!

DESTRUCTION OF GOVERNMENT ARMS AND STORES

FIVE FEDERAL SHIPS BURNT!

ESCAPE OF THE PAWNEE:

THE CUMBERLAND TOWED DOWN AND ASHORE!

EXCITING INCIDENTS, &c., &c.

Passengers from Norfolk last evening assure us that the amount of guns, stores and ammunition secured by the Virginia forces after the burning of the Navy-Yard, was enormous, and our correspondence confirms the fact. The guns in many instances were imperfectly spiked in the hurry and alarm of the Federal incendiaries, and are in no respects damaged.

THE DRY DOCK

Appearances indicated that it was intended to cripple this admirable and useful work, by blowing up the gates, but from some cause this work was not done, and the dock was found to be altogether unhurt.

We cannot bring ourselves to believe that an officer of a Navy, distinguished hitherto by a high sense of honor and chivalrous courage, could willingly condescend to such an inglorious mode of warfare as this. We rather regard it as an emanation from the wretched cabal at Washington, and a practical carrying out of the tactics laid down by the villainous Sumner, and other orators of the Black Republican party. Burn, sink and destroy is the word with them.

The Petersburg Express has the following by telegraph from Norfolk:

The prisoners taken this morning are Capt. Wright of the army, and young Rogers, a son of Commodore Rogers of the navy.

The enemy took two of our young men prisoners last night. They were reconnoitering on their own account.

To: Stephen R. Mallory
Norfolk, April 22, 1861

North left for Charleston to-day; I answer your dispatch. The *Pennsylvania, Merrimack, Germantown, Raritan, Columbia,* and *Dolphin* are burned to the water's edge and sunk. The *Delaware, Columbus,* and *Plymouth* are sunk. All can be raised; the *Plymouth* easily; not much injured. The *Germantown* crushed and sunk by the falling of shears. Her battery, new and complete, uninjured by fire; can be recovered. Destruction less than might be expected. The metal work of the carriages will be recovered; most of it good. About 4,000 shells thrown overboard; can be recovered. The *Germantown's* battery will be up and ready for service to-morrow. In ordnance building all small arms broken and thrown overboard will be fished up.

The brass howitzers thrown overboard are up. The *Merrimack* has 2,200 10-pound cartridges in her magazine in water-tight tanks. Everything broken that they could break. Private trunks broken open and officers' clothing and that of their wives stolen.

Glorious news! General Gwynn just read me a telegram; it comes from a reliable source; the New York Regiment, attempting to march through Maryland, was met half way between Marlborough and Annapolis and cut all to pieces.

—G. T. Sinclair

From the Journal of Lieutenant Thadeous Harwell:
April 20 and 21, 1861

What strange and awful spirits were abroad that night! Which our brave Captain sensed, and handing the field glasses to me did most nobly ask that I give him my opinion of just what mischief might be afoot! To my eye I put the glass. And what was that I saw? To our good captain said, "Indeed, there is some ignoble thing here! Something is rotten in the State of Virginia!"

And so on my urging the captain steered our humble vessel down the Elizabeth River to Norfolk. What is that we see? Just what the cowardly debased Yankees had wrought—not but utter destruction to the grand and valuable naval yard which by right and location does and should belong to the Sovereign State of Virginia, and the Grand Confederacy.

With never a thought toward his own life nor limb, our gallant Captain Bowater went at the head of his own small army and extinguished the very flame that would have destroyed the dry dock and rained down on the heads of those poor innocents abed in Portsmouth untold hundred tons of granite! And thus did the bold Bowater save for the Confederacy that grand edifice, the dry dock, with which we now might hope to build grand and vast men-of-war to sally forth and vanquish those sea-born vandals who have come south to do us gross injustice!

I made much protest that our bold captain should not thus expose his life to the cowardly fires of our enemies, but rather it was the place of his subordinate officer, myself, who so longed to charge into the lion's mouth with guns blazing. What is that that our brave captain replied? He would hear none of it, but did assure me (with that nobleness and honestness of character that is the birthright of those noble Sons of the South) that on the next occasion I should have my chance to distinguish myself in mortal combat with those who would deprive us of our liberties! O, how I long for that day, hour, moment!

Mrs. Bertrand Atkins
9 Elm Street
Culpepper, Virginia

Dearest Mother,

No doubt you will have heard of the terrific excitement we have had down here! I daresay it has been building for the past month, ever since my arrival here in Portsmouth, the way the storms build up in the summertime. You could just feel it, with more and more soldiers arriving in town, and talk everywhere of attacking the naval yard, and the Yankees making their preparations to leave. Two nights ago the storm broke, as it were. Of course I remained safe at home with Aunt Molly, well away from any danger, but the flames were perfectly visible, and the sounds of the gunfire and explosions quite clear, even though we were more than a mile away from the yard.

Now things are settling down some, with our troops in command of the yard and the Yankees fled to Fort Monroe and Washington. Still, it seems as if Portsmouth and Norfolk are to be the center of much activity, in the military and naval line, as the Yankees were not able to destroy as much as they thought. It is a very exciting place to be, during an exciting time, not unlike being in Boston or Philadelphia in 1776. But I am getting too full of all this excitement and playing the poet again, as Father has always accused me of doing.

I trust all is well with you and Father, and that Father has become more sanguine about my moving down here. Aunt Molly is well and sends her love, and I am well also.

Love to everyone there.
Your daughter,
Wendy Atkins

12

*The officers and men all being raw recruits, discipline was very galling to
them . . . but soon the boys began to learn the "Old Soldier" tricks and learned
to yield gracefully to the inevitable when they could not dodge the officers.*

—James R. Binford, 15th Mississippi Infantry

Lieutenant Robley Paine, Jr., trudged through the tent-lined,
makeshift streets of Camp Walker, bivouac of 3rd Brigade, of which the
18th Mississippi was now a part. The summer sun pushed him down into
the dusty path. He and his men had been there for two weeks already, but
it seemed much longer than that.

It was July of 1861, and Lieutenant Paine reckoned he knew most of
what soldiering was about.

He knew the weary, hot, dusty marching, as he and the rest of the
young men had tramped to Yazoo City and then north to Corinth, over
two hundred miles by paddle wheeler, by foot, and by rail.

He knew the muttering and the growling and the insubordination of
the men, silent and otherwise. He learned when to cajole and when to yell
and when to deliver a cuff to the ear or a boot to the ass. He learned how
to do it in such a way that it got the job done and left no permanent and
festering hatreds.

In Corinth he learned what an ungodly mess a cluster of officers could
make of trying to create an army from a rabble. Officers who, a month before, had been cotton planters and merchants and politicians.

But not all of them. There were a handful of real soldiers, men who had resigned their commissions in the old army and come south to fight for their states. These men Robley watched close, and imitated, and tried to learn what he could about real soldiering.

He learned about indecision and infighting, about intrigue, about toadying and backstabbing and bootlicking. By his own inbred good sense and natural aversion to such things, and the honor instilled in him by his father, he learned to avoid it all, and to go about his business and look after the welfare of his men.

As a result of that policy, Robley Paine remained an officer, because in the Confederate Army the men voted their officers in, with a democracy that harked back to the army of 1776. Robley Paine was a near-unanimous choice for third lieutenant.

At length, under the direction of General J. L. Alcorn, the disparate young men from Mississippi were formed into companies: Company A, the Confederate Rifles, Company B, the Benton Rifles, Company C, the Confederates, and so on. The boys from Yazoo County formed Company D, named, to no one's surprise, the Hamer Rifles. And finally the great lot of them were formed into the 18th Mississippi Regiment and sent north once again.

They traveled for eight days, marching, jostling onto railroad platforms, crushing into sweating railcars, rattling northeast. They covered nearly seven hundred miles and landed at last in the great *ad hoc* tent city of Camp Walker near Manassas Junction, Virginia.

Robley paused in his deliberate wandering, pulled off his kepi, wiped his forehead with the sleeve of his frock coat. He squinted around him, at the bored men on guard duty, the companies off in the distance, kicking up dust as they drilled, the men lounging around, reading, writing letters, playing cards. Things were getting mighty relaxed at Camp Walker. Laundry hung out in the sun, tables and chairs were set up outside the little tents, chickens ran around the dusty ground. They were only about twenty-five miles from Washington, D.C., the heart of the Union, and all the bluebellies gathering there, but no one of either side seemed overeager to do anything about it.

From the moment that he had signed his name to the enlistment roll, through the long march and wait and the endless drilling at Corinth, over the misery of eight days' travel to Manassas, Robley had known several fears.

One was that he would miss the great battle that would decide the war. That one was a common fear. It was the only fear that the boys would gladly own up to, and did, often.

But also, in his heart, tucked away, he harbored the secret fear that that was what he wanted, that he hoped to miss the battle, that he was afraid to stand up in that great fight. That, too, was not an uncommon fear, but it was not so popular a topic.

All of that seemed long ago, and those fears were smothered under the weight of drilling, guard duty, mess duty, general boredom, and now fear that he or his brothers would fall victim to the measles, which were spreading like plague through the 3rd Brigade. After weeks of dull camp routine, the possibility of battle seemed so unlikely as to not warrant concern.

Yes, Robley figured he had already experienced just about all there was to soldiering. There were only two things left, that he knew of. One was the misery of a winter march or encampment, and the other was the horror of battle. The former he reckoned he could do without. The latter he was desperately eager to try, to be done with it, if only to discover the truth about himself.

Robley put his kepi back on, trudged to the end of the 18th Mississippi's encampment. Coming from the other direction was Nathaniel Paine, alone.

"Couldn't find him?" Robley said.

"No, sir." Nathaniel pulled his kepi off, just as Robley had done, wiped his forehead. As soon as Robley had been promoted, Nathaniel had begun to address him as "sir," with not the least hint of irony.

Robley frowned, looked around again. Miles of identical tents, thousands upon thousands of men. The Confederate Stars and Bars hung limp from a flagpole near the center of the camp. The two-story brick home of Wilmer McLean, headquarters of Brigadier General David Jones, stood brooding over the rows of Lilliputian tents.

Far off in the distance they heard the flat boom of cannon fire, the artillery units around Washington, D.C., exercising at their pieces. It had caused a stir in camp the first time they had heard it, but now it was hardly noticed.

"Fella told me he saw him with his bird, heading for the South Carolina boys," Nathaniel added.

"All right. We'll try there." Robley headed off, with Nathaniel behind, and soon they crossed the largely invisible divide between the 18th Mississippi camp and the 5th South Carolina, with whom they were brigaded.

Near the center of the 5th South Carolina's camp the tents were arranged in such a way as to form a parade ground, and at the far end of the parade there was a cluster of men in a circle, and Robley had a good idea that Jonathan might be among them. He was not a fellow to miss a frolic of any kind.

The brothers crossed the parade, peered through the group of men standing and kneeling, and Robley was not surprised to see Jonathan at the center of the circle, holding the fighting cock he had been training up for a week now. Money was passing around the circle of men.

Jonathan was in his shirtsleeves and his kepi was tilted back and his face was red with exertion and excitement. His light brown hair was plastered to the sweat on his forehead and he was grinning, and even Robley could appreciate how handsome and vital his brother looked.

"What y'all say your chicken's name is?" Jonathan called to his opponent at the far end of the circle, a big Irish-looking fellow who also clutched a straining rooster. "Y'all said his name is Abe Lincoln, didn't ya?"

"Abe Lincoln, my ass. Yankee Killer. Gonna git himself some practice now."

"Yankee Killer? Well, hell, just put a uniform on him. He's as much a man as any of you South Carolina boys."

Robley could not help but smile. Jonathan had a quick wit about him. It got him in trouble more often then not.

Then, on some unseen signal, the birds were released. In a great welter of feathers and flying dust the fighting cocks fell on each other, flailing and lashing with dagger spurs. The roosters screamed and the men screamed and shouted and urged the animals on to greater violence.

A stream of blood made a red slash across the tan earth, and Robley winced and felt a rush of shame that he should have such a reaction. They were birds. How would he fare when men were being shot down around him?

The shouting of the men and birds built and Robley pushed his concerns aside, watched the battle of brilliant red and yellow and black feathers. Some of the watchers let out a wild, unearthly whoop, a pagan battle cry that came from some place deep inside, and it sent shivers down Robley's spine.

And then it was over and Jonathan Paine's bird lay in a crumpled heap of bloody feathers.

"What the hell you say the name of your bird is?" the victor taunted Jonathan. "Winfield Scott, ain't that what you said? Or wasn't it Bluebelly?"

Jonathan grinned. He did not get angry. He rarely did. He picked up the rooster's limp body. "His name, suh, is Stew Meat." Jonathan bowed, turned to leave the circle, saw Robley watching him.

"Ah, brothers, you had to witness my bird's ignominious defeat. He left a great string of dead fighting cocks in his path, and the one time you see him fight is when he gets beat by that cheating South Carolina son of a bitch."

"He left one rooster dead in his path, and I think that one was sick with consumption to start," Nathaniel said.

"Come on, Private," Robley said, "there's been a reassignment and you have picket duty tonight."

"Picket duty?" The three brothers stepped off across the dry, dusty parade ground. "If y'all are putting me on picket duty," Jonathan said, "you must reckon them Yankees'll be coming down the road tonight."

"You don't mind fighting them single-hand, do you?" asked Nathaniel.

"Who else is gonna do it?"

They marched back toward the 18th Mississippi's camp, slower now, as the sun reached its zenith. "Tell me true, Lieutenant," Jonathan said. When he used Robley's title with sincerity, it meant he was looking for a real answer. "When you think we're gonna be at them bluebellies?"

Robley stopped in the middle of the wide central street. His wool clothing itched intolerably and he wanted some relief.

"Can't be too much longer," he said, scratching with abandon, which got his brothers scratching as well. Robley heard enough talk around camp to know that speculating about future action was the quickest way to sound like an idiot. But with his brothers it was different. "Uncle Abe's three-month enlistments are up soon. He's got to do something, before his army goes home. Got to be a battle soon."

Nathaniel and Jonathan nodded. For all the casual, hunting-trip quality of Camp Walker, there was always that, the impending battle, hanging there. The Sword of Damocles, it would have to fall eventually.

"You afraid?" Jonathan asked Robley, and again there was a sincerity that the youngest did not generally show. Standing there, his dead rooster in his hand, he looked like the little boy that Robley remembered, holding a broken toy, a bit bewildered in a world where his father imposed no strict rules. The boys had always turned to Robley for structure in their lives.

Now Robley just shrugged, spit on the ground. "You mean am I afraid there won't be a fight?" he asked, though he knew that was not what Jonathan meant.

"No, I mean, you afraid of the fight?"

Robley looked away, collecting his words, making sure there was no one else to hear them. These were his brothers. He did not always have to be Lieutenant Paine in front of them.

"Yeah. I'm afraid of the monkey show. I'm afraid I'll run. Won't have the nerve to stand up to it."

Jonathan smiled, chuckled, shook his head. "That it? Aren't you afraid of being killed? I'm . . . seems to me a Yankee bullet's a more frightening prospect than doing a skeedaddle."

The words took Robley by surprise, and he realized that his thoughts had been so directed toward how he would perform when the bullets started to fly that the thought of being killed had never occurred to him.

"No, I'm not afraid of being killed, I don't reckon. Rather die with honor than live with the shame of running," he said, and that seemed true, but was it?

Here now was a whole new question with which he would have to wrestle.

13

I had purposed offering some remarks upon the vast importance to Virginia and to the entire South of the timely acquisition of this extensive naval depot, with its immense supplies of munitions of war, and to notice briefly the damaging effects of its loss to the Government at Washington; but I deem it unnecessary . . .

—William H. Peters, Commissioner, to John Letcher, Governor of Virginia

*H*ieronymus Taylor sat on the stool at his workbench and puffed his butt end of a cigar to life. The *Cape Fear* was riding at her anchor. The fires were banked in the boiler and the doors and vents of the deckhouse that enclosed the fidley, the section of the deckhouse directly above the engine room, were open to the afternoon breeze, and the engine room was almost comfortable.

Taylor shook the flame out on his lucifer and tossed the smoldering match onto the workbench. He never took his eye off of Fireman First Class James Burgess.

Burgess had spent the past half hour tapping threads into a hole he had drilled into the side of one of the shoes on the eccentric—a circular piece of metal mounted off-center on the crankshaft that worked the engine's valve gear. When the threads were cut, he screwed a bolt into the hole. Then he screwed an eyebolt into a deck beam a few feet above the eccentric.

All this Taylor watched without comment. He could not figure what Burgess was about. He thought about asking him, but the Scotsman was never very enlightening, even when questioned directly.

If it had been O'Malley fiddling with his engine without permission, he would have stomped him underfoot. O'Malley had no feel for engines. He suspected O'Malley's engineer's papers had been supplied by some fellow Mick working in some navy shithouse office.

Burgess was different. Burgess understood engines. With Burgess, Taylor just watched.

When the eyebolt was in place, Burgess pulled a length of quarter-inch manila line from his pocket. He tied a bowline in one end and looped it over the bolt on the eccentric, then threaded the bitter end through the eyebolt. That was as much as Hieronymus Taylor could endure. The chief slid off the stool, ambled over to where Burgess was working.

"Awright, Burgess, I give," he said to the Scotsman's back. "What in hell are you about?"

Burgess made a grunting noise that might have been a word. It sounded like "Wawarr." Then, when Taylor did not respond, he elaborated, saying, "Feer kaws."

"Forgive me, but I can't understand a goddamned thing you are saying."

Burgess turned around. He spoke slowly and deliberately, as if to a child. "Washer. Fer washin clothes."

Taylor nodded. "And how does it do that, exactly?"

Burgess pointed to the deck below, where the end of the rope dangled. "Put a barrel there. Fill it full of water. Get 'er good an hot with steam. Cut the barrel head down, put a ruddy great weight on it, hang it from the line."

Hieronymus nodded. That was all the explanation he would get. He knew that. But he understood. Dirty clothes go in the barrel of water, hot from the boiler. The round barrel head, cut down so there is clearance all around, goes on top. The line goes from an eyebolt in the barrel head, through the eyebolt overhead, to the bolt on the eccentric shoe. When the engine is turning the shoe goes up and down and the line from the shoe to the barrel head makes the barrel head go up and down, like the plunger in a butter churn. The clothes are agitated until they are clean.

"Well, damn. You are one clever son of a bitch. Fer a foreigner, I mean."

"Do it on errey Scottish ship," Burgess grunted and went back to his task.

Taylor smiled. This was a hell of an idea. "Moses!" he yelled.

"Yassuh?" Moses and a couple of the coal heavers were knocking clinker from the boiler grates.

"Git some of your boys topside, find us a barrel. Cut the head down, 'bout an inch around. Damn me, we gonna have the cleanest damned black gang in the navy."

"Yassuh." Moses left off what he was doing and took Billy and Joshua topside.

Taylor liked Moses. Moses did not argue and he did his work well without playing sullen, petty games, and he could sing like a son of a bitch, and that was about all Taylor could ask of a coal passer, or any man, for that matter.

"Chief?"

Taylor looked up. Jacob, Bowater's servant, was leaning into the deckhouse door, one deck up. "Captain's compliments, Chief. Dinner in twenty minutes."

"Aye." *Damn.* Taylor usually ate by himself, or with his engine-room gang. But once a week Bowater invited him to dinner, and much as he would have liked to, he did not think he could refuse. Bowater might be a blueblood, slaveholding navy martinet, a man incapable of action, a yachtsman who would rather lounge about on the deckhouse roof and dabble with his paints and have his darkie bring him mint juleps than fight a war, but he was still the captain.

Hieronymus tossed what was left of his cigar into the furnace, climbed grudgingly up the ladder and aft to his cabin. He wished Burgess had fin ished the clothes washer the day before. Taylor could not help but feel like slovenly white trash in Bowater's patrician presence. It annoyed him, and it annoyed him more that he let Bowater get to him in that manner. He wished they had a bath down in the engine room. Or a shower bath, that would be even better. Rig a barrel to the overhead, run a steam line into it, tap in a valve . . .

Taylor stopped in midstride, saw the whole thing form in his head. *Yes.* He wondered if Burgess or any of his damned Scots had ever come up with that one.

"Massa Samuel?"

Samuel Bowater looked up from the reports from department heads, Hieronymus Taylor's insufferably dreary description of the state of the engine.

"Yes, Jacob?"

"Dinner in twenty minute, suh. Chief Taylor and Missuh Harwell joinin' you, suh."

"Right. Very well. Thank you, Jacob. Please get my painting gear together. I'll be going ashore after lunch."

"Yes, suh," Jacob said, then, good servant that he was, disappeared.

Bowater sighed and set the reports aside. They had been puttering around the same ten-mile stretch of river, from Gosport to Sewall's Point, for two months now. Two months, while somewhere beyond that water-front, somewhere up the river and in the country beyond, the pressure of war built like steam in a boiler. Bowater knew it would blow soon, and he did not want to be at a safe distance when it did.

They had been busy enough; they had not been idle. At the end of May they joined in the effort to raise the remains of the *Merrimack* from the river bottom. They had sealed her up as best they could, pumped her out until her own buoyancy lifted her out of the mud.

With the *Cape Fear* alongside, she was eased into the flooded dry dock and her keel was allowed to settle down on angle blocks and her black-ened sides were supported with shores wedged between her timbers and the side of the dry dock. The water was pumped out of the dock. The *Merrimack*, charred on the topside and unscathed below, rested safe and dry in Confederate hands, while Confederate minds wrestled with the question of what to do with her.

Captain, now Flag Officer, French Forrest, whom Samuel knew from the old navy, had been given charge of the navy yard. Under his able com-mand the yard was made whole and defensible. The buildings that the re-treating Yankees had burned were rebuilt. Batteries were erected along the outer walls.

The *Cape Fear* and the smaller tug *Harmony* were set to work as ord-nance transports, hauling guns to the newly erected batteries on Craney Island and Fort Powhatan and Aquia Creek, distributing the largess that the Federals had left in their wake.

Twice they made the 120-mile trip down the canal through the aptly named Great Dismal Swamp to Albemarle Sound, past Roanoke Island and into Pamlico Sound. There, on the sandy, windswept Hatteras Island, south of the massive and blind Cape Hatteras light, the Confederate Army was erecting two sand-and-mud forts to keep the Yankees out of the protected sounds and the rivers that ran deep into Confederate country. The tugs from Norfolk brought guns, ammunition, supplies, all former property of the United States.

The work was hot, dull, uninspiring. The *Cape Fear* had hauled tons of ordnance, but she herself remained unarmed. There was no chance that she could be anything but a tug. And as long as that was true, then Bowa-ter knew he could be nothing more than a spectator to the greatest mili-tary undertaking he was likely to see in his lifetime. The thought made him desperate.

Samuel Bowater stood and stretched. He was certain that the others, Harwell and Taylor, blamed him for their inaction, thought that perhaps he was backward in his effort to join the fighting. They did not know about his constant requests of Forrest that the vessel be mounted with a gun for offensive action, his letters to the navy office at the new capital in Richmond for new orders, the repeated instructions to remain at Norfolk under Forrest's command until instructed otherwise. They did not know and he would not tell them, because it was not their business.

He smoothed his pants and pulled on his blue frock coat. Generally he ate by himself in his cabin, but today was the crew's day off and his weekly Saturday dinner with his officers. On so perfect a summer day, the roof of the deckhouse made a wonderful spot to dine.

Landsman Dick Merrow walked around the front of the wheelhouse and rang the bell, two sets of two. Four bells in the afternoon watch, two o'clock in the afternoon. Dinnertime. Bowater stepped out of his cabin, stepped through the door to the boat deck, which formed the roof of the deckhouse. Lieutenant Harwell was already there, trying to look casual but not too casual as he waited for his captain. Taylor was not yet there.

"Please, Mr. Harwell, sit," Bowater said, and the lieutenant nodded his eager head and sat to the right of the captain's place. The boat, hanging in its davits, cast a shade over the table, and that and the soft breeze made the setting most idyllic. The table was set with the silver and bone china service and crystal glasses that Samuel had brought with him for his captain's table.

Jacob stepped forward and poured wine for the two officers. "So . . ." Bowater began, but he was interrupted by the sound of Taylor's shoes pounding the ladder and he climbed up to the deckhouse roof.

"Forgive me, Captain, for my tardiness," he said, his tone just shy of insubordinate. He was dressed in his uniform coat and hat, though the coat was unbuttoned and hanging open, and the visor of his hat was creased and pulled low over his eyes. But he had made an obvious effort to clean up, and that was something, though he had stopped short of shaving.

"Damn." Taylor looked around, breathed deep. "It is a fine day indeed for dining *al fresco*," pronounced as if referring to a man named Alan Fresco. "I have got to get out of that damned engine room and up here on the boat deck more often."

"Please, Chief, be seated," Bowater said. "Have you decided to grow a beard?" He recalled the promise he had made to himself to be more tolerant of Hieronymus Taylor. He was a fine engineer, for what that was worth.

"Thankee, sir." Taylor sat. "Beard? Perhaps I will." He picked up the wine bottle before Jacob could get to it, poured himself a glass. "I'll just have a taste, here, if you don't mind, sir," he said.

"Please, Mr. Taylor, help yourself."

More shoes on the ladder, and the coal heavers Billy Jefferson and Nat

St. Clair appeared carrying silver trays with silver covers, their white gloves in sharp contrast to their dark skin. Behind them, imperious, Johnny St. Laurent fussed and directed, like an overzealous lieutenant dressing his lines.

When at last the trays were set to the cook's satisfaction, Billy and Nat stepped back while St. Laurent whipped off the covers with a magician's flourish. Underneath, a leg of lamb, roasted to a brown perfection and nestled in a bed of new potatoes. St. Laurent allowed them only a glance before he returned the covers and Billy and Nat distributed bowls of soup.

"We start wid a fine malecotony soup today, and for de main course, roast leg of lamb on a bed of *pomme de terre à la Maître d'Hôtel* and fresh asparagus, followed by a claret jelly and fresh fruit."

"Excellent, Cook," Bowater said, and the chef nodded, as if there was no question, then snapped his fingers and the servers disappeared down the ladder, with St. Laurent following behind.

"Well, hell, Captain, I don't know how I managed to find the one darkie cooks all this Frenchified stuff. Don't even know how to make a decent gumbo or fried chicken," Taylor said.

"Hardly a failing. Was he really the chef at the Château Dupré Hotel?"

"Aw, hell no. He was the fella mixed up the sauces or something. He's jest putting on airs. I reckon he learned a thing or two about cooking, jest watchin them real chefs."

"He did indeed. So how did he happen to come with you?"

"They was some mess he got himself in. Something to do with the wife of one of the cooks there at that hotel. I never did get the whole story. Just knew he had to get the hell out of New Orleans, but fast. I was heading to Wilmington, took him along."

Bowater nodded. "You were friends?"

"He used to shovel coal for me. Paddle wheeler we used to work, New Orleans to Vicksburg on a regular run."

"I see." Samuel could sense the layers upon layers of story that formed the bedrock of their acquaintance, Hieronymus Taylor and Johnny St. Laurent. He wondered briefly if there was anyone who would come to him if they were in dire need of help. No one that he could think of.

"Sir?" Harwell interjected. Bowater looked at the luff and could see that he had something to say and was ready to burst if he did not say it.

"Yes, Mr. Harwell?"

"When I was ashore this morning, sir, I found out what they are planning for the old *Merrimack*."

"Oh, yes?" Judging from the lieutenant's expression, it was something more than just rebuilding her as a steam frigate.

"Go on, Lieutenant," Taylor said. "I am like to perish with anticipation."

"Well, sir," Harwell said, addressing himself only to Bowater, "it appears they are going to rebuild her as an ironclad."

"Do you mean like that French monstrosity, *Le Gloire*?"

"No sir. No masts at all. More like a floating battery, but with engines. They will use *Merrimack*'s old engines. An iron casement and bows and stern, submerged I believe."

For a moment, no one said a thing, and in silence they considered that. An ironclad, with no sailing rig. A self-propelled floating iron battery.

"She'll look like a damned turtle," Taylor observed and grinned at the thought. "Be just like a turtle, slow and strong."

"She will be a vulgar monstrosity," Bowater said. *Merrimack*, with her shortened masts and her tall, black, ugly stack, was no beauty herself. All of these steam vessels, these hermaphrodites, half sail, half steam, lacked the grace and beauty of the old sailing navy. Was there any steamer that could compare to the beauty of a sailing frigate?

Once, not long after his graduation from the Navy School, Bowater had seen from the deck of his ship the USS *Constitution* underway, a full press of canvas to topgallant studding sails. The image was clean in his mind, like an etching. There was nothing else made by the hand of man that could compare to that for grace, beauty, and silent and unassuming power. She was from a different time, a more elegant time, and the men who sailed ships like that were very different from the men who mucked about in dark and filthy engine rooms.

"She will be ugly, Captain, but she will be lethal as well," Taylor said. "I'll take power over beauty any day."

"Of course you would, Mr. Taylor." It was what Samuel Bowater would expect from the engineers and mechanics of the world. A new direction for mankind, a rhumb line to the end of civilization.

"Anyway, they should have guns enough for her," Taylor said through a mouthful of lamb. "Don't reckon we've hauled away everything the Yankees left behind." Then, in another tone, *sotto voce*, he added, "Reckon there should be guns enough for any boat in the navy. . . ."

Bowater stiffened. It was not the words—he had not heard for certain what Taylor said—but the tone. Insinuation? Was the engineer hinting at something backward in Bowater's nature?

"What are you saying, Chief?" Bowater saw Harwell tense.

"I'm saying, if there was a gun on this here tugboat, we might stand a chance of getting into some fightin'."

Bowater leaned back, eyes on Taylor's unshaven face, his carefully arranged look of innocence.

What am I supposed to say? He had been pleading with Forrest since the flag officer's arrival to mount a gun on the *Cape Fear*'s foredeck, but Forrest had refused him every time, told him they could not waste ordnance arming tugs.

But Bowater could not tell Taylor that. It was none of Taylor's affair. He did not wish to set the precedent of inferiors asking after the captain's business. But neither could he let Taylor think he was shy about wanting to get into the fight.

Checkmate . . . with one question he has trapped me. . . .

"Chief, these questions are not the business of the engineering division. But let me say that I am attempting to improve our armament by way of the proper channels."

Taylor grunted, made a laughing sound. "Proper channels ain't gonna get you a goddamned thing, we both know it."

"And so that is an end to it."

"Is it?" There was a smoothness to Taylor's tone, like a snake-oil salesman, and it made Bowater wary and intrigued all at once.

For a long moment they sat there, silent, each holding the other's eyes, each needing the other for his existence and hating it.

Bowater spoke first. "Go on," he said. He said it softly, as if afraid to speak loud, afraid to admit that he wanted to listen. Here was forbidden fruit, Bowater could sense it. It frightened him, attracted him. He wanted to arm the *Cape Fear*, wanted it more than anything he could recall. He could feel that he was about to cross a line. He did not know what to think.

The ordnance house reminded Samuel Bowater of a buffet table laid out for the gods of war.

All of the guns that the retreating Yankees had spiked and rolled into the river had been recovered and the spikes removed from their vents. Stretched out in great rows were gun upon gun, some in carriages, some lying on the granite floor. There were massive 9-inch and eleven-inch Dahlgrens, howitzers of every size; twenty-four-pound, twelve-pound, six-pound. Long, sleek rifled barrels were lined up like fish on ice at the market, from the enormous, crushing hundred-pound Dahlgren through thirty-pound, twenty-pound, twelve, and ten.

There were James rifles and mortars and old smoothbores of antiquated design, the venerable thirty-two-pounders, and twenty-four-pounders, once the mainstay of the sailing navy's broadside. There were twelve-pounders, nines, and fours. But like the smoothbore rifles that so many of the infantry were carrying, North and South, those guns were of another age, quickly being eclipsed by the rifled barrel and the exploding shell.

"Well, damn, Cap'n Bowater," Taylor whispered. "I do not know where to begin." He said it soft. They had no business doing what they were doing.

"Not with the Dahlgrens, I shouldn't think," Bowater said. Taylor nodded. All the reinforcement in the world would not render the bulwark and decks of the *Cape Fear* strong enough to support one of those monsters.

They walked down the rows of guns, looking them over, like buyers before a horse auction. "It would be a waste of time to put a smoothbore on board," Taylor suggested, and Bowater concurred, so they moved quickly past the older guns.

They came at last to the Parrott rifles, and they stopped there and ran their eyes over the long tapered barrels with their distinctive reinforcement at the breech.

"Now this might be more of what we need," Bowater said. In fact, he had worked out long ago exactly what gun he would like to see on the *Cape Fear*'s foredeck, but for some reason he could not bring himself to admit as much.

Taylor nodded again. "Ten-pound Parrott weighs just under a thousand pounds. . . . That kind of weight would put the boat down by the head, I should think."

"It just might."

Taylor looked up and met Bowater's eyes, and there was something mischievous in his expression. "Might balance her a bit . . . one gun off the bow and another off the stern . . ."

Bowater took a deep breath. He and Taylor had worked out this *ruse de guerre* over dessert, in the shade of the boat on the *Cape Fear*'s boat deck. They talked in elliptical, half-finished sentences. Bowater could not bring himself to speak more boldly. This sort of trickery was antithetical to everything Bowater was and believed and was trained to be. If honor and ethics were a rope to climb, then he had just slid down many feet. But he had to get into the fight.

The two men looked down at the guns again.

"Ten-pound Parrott forward. Two twelve-pound howitzers aft," Bowater said in a tone that suggested the matter was settled.

Footsteps on the granite floor echoed around the building, and Bowater and Taylor looked up to see Commander Archibald Fairfax approach. Fairfax was in charge of ordnance at Norfolk, an able and active officer. He had managed to rework a number of the old smoothbore thirty-two-pounders, reinforcing their breeches and rifling them, bringing them into the modern age.

He was also in charge of fitting out the vessels stationed at the yard. "Captain Bowater, a pleasure, sir," he said.

"Commander, good day," Bowater said, extending a hand. "I do not believe you have met my chief engineer. Mr. Hieronymus Taylor, Commander Fairfax."

"Commander," Taylor said, shaking his hand. One glance told him Fairfax was old navy, through and through.

"What can I do for you, Captain Bowater?"

Bowater felt a tingling in his hands, an unsettled feeling in his gut. Up until now it had all been theoretical, which was bad enough. But now the moment was there. Now he had to lie to a superior officer, or give it up.

"We came by to see about the new guns for Fort Powhatan," Bowater said, and when Fairfax looked understandably confused, he added, "The ten-pound Parrott and the two twelve-pound howitzers."

There . . . that wasn't so bad. . . . He felt the rope slip though his hands.

Fairfax shook his head. "I was not aware that Fort Powhatan was to get more guns. Who gave you that order?"

"We were up there yesterday. Captain Cocke said he had sent word to you. He was under the impression it was all arranged."

"No . . . this is the first I hear of it."

"Well, hell, sir . . . beg your pardon, Commander," Taylor said. Bowater hoped he would not make a hash of things now. "I can draw the fires, but now we're going to have to take on more fresh water before we get head up steam again. We'll need more coal, too. Got just enough on board to steam there and back with steam up now."

"Very well, Chief," Bowater said. "There is nothing for it." He shook his head, turned to Fairfax. "I swear this happens every time, sir. One bureaucratic mix-up and we are set back two days."

"Well, perhaps not," Fairfax said. "If Cocke intended to ask for those guns, I should think the paperwork is somewhere. Be a waste for you to leave empty-handed. Why don't you take those guns aboard and I'll see what became of Cocke's requisition."

"Thank you, sir," Bowater said. "That sort of efficiency is not something you would have heard of in the old navy."

"No, indeed, Mr. Bowater. If we have any advantage at all over the United States Navy, it is that we are not so entrenched and somnambulant. Feel free to press whomever you need from the yard to help with the guns. Mr. Taylor, a pleasure to meet you. Good day, gentlemen."

"Good day," the officers of the *Cape Fear* said in chorus. Commodore Fairfax turned and walked away.

Done. They had their guns. And Bowater felt like a new-minted whore, just finished with her first trick. He wondered if that sort of thing got easier, and what the implications were if it did.

14

Our hands nervously toying with the hammers of our rifles, each one felt that his final departure was near at hand and busily repented him of his sins.

—Alexander Hunter, 17th Virginia, Blackburn's Ford, Bull Run River

A sharp jerk of alarm, a twist of fear. The long slide back into boredom. Alarm, fear, boredom, the cycle went round and round, a grindstone wearing Robley Paine down. Six days now. It was more exhausting than any drill or long march he had encountered yet.

He stood and stretched arms and legs, tore a piece of bacon off with his teeth. It was raw—fires were not permitted that morning—and the meat was chewy and slightly noxious, but he made himself eat. He followed the bacon up with a cracker, and then a drink from his canteen, filled with gritty river water.

The air was warm and sweet-smelling, the sky just growing light through the tangle of young trees along the riverbank. Over the muted conversations of the other soldiers, muttering over their inadequate breakfast, the incompetency of their leadership, he could hear the sounds of the Bull Run River, coursing through its choked and tangled bed, running over the shallow place they were protecting. McLean's Ford.

It was July 21, a Sunday, and though there would be no church service that morning, Paine did not doubt that there would be a power of praying going on. He had done enough of it himself already, and he reckoned there was more to come.

"Morning, Lieutenant." Jonathan Paine ambled up, scratching with one hand, rubbing his eyes with the other. "Got any more of that bacon?"

"Where are your rations, Private?"

"Ate 'em last night. I was fearful hungry."

Robley scowled at his youngest brother, but cut a slice of bacon from his own remaining piece and handed it over. Jonathan, skinny as he was, ate more than any other person Robley had ever met.

"Today's our day," Jonathan said through a full mouth, but it was more a question than a statement.

"I reckon." It had been six days since the great flurry of excitement that saw 3rd Brigade decamp from near the McLean house and tramp the mile down gently sloping hills and through clustered stands of young trees to the banks of the Bull Run. For six days they had been in the proximity of battle, but had yet to enter into it themselves, like so many Moseses looking down on the Promised Land.

On the day after they had taken their position at McLean's Ford, the firing started, muted, distant, and sporadic. It was Brigadier General Milledge Luke Bonham's 1st Brigade, lobbing shells at the pursuing Yankees as they fell back from Fairfax Courthouse to the Confederate lines behind the Bull Run.

It had been worse the following day. Then the Yankees had come in force down the road from the cluster of wood-framed houses known as Centreville. They hit James Longstreet's 4th Brigade hard and repeatedly, not half a mile from 3rd Brigade's left flank. The soldiers of 3rd Brigade grabbed up their rifles and rifles, yawned with nervousness, fiddled with their equipment, joked, prayed, waited for their orders to splash across the river, to turn the bluebellies' flank. But that order did not come.

Colonel Jubal Anderson Early's 6th Brigade, held in reserve behind Longstreet, came up in support and drove the Yankees back until they came no more. The men of the 3rd stood tensed, listening to the bang of artillery, the crack of small arms like a pitch-pine log in a fire, watched the clouds of smoke building over the trees. They stood ready until the tension began to ebb away and they headed down that slope to boredom, and there they would stay until the big guns began to fire again.

"We're in the right place for a fight, I reckon," Jonathan continued. He was nervous. The only time he showed any interest in what the army might do was when he was nervous.

"General Beauregard seems to think so," Robley said. Nearly all of the Confederate troops were massed at that end of the line, the Confederate right. Bonham, Longstreet, Jones, Ewell, Early, and Holmes had all been positioned there, strung out behind the Bull Run.

The day before, as brigades of Joseph Johnston's Army of the Shenan-doah had begun to arrive by train—to the great relief of the Confederates, from Brigadier General Pierre G. T. Beauregard, in overall command, to Private Jonathan Bonaventure Paine—they too had been massed near the McLean house. Now they stood in the rear of Bonham, Longstreet, and Jones, ready to come up to support the regiments along the river that would surely take the brunt of the Yankees' massed assault.

The sun was breaking the horizon and the sky above was blue, clear and blue, and promised more unrelenting heat. The 3rd Brigade, like a great animal coming slowly out of sleep, began to move and shift and shuffle into place. Nathaniel came up, carrying two canteens, one of which he handed to Jonathan.

"Morning, Lieutenant," he said.

"We drew cards to see who would fill canteens," Jonathan explained. Robley frowned and shook his head as an officer should.

He ran his eyes over his two younger brothers, recalled how they had looked standing under the big tree in the front yard of Paine Plantation, their uniforms new and perfectly fitted, the leather of their belts and cartridge boxes gleaming black, their faces red-cheeked and eager. They looked like theatrical soldiers then, boys in costume.

They did not look that way anymore. They had lost so much weight that their clothes hung loose on them, and they wore their uniforms with the casual air of professionals. The leather belts and cartridge boxes were cracked and dusty and faded. Only their rifles retained the luster of new-ness, and that was only through meticulous maintenance. They had been soldiers long enough to know what was important and what was not.

In the distance they heard a gun fire, the flat bang of a cannon, field ar-tillery.

"Shush!" Robley said to Jonathan, who was opening his mouth to speak. The three boys cocked their heads. The gunfire was far off, three or four miles at least.

"Sounds like it's up by the Warrenton Turnpike," Robley said in a whis-per, pleased for the chance to display a knowledge of the terrain. "Fifth Brigade might be getting it. . . ."

"You reckon that's the Yankees attacking?" Nathaniel asked, also whis-pering.

"No. It's a feint, I'll wager. Real attack is going to come here." And then, as if in support of his prediction, they heard artillery opening up much closer and to the north, a battery that must be aimed at them. Rob-ley felt the sharp jab in his stomach, the sweat break out on his palms. So many times had the charge of excitement come and then drained away that he thought he would never feel it again. But with the sound of the guns he was flashed up in an instant, ready to go.

"You scared?" Jonathan asked, speaking soft.

Robley considered his answer. "No. You?"

"No."

"I'm not either," Nathaniel offered, but they were all lying and they all knew it.

Captain Clarence F. Hamer came stamping up the line, his tall boots in high polish, his tailored gray coat buttoned snug around his midriff, the top of his kepi a swirl of gold lace. "Lieutenant Paine! Get the company in order! We move out in half an hour. You hear?"

"Yes, sir!" Robley fairly shouted. He turned to the soldiers closest to him—his brothers—and began to issue orders. "Fall in, there! Get ready to march, men!" The order to move, to actually move, pitched his excitement even higher. And when Nathaniel and Jonathan said nothing but "Yessir!" and stumbled off to fetch their gear, he knew that they felt the same.

It was an hour and a half after Hamer's orders that Private Nathaniel Paine splashed into the Bull Run River. The warm, brown water quickly filled his shoes so that each step was accompanied by a sucking, squishing feel. He wished he could shed them, go barefoot, as he had for half of his life, but Robley would not like that.

Nathaniel felt twisted up, alternately nauseated and jubilant. He wanted to get into the fight, he wanted to run, he wanted to move just to release the awful tension boiling inside. Robley could issue orders and yell at the beats, Jonathan could make jokes and get the ranks roaring with laughter. Nathaniel did not have those safety valves, so he marched, and that was some relief. But the pace was agonizingly slow, stopping, starting, stopping, until he wanted to scream with frustration.

They crossed through the river and trudged up the bank on the north side, and Nathaniel considered how he was now at the northernmost point on earth he had ever been. It was pretty, with the rolling green fields and the darker trees and the brown roads crisscrossing the country. Pretty, but not the place he would care to spend eternity.

Off to the left, northeast of their position, he could hear artillery making it a hot morning for someone. Longstreet's brigade, he imagined. Third Brigade was marching now, and he wondered where they were going, what they were trying to accomplish. March on Centreville? Hit the flank of a Union attack? What was it like, to hit a flank? It was an expression he had heard again and again from the many would-be generals in camp, but he had only the vaguest idea of what it meant.

Still, they were moving toward something, and that alone buoyed him. The marching was good, the final call to action. And just as his shoes were starting to dry, and he was taking some joy in the long, rhythmic strides of the army advancing, someone called a halt.

The sound of tramping feet died away, and in its place came groans of frustration, muttered curses. Some said, "Aw, now what the hell is it?" loud, so the words carried over the ranks.

Jonathan, at Nathaniel's side, shouted back, "We got to wait for the Yankees to change into their brown pants!" It was not a particularly funny reply, but in that charged atmosphere the men would have laughed at anything, and they laughed at that.

For twenty minutes or so they remained in place, on the road, standing ready to move out. Then slowly, like a cube of sugar in coffee, the tight ranks began to dissolve. Men leaned on rifles, then sat on the road, then stretched out on the roadside with their heads on their knapsacks and fell asleep. Others wandered down into the fields that bordered the road and began to eat the ubiquitous blackberries off the tall, dense, thorny bushes.

To the northwest the artillery continued to pound away, and farther off, five miles or so, on the Confederate left, where there was not supposed to be a battle, they could hear sounds that sounded very much like a battle indeed. Over the tops of the trees, smoke like low-lying fog rose from the field and hung there. And on the Confederate right, where the 3rd Brigade waited, the insects buzzed in the grass, the songbirds flashed through the trees, and the men ate blackberries and dozed.

The morning grew hotter, the men more lethargic, and the gunfire off to the far left grew more intense. Jonathan sat on the road, leaning on his knapsack, and Nathaniel sat beside him. From his knapsack he pulled a battered leather-bound journal and the pencil that he kept stuck in the binding.

July 21. Woke up and called to arms. Thought we were going into battle for sure, and it made me damned scared, I'll admit it. Jonathan joking around as usual, but I think he is scared too. He tricked me into filling our canteens. Robley is ordering everyone around, but that is his way and I think he is just nervous and does that to shake the nerves off.

"You writing to Ma?" Jonathan asked.

Nathaniel looked up with a flush of embarrassment. "No."

"Well, you should. And when you do, tell her I love her too, all right?"

"Why don't you write yourself?"

"I will. But you're the one always writing. You planning on publishing your memoirs? Get rich that way?"

"Might. Once I get famous."

"Oh? When you gonna get famous?"

"Once I get a chance to start licking Yankees."

"Humph. Good thing your daddy's got money."

Nathaniel put the book and pencil away, lay on his backpack, and pretended to sleep. At last the officers came riding and racing down the line, stirring the men of 3rd Brigade, urging them back into ranks. Nathaniel felt the languor drain away as he snatched up his rifle, shuffled back into line. He could see grins on the other men's faces, nervous shuffling of feet as they prepared to plunge forward.

But they did not. Rather, they were ordered about, marched back toward where they had come from. Fifty-five minutes later, Nathaniel Paine's now dry shoes once again plunged into the lazy Bull Run. Twenty minutes after that, he found himself at approximately the same place he had started that morning. If his rifle had not been loaded he would have thrown it down in disgust. The fight was out of him now. Not spent but worn away, and he did not think he would get it back, not that day.

Jonathan Bonaventure Paine saw the disgust on Nathaniel's face and told himself that he felt the same. And he did. To a degree.

He leaned on his rifle, took off his kepi, and wiped his forehead with his sleeve. It was terribly hot, and not yet noon.

"Hey, Nathaniel?"

"What?" His brother's tone disgusted, resigned, weary.

"Got any water left in your canteen, there?"

"Yeah." Nathaniel pulled the half-empty canteen off his shoulder, handed it to Jonathan. Jonathan took it, tipped the water into his mouth. It was warm, near hot, and he could taste the mud of the Bull Run, but he was grateful for it.

Here was the difference between them, Jonathan thought. Nathaniel had saved half his water, while he had drained his an hour ago. He imagined that if they checked Robley's canteen they would find it near full, that the lieutenant was saving the entire thing for when it was really needed.

Jonathan handed the canteen back, looked off to the country that lay south of the Bull Run. That morning there had been regiments spread out around the McLean house, held in reserve for the attack that was to come their way. They were not there now. They had been ordered off to reinforce the left flank, when it became clear that that was where the fighting actually was. Only the trampled grass and the dark circles where fires had once burned indicated that armies had once bivouacked there.

He turned and looked toward the northwest. The smoke was thick over the low hills, and the sound of the firing, soft and distant though it was, was continuous. Someone was catching hell.

"Reckon they were right about a battle today," Nathaniel said. "But someone was wrong about where."

"Reckon." Cresting one of the low hills between themselves and the battle line, and about a mile away, Jonathan could see a battalion heading for the fight. They were marching fast, a long, gray line, the sun glinting off bayonets. The sight moved him in a strange way, and he felt the emotions rush one way and another until he thought he might go quietly mad, standing there in the Virginia sun.

It had frightened him, marching across the Bull Run. And yet he had been disappointed when they halted, confused when they were ordered back over the river. At one moment he wanted to be at the Yankees, the next he wanted to skulk off into a stand of trees and hide.

There was Nathaniel, obviously angry about missing out on the fight. Jonathan had always thought his brother felt as he did, though they certainly had never discussed it. But in the final instant, he wondered, was Nathaniel more of a fire-eater than he?

Robley was afraid, he had said so, but he was afraid of running, not of stopping a bullet. Well, Jonathan was afraid of that too. He was afraid to miss the fight, afraid to join the fight, afraid he was a coward, unsure how he measured up against the others. He wanted to take the butt of his gun and bash himself on the head, just to drive the thoughts away.

He looked at the distant brigade, the diamond flashes of sun on polished steel, and in that instant, with no consideration given to it, he made a decision, and with that decision, everything else was wiped away. There was no more room for any of it.

"Nathaniel, see that brigade yonder?"

"Yeah. Jackson, I reckon."

"I'm gonna go join up with them."

Nathaniel had no reply to that. Finally he said, "What are you talking about, Jonathan?"

"I'm going to go. Right now. Catch up with them. Go see the monkey show."

He pulled his eyes from the bayonets, looked his brother square in the face, and to his surprise, he saw a smile growing on Nathaniel's face.

"Damn . . . I'm going too."

Jonathan bit his lip. How many times had he instigated Nathaniel into joining him on some stupid venture or other, only to catch it from Robley? Here it was again, and while this was surely different from lighting fires in the woods, or taking off down the Yazoo River on a homemade raft, it was the same thing as well.

Jonathan grinned. "Let's go!"

The boys picked up their knapsacks and rifles, shuffled out of what was left of the line of march. The men of the 3rd Brigade were spreading out again, going after blackberries, ambling down to the river to fill canteens. There were no officers that they could see, so they walked along, slow and inconspicuous, as if they were in search of a blackberry bush of their own.

"Hey, you." Jonathan heard a voice, Robley's voice, behind.

Damn . . . He turned around. "Lieutenant! Are we going to attack them Yankees, or what?"

"Where y'all going?" Robley ran his eyes over his brothers. "Nathaniel, where y'all going?"

"Looking for blackberries," Jonathan supplied, because he knew Nathaniel could not lie with conviction.

"That's a damned lie. Where the hell you going?"

Nathaniel straightened a bit. "We're going to join that brigade yonder. Going into the fight."

Robley squinted at them, shook his head. "You can't do that. This here's your regiment. You can't just go off where the hell you like. This isn't playing soldier back home."

"Well, goddamn it, Robley, there isn't anything going on here!" Jonathan replied. "I'm not going to spend the whole damned war marching back and forth over that infernal river."

"There is a reason we are here, you ever think about that? What if them Yankees come down that road, try and flank us?"

"The Yankees aren't coming down that road! The Yankees are over there! That's why every damned brigade but us is over there. I'm going. You can come or not, but I'm going."

"I order you to get back in line!" Robley pointed back to where the 18th Mississippi was milling about.

"There's no damned line. I'm going. Have me arrested or don't, but I'm going." He tossed his rifle over his shoulder, turned on his heel, as he had been taught in drill, and marched off on the double quick, his eyes on the tail end of Brigadier General Thomas Jackson's 1st Brigade, Army of the Shenandoah.

Robley Paine scowled, clenched his teeth, balled his fists in fury at the sight of Jonathan, marching double-quick away. Issuing another order was pointless. He could summon the provosts, have his brother arrested. If they charged him with deserting, he could be shot. The thought made Robley sick.

Besides, Jonathan was not deserting. In a way, he was doing just the opposite.

Robley turned and glared at Nathaniel, who remained where he had stopped. He was about to say something about Jonathan's damned insubordination, how he would regret it, but the expression on Nathaniel's face stopped him. Nathaniel looked apologetic, and sorry, and determined, all at once.

"Nathaniel . . ."

"I'm sorry, Lieutenant. I have to go." He snapped to attention, gave a flawless salute, then turned as Jonathan had and hurried after his brother.

Robley stood alone and watched the two boys march away, and for that moment he hated them, hated them profoundly. He hated them for ignoring his orders and making a mockery of his rank. He hated them because they were going off to be in the fight and he was not, and they would find out if they had the brass for this work, and he might never know.

He hated them because they were privates and could get away with what they were doing, but he was an officer and could not.

And mostly, he hated them because he knew that he was using his lieutenancy as an excuse. He could follow them if he chose. There were nearly three thousand men in the 3rd Brigade. No one would see him, no one would care. At the core of it all, they had the courage to do the thing that they were doing, and he did not, and he hated them for it, and he hated himself.

15

They look for a fight at Norfolk. Beauregard is there. I think if I were a man I'd be there, too.

—Mary Boykin Chesnut

*S*unday was perfect, the sun just shy of being too hot, a light breeze off the water, but Bowater felt guilty and exposed as he crossed the naval yard and left through the iron gates. He was still reeling from the terrible thing he had been led into doing, pulled apart by the opposing forces of his humiliation over having lied—there was no other word for it, no softer term—and his delight at seeing the big guns lowered onto the deck.

Bowater skirted the wall of the navy yard to a little waterfront park just to the north of the shipyard. It was no more than a strip of grass and a few trees and benches running along the Elizabeth River, but it afforded a nice view of the water and the town on the far side, a pretty view that Bowater had been working to capture on canvas for the past four Sunday afternoons.

He stopped at the place he had been working, set up his easel, and placed the half-finished canvas on it. He dabbed paint on his palette, stared at the canvas, the river, the canvas. It was the same view he had been staring at from the deck of the *Cape Fear* for over two months. He wondered why he had thought to paint that scene when he was already so sick of looking at it.

He wondered why he bothered to paint at all, when he was so utterly incapable of capturing that essence that he was seeking. The colors were rendered true, the proportions, the perspective. There was a nice sense of framing with the after end of one of the yard tugs taking up the foreground. It should have been a nice painting, but it was not. Something was not there, like a forgotten word on the tip of the tongue, tantalizing, but he could not find it.

Maddening. Painting was supposed to be his passion, the thing that drew his mind away from the horrible sameness of the rest of it. Now it, too, was becoming a burden.

He dabbed at the oil-paint river, coaxing some of the reflected sunlight out of it, and soon, despite his frustration, he was immersed in the work. There was no *Cape Fear*, no Hieronymus Taylor, no war that he was in danger of missing, no shame in compromising his integrity. There was only him and the river in front of him and the river he was making appear on the canvas.

"I should not have done that, but the effect is interesting." A woman's voice behind him, as if they had been carrying on a conversation, and Bowater jumped, nearly ran his brush right over the canvas.

He turned around. The speaker was perhaps in her mid-twenties. Long, dark hair fell out from under a wide straw hat. She wore a short jacket and skirts—no hoops. Drops and splatters of paint dotted her clothing.

"I'm sorry. I didn't mean to frighten you."

"You most certainly did not frighten me."

"Startle you then. That's not bad." She nodded toward his painting. Samuel felt himself bristle.

"Thank you, ma'am, for so insightful a commentary."

"You needn't get in a huff. Just a friendly critique, one painter to another."

She took a few steps forward, bent and studied the painting while Samuel Bowater studied her, tried to think how this person had managed to squeeze so many damnably irritating comments into two simple sentences.

"If you don't mind . . ." Bowater said. The girl straightened, said, "Oh. Sorry. My name is Wendy Atkins."

She held out her hand in a very masculine gesture and Samuel took it, shook, said, "I am Lieutenant Samuel Bowater, at your service."

" 'Lieutenant'? An army officer?"

"Confederate States Navy." Samuel heard the irritation creep into his voice, and Wendy heard it as well.

"Forgive me, *Lieutenant*, I don't want to interfere with your artistry."

She turned and walked off, and Samuel watched her, despite himself. There was something about her, something of the libertine, that made Samuel think of the suffragettes or one of these radical, thoroughly distasteful women's groups.

Forty feet away she stopped and set up an easel and rested a canvas on it. She had been holding a paint kit and canvas in her hand, but Samuel had not even noticed, and he only now caught her phrase "one painter to another."

Samuel had been watching her preparation, the graceful, practiced way that she set out her paints, but his eye was drawn to the canvas. It was not a big painting, twenty inches by twelve, perhaps, and hard to make out at that distance. It was approximately the same view that he himself was painting. But even from forty feet there was a quality that seemed to radiate from the picture, an ambiance that dovetailed perfectly with the actual river in front of him, the smell of the trees and grass and hints of smoke. It seemed to have . . . Bowater did not know the word. It.

He frowned. Now he would have to deal with the distraction of having her close at hand, along with all the other damnable distractions that made his life a misery and his painting a mediocrity.

He turned back to the canvas, and soon the world and his own self-pity were lost in the pure focus of applying paint to canvas. He touched the tiny buildings on the far shore—darks and lights, brick reds and pale yellows—the suggestion of buildings. He ran an eye over what he had done, gave a tiny nod of approval.

"Nice, nice . . ." Wendy's voice again, and again Bowater jumped.

"I'm sorry, did I frighten . . . startle you again?"

Bowater rounded on her, and the first thing that leaped into his throat was the kind of tongue-lashing he was accustomed to giving a subordinate, but he held it back. He cleared his throat. "I find such peering over someone's shoulder to be the height of intrusiveness," he managed.

"Oh, come now. People do it to me all the time. It doesn't bother me."

"What people do all the time, ma'am, and what you are willing to tolerate are hardly benchmarks for decent society." He had meant for the words to cut her like a very sharp knife, but instead they sounded pompous and absurd, and Wendy just smiled and leaned over again and looked at his painting.

"And yet . . ." she said.

"What?"

"I don't know . . . technically it is quite right, you know, except perhaps for your color choice there . . ." she pointed to the water in the shadow of the far shore. ". . . but there is something . . . I don't know . . . missing."

"The painting is not complete."

"Are you familiar with Fitz Hugh Lane?"

"Yes."

"I should think that sort of thing . . . why do you not paint naval subjects?"

Bowater was thrown off by the question, and forgot to be indignant about this entire line of interrogation. "The navy is my entire life. I paint, in part, to forget the navy for a while."

"Perhaps that is the problem."

"What?"

"Well, you do not let your real life get into your painting."

This was absurd, and moreover it had destroyed Samuel's enthusiasm for painting for the day. He took out his bottle of turpentine and began to wash his brushes.

"I do hope I have not chased your muse away," Wendy said. Bowater looked up, tried to give her an *Are you still here?* expression.

"My muse, I fear, did not choose to come south with me and is now trapped behind enemy lines."

Wendy laughed, flashed white teeth. "A sense of humor! Who would have thought it of the stoic lieutenant. On what ship do you serve?"

"The gunboat *Cape Fear*." He almost said "tugboat" but did not. "I am her commanding officer."

"Indeed? I have always been drawn to the sea."

"Then it is a pity you were not born a man." Bowater put his paints away and set his canvas on the grass. This Wendy seemed the type who might not realize she was not born a man.

"I have never been aboard a naval vessel," she said.

"I fear you have missed your chance," Samuel said. "On board the larger ships, it is not uncommon to stage entertainments that are appropriate for ladies to attend. But the larger ships are all in the Union navy. The gunboats of our Confederate Navy are hardly appropriate places for a woman."

"Including your *Cape Fear*?"

"Most certainly including my *Cape Fear*. Good day now, and good luck with your painting."

Bowater left her there, walked back to the navy yard, caught a boat to the *Cape Fear*. He needed the mental holiday that painting afforded him, but his afternoon had been ruined by that Wendy Atkins person. Her words seemed to buzz around his head like a swarm of bees, as noisy and as hard to get rid of. Why, he wondered, did the mind have such a capacity for self-torment? He had allowed himself to be pulled into Taylor's confidence game, and he had been beating himself over it ever since. Now, try as he might to stop them, his thoughts kept coming back to the person he least wished to think on.

Wendy Atkins dabbed paint on the canvas, looked out across the languid water of the Elizabeth River. There was no traffic moving, not much going on.

She glanced south, toward the navy yard. Wondered if Lieutenant Bowater would make an appearance. It was three weeks ago that she had met him, and she had seen him twice since. They had exchanged something like ten words. He had returned again and again to her thoughts.

She pulled in a big lungful of the brackish air, reveled in it. Wendy was drawn to the sea, though she did not know why. There were no sailors in her family, no grizzled old grandfathers to balance her on their knee and tell her tales of far-distant lands, of storms and golden sunrises at sea, no brothers returning from year-long voyages bearing exotic gifts. Her people were farmers and storekeepers. They showed little interest in traveling to the next town over, let alone distant lands.

Yet there it was; dreams of the romance and beauty of the sea wrapped around her like an old quilt, ever since she was a little girl. Growing up in Culpepper, Virginia, 160 miles from salt water, she based her first childish paintings of ships on magical voyages entirely on woodcuts in books and magazines and on her own imagination, since she had seen neither a ship nor a sea. She filled in the colors absent in the black-and-white images: golden hulls and red and green and yellow sails, oceans of brilliant aquamarine.

The reality, first observed at age thirteen on a visit to her paternal aunt in Norfolk, had been both a thrill and a disappointment. Ships, and the sea on which they traveled, were much more chromatically understated than she had imagined, yet much grander than she could ever have guessed.

She chafed through her teens, chafed through her early twenties, eager to return to the sea, to live by salt water. She read whatever she could get her hands on, stories of Columbus and bold Francis Drake, of John Paul Jones and Nelson. Her fantastic ships became peopled by fearless sailors who strode the quarterdeck in gales of wind and flying metal.

Wendy could not go to sea, she could not even live by the sea, but she could paint. Ships and seascapes done from memory, and the mountains as well and the people in her family, she painted them all with a skill that grew year after year. By the time she was seventeen there was nothing more that anyone in Culpepper or the surrounding area could teach her, because she knew more about art, and painted with more skill than anyone she knew.

She fended off suitors, defended against becoming trapped in Culpepper with a husband and children to care for. And after a while, as her reputation as an eccentric grew, the young men stopped coming, which was fine. They thought of her as some sort of bluestocking, assumed her to be a suffragette, which she might well have been if she had cared enough about politics to pay attention.

But she did not. Painting. The sea. Those were the things she loved. And when the war came, and the possibility of the grand men-of-war sailing from Southern ports, she could stand it no more. Weeks of arguing, pouting, stubbornness won her her parents' approval to move to Portsmouth and live with her Aunt Molly. Despite the fact that Molly was, in many ways, as suspect as Wendy.

She took the carriage house behind Molly's larger place as her own, began painting the ocean and river views around Portsmouth and Norfolk. In the month that she had been there, the place had provided more excitement than over two decades in Culpepper. The energy was palpable.

When it exploded on the 20th, Wendy was there, down by the naval yard, walking the streets, unescorted, but she did not care. She let herself get caught up in the swirl and madness of the crowd. Sucking it down. The shouting, the gunfire, the bitter smell of smoke, rolling over the low walls surrounding the yard, the towering columns of flames—it was all so thrilling that she could barely tear herself away with the coming of dawn and the bone-weariness that dragged her back to her little carriage house.

Living in Portsmouth, she was learning a great deal about the reality of the maritime world, discovering that real sailors were not necessarily the gentleman heroes of her dreams, the lovable rogues.

But Wendy Atkins was a romantic, and like any good romantic, she would not let the empirical truth trounce the fine fantasy world she had created. She longed, above all, to get underway on a ship, a man-of-war. She still felt there was romance and excitement to be found there. She longed to see it from beyond the passenger's perspective. But that did not seem possible.

Or had not seemed possible. She was growing more hopeful of her chances. There were a lot of navy men around. And while none of them was the Hawkins or John Paul Jones of her dreams, there were some possibilities there.

She seemed to draw them like a lodestone, standing on the bank, brazen with her hoopless skirt and paint-spattered clothes, painting. They were an odd lot; boys who would look over her shoulder and try and fail to think of some insightful comment; they usually ended up with something along the lines of "Boy, ain't that pretty!"

Those she dismissed out of hand.

There were others who were more intriguing, officers, mostly, some of whom knew a thing or two about art. And officers, she understood, were the ones to know if one wished to see a man-of-war in some significant way.

And there was Samuel Bowater. Most intriguing of all, because he was a painter, and not an altogether bad one. He did not make an attempt on her affections, hardly spoke to her when he did see her, and she did not know if that was his means of piquing her interest or if he genuinely did not care.

Wendy laid her thin brush aside, picked up the thicker one, touched it to the white paint, and began to build high cumulus clouds. There were some men who were more subtle. By way of example, the man sitting on the bench twenty yards away, ostentatiously tuning his violin. He wore a blue frock coat with some kind of shoulder boards, but what rank or position he might hold she could not imagine.

He dragged the bow across the strings, made a horrible noise that set her teeth on edge as he fiddled with the pegs.

If he can't play that thing, I am going to have to move, she thought. Her concentration could not suffer through amateur fiddling twenty yards away.

Finally the man stopped tuning, rested the bow on the strings, looked out over the water. Wendy stole glances at him. Unkempt, to some degree, he could use a shave, but his features were strong and he was not unattractive.

He closed his eyes, moved the bow across the strings. Wendy paused, brush hovering over her painting, listened. The tune was familiar, some folk song, though this fellow played it slow and solemn, not the way she had heard it before.

She listened. He was no amateur, he made the instrument speak, threw in delicate fingerwork, flourishes of music where the original, simple melody had none.

"Rosin the Beau," Wendy realized. That was the tune, "Rosin the Beau." Her father used to sing it to her when she was a girl. But there was magic in the way this fellow played it, the simple folk tune as foundation, the clever but subtle improvisation on the old song.

Wendy went back to her work as the music floated over her, as if it was the leitmotif of her art, orchestral accompaniment; it dovetailed with her mood, or pulled her mood along with it, she did not know which. The effect was the same.

She built oil-paint clouds and the violinist ended his song, moved on to

"The Dark-Eyed Gypsy" and from there to the tunes she knew as "forebitters," the songs of the sailor men, not the chanties, the work songs, but the plaintive songs they sang on the forecastle head at night. The music entranced her.

She painted on, wrapped in the sound, and then somehow the folk songs and the forebitters were over and she was getting snatches of Mozart and Bach and Beethoven. She smiled as she dabbed paint. And then the music stopped and soon she heard footsteps. *Here we go . . .* she thought.

"Forgive me, ma'am," the man said, and she turned and he tipped his hat, a wool cap with a leather visor, the kind the naval officers wore. "I have been terribly rude. I do hope I haven't disturbed you." His accent was not Virginia, but Deep South.

"Your question is disingenuous, I think," she said, turning back to her canvas.

"Pardon?"

"You are being disingenuous. It means . . ."

"I know what it means."

"Then you know you are being that." She turned to him and smiled. "You play wonderfully, and a very catholic repertoire, but I do not think you were worried about disturbing me."

The man lifted his cap, scratched his head, gave her an odd sort of smile. "Maybe not."

"Are you just a musician, sir, or do you fancy painting as well?"

"Oh, I don't know much about painting . . . I know what I like." He looked at Wendy's painting, all but finished. "I could say somethin' like 'My, ain't that pretty,' but I don't reckon that would be what you call an insightful comment."

"I reckon not."

She turned back to her painting, let the man hang in the uncomfortable silence, and just as she heard him begin to shuffle in preparation of walking away, she said, "Are you a naval officer, sir? I do not recognize your insignia."

"Well, they still gettin all that insignia nonsense straightened away. I am a naval officer. Chief engineer on a gunboat."

"Chief engineer . . ." Wendy had never cared for engines and such. She thought them dirty and vulgar. They were the barbarians at the gate, ready to drive off the tall, elegant sailing ships of which she had dreamed for so long.

"That's right," the man said, as if reading her mind. "I am one of those loathsome and dirty mechanics who labor in those Stygian depths."

Wendy turned and met his eyes. He was smiling at her, playful and ironic. She tried to see into him, tried to look through his brown eyes. *He is a tricky one*, she thought. If Samuel Bowater was a hard man to plumb, this one seemed more complicated still. *Stygian?*

"My name is Hieronymus Taylor," the man said, held out his hand.

Wendy took it and shook. Most men did not offer to shake hands with her. "Wendy Atkins, a pleasure. 'Hieronymus'?"

"Now, you ain't gonna ask if I'm named after some ol painter, are you?"

"Well, yes . . . I was. Were you?"

"Damned if I know . . . beg pardon. My daddy never did tell me, an he's dead now, so I reckon it's too late to ask. Though where the old man would have heard of a fella like that, on the docks of N'Orleans, I can't figure."

Ahh . . . Wendy thought. *New Orleans, waterfront, dock rat* . . . She filed him away in the right pigeonhole. "Wherever did you learn to play the violin like that?"

"Old black fella taught me. Rollin Jones was his name, somethin of a legend down in the delta. He seen I had a natural ability, taught me up."

"Surely he did not teach you Mozart."

"No. Was I playin Mozart?"

"Yes you were. How could you not know that?"

"Well, I hear bits of music, they stick in my head. Can't forget 'em if I try. Guess I heard that somewhere. Which one was Mozart?"

Wendy hummed a few bars and Taylor took up with her and they hummed together. "Right, right . . . I sure do love that bit of music."

"It is lovely," Wendy said, and she was quiet again, but it was not uncomfortable now. "You know," she continued, and the words came out way ahead of any thought, "I have always wanted to sail aboard a man-of-war. Just once."

Taylor nodded. "You might be talkin to the right fellow."

"During a fight at sea," Wendy added, firing the second barrel. *Insane* . . .

Taylor laughed out loud. "That's getting a bit trickier."

Wendy nodded. "Forgive me. Girlish daydreams of Lord Nelson and such. I don't know where that came from."

Taylor folded his arms and regarded her with a curious look. Then, to Wendy's full amazement, Taylor clarified. "I said that was a bit trickier. I didn't say it was impossible."

16

Our brave men fell in great numbers, but they died as the brave love to die—
with faces to the foe, fighting in the holy cause of liberty.

—Captain Thomas Goldsby, 4th Alabama

*J*ackson's brigade was moving fast, honed by months of hard marching through the Shenandoah Valley. Jonathan and Nathaniel Paine hurried to catch up, but the long gray line was like a mirage, and no matter how fast they tramped, they seemed to get no closer to it.

Sweat was running freely down their faces and under their wool shell jackets and down their legs. There was nothing they would have liked more than to strip naked, to leap into cool water, as on hot summer days when they were boys on the plantation.

They tramped downhill from the McLean house, across grass that crunched under their shoes, dried to tinder from the heat. They crossed a narrow stream, some branch of some branch that trickled into the Bull Run. It was hardly deep enough to get their shoes wet, but they managed to shove the canteens into the mud so far that the brown water ran into them. They drank as much as they could stand, filled them again, and continued on.

At last they came to the dry, brown dirt road down which Jackson was leading his men, three regiments of Virginians, the 2nd, 27th, and 33rd. The boys hurried on in pursuit. The dust from the tramping brigade hung in the air, rising up above the men like their own personal dust storm, and the Paine boys felt it stick to their faces and clog noses and chafe throats as they pressed on. They had come about a mile, and had three more to go to get where the fighting was.

Along the route of the march they encountered men who had fallen out, some from Jackson's brigade and others from the 2nd and 3rd Brigades of the Army of the Shenandoah, which had come before. Some sat and some lay passed out, perhaps dead, from the heat. Some leaned on their guns and watched with no interest as the boys hurried past. Occasionally one would call out to them for water, but they had no water to spare, and even if they had, they would not have shared it. They had no interest in beats who had dropped out of the fight when they were so eager to get into it.

They marched on in silence for as long as they could, and then, by tacit consent, stopped and had a drink of hot, silty water.

"Reckon we're catching them up," Nathaniel huffed. His face was a worrisome shade of red, his hair plastered to his forehead, wet as if he had just come from a swim.

Jonathan just nodded, not ready to speak. He looked up the road. The tail end of the brigade did appear closer. Hard and conditioned as Jackson's troops might have been, a brigade on the march could not move as fast as two motivated and well-rested young men.

"It would be an unhappy irony," Jonathan gasped at last, "if we was to die of the heat just before we get to tangle with them bluebellies."

Nathaniel nodded. With his mouth hanging open and his eyes glazed he looked remarkably like a dead fish. "Let's move it out," he said, and the boys shouldered their rifles and headed off again on the double quick.

They could not see the fighting, but still they were in no doubt that the battle was joined, and the fighting was hot and intense. Beyond the low, rolling hills, the lines of forest that ended abruptly where the farmers' fields began, they could hear the gunfire. It was not the burst of fire, followed by quiet, that they had heard the day before, as skirmishers and pickets felt each other out. This was a blanket of noise, a mosaic of noise, a single whole made up of thousands and thousands of tiny parts.

And through the wall of sound, the big guns blasted away like kettledrums punctuating the lighter melody. The clouds of smoke rose in the still air, great banks of gray, roiling smoke, rising up from behind the patchwork hill and settling in a thick layer.

On the road ahead of them was a house, a big, imposing affair with massive brick chimneys on either side. But Jackson's brigade had turned off the road and was now making its way across open fields and up the slope of a hill—what appeared to be the final hill—between them and the great battle of the war.

"I swear . . ." Nathaniel said, "I swear, I expect to see them Yankees come swarming up over that crest, any second now."

"Well, we still got the Virginians between us and them, if they do."

They tramped on, heads down, through a patch of piney wood. The shade of the trees was a relief from the sun. And then they broke out and Jonathan said, "Lookee here, brother." Jackson's brigade had nearly reached the crest of a hill and stopped. Mounted officers were riding in the front of the battalion, spreading the men out into a line of battle, until the serpentine mass of troops, marching toward the fight, was now a wall of men, poised just below the high ground, ready to sweep forward.

"Come on!" Nathaniel said, quickening his pace, and Jonathan did likewise. Jackson's men were spread along the rise, the far end disappearing into a tangle of scrub and trees. If 1st Brigade was going forward, the boys did not want to miss it. They were no more than a couple hundred feet behind the line when Jackson's men did the one thing they would not have expected. They lay down.

"Now what in hell? They having a little nooning?" Jonathan huffed.

"Beats me."

The two boys quickly covered the distance, came up with the troops near the crest of the hill, spread out over a thousand feet of hilltop and packed tight. They found a gap in the line into which they stepped and fell to the ground with the others. For some time they did nothing, just lay there and gulped air, grateful to be done with marching.

Overhead, the shells screamed by, nearly deafening as they passed, the bullets whipped by with a wild buzzing sound, so it seemed as if there was a great current of flying metal just feet above them, as if, were they to stand, they would instantly be caught in the maelstrom and hurled clear down the hill, carried away on the riptide of artillery and rifle fire.

At last Jonathan rolled over, propped himself up on his elbows, turned to the soldier on his right-hand side. "Say, pard, what's going on here? What're y'all doin?"

The soldier looked at Jonathan, said nothing, just chewed a stalk of grass he held in his teeth. He did not look like the men of the 18th Mississippi looked. He looked more like what a soldier should look like, by Jonathan's lights. He was lean to the point of looking unwell, but there was a hardness in his gaunt face, an unhurried professionalism in his demeanor. His uniform, such that it was, was torn in some places and patched in others. His kepi had a dark and permanent sweat stain an inch high all around. The butt of his gun was chipped and the finish nearly worn off, but the metal gleamed in a way that spoke of the care the weapon received.

At last the soldier spoke, as unhurried as if he was leaning on a rail fence, talking with his neighbor of a summer evening. "We're layin down," he said.

Jonathan nodded. "Why are we laying down? Isn't there a battle going on over there?" Jonathan nodded toward the crest of the hill.

The soldier considered him for a minute more. His eyes wandered over Jonathan's uniform. "Where the hell *you* come from?"

"Eighteenth Mississippi. We were down at McLean's Ford."

The soldier sat up on his elbow, looked back down the hill, toward the woods. He looked back at Jonathan. "Where's the rest of your regiment?"

"Back at McLean's Ford, I reckon. My brother and I, we didn't want to miss the fight."

The soldier nodded. "Y'all ain't seen the elephant yet?"

"No. And now we're just laying down. What does a fella have to do to kill a few Yankees around here?"

The soldier smiled at some private joke. "Don't you worry, young Mississippi. You want fighting, you come to the right goddamned place." Then his expression seemed to soften a bit, and he said, "Say, you got any water in that canteen?"

"Some." Jonathan struggled out of the strap, handed the canteen over. "It's half mud."

"No matter. Hour ago I was drinking out of a hoofprint, and glad for it." The soldier took a couple of swallows, with evident pleasure, and handed the rest back.

Jonathan looked to his left. Nathaniel was lying on his back, looking up at the artillery screaming overhead. Somewhere down the line to their right, a Confederate battery was returning fire. They could feel the concussion of the heavy guns going off, feel the rumble in the ground.

"I sure as hell would like to know what was going on in the front there," Nathaniel said.

Jonathan looked up at the crest of the hill, twenty feet away. He could see nothing but blue sky through the tall, coarse brown grass, and the black streaks of shells screaming past.

Let's go have us a look. He thought the words, almost spoke them, but checked himself. He was having doubts about this whole thing, now. It was bad enough that he might have made a grand mistake with his own skin, but he had got Nathaniel in on this as well. He felt a flush of guilt for having once again lured his brother into some mischief.

Mischief, hell . . . I might've got us both killed. . . .

This was not their regiment, of course, not where they were supposed to be. Were they obligated to go forward, if the others did?

What was going on out there? *Am I my brother's keeper?*

"Hey, Nathaniel . . ."

"What?"

"I'm gonna crawl over to the edge of the hill there, see what's what."

Nathaniel was quiet for a second. "I'll come, too," he said at last.

The two of them crawled forward, walking on elbows and pushing with knees. Over the crest of the hill behind which they were lying, through the tall, stiff dried grass, they could see there was a dip in the ground and then a second rise, thirty feet away.

They stood straighter, ran down into the dip and up the farther slope, dropping and crawling as they approached the crest. They came up over the last rise, approached the top carefully. Beyond the last rise the land was flat for a couple hundred feet and then it sloped away steeply. To the right was a small white house, riddled with holes from the Yankee guns. Beyond that was a great sweep of countryside, brown fields and patches of trees, a dusty road running off to the north.

And the enemy.

"Sweeeet Jesus! Look at all those damned Yankees . . ." Nathaniel said.

It was nothing that Jonathan could have imagined. The wounded and dead were everywhere. Hundreds upon hundreds of men scattered like heaps of tossed-off rags and spread over the hill. Before he saw the Yankees, thousands of them, before he saw the field artillery blasting holes in the Confederate lines or the Confederates giving ground to the blue-clad hordes, before he saw any of that, he saw the dead and he pictured himself among them.

He looked off to his right. Thirty feet away, a soldier lay on his back, eyes and mouth open and his lower half turned away at an odd angle, as if he had been broken in two and his insides spilled out. Jonathan looked long enough to understand what he was looking at, then turned his head quick, squeezed his mouth and throat closed tight to fight the rising in his stomach.

"Jonathan!" Nathaniel slapped him on the shoulder. "I said, did you see all them damned Yankees?"

Jonathan looked down the hill, avoiding the dead men, avoiding the horror to his right. Thousands upon thousands of bluebellies were massing at the base of the hill, and many, many more behind. Not disorganized clumps of men, but neat blocks of soldiers, marching regiments, coming on in a relentless way. They fired by volleys, shot clouds of gray smoke out in front of them, like some fire-breathing creature of mythology. Some were coming on, but most were marching to and fro, getting into formation, assembling into a grand and unstoppable line of men and guns, ready to sweep forward and roll over the weakened Confederate lines.

There was another, smaller hill beyond the one on which they lay, and between the points of high ground, a thin tributary of the Bull Run River wound itself, crossing and recrossing a turnpike that ran in a straight line between. From the distant hill, perhaps a mile away, a Union battery was pouring shot and shell into the Confederate lines.

More big guns were coming. Jonathan could see teams of horses dragging field artillery across the turnpike and up the grassy fields of the hill from which they watched, ten guns churning up dust with the big wheels of their carriages and leaving twin lines in the grass as they were hauled along.

"I don't think this is our day, Jonathan!" Nathaniel shouted over the din.

"Those guns are going to knock hell out of us, once they're in place!" Jonathan replied.

The Confederate line, such as it was, was backing away from the Union march, backing up the hill toward where Jackson's men were lying. Some units were retreating in good order, but others were breaking and running for the Confederate lines, desperate to put the hill between themselves and the killing volleys.

The panic was infectious. One by one the units broke and ran, and the Union juggernaut came on, slow and relentless and seemingly unassailable.

"Look there!" Nathaniel said, pointed down the hill. In the wake of the artillery, which was now moving up the hill to a position not 200 feet away, came a regiment of Yankees. Their jackets were blue, but their pants were bright red. Others were clad entirely in brilliant crimson, short jackets and pants that were loose-fitting from the waist right down to where they were drawn in tight by white gaiters.

"Zouaves . . . damn . . ." Jonathan said.

The regiment was a thing to behold, a thing of beauty on that field of horrors. Their lines became muddled as they made their way over a rail fence, but once on the other side they reformed with startling symmetry and marched on, uphill, coming in support of the battery.

"They'll make better targets with them red outfits, anyway," Nathaniel said.

"I reckon . . . I reckon it's time we got out of here."

They did not take their eyes from the field below, as if the enemy was waiting for them to turn their backs before shooting them. Instead they backed away, crawling backward, and slowly the crest of the hill came up between them and the fight beyond. When at last they could see nothing but sky, they turned and scrambled back to the lines, hunched over, half crawling, half running, until they were once again part of the line of waiting men.

The soldier with whom Jonathan had spoken turned to him now. "You seen the elephant? What'd he look like?"

Jonathan opened his mouth for a flip response, but the image of the dead man, torn apart, swam in front of him. He closed his mouth and shook his head. No words would come.

The soldier nodded. "He gets uglier," was all he said.

Then with a roar that made Jonathan jump, the Union artillery opened up. The gunfire was from nearly in front of them, but the Yankees were aiming elsewhere, and only the intimidating sound of the blasts threatened the men with whom the Paines had joined.

"Them Yanks brought up some guns, I reckon," the soldier at Jonathan's side commented.

"Yes, a dozen or so." Jonathan was eager to tell this man something that he did not know. "And Zouaves to support them. You should see their red uniforms!"

The soldier smiled. "Pretty uniform don't make a soldier. I hope for their sake them uniforms is bulletproof."

An officer came running down the line, waving a sword over his head. "Stand and prepare to fire! Stand and prepare to fire!" he shouted.

The soldier looked over at Jonathan and smiled. "Here we go, boy," he said, and Jonathan, who thought he would be sick with the thought of standing up in that hail of iron, got some comfort from the words and the calm in the man's voice.

All along the line, soldiers rose to their feet, shouldered weapons, pawed at the ground with battered shoes.

"I don't know, Jonathan," Nathaniel said in a low voice. "I'm so scared, I'm like to shit my pants. . . ."

"Yeah, me too."

Then from somewhere came the order to advance. Jonathan did not hear it, but suddenly everyone was moving forward, and so was Nathaniel. And he was, too, though he still had not decided whether he would go. They tramped forward to the crest of the hill, over the ground they had just covered on their stomachs. To their left, more men were emerging from the trees and scrub, and before them, terribly, terribly close, the Union battery, with the red-clad Zouaves out in front to protect it from the Southern threat.

The same officer who had ordered them up was back, telling them to halt, which Jonathan did, gladly, and when all the line was stopped the order came to prime.

Jonathan's hands moved with no thought, so often had he gone through this routine. His right thumb pulled the hammer back to half cock, then he reached for the percussion caps in his pouch, fished one out, pressed it onto the nipple.

"Ready! Aim!"

The gun came up to Jonathan's shoulder and he sighted down the barrel, was dimly aware of red-clad men swimming at the end of his muzzle.

"Fire!" The word was not all out of the officer's mouth before Jonathan squeezed the trigger, felt the familiar jar of the butt plate against his shoulder.

The smoke and the noise and the concussion of the whole line firing at once was unlike anything Jonathan could have imagined, the numb calm that he felt now unlike anything he might have guessed at. He was standing up in the flying river of iron, the minié balls and shells screaming past, making their terrible sound, and his arms and hands were performing the manual of arms, and he was hardly aware of any of it.

He felt the paper cartridge in his teeth, tasted the powder as he bit into it and tore off the top, but he was not sure how it had come to be in his mouth. His thoughts, such as they were, revolved around the stunning fact that he had just aimed his rifle at a human being and pulled the trigger. He had tried to kill the man, and he seemed not to care. He was more like a distant observer, watching this young man perform in his first battle, than he was a part of the scene.

His rifle came up again to the firing position, but this time he hesitated and looked at the scene beyond the shining barrel. The smoke was lifting and he could see the line of field guns, but the former military perfection was gone.

There were dead men everywhere, humps of crimson cloth and red legs sprawled out at odd angles and terrified horses and wounded horses screaming, an ungodly sound.

Some of the troops, the Zouaves and the red-pants regiment, were standing to fire, then dropping to their knees to reload. Still more were backing away down the hill, and some actually running, leaving the artillery units unprotected. And still the guns fired, as if they were unaware of the battle among foot soldiers taking place around them.

Jonathan looked to his left. Nathaniel was going through the drill, biting cartridge, pouring powder down the barrel, ramming the ball home.

Someone raised a shout, somewhere down the line, and a ripple of excitement moved through the men and Jonathan checked himself as he put his rifle to his shoulder and looked down the hill. From the woods on the left burst ranks of horsemen, Confederate cavalry, and with sabers flashing in the sun they charged down on the retreating Zouaves.

Jonathan watched, transfixed, as the battle played out just a few hundred feet away, horses prancing and whirling and sabers hacking up and down and the men on foot lunging with bayonets and firing up at riders, knocking them from the saddle. It was a macabre ballet, and the music to accompany it was the crash of artillery, the scream of minié balls, the wail of shells passing overhead.

Jonathan remembered the rifle in his hands. He shouldered the weapon, pointed it in the general direction of the battery, fired. The butt dropped to the ground, his hand found a cartridge.

The dance of horse and infantrymen was over, the cavalry retreating back to the woods, the Zouaves moving farther down the hill.

And then that officer was there again, racing down the line, sword raised, and he was shouting, "Advance! Thirty-third Virginia, advance!"

The line of men took a step forward, the great mass of soldiers building the first bit of momentum. The officer turned toward the front and then his head seemed to explode, as if a charge in his brain had been fired off. He flew back, landed on his back, arms outflung, sword still in his twitching fist, but the Confederate line pushed past him and moved down the hill.

Jonathan looked at the dead man, half his face and head gone, the one remaining eye staring at the sky, but he felt nothing, no sensation in his gut, just a casual interest, and then his eyes were forward, on the artillery park, because that was where they were going.

Over the crest of the hill and they climbed over a rail fence and on the other side the officers formed them up in a line, shouted some words that Jonathan could not hear.

"Here we go, now!" Nathaniel yelled. Jonathan turned to look at his brother. He was grinning an odd grin and Jonathan knew his brother was as charged as he, as ready to go forward.

"Advance!" the word came rolling down the line and then the 33rd stepped out, and Jonathan and Nathaniel with it. A few hundred feet from the artillery and Jonathan could see two of the big guns swing around, their round mouths pointing at the Confederates, and he tensed, turned his head slightly away, readied himself for the blast, but it did not come.

One hundred and fifty feet and the colonel of the 33rd neatly turned the regiment so they were coming more directly at the battery. The two guns still stared silent at them, but now some of the other guns were being limbered up, ready to move. It seemed all confusion among the artillerists. Jonathan wondered why they did not fire. He wondered if the 33rd's blue uniforms were confusing them.

The Zouaves at the bottom of the hill were massing, and now someone was swinging one of the guns around to bear better on the advancing Confederates, and Jonathan thought, *That's it, then, the jig is up.*

"Fire! Fire!" The order moved along the Confederate line and as one they stopped, shouldered weapons, fired from just over a hundred feet. The last rifles were still going off when the Confederate line rolled forward again, and as they jogged through their own smoke they could see the destruction and panic they had wrought. Dead men were everywhere, Zouaves, red-legged infantrymen, artillerymen. Horses thrashed out their lives still bound by their traces. Hundreds of men raced down the hill, tossing aside any encumbrance—knapsacks, rifles, canteens.

The 33rd rushed into the gap and then they were among the guns and only the dead and wounded of the Yankees remained behind. The rest were racing for their lines. A cheer went up from somewhere on the left and it was taken up along the line and soon among all of the 33rd, and Jonathan and Nathaniel Paine were shouting like madmen, whooping it up over their captured artillery.

A gang of soldiers tossed their rifles aside, grabbed the trails of one of the guns, swung it around to bring the weapon to bear on the fleeing Yankees. Others busied themselves pulling shoes of likely-looking size off the bodies of the late artillerymen. And off to the right, the rest of Jackson's 1st Brigade began to move forward. The Confederates, on the verge of being crushed, were now on the offensive.

But the Yankees had some fight left in them. Even as the jubilation of taking the battery was fading, Jonathan became aware of small-arms fire. Minié balls were whipping past, buzzing by, at a furious rate, the noise much louder, the air even thicker with iron and lead. He looked down the hill. A regiment of bluecoats was making its way up the hill, firing in volleys as it came. A Virginian not ten feet away was knocked from his feet, a dark hole in his chest. Another screamed as his leg buckled under him, his knee shot through, and he fell to the dry grass, landing on top of a dead Yankee.

"Here they come!" Nathaniel shouted, raising his rifle and firing, dropping the butt to the ground and reloading.

Damn, damn . . . Jonathan had forgotten about his rifle. He set the butt on the ground, reached for a cartridge. Fingers were plucking at his sleeve and his pants and he looked to see who it was and saw nothing but a series of holes where bullets had passed.

Damn . . . The calm was deserting him, and he could feel panic rising up like the sickness he had felt before. He took a step back, could see more of the 33rd backing away from this onslaught. He raised his rifle and pulled the trigger.

To his left he heard his brother grunt, as if he had stubbed his toe, and he turned but Nathaniel was not there.

He looked in the other direction, but his brother was not there either, and he wondered if Nathaniel had panicked, had run for the crest of the hill. And then he thought to look at the ground.

Nathaniel was lying half on his side, turned away from Jonathan, as if sleeping. Jonathan dropped his gun, dropped beside him, rolled him over.

The bullet had hit Nathaniel in the chest, just to the left of his breast-bone. Blood gleamed through the rent in the fabric of his shell jacket, spread a dark stain through the cloth. A line of blood trickled out of the edge of his mouth.

"Nathaniel . . ." Jonathan did not know if he had thought the name, or whispered it or shouted it. His brother's eyes shifted over and then they were looking at one another, looking into each other's eyes.

Nathaniel blinked once, slowly. His mouth opened and Jonathan leaned closer, to hear what he would say. But no words came, just a soft gurgling sound, a horrible sound, then a rattling noise. Jonathan leaned back. The life was out of Nathaniel's eyes.

Jonathan's eyes filled, the tears made hot wet tracks down his cheeks. He felt them fall on his hands. "Nathaniel, Nathaniel, what have I done, what have I done? Oh, God, oh, God, forgive me . . ."

He looked up to the sky, the blue, blue sky. A bullet screamed past, he felt it graze his scalp, tear through his hair, but it made no impression on him. He had no thought of moving, could not even if he had wished to. There was nothing for him to do but to wait there with his brother. He could not leave Nathaniel, not after he had brought him so far.

A hand grabbed him by the collar, jerked him to his feet as if he was a doll, shoved him on his way, never letting go. Jonathan found himself running, half pulled, half dragged up the hill. The rail fence swam in front of him and then he was on it and someone was shoving him over the top. He fell in a heap on the other side, looked up. The soldier with whom he had shared his water was climbing after him. He landed beside Jonathan, scrambled to his feet, pulled Jonathan up again. "Come on, boy!" he shouted.

"My brother is dead!" Jonathan shouted back, even as the man pushed him back into a run for the crest of the hill.

"Don't mean you have to be!" the soldier replied. They huffed up the hill, Jonathan staggering, nearly falling, running only because this man was pushing him along, not through any will of his own.

And then they were past the crest of the hill and the man stopped and gasped for breath and let Jonathan Paine collapse at his feet.

The tears came fast now, the grief so consuming that it was like a pressure inside, with no way to get out. "My brother is dead . . ." he said again.

"He ain't the only one," the soldier replied, but there was kindness and sympathy in his voice.

17

The top of the hill was occupied by a battery of artillery, and a body of infantry, belonging to the Federal Army. We sprang out of the ravine and went up the hill at a double-quick. The Federal battery and infantry opened fire on us as soon as we emerged from the ravine, killing and wounding a number of us as we climbed the hill.

—Private George Gibbs, 18th Mississippi,
describing the Battle of First Manassas

Jonathan Paine lay in the coarse grass. Eyes closed, floating in a world of noise and grief. He could make no sense of the sounds around him. The minié balls, the shells, the shouts of officers, the screams of wounded, all melded into one horrible din of war.

He had left Nathaniel there on the field, his beautiful brother, tall and strong, all life and potential. Now he was nothing, just a corpse, everything that was Nathaniel blown out of him.

"Hey, Mississippi . . ." the soldier said. Jonathan looked up, saw the man as if looking through rain-streaked glass. "Looks like we're advancing again. You want to kill some Yankees for your brother, best come." He held out Jonathan's rifle, which he had, apparently, snatched from the field. Jonathan could not recall.

Jonathan got on his feet and the soldier handed him his rifle and he looked at it as if for the first time. *Kill some Yankees for your brother. . . .* It would do Nathaniel no good that he could think of. He was not sure, for all his high talk, that Nathaniel had ever really wanted to kill Yankees. He, Jonathan, might well be shot down too, and his body and Nathaniel's would be rolled into a common grave and their bones would mix with the bones of others and there would be no indication at all that they had ever been.

Nathaniel buried in an anonymous grave. The thought horrified him. Their father and mother never having a notion of what had become of their son, their beautiful Nathaniel. He could not let that happen.

The soldier was five paces ahead and walking away and Johnathan chased after him, fell into step at his side. The man looked up at him, nodded his approval, then turned his eyes to the front, where the enemy waited.

They were up at the fence again. Jonathan looked to his left and right. He could see Jackson's brigade stretched across the crest of the hill, thousands of men in various shades of gray and blue, thousands of men who were ready to kill, men who were prepared to walk into that flying river of iron, when sane people would cower or run.

First Brigade poured like a river over the fence. They paused and shouldered rifles and pointed them at the blue lines in their front. Jonathan saw cannons and horses over the top of his barrel. He pulled the trigger and the hammer snapped down on the nipple but the expected jolt did not happen because the gun was not loaded.

He dropped the butt to the ground, reached for a cartridge. He could hear bullets splinter the rail behind him. His kepi moved a bit as some flying ordnance passed by. He felt as if he himself was in a different place, some place where those bullets could not reach him.

He finished the manual of arms, raised the rifle, pulled the trigger, stepped off with the rest as they advanced on the bluebellies. The bullets danced on the dry ground and sent up tiny dust clouds like the first drops of heavy rain on a dry summer afternoon. The thunder of the guns rolled on and on.

The line stopped and they loaded and fired and moved on, their advance accompanied by the weird yelping battle cry that had spread through the army. The Yankees seemed to be backing away. Advance, stop, fire, advance; the Confederates slowly gained back the ground they had already won and lost once that afternoon.

Jonathan could see the artillery park now, the heaps of dead men and horses, the guns that the Yankees had not managed to pull back to their lines. He could see Nathaniel, lying as he had left him, on his back, arms flung out, and he started toward him.

"Hey, Mississippi, where the hell you going?" the soldier called, but Jonathan just crouched and ran forward, as if running through a hailstorm. A bullet grazed his arm, it felt like a cut from a knife, but it did not slow him.

Jonathan covered the distance fast and then he was among the dead and the guns, kneeling at Nathaniel's side, crouched low as the bullets whipped over his head. He rolled his brother's body half over. It felt stiff and unyielding, not like a living thing at all. He plunged his hand into Nathaniel's pack, felt around for the old journal he knew was there. His fingers brushed against the soft leather cover and he grabbed it and worked it out of the knapsack, held it in his hands, glanced up.

The Yankees were still falling back in the face of Jackson's advance, but there were more bluebellies forming at the base of the hill and tramping up, their units still in good order, tight squares of marching men.

Jonathan paused in his task long enough to load and aim and pull the trigger once more. He laid his rifle aside, snatched up the notebook. He flipped to a blank page, pulled the pencil out of the binding.

Nathaniel James Paine, Company D, 18th Mississippi, 3rd Brigade, son of Robley and Katherine Paine, Yazoo, Mississippi. Please God send me home to be buried in my native earth.

Jonathan tore the page from the journal and tucked it in the front of Nathaniel's shell jacket. He felt an easiness in his mind. It was not peace, not by any means. He did not think he would feel at peace ever again, not after luring Nathaniel to his death, not with the things he had seen on the battlefield that day.

He looked at his brother's face, gray-colored, mouth open, the skin growing tight around his features. Jonathan wondered how many Yankees he himself had killed, how many young men had been turned into so much clay by his bullets.

He looked up. The Confederate line was approaching, the Yankees falling back, but he was still far out ahead of his own people. He snatched up his rifle, reached for a cartridge. He bit the top off and tried to spit it out, but his mouth was so dry he could not spit at all, so he pulled the paper out with his fingers, then poured the powder down the barrel and pushed the bullet in. He pulled out his ramrod and thrust it down the barrel but he could not push it even halfway in. He slammed the ramrod down the barrel, twisted it, but it would not go.

He stared dumbly at the thing, tried to recall if he had been putting percussion caps on the nipple. He could not recall having done so. Was his rifle filled with unfired bullets and power?

He shook his head, tossed his weapon away. No time to puzzle it out. He grabbed up Nathaniel's rifle, lying beside his brother. He paused. Nathaniel was forever getting mad at him for borrowing things without asking. He had been apoplectic the time Jonathan took his painting kit and used it to create genuine Red Indian designs on their canoe.

"Sorry, brother," he said and took the rifle and ran, crouching, for the Confederate lines.

The gray- and blue-clad Virginians were still advancing, walking slowly into that murderous fire. Men took bullets two and three at a time, twisting in their macabre dance that ended with them crumpled and left behind by the advancing line. The shrieks of agony were like nothing Jonathan could have imagined, but they were far less disturbing than the pitiful cries for help, for water, for mother.

Jonathan loaded and placed a percussion cap on the nipple and looked through bleary eyes over the barrel and fired. The butt of the gun slammed into his shoulder, and something else slammed into his side and half spun him around. He looked down and saw strips of his shell jacket hanging down and blood and torn skin. He put his hand on the wound. It felt warm. He pulled his hand away, and his palm was bright red with blood. He stared at it for a moment, then stepped off again with the advancing Confederates. He could not think of anything else he might do.

Load, fire, advance. The bluebellies had been joined by more troops coming up the hill, and now the Virginians were not stepping forward so fast, and in places they were even beginning to back away.

Jonathan pulled a percussion cap out of his box and placed it on the nipple and then his right leg was swept out from under him and he fell and twisted as he went down, saw the blue sky, the blinding sun, swirl past, and he hit the ground, screaming, screaming.

He propped himself up on his elbow. His leg from the knee down was hanging at an angle that was not right. He could see white, jagged bone sticking out from rent gray cloth and bright blood, and he screamed again.

Can't fall here . . . can't fall here . . . The words ran through his head. He could not stop there, right in the line of the Yankees' advance. He rolled over, grabbed up his rifle, and held it like a post in the ground. He worked his hands up its length, pulling himself up on his one good foot. The pain was like a brilliant white light in his head, eclipsing everything, but he gritted his teeth and he screamed when he had to and he pulled himself up.

He balanced on his remaining foot and flipped the rifle over so that it was more or less like a crutch. He tucked the butt under his arm, took a hop forward. The pain ripped through him, not just in his leg but all-consuming. He screamed, panted, waited as the pain passed. Much more of that and he would pass out, he knew.

He gasped for breath, looked around. The Confederates seemed to be falling back, he seemed to be alone on the field, save for the writhing wounded and the dead.

He looked in the other direction. The Yankees were coming strong up the hill, firing in volleys, advancing.

Oh, hell, hell . . . He had to move, but he knew what the pain would be and he could not bring himself to do it. He looked at the advancing blue line, and out of all of those men, he saw one look at him, look right at him, and raise a rifle to his shoulder.

Son of a bitch . . . that Yankee son of a bitch is trying to kill me. . . .

Three hundred feet away and he could see that little round black spot that was the muzzle and for the briefest instant a blossom of red and yellow, and then nothing.

For Lieutenant Robley Paine, Jr., it had been the worst day in memory. Twice more the battalion had shuffled into line, marched forward, splashed through the Bull Run River, then stopped. They milled around, the lines drifted away, and all the shouting of the officers could not keep the men in order. It was as clear to the men as it was to Robley that they were not going into a fight.

Robley did his share of shouting at them, more than his share, despite his own admission of the futility of it all. He kicked men in the ass to get them back in line and in the legs when he caught them sleeping in the grass, shoved them back into formation. Once he made his company go through the manual of arms. He was furious and taking his fury out on the men and he knew it and did not care.

All the day long, taunting him, the sounds of the fight off to the left grew louder, the cloud of smoke denser. From the south and the east and the north they could see dust clouds where more and more regiments rushed to the battle, and all the while the 18th Mississippi crossed back and forth at McLean's Ford, or sat and did nothing at all.

With each hour that crawled by, with each muffled escalation of the fighting off to the left, Robley grew angrier by degrees. He felt utterly betrayed, that his brothers should march off and leave him that way. He felt sick at the thought that they might well be in the thick of the fighting, while he sat on his hands.

How would it be if this was the first and last battle of the war? How could he endure it, the rest of his life, listening to his younger brothers tell tales of the fighting they did while he sat silent? And when pressed, he would say only, "Third Brigade, we never did get into the fight."

But your brothers were in 3rd Brigade. How did they get into the battle?

He almost went off to the fight himself, half a dozen times at least. Once he even took two steps in the direction of the gunfire, but even then he stopped. He could not do it. He was an officer, it was not his business to go. He felt as if his soul was being drawn and quartered.

It occurred to him, more than once, that his brothers could be wounded, terribly disfigured, perhaps dead. But even that thought did little to mitigate his misery. How would it be, back home, if his brothers were killed in the fight, and he never even showed the courage to go? Would he be able to make the others understand that he could not go? That his duty lay in doing as he was ordered to do?

He says it was his duty, but Jonathan and Nathaniel, they went into the fight anyway. Gave their lives for the cause. They understood the real meaning of duty. And honor. That was what people would say. Could he ever convince himself that duty, and not cowardice, had held him back?

The long afternoon dragged on, and Robley sank deeper into his funk. He found himself engaged in mock arguments in his head, eloquent explanations of why he had not left his regiment to join the fight, discourses on how, heroic as his brothers might seem, it was he, Lieutenant Paine, who was the real soldier, for wars could not be fought with renegade troops, rushing off where they pleased, but by steady, reliable men who obeyed orders.

As the sun was moving toward the horizon, and the sounds to the left of the line changed once again, two rumors ran through the 3rd Brigade, one to fill Robley with horror, one with hope.

The first was that the enemy was routed, that Jackson and Evans and Bee and the rest, aided by the timely arrival of reinforcements and Stewart's cavalry, had sent the Yankees fleeing for the Bull Run and the defenses of Washington. The word was that it was not a retreat but panicked flight, that the great Union army had crumbled completely, that it was every bluebelly for himself.

Robley could think of no news that he less wanted to hear. The Yankees whipped, his brothers a part of it, and him having not fired a shot? It was too much to bear.

Then on the heels of that dreadful news came word that the 18th Mississippi was moving out, going in support of Longstreet's 4th Brigade. They would be advancing on Centreville, hitting the Yankees from the other side, cutting off their retreat. It would be real fighting, finishing off what the men on the left had started.

Oh God, oh, God, let it be so. . . .

Twenty minutes later they were moving out again, following the Bull Run River northwest to join up with the 4th Brigade, which even now was halfway across Blackburn's Ford and marching north.

There was artillery fire somewhere ahead, from the direction in which they were marching, and Robley felt the sound lift his spirit. This could be it. He looked to his left. The sun was moving fast toward the horizon. Soon this long day would be over, but there was still time for them to get into it, if they would only hurry.

The 18th Mississippi splashed across Blackburn's Ford and marched up a narrow, dusty road flanked by scrubby trees. Robley could feel the line tense as the marching men waited for skirmishing fire to burst from the undergrowth. But there was no fire, and they marched on, and to Robley's joy the artillery fire increased with every yard they covered.

They broke out into open country and Robley could see that the men were spreading out in a line of advance. The sun was lower now, washing the fields and the trees in orange and casting the lines of men in lovely, warm tones as they stood ready to advance into the face of the artillery.

He could see the Union guns up ahead, or more precisely the muzzle flashes, brilliant in the gathering dusk. The gun smoke was pink and orange and the guns belched their pinpricks of light and now the shells were screaming by. For the first time that day, Robley considered the reality of what he was doing. Suddenly the discomfort in his gut was not from fear of missing the fight, but from fear of the fight itself.

Ah, hell . . . he thought. His personal demons had worn him down.

Captain Hamer was issuing orders now for Company D to take its place in the line, and Robley echoed those commands, directed men here and there, shuffled them from a marching unit to a unit ready to attack. They moved forward, stood among the yawning men, the grim men, the pale-looking men who faced the Union batteries and readied themselves to advance into the guns.

Robley took his place in the front and off to one side of his company. He scuffed his feet in the dirt, checked the percussion cap on his rifle, checked to make certain the company's line was dressed properly. And finally, there was nothing to do but wait.

The artillery was firing faster now, the muzzle flashes getting brighter as the daylight grew more dim, the shadows deeper. The order came to advance, and there was no room for anything else in Robley's mind, there was only himself and the line of guns and the broken, uneven ground between them, the real estate he had to cover to get to those guns and make them stop.

The long line of men moved forward and the pace began to build and Robley saw the Confederate Army as one solid whole, and himself one small part of that, and he saw the whole as an unstoppable force, rolling forward. Other men were yelling, the peculiar yell that had become so popular in the camps, a weird, twisting, yelping sound. A frightening sound. Then Robley found himself doing it too as his pace built from a walk to a fast walk and the line of guns on the road ahead grew closer.

The shells were screaming overhead. Robley could feel their wind as they passed and the shriek filled his head so that no other noise, not even his own voice, could get through the sound.

He looked to his right, at H Company, to see that they were advancing evenly, and it was only then that he realized the artillery was finding its mark. There were big gaps in the line, as if God had cut away a section of men with a shovel, just scooped it away. Even as he watched he saw a shell plow through the line not fifty feet away, saw men and parts of men tossed into the air, heard the screams of the wounded take up where the shriek of the shell left off.

Dear God . . . Robley thought. *Dear God . . .* He had never conceived of anything so horrible. He pulled his eyes away, fixed them on the guns, the flashing muzzle, marched on with determined step.

Perhaps it was an illusion, perhaps the Yankees were being reinforced, but Robley could not help but think the artillery was coming faster now, the guns served quicker, the scream of the shells and the buzz of minié balls nearly continuous. The Yankees' guns were telling more. With the Confederate lines so close they could hardly miss.

Robley could feel the momentum wane, could see the men slacken their pace, wince as the guns went off, shy away as if turning a shoulder to a cannon could ward off the shot. He had heard of how panic could sweep a unit, how they could, as if by mutual consent, turn and run. He could sense that they were there, that Company D would, at any second now, stop going forward, and when the forward momentum stopped, it was only a matter of time before they ran.

"H Company! Hamer's Rifles! Stand fast!" Robley shouted, holding his rifle above his head, his voice competing with the artillery fire, the blast from the guns and the song of the shells.

"Men of Yazoo! Advance!" Robley turned determinedly toward the guns, stepped into the onslaught of shells. He wondered if Captain Hamer had been killed, wondered why he was not rallying the troops. No matter. He, Lieutenant Paine, was doing it. Through the fear, the numbness, the confusion brought about by the relentless noise, he felt a spark of pride. He had not flinched, he had not run. When he saw his company ready to break, he had rallied them, led them forward. Two hundred yards and they would be swarming over the artillery and he, too, would be a victor that day.

"Advance!" He turned to make sure the lines were dressed properly and instead saw nothing. He was alone. He turned farther. The Confederate line was twenty feet behind him and backing away. Not breaking, not panicking, but backing away from those lethal guns.

"No! Hamer's Rifles! To me!" he shouted, but if anyone heard him, no one responded.

"Son of a bitch!" he shouted. He was on the verge of heroism and his men were leaving him. "Son of a bitch!"

He whirled around, looked right at the guns. He would charge them himself, come in like a fury, drive the gunners away. The others would join him when they saw his courage, saw how real determination could win the day.

He took a step forward. *This is madness*, he thought. The shells screamed past him and he stood in the middle of their hail and he was locked in indecision.

He glared at the guns, hating them. In the gloom he could hardly see them, save for when they fired and threw their flash of red and yellow light over the black barrels.

A gun directly ahead fired, the sound of the shell close and simultaneous with the flash of the gun. And in that flash he saw the gun beside it, and realized he was looking right into the muzzle.

Goddamn you . . . Robley Paine thought. A shout built in his throat and he ran forward, hating that gun, hating the bluebellies, ready to kill them all himself.

And then the gun fired. Robley Paine saw the flash of red and yellow as it discharged its canister shot, and then a thousand rifle balls tore him apart.

18

I deem it proper to bring to the notice of the Department the inefficiency of the battery of this ship when exposed to the fire of heavy rifled cannon, as was clearly shown in the attack . . . by a very small steam propeller, armed only with one large rifled gun.

—Captain J. B. Hull, USS *Savannah*, off Newport News,
to Hon. Gideon Welles

Flag Officer's Office, Dockyard,
Gosport, Va., July 21, 1861

Sir:

You are directed to take the steam tug *Cape Fear,* currently under your command and mounted with one rifled gun and two howitzers, and carry with you all the projectiles you deem necessary, as well as such additional hands as you might require, to be secured from among the company at the dockyard, and proceed along the coast in shoal water to Sewall's Point; to exercise your best judgment in an approach to the enemy's vessels at anchor off Newport News or Hampton Roads, and take a position out of reach of their guns, to try the range of yours, to near the enemy cautiously and do them as much damage as possible. You are at all times to exercise your best judgment and above all to avoid loss of your crew or your vessel to the enemy. Upon completion of whatever action you deem appropriate you are to return to the dockyard and report to me.

Respectfully,
Captain French Forrest,
Flag Officer, etc.

Captain Samuel Bowater, CSN
CSS *Cape Fear*

Bowater read the orders over again, and then a third time. They were fairly typical, in his experience, ranging from the obvious ("exercise your best judgment") to the absurdly obvious ("avoid loss of your crew or your vessel to the enemy"), but beyond that they really said nothing, other than ordering him to attack the enemy as he saw fit.

He stared out the window of the wheelhouse, down at the ten-pound Parrott rifle mounted in the bow. He had come to loathe the sight of the gun. Every time he looked at it, it reminded him of his shame and humiliation, scheming like some criminal, lying to a superior officer. And just as bad—worse, perhaps—allowing himself to be talked into the act by Hieronymus Taylor, of all men. How had he come to a point where he would follow the lead of men like Taylor?

He had come to loathe himself, loathe Taylor, loathe the gun for what it represented. But now, orders in hand, he was not so certain.

It had come to a head that very morning, Commander Archibald Fairfax giving him a verbal keelhauling the likes of which he had not endured since his first year at the Navy School. But it was no more than he deserved for playing the low trick he had played, and so he faced up to, and to some extent even welcomed, the humiliation he suffered.

Those issues of honor and humiliation so occupied Samuel's thoughts that he hardly heard a word that Commander Archibald Fairfax said, or rather shouted, neither the commander's insinuations concerning Bowater's fitness for command nor threats of dismissal from the service.

Samuel stood in Fairfax's office, in front of the commander's desk. Fairfax, seated, ranted and jabbed a pencil in the air as if he was trying to stab it through Bowater's chest, if only Bowater would come a bit closer.

It was not until Fairfax demanded a response from him that Bowater came back to the reality of the moment.

"It was a . . . fabrication, was it not? The whole thing?" Fairfax would not go so far as to say "lie." Even military discipline had its limits where a man's honor was concerned.

"Yes, sir. A fabrication. There was no order from Captain Cocke. I fabricated the entire story simply to secure those guns for use aboard the *Cape Fear*."

Once Fairfax had, under false pretenses, given Bowater and Taylor permission to load the guns aboard, they rounded up a dozen yard workers, augmented them with the crew of the *Cape Fear*, and set them to it. It had taken all of the afternoon and into the evening to wrestle the ordnance aboard, the ten-pound Parrott rifle, six and a half feet long and weighing nearly nine hundred pounds, and the twin twelve-pound howitzers, two feet shorter but almost as heavy.

It would have been easiest, of course, to set the gun carriages down first, and put the guns right in place. But that would have looked as if they intended to arm the *Cape Fear* all along, and not carry artillery to Captain Cocke. Instead, to maintain appearances, they set everything on deck and lashed it in place and then steamed away, up the Elizabeth River in the general direction of Fort Powhatan.

They returned the next day with the guns still conspicuously lashed in place. It seemed to Bowater that there was something particularly unethical, even unseemly, about concocting an excuse in advance. He figured, if pressed about why the guns had not been delivered, he would count on his ability to fabricate some innocuous explanation on the spot.

To his relief, no one asked. For three days they steamed around with the guns lashed in place while, unseen, the men strengthened the deck and bulwarks that were to become gun stations and Eustis Babcock was set to work making up train tackles and breeching.

When that was done, and sufficient time passed, they put the gun carriages in position and with the aid of improvised shears lifted the barrels onto them. In that way they cunningly transformed their tug into a man-of-war.

Unfortunately, they had not fooled anyone. Least of all Commander Archibald Fairfax, who did take the precaution of inquiring of Captain Cocke if he had, in fact, requested the guns, before ripping Bowater apart like a bear.

"Would you care to tell me why, Lieutenant? Why you felt the need to participate in this elaborate charade?"

"I hoped that arming the vessel, sir, would lead to our engaging the enemy."

"This navy will decide whether or not you engage the enemy, with no prompting from you. For the moment, Lieutenant, you command a tug. And you are hardly fit for that. Do you understand?"

"Yes, sir."

Samuel Bowater was not terribly concerned with losing his position or his command. He was going mad, puttering around Norfolk while the war was being fought elsewhere. He had even toyed with the idea of resigning, of looking for a berth, or whatever one called it, as an officer in an artillery company.

"I apologize, sir," Bowater said.

Fairfax stared hard at him, and Bowater stared at a point just above Fairfax's head. At last Fairfax made a snorting noise and tossed the pencil on the desk.

"Your apology is accepted. And you may rejoice to know that your scheme is working out just as you had anticipated," he said, and the change in his tone caught Bowater's attention. "Seems Forrest saw the way you loaded your boat down with guns and liked the looks of the thing. He intends to send you upriver, see what you can accomplish against the Union fleet."

For a moment Samuel did not know what to say. He was not certain he had heard correctly. "You mean, sir . . . send us upriver to fight?"

"Fight? I don't know what the hell kind of fighting you envision, Lieutenant, a tugboat against all the fleet there at Fortress Monroe. I think he had more in mind a reconnaissance, and a few shots if you can take them." Fairfax's anger had moderated considerably, Bowater noted. He wondered if the commander had been genuinely angry at all, or if he had simply felt obligated to berate an inferior for trying to pull the wool over his eyes.

"This might be an opportunity for a little more action in the offensive line," Fairfax continued. "Forrest is talking about arming the *Harmony* the same as you have done the *Cape Fear*. Let me take her upriver and get my blows in as well."

Ahhh! Bowater thought. His insubordination had put a new thought in the head of Captain French Forrest, flag officer in command of the dockyard. And that thought might lead to Fairfax's getting the opportunity to take a vessel in harm's way, a thing denied to most Confederate naval officers.

No wonder you're not so mad as you make out . . .

"In any event, Bowater, it looks as if you get to keep the guns you so cleverly acquired. I wish you joy with them. Do you have steam up?"

"The fires are banked, sir."

Fairfax handed Bowater a sealed envelope. "Here are orders from the flag. I don't know what is in them, but I suspect you will want to get a head up steam." He lifted a canvas bag from the floor, dropped it on his desk. "And here is your crew's mail. You are dismissed, sir."

"Yes, sir. Thank you, sir."

"And Bowater?"

"Sir?"

"I reckon you know better than to ever try and pull such shit as this again? At least with me?"

"Yes, sir," said Bowater, far more contrite this time, and far more sincere. He snatched up the mail bag, saluted, turned, and left quick, before Fairfax could say anything that might ruin his newfound happiness.

Now he looked at the orders in his hand and the gun on the bow and he felt quite differently about the once despised ordnance. The gun had led to the order he had dreamed of, a chance to show some initiative and dash. No more hauling guns, now he would be a fighting captain. Fourteen years in the United States Navy had nearly worn his initiative away to nothing. The Confederate States Navy was threatening to do the same. But now this. It was the chance he had hoped a fledgling service would provide.

But the *Cape Fear* could not move until the boilers had head up steam, and the speed at which water turned to steam was ordered by the laws of physics, not Samuel Bowater.

He had to move, to expend some of his restless energy. He climbed down the ladder, around the side deck. Find out how long until steam was up? No, he couldn't ask Taylor that. Couldn't show his eagerness. Think of something that would lead to the answer.

He opened the engine-room door, looked down the fidley. Chief Taylor was not there, not that he could see. He closed the door, walked farther along to the door of Taylor's cabin. He wrapped on the door, which swung open under the tap of his knuckles.

"Chief Taylor?" Bowater leaned into the room. It occurred to him that he had never seen the inside of Taylor's cabin. "Chief?" No response.

The yellow sunlight spilled in from the cabin's only window. On the desk beside the door, a big, leather-bound book lay open, with papers and pencils scattered about.

"Hmm . . ." Taylor did not strike Samuel as a reading man. He took a step closer, lifted the cover. *The Principles and Practice and Explanation of the Machinery Used in Steam Navigation; Examples of British and American Steam Vessels and Papers on the Properties of Steam and on the Steam Engine in its General Application, Originally compiled by Thomas Tredgold, CE. MDCCCLI.*

Bowater laid the book down again, read part of the page to which it was open. *Let t_1 be the temperature of the water at a dangerous pressure; t the temperature at the working pressure; Q the quantity of heat, in British units, transferred to the water per minute—then the equation $T=\underline{W(t_1-t)}$ is approximately correct.*

He shook his head. Hieronymus Taylor was the kind of engineer who started as a coal passer and picked up bits and pieces along the way— learned how to clean a grate, wield an oil can, rebuild an air pump, until at last he was running the black gang. Perhaps he had an aptitude for such things, which would help. But Samuel did not think him the kind of engineer to delve into such theoreticals. He would not have credited Taylor with the education to read even the title of that book.

And yet there were the notes and equations and comments on the text, written in the cramped scrawl that Samuel recognized from countless engineering division reports.

Curious as he was, Bowater recalled that he was doing something utterly improper. He stepped out of the cabin, eased the door shut. Walking forward, he met Chief Taylor coming aft.

"Ah, Chief. I was looking for you. I just wanted to double-check that we had clean fires for our work today."

Taylor was in shirtsleeves, and with the sun full on him it was difficult for Bowater to look directly at his white shirt. He had noticed, just in the past week or so, that the formerly unkempt black gang were now wearing uniforms and work clothing of pristine cleanliness. Not just Taylor and the firemen, but even the Negro coal passers seemed to have crisp, clean outfits when they gathered on the fantail for their evening sing-alongs.

Bowater's clothes were washed on the foredeck by Jacob, who also washed Mr. Harwell's clothes as a courtesy. The deck crew were given buckets and soap and allowed to do their wash once a week, dipping fresh water straight from the river. But Samuel never saw any of the engineering department wash their clothes, and yet, here they were, the cleanest on board, even though they worked in the filthiest environment.

Samuel did not begrudge them their superior cleanliness, but he was damned curious as to how they did it. He would not, of course, ask, because he was certain Taylor wanted him to. He would rather not know.

"Grates are all clean, bunkers full, black gang scrubbed and dried. Head up steam in one hour. I have some of my boys ashore, gettin' some piping I need. Boat should be back, twenty minutes or so."

"Very well. See that they are. I want to be underway the minute steam is at service gauge."

"The very minute, Cap'n," Taylor smiled.

Bowater climbed up to the wheelhouse, sat at the small desk in his cabin. Mail had come that morning. He picked up the letter on top, smiled as he looked at the printed stationery. NAVY DEPARTMENT, WASHINGTON, D.C. He had received enough of those over the course of his career. He had not reckoned on receiving any more.

He snatched up his scrimshaw whalebone letter opener, cut the letter open. He could well guess at its contents.

NAVY DEPARTMENT, May 7, 1861

SIR: Your letter of the 22d ultimo, tendering your resignation as a lieutenant in the U. S. Navy, has been received.

By direction of the President your name has been stricken from the rolls of the Navy from that date.

I am, respectfully, your obedient servant,

GIDEON WELLES
Secretary of the Navy

Bowater read the terse words, read them again and again, and an unexpected sadness came over him, a touch of shame, that all the arguments about the legitimacy of his actions could not entirely erase.

An officer had always held the right to resign his commission. There was nothing dishonorable about it. If the officer's conduct was under question, however, there were several options available to the navy by which they might censure that officer, even at the very moment he moved beyond their grasp.

One such punishment was dismissal from the service, throwing him out before he had the chance to honorably resign. Worse, dismissal with striking the officer's name from the record, as if he had never been.

But the ultimate censure was the one that Bowater held in his hands: dismissal and striking of the officer's name by order of the President. There was no equivocation, no appeal. The officer was cashiered.

In the early days of secession, officers had been allowed to resign without dismissal of any sort. When Gideon Welles took over, that changed. His was a scorched-earth policy, no quarter given.

Bowater stared at the note. He had never really expected anything else, had never thought to preserve his place in the old navy in case seccession didn't pan out. Still, an Academy education and fourteen years of service were not so easily dismissed.

To hell with you, Gideon Welles, my "obedient servant," he thought, and crumpled the letter up and tossed it in the wastebasket. That was the past, a life that was gone, and he was blessed to have a second life now, a thing denied most men. *I do believe I will go punch a few holes in your ships, Mr. Secretary.*

He looked at the next letter, from his father, and opened it up. It was written in the neat, tight hand that Samuel knew so well. He read it through. It was a very businesslike report: effects of the blockade, the state of Charleston's defenses, who was off in military service, price increases. Samuel smiled despite himself. William Bowater, Esq. He wondered sometimes if his father had not been some dour Boston Puritan in an earlier life, as those dabblers in mysticism were wont to believe.

He went through his father's letter again. There was something comforting in the stolid and unexcitable prose. With everything falling apart, with the entire order of his universe in flux, it was nice to see that one thing at least remained unchanged.

Lord, he is a stoic, and I am some kind of damned poet . . . He hated the thought as he thought it. The idea of himself as an artist felt facile and shallow.

From the top of the ladder, Hieronymus Taylor could look down the fidley on his engine room and his beloved engine, with the great maze of pipes: steam and return water, eduction pipes and intake pipes and discharge pipes, running to cylinder, air pumps, hot well, condensers, boiler, feed water, so amazingly complex, such a tangled web, unfathomable to the uninitiated, and yet not an inch of it that he did not fully comprehend, and hardly a bit of it that he had not laid hands on at one time or another.

A thing of beauty, like a symphony wonderfully written and wonderfully played, all the disparate parts, iron and steam, working together to create that final whole, *pssst, clunk, pssst, clunk, pssst, clunk*, thirty rotations per minute.

He ran his eyes over the entire space, the engine room, the boiler room on the other side of the open bulkhead, the bridge from one side to the other, the deckhouse with its windows and skylight and vent above, enclosing the fidley. Gloomy, hot, bad-smelling, and loud, it was his fiefdom and he was well pleased with it.

At the workbench below, fireman Ian O'Malley was seated on Taylor's stool, his face hidden behind a newspaper, and the sight of the man deflated the good cheer the chief felt at looking upon his engine and its domain. He clattered down the ladder and across the engine-room deck.

"Y'all hold her dere, now . . ." Moses's voice came from behind the engine, a place deep in the recess of the engine room, inconspicuous and hard to see from the engine-room door above. "Good, now gimme dat wrench. . . ."

Taylor ducked under the piping for the condenser and straightened. Coal heavers Joshua Beauchamps and Nat St. Clair were holding a three-foot-square metal box, the hot well from a small steam engine, against the overhead, while Moses bolted it to the deck beams. The hot well had been Moses's idea—he had noticed it in the yard one morning while they were taking on coal, and Taylor agreed that it was an improvement over his initial idea of a barrel as a water tank.

He watched for a moment while Moses tightened the bolts, then said, "Secure that tank, then belay the thing, Moses. We got to get underway."

"Damn!" said Moses, never taking his eyes off the bolt head. "Can't we ever finish one damned thing 'round here?"

"Not as long as we got a master's division."

"Massa's division?" Moses tightened the bolt until it was snug, then lowered his arms and stepped back. "You de only massa we gots, Massa He-ronmus. You de massa of dis whole fine plantation here." With a sweep of his arm he gestured toward the engine and boiler rooms.

"And don't you forget it, neither. Now hurry it up."

He left them at it, ducked back under the piping, ambled over to where O'Malley was lounging. "Morning, O'Malley," he said cheerfully.

O'Malley looked over the top of his paper. "Morning, Chief," he said and raised the paper again.

"Say, O'Malley . . . the captain has a notion to get underway. Think you might stoke up them fires?"

O'Malley lowered the paper once more. "I reckon one of them niggers can do it," he said and raised the paper again.

Taylor smiled, nodded, waited until the urge to pull the paper from O'Malley's hands and stuff it down his throat had passed. "I can see you wouldn't care to get them new dungarees all covered with coal dust. Where'd y'all get 'em?"

O'Malley lowered the paper. "I got 'em up to Norfolk last Saturday, and a right bargain they were. Are they not the handsomest you've seen?"

Taylor nodded. The cloth was dark blue, and the light from the skylight overhead danced on the new steel buttons. "Very nice. It grieves me to ask you to get them all soiled, but Moses and the others are still working on the shower bath." *Which*, he added silently, *I told you to do, you lazy Mick.*

"Ah, very well," O'Malley put his paper down with a sigh. "I'll do it meself. Easier than trying to get a bloody darkie to do a job of work. . . ."

He slid off the stool, ambled over to the boiler, on the other side of the open bulkhead. " 'Tis no great hardship, soiling me clothes, now that me and Burgess have that famous clothes washer set up."

The Irishman whipped a rag around his hand, opened the door to the furnace. He picked up a shovel and spread out the coals banked in the firebox, then began to scoop more coal from the hopper and feed it to the glowing orange bed.

Taylor picked a match up off the workbench, scratched it, and lit his cigar. He leaned back to watch the fun.

O'Malley continued to feed coal into the firebox, and Taylor heard the first hiss of steam beginning to form.

"Easy with the coal, O'Malley. Don't smother it. Want to get her nice and hot."

"I'm not goin ta bloody smother it," O'Malley growled. He paused in his shoveling because in fact he was.

The fire was getting hot, Taylor could feel it from the engine room. O'Malley was starting to do a weird little dance, squirming a bit, as if something might be in his pants.

"We'll need some speed today, O'Malley. Get her good and hot!"

"Aye!" O'Malley called, his back to Taylor. Taylor hurried to where the coal heavers were working on the shower bath. "Moses, you all, come see this!" He got back to his stool in time to catch O'Malley give a little jiggle, as if he was trying to shake something out of his new dungarees.

"Good and hot, O'Malley!" Taylor prompted, grinning around his cigar.

"Aye!" the Irishman shouted, more irritated this time. He scooped another shovelful, then another, leaned forward to spread the coals out. He paused for a second, then dropped his shovel and whirled around.

"Ahh! Ahh! Ahhh, bloody shit, bloody hell!" He leaped up and down, plunged his hands in his pants, screamed again, pulled his hands out. "Ahhh!" He jerked his belt loose, tore the buttons of his pants open, and dropped his dungarees around his ankles. He stood there, mindless of who might be watching, and clasped his private parts, sighing with relief.

It was a minute at least before Hieronymus Taylor could open his eyes and wipe the tears from them enough that he could see. What he saw, not surprisingly, was Ian O'Malley, staring hatred at him.

"Do ya think it's bloody funny? A man burns himself, acting on your rutting orders?"

"O'Malley, you stupid bastard. Every coal heaver been on the job a week knows you don't wear pants with goddamned steel buttons. Burn your pecker clean off, if you got one. Where the hell did you get your papers?"

"Shut yer bloody gob, you bastard, I'll do for you."

Taylor stood, spread his arms in a sign of welcome. "I'm waiting . . ." he said, but O'Malley just stared and said nothing.

"That's what I reckoned," said Taylor. "Now go and put some engineering pants on and get your ass back here. We got a war to fight, in case you ain't been informed."

"Chief?" Johnny St. Laurent called down the fidley. "Boat's puttin off, Chief!"

"Thank you, Johnny." O'Malley forgotten, Taylor climbed up the ladder and onto the side deck, walked quickly around to the fantail. He could see the boat pulling for them, brilliant white on the blue water. In it, the hands he had sent ashore. And one he had not.

He waited impatiently, glanced up at the wheelhouse, but neither Bowater nor Harwell was to be seen. He drummed his fingers on the cap rail. At last the boat pulled alongside and the sailor in the stern sheets called, "Toss oars!" and the boat came to a gentle stop at the Cape Fear's starboard quarter.

One by one the men hopped out. Taylor met Wendy's eyes, gave her a quick wink, then paid her no more attention. He resisted helping her out of the boat, and she managed well enough without his help, despite an obvious unfamiliarity with watercraft.

The bowman pushed the boat off, and Taylor was able to get a better look at her. She was dressed in sailor garb, the wide-bottomed trousers, loose-fitting frock, and wide-brimmed straw hat; the uniform of men-of-war men the world over. She looked like a kid playing dress-up.

"Come on," Taylor said, led her forward and then down the fidley ladder to the engine room. It was only there, in his fiefdom, that he finally felt safe to turn and look at her directly, and address more than two words to her.

"Everything go all right?" he asked.

"Perfect!" she said low. He could see she was thrilled by the adventure of the thing. They had been planning it for weeks, had put all the elements in place. Taylor had needed only to hear that they were going into battle. He was beginning to think it would never happen. And then, that morning, Bowater had informed him of their orders. Johnny St. Laurent was dispatched to town with a confidential message, on the pretext of buying fresh galley stores, a mission that Bowater the gourmand, who adored all that hoity-toity slop, would never refuse or question.

"Welcome to my little kingdom! Burgess, Moses, this here is Ordinary Seaman Atkins. He's gonna sail with us today, observe, if you will."

Burgess and Jones nodded to Wendy, their faces expressionless, and Wendy nodded back. She looked around the engine room. "It's very nice," she said, her voice uncertain.

"Oh, that it is!" Taylor said with enthusiasm. "Let me show you around." He was warming to his subject. "The engine is a horizontal-mounted compound . . ."

"Chief," Burgess interrupted, the word like a grunt. "Service gauge."

"Forgive me for a moment, Seaman Atkins," Taylor said with a little bow. "We gots to go to war."

19

SIR: I have the honor to report that at 11:45 a.m. this day a small steamer under the Confederate flag . . . approached this ship and commenced firing upon us with a rifled gun from her bow, our ship being at anchor.

—Captain J. B. Hull, USS *Savannah*, to Hon. Gideon Welles

Able-bodied seaman Seth Williams rang four bells in the afternoon watch.

The *Cape Fear* was vibrating with the thrust of her propeller as Bowater backed down on her spring line and swung the bow off the seawall. He grabbed the cord that communicated with the bell in the engine room and jerked twice, two bells, slow ahead. He felt the vessel shudder as somewhere below Taylor shifted the reversing lever, changing the rotation of the screw instantly from turns for slow astern to turns for slow ahead.

The tug stopped dead, and Bowater could hear the water churning up under her counter, a wonderful sound, the sound of a powerful vessel digging in, and then she gathered way.

"Cast off!" he heard Babcock shout. Bowater stepped out of the wheelhouse, looked down as the seawall slipped away and the lines that held them to the dock were brought dripping aboard. It was two o'clock in the afternoon, a bright, hot July afternoon, and they were going to war.

"Come left, leave *Harmony* to starboard!" Bowater called into the wheelhouse, and Littlefield replied, "*Harmony* to starboard, aye!" and eased the wheel over. Bowater stepped back into the wheelhouse, rang up more speed. Moments later he felt the turns increase, felt the stern dig deeper, as the deep-draft tug gathered more way.

"I'll give the chief this much," he said to Harwell, who was just stepping up onto the deckhouse roof. "He knows when he can ignore commands from the wheelhouse, and when he cannot."

"Mr. Taylor, sir, if I may be so bold, thinks a little too highly of himself and his engineering division. He would have us believe he was doing us a favor, getting steam to service gauge and turns on the propeller."

There was more bitterness in the lieutenant's tone than perhaps he had intended. Harwell's was not a personality that could easily suffer the likes of Hieronymus Taylor. Bowater did not have an easy time of it himself. But Bowater could ignore attitude—to a degree—if a man did his job, and Taylor was scrupulous about the maintenance of the engine and all the *Cape Fear*'s systems. Also, Bowater was captain. Taylor might get the last word, but that last word would always be "Yes, sir."

"Had we sails, like a proper ship," Bowater said, "Mr. Taylor would not be in so commanding a position."

"Yes, sir. Sir, may I drill the men at the guns?"

"Yes, please. You have . . ." Bowater looked up at the sun. ". . . about three hours to get them ready to fight."

Harwell hurried off, and Bowater stepped forward, leaned on the rail that ran along the forward edge of the deckhouse, and watched the city of Norfolk to the east and Portsmouth to the west slip past. Below him, up at the bow, Harwell was arranging the gun crew like a little girl setting her dolls around a toy table for make-believe tea.

They had taken on coal at the Gosport Naval Shipyard, and as many shells for the guns as they could lay hands on, around a dozen for each gun. They had requested twenty volunteers to augment their crew, enough to work the ship and all three guns at the same time. Thirty-seven men had stepped eagerly forward, and Bowater had had to choose among them. He was not the only one chafing at the inactivity of the dockyard.

Craney Island was in sight when Hieronymus Taylor climbed up to the deckhouse roof, squinting in the brilliant sun. His shirtsleeves were rolled up over powerful forearms and he wore only his gray vest, cap, and trousers. His formerly bright white shirt was wilted and smudged now. He stopped, took a long look around, puffing his cigar like a locomotive getting up speed.

"Beg pardon, Cap'n," he said at last. "I was wonderin, and I ask purely to increase the efficiency of the engineering division, but what're you plannin for this day's activities?"

"Well, Chief . . ." Bowater equivocated. "I wish I could tell you exactly what we will be doing, but I cannot. The circumstance of the Union fleet will dictate our actions."

"No, really, Cap'n," Taylor said. "What're you meaning to do, now?"

"I mean to steam up to the Union fleet, Mr. Taylor, and blast away and see what mischief we can do."

"Ain't much of a plan, if you'll pardon my saying so," Taylor said. His cigar was clenched in his teeth, but his mouth seemed to be smiling around the obstruction, and his tone suggested more approval than concern over Bowater's boldness.

"I am willing to take suggestions, Chief."

"No, no. I don't presume to know better, Cap'n. For a man of your breedin, you seem to have an aptitude for this sort of craziness."

"I would thank you for the compliment, Mr. Taylor, were I certain it was one. Now please see to your engine." He wondered if perhaps he was winning the respect of First Assistant Engineer Hieronymus Taylor. And if so, he wondered if that was cause for concern.

For an hour they steamed north, up the Elizabeth River, then rounded Craney Island and stood out toward the middle of Hampton Roads, that wide patch of water where the James, Nasemond, and Elizabeth rivers joined forces to pour into the Chesapeake Bay.

A good portion of the seaborne power of the United States was arrayed out in front of him, stretching in a loose line of anchored ships from Newport News Point across Hampton Roads to Fortress Monroe.

He could pick out the sailing ship *Savannah*, and the *Cumberland*, towed to safety the night that the dockyard burned. There was the *Wabash*, which had arrived since the last time Bowater had been up that way, the mighty USS *Minnesota* and the screw steamer *Seminole*, the *St. Lawrence* and the *Congress*. In the distance he could pick out the *Harriet Lane*, which he had last seen off the Charleston Harbor entrance, mere hours after the start of the Rebellion.

There were other ships as well, transports and tugs, schooners, store ships. It seemed as if more and more vessels arrived all the time, massing for something or other, ready to fall on some Southern shore.

They plowed northwest, through the blue-green water and the lovely late afternoon, looking for all the world as if they were heading up the James River, a little Union tug out on some job or other. The sun was moving fast toward the west, lighting the Union ships up with a soft, rosy tint. From a distance they looked tranquil and quiet.

Bowater put his telescope to his eye. Up close the ships still looked tranquil and quiet. Not a wisp of smoke from any stack, not one of them had steam up. The *Cape Fear* was two miles distant and he could detect no alarm on any of the decks, no frantic running as men raced to quarters, no bells, no rattles, no drums.

"Helmsman, start coming right. Slowly."

"Slowly right, aye . . ." Littlefield turned the wheel right, one spoke, two spokes. The *Cape Fear*'s bow swung to starboard, bit by bit, and her course changed from northwest to northeast, and soon her bow was pointing not up the James River but rather at the anchored fleet.

Bowater swept the ships with his telescope. Still no alarm. He looked down onto his own foredeck. The wheelhouse cast a shadow all the way forward, to the breech of the ten-pound rifle. The sun was setting behind them. It would not hide them, but it would make it more difficult for the Union gunners to aim.

The gun crew were sitting and squatting on the deck, out of sight behind the bulwarks. Bowater could see the tension on their faces, the nervous tapping of fingers, feet wagging back and forth like a dog's tail. He felt it himself; the sweating palms, the quickened pulse, the sense that everything appeared sharper. He had chosen his side and he was fighting and he felt alive, and he had not felt that way in a long, long time.

Lieutenant Thadeous Harwell crouched behind the bulwark with his forward gun crew, though he did not know if he should. He was not certain an officer should be crouching. But the captain had said crouch, and he did not say for the luff not to crouch, nor had he expressed any obvious displeasure with an officer crouching, so Harwell continued to crouch.

This is it, this is it, this is it . . . Harwell had never been in combat. He had missed the Mexican War. That conflict had been no great shakes in the naval line in any event, and only a few had managed to distinguish themselves, such as the young Ensign Samuel Bowater. But still it was a war, which Harwell had never seen.

He had suffered with his fear that he would not see war, would never find out if he had the stuff to be a Nelson or a John Paul Jones. He had pictured himself often enough with upraised sword leading a screaming horde of bluejackets over the rail of some first-rate ship of the line. Harwell's Patent Bridge. He knew it was foolish, that those days were over, that armor-clad steamships were spelling the death of the great sailing navies, with their thundering broadsides and boarders swarming through the smoke. But logic did not stop the dreams.

I regret . . . no, no . . . Gladly do I give my one life . . . "one life" *. . . that hardly needs saying . . . Gladly do I give my life for this, my beloved land . . .* Great last lines did not, Harwell believed, happen spontaneously. Hadn't Nelson uttered one each of the many times he thought he was done for?

Sure he must have practiced ahead of time. Harwell would not allow himself to be caught short.

Gladly do I lay down this life for my beloved Southern home, and only regret that I shall not live to fight on. . . .

That's not so bad.

Gladly do I lay down this life for my beloved South . . .

Good . . . so even if I only get the first part out, it will still stand.

"Mr. Harwell!"

The lieutenant looked up. Bowater was standing at the forward edge of the deckhouse roof, calling down. He felt his face flush. How many times had the captain called his name?

"Sir?"

"You may remove the cover from the gun, lieutenant, and prepare to fire."

"Aye, sir!" Harwell leaped to his feet, figured the order to cease crouching must have been implicit in the order to fire.

"Your target will be the large ship to the south."

"Aye, sir! *Wabash*, sir?"

"Yes, that is correct. The *Wabash*."

"Aye, sir!" The *Wabash*. He had served for five years aboard that ship, gone from ensign to lieutenant on her decks, boy to man. But sentimental pining for ships was an emotion of the lower deck, not fit for an officer.

Gladly do I lay down this life for my dear . . . no . . . my beloved Southern home, and regret only that I shall not live to fight . . . to struggle . . . on . . .

They were within a mile of the nearest ships of the Union fleet, the *Savannah* and the *Wabash*, and, incredibly, Bowater could see no sign of alarm. It was beginning to make him nervous.

On the *Cape Fear*'s foredeck, the canvas was peeled off the ten-pound Parrott and the crew bustled around the big gun. Seth Williams, designated gun captain, hooked a friction primer to the lanyard and inserted the primer into the vent, then stretched the lanyard out. The lanyard was a pretty bit of ropework, with Flemish eyes tucked in either end, coach whipped and capped with Turk's heads and ringbolt hitching around the eyes. It had been lovingly crafted by Eustis Babcock, starting the moment the gun came on board, so that the *Cape Fear* might have something attractive and seamanlike with which to fire her heavy ordnance.

Lieutenant Harwell mounted the ladder to the roof of the deckhouse and stood beside Bowater, who was pressed against the forward rail. "Ready to fire, sir," he reported, even before he was done saluting.

"Then fire away, Lieutenant," said Bowater, with a calm he did not feel.

"Take aim and fire!" Harwell shouted.

"Aim and fire, aye!" Williams shouted. He sighted down the gun, called for a bit of an adjustment, stepped back, bringing the lanyard taut.

Bowater felt the excitement build, clutched the iron rail tight, pressed his lips together. They were still approaching, their distance-off less than a mile, and the big Parrott was accurate up to a mile and a half. What . . .

Bowater's thoughts were interrupted by the blast of the gun, the jet of gray smoke, the surprisingly violent recoil as the gun flung itself inboard, making the *Cape Fear* shudder from keel up.

Harwell was staring at the *Wabash* through his field glasses. He pointed to the sky and Williams waved his acknowledgment.

"Over, sir," Harwell explained to Bowater. The gun crew jumped back to their places, swabbing and ramming home another shell.

A little more than two minutes passed before the big gun was run out again. Williams adjusted the elevating screw to his satisfaction, then stepped back and pulled the lanyard taut. A pause, and then he jerked the rope and the ten-pound Parrott roared out again.

Bowater kept his glass pressed to his eye, the *Wabash* filling the lens, and to his delight he saw a hole appear in her bulwark, blue sky where before there had been black hull, splinters big enough to see from a mile away tossed into the air.

"Hit!" shouted Harwell and the men cheered, waved hats, then fell to loading again.

"Well done, Lieutenant!" Bowater fixed the *Wabash* in his field glasses. It was chaos, as he reckoned it would be, an anthill kicked over. From less than a mile, Bowater could see perfectly well what was happening on the big steamer's deck. Men were racing about, officers were crowding the quarterdeck, waving arms, men rushing over the foredeck and up the rigging. It was bedlam, Gulliver waking to find himself the captive of the Lilliputians.

Wabash carried nine- and ten-inch Dahlgrens. But her guns were not rifles, but smoothbores, already antiquated. After hundreds of years during which little changed in the way of naval warfare, things were suddenly developing so rapidly that it was difficult for any navy to keep pace.

Still, smoothbore or no, the *Wabash*'s guns could blow them to kindling with one broadside, if *Wabash* could come to grips with them.

The *Cape Fear* hurled another shell and a hole appeared in the *Wabash*'s side, and Bowater wondered what destruction that must have done to the lower deck. He wondered if *Wabash* was getting steam up. It would do them no good. *Cape Fear* would be gone before their screw bit water.

The forward gun went off once more, and Bowater saw wood fly off the after rail. *It is like a turkey shoot, just an absolute turkey shoot.* And once again, he found that the ease with which they were attacking the Union fleet left him feeling edgy and nervous.

He crossed over to the port side, looked out at *Wabash* with his telescope. There was another vessel now, a smaller one, side-wheeler, schooner rig, steaming around from behind the big steam sloop. Not much bigger than the *Cape Fear*. Was she going to tow *Wabash* off?

Bowater shifted his focus from the ship to the side-wheeler. Not towing *Wabash* off. She was, in fact, coming bow on to the *Cape Fear*. And then the puff of smoke, the scream of shell, the water plowed up forty yards away, and with it, at last, the flat report of the distant gun. *A gunboat!* For all the Yankees' sea power, the only vessel that could get underway fast enough, the only one with a rifled gun that could reach out that far, was one not much larger than the Confederates'.

Harwell, beside him, was dancing with excitement. "Mr. Harwell, please have your gun crew redirect their fire to the gunboat."

"Aye, sir!" Harwell practically shouted, and relayed the order.

They were closing fast, both vessels charging like knights-errant. The *Cape Fear* fired, missed, but not by more than a dozen yards. The Yankee fired again and charged on.

He must have more shells than we do . . . Bowater was counting the valuable projectiles as his gun crew blasted away. He wondered if the Yankee captain had to do the same. He wondered if he knew the Yankee captain, if they had been shipmates once.

The *Cape Fear*'s gun went off, the deck shuddered under Bowater's feet, and in the deafening blast, the Yankee's gun seemed to fire in absolute silence, less than half a mile away. The last of the reverberations from the *Cape Fear*'s rifle were dying, and from that noise rose the scream of the Yankee's shell, fast and loud. Bowater could see the black streak in the sky, right in line with his vessel, and then the shriek was like sharp pegs in his ears and the shell crashed through the cabin behind him, exploding in a great shower of shrapnel and wood and glass.

Before Bowater's shocked face, an image of painted wood and dark paneling and Littlefield the helmsman, all exploding as if from some internal force. And then he was down, and the darkness washed over him, like the cold water in the dry dock, and once again he could not crawl free.

Hieronymus Taylor did not care for this, did not care for it at all. He paced back and forth, worried the cigar in his mouth, glared at the wheelhouse bell.

Generally, he preferred to be below. He would rather be in his engine room, surrounded by his beloved machinery, than up there in the light with the idiots and prima donnas of the master's division. He preferred the precision of machinery to the vagaries of wind and tide and politics and chains of command.

It was a preference, and a passion, which he tried to convey to Wendy. He gave her a tour of the engine room, spoke passionately about Scotch boilers and fire tubes and blowdowns. He was absolutely poetic on the subject of winging fires with slice bars, on hot wells and feed water, on Stephenson links and trunks and rods and shafts and pillow blocks.

There was so much he wished to convey to her. He wanted to tell her about the monster that he and his men were able to conjure up, like wizards in storybooks. How they made this monster rise in the boiler, how they drove it under pressure through the pipes, made it work for them, contained it, dangerous beast that it was.

He wanted to tell her how the monster—invisible, deadly hot—was forced into the trunk, made to push the piston, and there it died. He wanted to tell her how the watery remains of the beast were pumped back into the boiler and the thing was raised again from the dead, how they performed this miracle in a continual circuit, again and again, drove this gunboat along in that manner.

It was just like the fellow said, "What immortal hand or eye, could frame thy fearful symmetry . . ." Except it wasn't an immortal hand at all, just a man, an engineer. That was the miracle of the thing.

He wanted to tell her because he thought she would understand. He had never shared that vision with anyone, never tried. The beats that haunted engine rooms would have looked at him as if he had two heads. The general run of mechanics and engineers could never see the poetry in the machine. They saw pipes and valves and condensers and such, but they could not see the magic, the absolute beauty, in such mechanical perfection. There were times when Hieronymus Taylor would look on his engine, with all its parts running with interlocking grace, knowing that inside those pipes and trunks and hot wells and condensers the beast was living and dying, and he would tear up—actually cry—for the sheer beauty of the thing.

That was not something you shared with the black gang.

But Wendy, she was a different matter. Women by their very nature were more attuned to such things, more able to recognize beauty where men could see only function. And a girl with the imagination to paint as well as she did, and the grit to dress as a sailor and sneak aboard a man-of-war going into battle, she, of all people, should have the ability to see in the engine the elegance of mathematical grace. If anyone could get it, Wendy should.

But Wendy did not get it. She nodded as Taylor pointed out the steam dome and traced the main steam line aft, said "Indeed?" as the chief showed her the throttle and Stevenson links, looked politely at the things Taylor pointed out. But there was no passion there, only politeness. She asked intelligent questions until somewhere around the hot well pump her eyes began to look as if they were encased in thin glass. For all her imagination, she could not see in the machine what Hieronymus Taylor saw. She was not interested.

Taylor stopped his tour of the engine before coming to the part where the water returns to the boiler, and Wendy did not even notice. "Reckon if you want to see somethin, you best get topside," Taylor said, a muttered, taciturn admission of defeat.

"Topside? On deck?" Wendy looked by parts elated and afraid. "But sure I'll be discovered there."

Taylor shook his head. "More'n half the hands we got aboard are shippin the first time today. Doubled our crew for this here excursion. Ain't no one knows everyone aboard. Jest keep out of the way, act busy if you can. Won't be no problem."

Wendy smiled, and the look nearly compensated Taylor for his disappointment. "Thanks, Chief!" she said and scrambled up the ladder, left him alone, as he usually was, with his passions.

Now things were heating up, and he was not sure about it. He had been below before during times of great excitement—steamboat races, violent storms, collisions with other vessels—and still he preferred his engine room above all things.

But this was different. This was fighting, killing Yankees. Arrogant damn Yankees, like used to swagger around the docks at New Orleans, off their Boston-built ships, loading cotton for England, treating them all like they were field hands, white men and black.

Bowater. He was not much better. Just the fancy Dan that Taylor had expected, prim as Queen fucking Victoria, but now he was driving this little boat into combat, going to kill Yankees with unprecedented boldness, and Taylor wanted to be part of it. Not down below, not this time, but up on deck. This time he wanted to see the fun, because there had never been this much fun before.

It was crowded now in the engine room. Normally, there would only have been one fireman, Burgess or O'Malley, and one of the coal heavers, along with Chief Taylor. But now, at quarters, both firemen and all three coal heavers were down there, standing by for an emergency.

Navy fashion . . . Taylor thought. *Six men to do the work of two.* "What the hell you starin at, Moses?"

"Well, Massa Taylor, I ain't ever seen you in sich a state. You ain't afraid of dem Yankees, is you?"

"Afraid? Shut up, ya damned darkie."

Moses smiled at that, which just further infuriated Taylor. "Clean the ash out of that damned boiler, you lazy son of a bitch," he said and stamped off.

Taylor stood by the wheelhouse bell, peered up through the fidley. The sky beyond the skylight in the deckhouse roof was clear blue, as if the glass was painted that color. Behind him, he heard Moses's shovel scraping up the ashes, heard the black man singing, just loud enough so that Taylor could hear, a song to the tune of "Dixie."

> *O, I wish I was clear of ol' Chief Taylor*
> *Lock you down like a mean ol' jailer*

And the other stokers joined in, soft,

> *Heave away, heave away, heave away, Taylor-man.*
>
> *Well the engine room, it's his frustration,*
> *Thinks he's on a fine plantation*
> *Heave away, heave away, heave away. . . .*

Taylor turned, ready to put a stop to their nonsense. He was in no mood for it. Then, overhead and forward, the ten-pound Parrott fired with a roar that sounded through the vessel like the end of the earth. The deck below their feet shuddered and the blast of the gun echoed and died and suddenly it seemed very quiet below, despite the roar of the fire and the hissing and clanking of engine and pumps. Everyone stopped and stared up at the roof overhead, as if they could divine something from looking at it.

For a long time they stood like that, staring up at the deckhouse roof. The Parrott went off again, with its visceral roar. It was more than just sound. It was sound and reverberation down to the ship's fiber, a shudder in the deck, the smell of spent powder in the air, sucked below by the boiler's air intake, mixing with coal dust and oil, a full sensory experience as up in the sunshine the gun crew blasted away at the Yankees.

"Goddamned . . ." Taylor muttered, not certain who or what he was damning. He pulled his eyes from the overhead, paced back and forth, paused in his pacing. "Burgess, ya Scots ape, get some oil on them drive gears, they're squealing like a couple of rutting pigs," he shouted—a problem the Scotsman was well aware of—then set in pacing again.

The gun crew, raw as they were, were getting their shots off every two minutes. Taylor kept count without realizing he was doing so—three, four, five; he wondered if they had found their target, if he was justified in going topside to see.

Gettin' to be like a damned old woman . . . Taylor thought, and then a crash from above, the shattering of wood, an explosion as some part of their ship was blasted apart.

The *Cape Fear* shuddered again, an entirely different sensation, and Hieronymus Taylor was on the ladder, racing topside, shouting, "Burgess, you're in charge here! Look to the bells!" as he burst through the fidley door and onto the deck.

Taylor stepped into a scene of confusion. He looked forward. Men were crowded on the side decks, staring around. No one moved.

He looked aft. Wendy was there, by the door. She looked frightened. She opened her mouth to speak, but before she could Taylor said, "What happened?"

"A . . . bomb . . . of some sort hit. Up there." She pointed to the wheelhouse.

"All right. Come with me." He turned and ran forward, heard a few hesitant steps before Wendy caught up. He did not know why he had told her to come along. He would figure that out later.

A quarter mile ahead, a paddle wheeler was bearing down on them, pushing aside the smoke from her bow gun, churning the water white under her bows and her paddle wheels. One of the ad *hoc* Yankee river fleet, slapped together to combat the ad *hoc* Confederate fleet. The Yankee fired again, flame and smoke shooting from her forward gun, the shell screaming so close overhead that Taylor flinched and ducked, involuntarily.

Where the hell is Bowater? Taylor pushed through the stunned and stupid men toward the bow and the ladder to the top of the deckhouse. Could the vaunted Samuel Bowater be frozen in terror, unable to issue orders, stammering with indecision?

Son of a bitch patrician son of a bitch . . . Taylor raced up the ladder and when his head cleared the deckhouse roof he paused. The entire after end of the wheelhouse—the master's cabin—was blown to splinters. There was nothing more than jagged bits of bright-painted wood sticking out at odd angles, and the cabin roof, caved in in the middle and draped like a shroud over the wreckage

Taylor took the last few steps slower. What was left of Able-Bodied Seaman Littlefield was flung half out of the wheelhouse and was hanging on the window frame, shredded clothing and skin draped over a spreading pool of blood on the deck below him. Lieutenant Harwell was lying toward the starboard side, a pool of blood spreading around his head. The blue-gray heap to port was Bowater, apparently. There was no one moving on the upper deck.

20

SIR: I deem it proper to bring to the notice of the Department the inefficiency of the battery of this ship . . . as was clearly shown in the attack . . . by a very small steam propeller, armed only with one large rifled gun.

—Captain J. B. Hull, USS *Savannah*, to Hon. Gideon Welles

For a second, Taylor did not move either. He had dealt with any number of emergencies—fire, taking on water, boilers on the edge of exploding—but this, fighting a ship, was something new to him, and he knew no more about it than he did about celestial navigation or requisitioning barrels of beef.

On the port side of the boat deck, Wendy was kneeling and vomiting, and that did not help his concentration.

Just stop . . . got to just stop and sort this here mess out . . . They were steaming head on toward the Yankee gunboat, and that did not seem like a very good idea. Taylor reached through the wreckage of the wheelhouse windows and grabbed the bell cord, jerked it for one bell, slow ahead.

First time I ever pulled that damned thing . . . Hieronymus mused. From ahead, another shot, and the shell screamed by so close he felt he could have caught it like a baseball.

What the hell now? And then he heard a voice, Bowater's voice. It lacked that clear and commanding tone that Taylor associated with Bowater and all those who felt they ruled by birthright, but it was strong enough, and Taylor was glad to hear it.

"You men!" Bowater shouted down to the men on the deck below. "Do you want to be blown out of the water? Quarters! Load and run out!"

Bowater had pulled himself to his feet, was leaning heavy on the rail, but even as he shouted his strength seemed to come back to him. He stood straighter, then pushed himself off the rail, took a step toward the wheelhouse, moving carefully, as if the tug was rolling hard, and not in a near dead calm.

He noticed Taylor for the first time. "Chief, what in hell are you doing here?"

"Reckoned someone had to run the damned boat."

"Where's Harwell?"

"Starboard side. He's out, don't know if he's dead. I'll check."

"No, leave him, no time for that." Bowater was standing straighter now, the strength and presence of mind returning. He stepped into the wheelhouse, seemed not to notice the wreckage. He laid a hand on the big polished wheel, miraculously preserved, and gave a half turn to starboard. "What is the state of the engine?"

"All's well. I rung slow ahead."

Bowater said nothing. He grabbed the shredded jacket of Seaman Littlefield and jerked the body off the windowsill. He spun the corpse around, and as he did Taylor was presented with the full view of the horror of what had happened to the man and he thought he might be sick. Then Bowater tossed the body aside as if it was so much dunnage, rang up full ahead.

The *Cape Fear* began gathering way. Taylor could see the water slipping by as the big prop churned a wake under her counter. One, two, three knots, they were building speed, running straight toward their attacker.

"You gonna run her right up to the Yankee fleet, Cap'n?" Taylor asked, genuinely curious. He was feeling chastened by his own inability to think tactically. He wondered if Bowater would do any better.

"Got two shells left. We'll make the best use of them."

The Yankee fired again, but the shell flew clear. Bowater grabbed the wheel, looked over at Wendy for the first time. "Who is that, Chief?"

"Coal passer. Brought him with me, case we needed a hand."

"You there!" Bowater called, and Wendy looked up. Her face was streaked with soot, her eyes red. She wiped her mouth on her sleeve.

Least she sure as hell don't look like a woman, Taylor thought.

"Take the helm! Chief, go forward and see the gun crew ready to fire. Williams is captain of the gun, if he's still alive. We have two shells. That's all." Bowater issued the orders clear and calm, as if he was calling for the tug to be washed and the brass polished.

"Hell, Cap'n, I don't know nothing about cannons."

"Just see the gun crew doesn't panic." Bowater looked over at Wendy, frozen with fear and uncertainty, and for a sick moment Taylor thought he would see through the clothes and the dirt. But instead, Bowater shouted, "I said, take the helm!" and Taylor, behind his back, pointed at the wheel and jerked his head in that direction.

Bowater followed her with his eyes as she stepped into the wheelhouse, laid her tentative hands on the helm. Her eyes were wide. The vomit was imperfectly wiped away.

"And send up someone who knows what the helm is."

It was unreal, far worse than any nightmare. Wendy Atkins felt the warm, oiled wood of the wheel under her hand, had absolutely no notion of what to do with it. From the corner of her eye she could see the shoes and legs of the boy who had held the wheel before her, she could see the horrible thing that had once been his face. Her gorge rose again and she focused on other things.

Samuel Bowater! It was too much to believe! It had never occurred to her to ask Hieronymus who the captain of the boat was, had never dawned on her that it could possibly be Bowater. But now, as she made herself concentrate on things remembered, made herself not think of the dead boy or how she would look when the next shell hit, or what she would do if Bowater gave her an order, she could recall they had both said "gunboat," but since the term was largely meaningless to her, she had ignored it.

Samuel Bowater. Standing at the forward rail, hands clasped behind his back, looking out at the approaching enemy as if he was taking in the view of the gardens at Versailles. *How could he be so calm in all this?* She thought of the way he had tossed the boy's body aside. *What kind of monster is he?*

"Come left, two spokes," Bowater said. She heard him clearly, as there were no windows left in the wheelhouse. She wondered to whom he was issuing these imperious orders.

He hands down orders like Caesar on the throne! Wendy thought. She had always envisioned naval officers of steely calm, but now, presented with real calm in the face of such carnage, she was not so sure. Surely some sense of humanity was appropriate? She thought perhaps she despised Bowater, so callous with human life.

Then suddenly he turned on her, as if she had done something wrong. "Come left, two spokes, damn it!" he said, his voice near a shout.

"I . . . I . . ." Wendy had not even realized he was speaking to her. Then with a sound like disgust in his throat, he stepped into the wheelhouse and grabbed the wheel, turned it, just a bit, said, "Just hold it like that!"

She grabbed the spokes hard to keep her hands from shaking. She had never been so afraid. Bowater had looked her right in the face—how could he not recognize her? But apparently he did not, because he turned his back on her once more, looked forward.

Somewhere beyond the edge of the deckhouse the big gun fired, so loud that Wendy jumped, let out something like a scream, which was thankfully muffled by the thunderous cannon. She thought she might vomit again, if there was anything left in her to vomit. It was such insanity, such confusion. Noise, bloody death, smoke, shouting, screaming, how could anyone think, how could anyone do anything but cower in a corner and hide?

But she was not cowering, she realized. Frightened as she was, she was not hiding from the gunfire, but rather standing straight in the very spot where another had met brutal death just minutes before. And with that she felt an odd calm come over her.

A sailor came bounding up the steps, paused and saluted Bowater. "Tanner, sir, here to relieve the helm!"

Bowater jerked his thumb over his shoulder, did not look back.

Tanner stepped into the wheelhouse, said in an official tone, "Here to relieve the helm." He paused, as if waiting for a response, and when Wendy could think of none he said, "What course?"

"Course?"

"Where are we heading?"

Wendy shook her head. "I have no idea."

Damn, damn, damn . . . Taylor watched their penultimate shell pass close over the side-wheeler and plunge into the sea three hundred yards astern. Close. Not close enough.

He was standing behind the gun, having raced down the steps from the wheelhouse. Harwell was moving a bit, he noticed, was not dead yet. A gash on his head, blood matting his hair. Taylor could not tell how bad it was and did not pause to investigate. He had grabbed the rails of the ladder and slid down to the deck, pictured Bowater tossing Littlefield's body aside. *Cold son of a bitch. . . .*

The gun crew was swabbing out, ramming home, going through the drill which Mr. Harwell had tortured into them.

"Ready!" Williams stood back, lanyard taut.

From on high, Bowater's voice. "This is your last shot, Mr. Taylor!"

Last shot, Mr. Taylor? How the hell did this become my responsibility? He stepped up to the gun, sighted over it. *I should have stayed in my damned engine room!*

The side-wheeler, bow on, was right in the sights. But, Taylor recalled, it had been before, and the shot had gone over. He grabbed the elevating screw, cranked it up, depressing the muzzle, thought, *If this gun goes off now I am one dead bastard.* . . . Heard Williams make some noise, but the devil take him.

"Give me that lanyard, Williams!" Taylor demanded. Williams paused, could see resistance would be futile, if not dangerous, handed the fancy line over. If Bowater was going to make him responsible, then he was not going to let anyone else make a hash of it.

He looked over the barrel again. The *Cape Fear* and the Yankee were coming bow on, both armed the same, both equally vulnerable.

But not quite. *That Yankee whoremonger has side wheels! Gotta take out one of them side wheels!* "You there!" he shouted to the men with the hand-spikes. "Move this here around to starboard, just a hair!"

The handspike men jammed their bars in the deck, levered the gun over. *There it was!*

"Git back! Git back!" Taylor shouted, and he jumped back and the handspike men jumped back and Taylor pulled the lanyard. The gun went off with a terrific roar, painful, since Taylor had forgotten to clap a hand over his ear. It leaped back against the breeches but Taylor's eyes were on the side-wheeler alone, the side-wheeler steaming down on them, the side-wheeler whose port wheelbox suddenly burst into a spray of shattered wood and broken buckets and twisted metal, flung up in the air.

"Sum bitch! Sum bitch! Yeeeeha!" Taylor shouted, and he knew he was shouting as loud as he could, and so were the men around him, but he could hear only a muffled version of the noise, as if he was listening from underwater. No matter. They had hit him, right where it hurt.

The side-wheeler slewed around to port as the starboard wheel drove her on, then stopped dead as her captain rang out all stop to sort out the damage.

Now what? Taylor wondered. His blood was up, he was ready to go and board them like pirates of old. He looked up, grinned up at Bowater, but Bowater was staring forward at the disabled Yankee, hands behind his back, expressionless. He was not shouting.

Cold son of a bitch. . . .

Samuel Bowater stepped into the wheelhouse, eyes still on the disabled Yankee, rang slow ahead. Close enough. Decision time.

He wanted to shout. He wanted to yell and wave his hat the way the others had. But of course he did not.

"What's your name, sailor?" he said to the new helmsman. This one had the hard, casual look of a real sailor, not the whimpering incompetence of that boy Taylor for some inconceivable reason had dragged up there.

"Ruffin Tanner, of Mobile, sir, by way of the *Congress*, which were my last ship."

"Welcome aboard the CSS *Cape Fear*, Tanner. How do you like it so far?"

"I like it fine, sir, mighty fine." He gave the wheel a quarter turn, brought it back amidships. "Man's blood gets a bit thick, sittin' around one of them Yankee men-of-war."

"Indeed." Bowater remembered Harwell, lying in a pool of his own blood, remembered his own shocking disregard for the man. In a flush of guilt he stepped out of the wheelhouse and around the front, knelt beside the lieutenant, lifted his head.

"Mr. Harwell? Mr. Harwell?" The lieutenant's eyes opened, his lips moved to say something, but Bowater could not make out the words, so he ignored him, examined the wound on his head.

A splinter had opened up a nasty gash, which had bled profusely, and had no doubt rattled the luff's brains, but as far as Bowater could tell, he was not seriously injured. He was a horrible sight, with the blood streaking his face and congealed in his hair. He looked as if he had no business being alive, but he did not seem mortally wounded.

"I'm . . . I'm all right, sir . . ." Harwell said in a stronger voice, and put a hand down on the deck to prop himself up.

"You just rest here, Lieutenant, as long as you need," Bowater said. Harwell looked as if he was going to protest, but happily he passed out again and that was an end to it. Bowater laid him out, stepped into the wheelhouse again.

From the long black side of the *Wabash*, a puff of smoke, and then a shell plunged into the water nearby, and then another puff, another shell. They had steamed right into the range of the smoothbores.

"Hard a'port, Tanner," he said and rang up four bells, full ahead. Time to leave.

It was 114 degrees in the engine room, hotter than that in the boiler room, and the firemen were struggling to get the fire hotter still.

Hieronymus Taylor wiped his forehead with a filthy rag. It was bad enough when you were in the engine room all day, but coming from the relative cool of the upper deck made it seem much worse.

He wiped the face of the pressure gauge on the front of the boiler. Nineteen pounds and building. That was just about all the pressure the boiler would take. He turned to Moses. "Get some more coal on, spread her nice and even, she'll take more than this!" he shouted.

"Oh, we cookin now, boss!" Moses shouted, spreading the white-hot coal with his shovel.

"Goddamn it, man!" O'Malley shouted. "Yer gonna blow us all to hell, damn it! The boiler can't take it!"

"What the hell do you know about it, Ian? You just make sure there's water enough, and you can bet I'll kill you before the boiler does!"

"You're mad!"

"Get!" Taylor pointed toward the boiler and its gauge glass. O'Malley scowled, turned, and stamped off, his boots loud on the metal plates on the deck, even over the groaning, straining, hissing, clanking engine.

Taylor resumed his pacing fore and aft. Through the fabric of the hull, he heard something, some muffled detonation. The *Cape Fear*'s hull was like an eardrum, picking up the vibrations, turning them into something else. Taylor could not tell what it was—he had never heard such a thing— but he guessed it was ordnance exploding in the water. The side-wheeler or the *Wabash* getting in her shots. *Might be time we got out of here*, he thought, and as he did, the bell rang four times, full ahead.

"Here we go!" Taylor shouted, twisting the throttle open. He felt the deck plates tremble with the increased turns of the engine, and then the helm was put hard over, the *Cape Fear* heeling into the turn.

Taylor managed to grab hold of a stanchion and keep himself from tumbling to the floor. Billy Jefferson, shovel jammed in a coal pile, stumbled, fell sideways, put his hands out to steady himself, flat against the steam pipe. Smoke rose from his palms and Billy screamed, a piercing, high scream that made Taylor wince.

He launched himself off the post, raced forward, but Moses was there first, grabbing Billy around the waist, pulling him back from the boiler to the deck.

"St. Clair! Water! Cold water, here!" Taylor shouted. St. Clair hurried off and Taylor looked quickly around, counted heads. Some of his men were standing, some lying where they had fallen, but he could see no other injuries.

He stepped back to the pressure gauge. With the throttle opened, the pressure in the boiler had dropped off, but it was still high.

"Moses! Let St. Clair tend to Billy there! You stoke her up! Coal now, you hear? O'Malley, bear a hand there!"

"Yassa!" Moses knocked open the firebox door with his shovel. The fire was white-hot, an undulating bed of heat, throwing weird shadows and light through the gloom of the engine room, the eternal twilight of that lower region.

Burgess was there. "Bearins runnin hot," he grunted.

"They'll hold for now."

"Lotta damned pressure," he said, nodding toward the boiler.

"That's why we have safety valves."

Actually, they didn't. Taylor had tied them down, figured he knew better than a damned bit of iron and springs when he was pushing his boiler too hard. One of the advantages of the navy, he found: no damned inspectors poking around his engine room.

"O'Malley!" Taylor shouted. The Irishman was sulking in a corner. "I told you to tend the water!"

"What? I'll not go near that damned boiler, and you running twenty and more pounds of steam! That's work for one of the niggers, that is!"

"Niggers are too busy, and if there ain't any niggers we got to use a Mick! Now go!"

O'Malley stamped over to Taylor, but he did not seem inclined to check water levels in the gauge glass.

"I've about had it with yer abuse, do ya hear? I'll not stand for it, and me, a white man, and treated worse than yer darling niggers!"

"You work as hard as my niggers, I'll treat you as well as my niggers," Taylor said, stopped as he heard a hissing sound—water or steam getting away. He looked up just in time to see the crack in the feed-water line opening like a grinning mouth, hot water—not boiling, but hot enough—spewing out.

"Ah, shit! Stand clear!" Taylor shouted, and Burgess and O'Malley and Moses and St. Clair scattered and the pipe burst with a groan and a snap and the feed-water pump forced hot water in a great spray over the engine room, hissing off the pipes, showering the floor plates, spraying over Billy Jefferson, who lay beneath it, screaming and trying to shield himself.

"Damn it! Get the valve, Burgess!" Taylor held his arm over his face, raced forward, slipped on the wet steel plate, and came down in a heap, skidding to a stop with feet against the boiler face. The hot water was lashing at him, burning his face like snake bites, and Billy was screaming, unable to stand with his burned hands.

Water was spewing from both ends of the broken pipe, pushed out by the feed-water pump and draining from the boiler, and if the water in the boiler got too low, there would be hell to pay. The fusible plug would melt, but that would be the least of their problems.

Taylor looked up as best as he could, trying to keep his face from the blowing, scalding water. He rose unsteadily to his feet, the slick decks and the hot water and the burning pipes threatening from every direction. He grabbed the valve on the boiler face—it was painfully hot but Taylor was accustomed to that—and he cranked it shut, heard the sound of the water flow die off.

He turned and looked aft. Burgess, his face red from the hot water, had reached the feed-pump valve. The water was off. Billy was lying on the floor plates, whimpering in pain. O'Malley was nowhere to be seen.

"Burgess, check the gauge glass, keep an eye on that boiler!" With no water going to the boiler, and quite a bit lost, they did not have too much steaming left before the thing began to melt down.

There was a snap to his right, a crack like metal giving way. Ten inches from where he had been standing, the steam gauge blew clean off the pipe, flinging itself up and off to one side. The flying gauge shattered against the boiler-room bulkhead and a whistling white plume of condensing steam came bursting out of the hole where the gauge had been.

Might be pushing it now . . . Taylor admitted to himself. "Moses! Shut off the valve to that gauge," he shouted as he moved quickly aft, "and close that damper on the fire door, you hear?"

"Close the damper!" Moses called, and Taylor heard the reassuring sound of the damper slamming shut and hoped he had not pushed his luck too far.

Hail Mary, Mother of God, the Lord is with thee . . . he muttered, feeling like the Lord's own hypocrite, but childhood training died hard and he hoped the prayer might do some good.

He looked around, at the dripping engine room, the dripping, burned men. Burned but still alive. "Damn," he said. That was all he could think to say.

Ian O'Malley raced up the ladder, desperate to get out of the engine room before the boiler blew. He was frightened, to be sure, and angry and wounded in his pride. But most of all he was bitter about the treatment he received. He had spent the better part of his life being bitter about the way he was treated. The emotion fit him like a well-worn pair of trousers, enveloping and comfortable.

Bloody bastard . . . he thought, throwing open the fidley door and stepping aft, stomping through the sunshine and relatively cool air.

Bloody Southerner and he treats his niggers better than me . . . and me a fireman first class . . .

That was another sore spot. His mother's second cousin, chief engineer of an oceangoing packet, no less, had given him recommendation enough that it should have garnered him first assistant engineer's papers, at least, despite what little experience he actually had. It should have been him telling Taylor to check the feed water and clean the damned grates . . .

Suddenly he was aware of gunfire. Far off, but he could hear it, shells whistling past. He looked outboard. They had turned, and he could see the Yankee ships astern, and the big one was firing.

I made a bloody mistake, didn't I? he thought. *Should have joined with the bloody Yankees . . .*

He heard a voice behind, a soft voice. "Mr. O'Malley?" He turned. The boy Taylor had brought with him was there, but O'Malley had his suspicions. In fact, if he was right, it would be enough to get Taylor cashiered from the navy, which would be justice done. "You . . ." O'Malley said, took a step toward the speaker, hand reached out, and then his whole world was consumed by the whistle of a shell that seemed to suck the air out of the day, and then it blew up.

Wendy felt an odd sort of calm as she walked around the decks, even with the iron flying. It was like being in a bell jar, looking out, able to see everything, protected. It was an illusion, a dangerous one, and she knew it and told herself as much, but she could not shake it, so instead she enjoyed it, experienced it.

After fleeing the wheelhouse she had hunkered down by the forward end of the deckhouse, watched Taylor lay the gun, disable the Yankee. She had cheered with the rest, spontaneously, until she realized her voice might give her away. But Taylor had been right. No one seemed to care who she was or what she was about.

She watched Taylor go back into the engine room, but she could not bear to go down there. She had remained on deck, inconspicuous, reveling in her genuine taste of battle. It was exhilarating, now that it was over, now that the gunboat had turned and was steaming away from the Yankees.

Wendy was buoyant as she walked down the side deck, unconcerned about the last desperate shots the Yankees were taking. She saw Ian O'Malley storm out of the engine-room door, and she even felt kindly disposed to him, though she had seen in him a sullen malingering villain. Still, she looked on him, and all the men aboard, as her shipmates now, her Band of Brothers.

"Mr. O'Malley?" she said. O'Malley turned and his face was not a kind one, and she could see the anger in his eyes, the suspicion as he squinted at her, took a step toward her. She took a step away, the fear suddenly back. O'Malley sneered, said, "You . . . ," hand reaching for her, and then the distant whine of a shell grew suddenly to an overpowering scream, a noise that cut right through both of them, and then the forward end of the deckhouse exploded in a burst of wood and glass.

Wendy saw the sides of the cabin blow out and O'Malley lunged at her and she screamed, thought he was going to kill her. His eyes were wide and he hit her, full-body, knocked her back, and he was on top of her, and she swung and punched at him, kicked as they went down, but it had no effect.

She hit the deck hard, flat on her back. Felt the impact through her whole body. It stunned her, but all she could think was to get O'Malley off her, to get away before he killed her. She pushed him off, and to her surprise he moved, did not resist, and she scrambled to her feet.

She jumped back, pressed herself against the deckhouse, ready to kick O'Malley if he came for her. She looked down, saw he would not.

A shard of wood, three feet long, part of the frame of the cabin, was jutting from his back, and now that she looked she could see the jagged forward tip sticking out from his chest where it had gone clean through. A trickle of blood ran from his mouth.

Wendy stared at the lifeless eyes, the dead man in a growing pool of blood, and she felt nothing. She felt like Bowater, tossing the dead helmsman aside. *Oh God, is this all? Is this all it takes, for a person to lose humanity entirely?*

Taylor came up the engine-room ladder, stepped out onto the side deck. Wendy was there, pressed up against the deckhouse. O'Malley was dead at her feet. For a fleeting instant he thought she had killed him, but then he realized that was absurd.

"What happened?"

"Shell hit, up front, there. That piece of wood went right through O'-Malley."

Taylor nodded. She did not seem as upset as he might have thought she would be. "You best go down to the engine room. We'll be heading in now."

They looked at one another. There was something strange in Wendy's eyes, something that had not been there that morning, and Taylor was suddenly afraid that he had made a great mistake, allowing her to see this. She pulled her eyes from his and disappeared below.

Taylor stepped forward again. Through the gaping hole that had once been a wall, Taylor looked in at the space that had once been the galley. The place was unrecognizable; only a few bits of cookware and sundry pieces of twisted gear looked at all familiar. The destruction was incredible, as if someone had picked the *Cape Fear* up and shaken her, then dropped her again. And right in the middle of it, sitting on a twisted and cracked stewpot, sat Johnny St. Laurent, wide-eyed, shaking his head, seemingly oblivious to the battle still raging.

He looked up and met Taylor's eyes, shook his head in disbelief. How he could still be alive Taylor could not imagine. Then St. Laurent said, with evident grief, "All morning . . . I have been making *de homard à la crème* with a Felbrigg sponge cake for dessert, and now . . ." He spread his arms to indicate the destruction of his fiefdom.

"We'll set her to rights, Johnny, don't you fret," Taylor said, as soothing as he could be, then left the galley and went up the ladder to the wheelhouse. "Cap'n, we lost the feed-water line, we gonna have to shut her down, ten minutes or so."

Bowater nodded. "Ten minutes will be all right. More than that I do not think will do. We are not in the best place to be drifting."

"Ten minutes."

"Very good. What was the damage from that last shell?"

"Galley's a wreck. Lunch is ruined. O'Malley was killed. But nothing beyond that, I don't reckon."

"The *homard à la crème*, ruined?" Bowater met his eyes for the first time. "Devil take those shopkeeping, mudsill Yankees. . . ."

The sun was an hour gone, and the last orange strips of sky fading in the west, when the *Cape Fear* came alongside the seawall at Gosport Naval Shipyard and Babcock saw to the dock fasts. The damage to the vessel was considerable, but they had inflicted worse than they received, had crippled one of the Union's James River fleet, had put a few shells through one of the Federal navy's most powerful men-of-war, had shown the Confederate flag on waters that the Union had considered inviolably theirs. Samuel Bowater was eager to report all of that to Flag Officer Forrest.

Even as the *Cape Fear* had steamed her way down the Elizabeth River, Bowater had thought of his uniform. He and Jacob rummaged through what was left of the master's cabin, and it was not much. Nearly everything that Bowater owned was now in more parts than it had been that morning. His uniforms were charred and shredded. Only a quarter of his oil painting of Newport remained, but he was not sorry to see that gone, and might well have done the same to it himself.

So, when the tug was tied alongside, Bowater was still wearing the uniform he had worn during the fight, and though he was openly unhappy about appearing in such tattered attire, he was secretly proud of the numerous burn marks, bloodstains, and sundry tears in his frock coat and pants. They were clothes that showed hard fighting.

He stepped through the shredded wheelhouse, climbed down the ladder to the foredeck. The Parrott rifle was secured now, the giant put to bed, and for the first time since it had come aboard, Bowater looked on it with pride. He had washed himself clean of the guilt and shame, burned away the humiliation in the fire of battle. He may have allowed Hieronymus Taylor to talk him into the ruse, but he, Samuel Bowater, had led them into the fight, and the gun and the armed *Cape Fear* had proved their worth. He felt better than he had in a long, long time.

He stepped quickly across the shipyard. He intended to try Forrest's office first, but was not confident of finding him there. It was, after all, nearly nine o'clock on a Sunday night.

Bowater could see lights in various windows, could hear people moving about, shouting. There was a charged quality to the air, an atmosphere of excitement, and Bowater wondered if news of his fight had reached the shipyard already, if the word of their deeds had preceded them.

He reached the administration building and stepped inside and he could see, at the far end of the hall, that Forrest's office was occupied, which made him think all the more that news of his battle had reached the flag officer.

Samuel Bowater stepped up to the office door, looked inside. Forrest was there, along with Fairfax and several others of the shipyard's ranking officers. He knocked on the doorframe.

"Sir?" he said.

Forrest turned, his lined, weathered face spread with joy. "Bowater! Bowater, come in. Are you just back now?"

"Yes, sir." Bowater stepped through the door. The room seemed to be bursting with joy, and Samuel wondered if his actions were regarded as grander heroics than even he had dared think.

"Well, you have not heard then!" Forrest said. "It just come in over the wire. Beauregard met the Yankees at Manassas, fought 'em all day, and absolutely routed them! Sent 'em on a grand skedaddle clear back to Washington, the dirty dogs! They are saying it is the greatest victory since Waterloo!"

Forrest looked around at the others, as if for confirmation, and the other officers nodded their delighted agreement. Then Fairfax looked Bowater up and down and said, "Dear Lord, sir, what has happened to you?"

21

Great Battle and Glorious Victory
The greatest battle since that of Waterloo was fought yesterday, in the neighbor-
hood of Manassas, between 50 and 60,000 Southerners on one side and 95 to
100,000 Yankees and Hessians on the other. The loss is not known, except that
it was great on both sides.

—*Richmond Whig*, July 22, 1861

The Great Battle was two days gone when word reached Paine Plantation, just south of Drumgould's Bluff on the Yazoo River. Robley Paine read about the event with a strange back-and-forth pull of emotions. It was the birth of his nation, and like the birth of his sons a bloody, wrenching, frightening affair. Like the birth of his sons, it should have filled Robley with an irrepressible joy.

But that was not what he felt, sitting on the wide porch, under the blue-painted ceiling, reading the newspaper accounts, the bold type that heralded victory, last-minute arrivals that turned the tide of Yankee and Hessian attacks.

What Hessians? Robley wondered. All the papers were filled with allusions to the Hessians.

Despite these accounts of Southern heroism, brilliant leadership in the field, feats of courage, Robley's eyes moved again and again to the single line: *The loss . . . was great on both sides.*

How will I know about my boys? he wondered. *If they are hurt or killed, will the army write me? If not, I will have to wait until the boys themselves write, to find out what has become of them.*

Paine thought of the boys' mother. He glanced up at the front door, as if she might be standing there. His sons had not been overly vigilant about writing, as he had suspected they might not. That silence had only added to Katherine's already great misery. News of the battle had sent her to her bed. He wondered if she could endure a long wait to hear from the boys.

What if they are hurt? Or . . .

The papers were reporting that nearly 160,000 men had participated in the fight, Union and Confederate. Even if twenty thousand were casualties, that was still only one man in eight. And of those, most would only be wounded. An even smaller number would actually be dead.

When his boys marched off, Robley Paine had been dreadfully worried that they might receive wounds, but now that was hardly a concern. *It would not be so very bad if they were wounded,* he caught himself thinking. *Not so much as to cripple them or kill them, just enough that it took them out of the fighting, let them come home with honor.*

He shook his head, tried to distract himself from those dark thoughts. There was a dispatch from Norfolk, the paper reporting some minor victory by an armed tug of the Confederate States Navy. Robley smiled at the thought of the Confederate States Navy, wondered at what a motley collection of tugs and paddle wheelers and barges old Mallory was calling a navy. Still, they had managed to effect something, this navy, so there must be some merit in the idea.

He could not concentrate. He put the paper down, stepped down off the porch and walked the familiar downward slope to the riverbank. His beloved Yazoo rolled on past, that wide, disinterested stream. Did she care if the Yankee vandals were coming, if Yankee steamers would part her with their sharp bows? No, she was just water.

Paine turned back to look at the big house, the open-armed oak, his favorite view in the world. He imagined his boys tramping weary home from the war, seeing that big tree, its limbs like open arms, welcoming then back to the one place of earth that would always be their sanctuary. How much more beautiful would that tree look after the terror of war? Robley ached for that day to come. He ached to get word of his boys.

Four days later he did.

The letter was from Richmond, a printed envelope with the name of the Department of War. The very look of the thing was ominous, loathsome. Robley carried it unopened into the library. He felt sick to the point of nausea just holding the horrible thing, still sealed, in his hand. Finally, with trembling fingers, he tore it open.

Dear Sir:

We regret to inform you of the death of Lt. Robley Paine, Jr., Company D, 18th Mississippi Regiment, 3rd Brigade, during the late Battle of Manassas. Lt. Paine fought bravely in defense of his country.

Regretfully,

E. R. Burt, Colonel, 18th Mississippi

Robley fell back in the winged chair, staring at the stark, cold, typed words. He thought of his beautiful boy, four years old, blond hair and smudged face, running across the lawn, whooping like a wild Indian. He thought of him in his lieutenant's frock coat, lying splayed out on the battlefield, dead eyes open and staring skyward, flies buzzing around open wounds. Robley Paine had seen enough battlefield casualties to know what they looked like, to guess how his lovely, handsome boy had ended up. The tears rolled down his cheeks and the sobs rose from his chest.

He heard soft steps in the hall, approaching the study, and he panicked. He did not want his wife to see the letter, but he could not hide it, and he could not lie to her.

"Robley, whatever is it?" But he did not have the strength to reply, or even move. She crossed quickly, plucked the letter from his hand. She gasped, dropped the paper, fled from the room.

It was several hours before Robley could find it in himself to stand up, to drag himself upstairs to the bed on which his wife had flung herself in her grief. He tried to comfort her, but there was little comfort in him.

Three days dragged by in a purgatory of grief, and then another letter arrived and it was in an envelope like the first. Robley opened the envelope in a numb, mechanical way, thinking vaguely that the regiment had by accident dispatched two letters announcing Robley Junior's death. He unfolded the letter.

Dear Sir:

We regret to inform you that, as of this date, Private Nathaniel Paine, Company D, 18th Mississippi Regiment, 3rd Brigade, and Private Jonathan Paine, ditto, are missing. As their names have not appeared on any of the lists of prisoners taken by the enemy, we fear they must be presumed deserted or dead.

Regretfully,

E. R. Burt, Colonel, 18th Mississippi

Robley did not know what to think. Even if his mind had not been so muddled with grief for his eldest son, he would not have known what to make of it.

Not prisoners, so deserted or dead. For a hopeful second he thought that perhaps they *had* deserted, perhaps they had left the army, were coming home that very moment, coming back to the proper side of their moat, their Yazoo River, where he would keep them safe. Let a provost try to extract them from Paine Plantation. It would never happen. The Yankees would seem a trifle compared to the way Robley Paine would fight to protect his boys. They would be safe there, within the family kingdom.

No sooner did that happy thought occur to him than he banished it away, and in its place came a new level of grief. His boys would not desert. He knew them too well to find hope in that thought. They would willingly die, side by side, but they would never desert.

And that left death. Their perfect bodies shot down by Yankee killers, left to rot in the hot sun. Robley Paine had seen the bloated, bursting corpses, the black faces of the battle dead. He saw his boys in their toy-soldier outfits, shot dead in some thick tangle of brush, some impenetrable wood where they would never be found, where their flesh would become carrion.

Robley felt the sickness and the tears coming again. He stood up quick from his wing chair, paced vigorously for a few moments. The letter said nothing of the sort, just that the boys' whereabouts were not known. No reason to give in to more grief. Certainly no reason to tell Katherine, who had just that morning emerged from their bedchamber, dressed in black, sallow and sunken-eyed, but nonetheless up.

He crumpled the ambiguous note, tossed it into the wastebasket. He would give no thought to the younger boys until he had some definite news, something irrefutable.

Two days later it arrived, in an envelope wrinkled, smudged, battered from hard use. The handwritten address said only "Robley and Katherine Paine, Yazoo, Mississippi," but it had found them. The return address read "Headquarters, 1st Brigade, Army of the Shenandoah."

Robley took the envelope, carried it into his library, staring at it the whole time, as if trying to divine something from the terse address. *Army of the Shenandoah?* He did not see how this could have anything to do with his boys. But any correspondence from any army was cause for dread.

At last he tore it open and extracted a piece of paper more wrinkled and dirty than the envelope, and splotched with the chocolate brown of dried blood. It was written in pencil on lined paper imperfectly torn from a notebook. It was in Jonathan's hand.

Nathaniel James Paine, Company D, 18th Mississippi, 3rd Brigade, son of Robley and Katherine Paine, Yazoo, Mississippi. Please God send me home to be buried in my native earth.

"Oh, God, oh, God, oh, God . . ." Robley stammered the words as if gasping for breath. Dumbly he stared at the other paper enclosed in the envelope.

Dear Sir:

The enclosed note was found on the remains of a private soldier from Mississippi who had apparently joined with our brigade in the great battle at Manassas. I regret that the exigencies of our current military situation make it impossible for us to comply with the request herein. Please be assured that Private Paine fought nobly and was given a Christian burial.

Regretfully,
Colonel A. Cummings
33rd Virginia

Robley's head fell back. The letters slipped from his fingers, fell fluttering to the floor. There it was. His boys had gone off with another regiment, thrown themselves into the hottest fighting, had died for their enthusiasm.

That was his Nathaniel, his Jonathan. Not deserters, quite the opposite. They had joined with another regiment, another army, had died unrecognized among strangers. If Jonathan had not lived long enough to scribble that note, then they would have simply disappeared, tumbled into unmarked graves.

A great deadness spread over Robley Paine, Sr., spread from his chest to his arms and legs and his head. A deadness that was more than death, because in death, he knew, his spirit would take flight, would join his beloved boys in Paradise. But now his soul was trapped on earth, trapped in this aching mortal coil, on this horrible, wretched earth, where Yankees could come down from their filthy cities and kill his beautiful boys.

He heard the swish of silk and his eyes shifted to the door of the library and he wanted to stand, to do something, to hide this from his wife, who could not take another of these hammer blows, but once again he could not move.

She stepped into the doorway, stood there in her black dress, stared at him with sunken eyes, and he stared back, silent. Robley wondered if this was how it had been for their Savior, Jesus, staring down from the cross into his mother's eyes. Such unspoken grief passing between them, grief far beyond words.

Katherine Paine's eyes shifted down to the letters on the floor, then back up to her husband's. She stood there, unmoving, and Robley could see that she understood, even without reading the letters that lay on the rich carpet at his feet, she knew. She probably knew all along. Without a word she turned and glided away.

After a while, Robley stood and wandered out of the library. He had no notion of how long he had been sitting there, whether that time could be measured in minutes or days. His feet took him down the hallway and out the front door, onto the wide porch and its view of the Yazoo River.

He stepped down off the porch and walked the green lawn, down, down to the water. For a moment he thought he might throw himself in, let the water envelop him, sweep him away. He thought he might let himself sink down into the river's warm embrace, but he was not certain. He seemed to have no power one way or another, as if it was not his decision to make. He would just have to wait and see what happened.

He stopped at the edge of the stream and stared into it and realized that he was not going to throw himself in, though he was not sure why not. Perhaps there was something else he was supposed to do.

Robley turned, as he always did, looked back at the house, the great oak tree with its spreading limbs. He squinted at the tree, cocked his head. There was something not right with it. He could see nothing different about the tree, but still there was something not right.

And then it occurred to him: the spreading branches, the welcoming arms. Who was it that the tree would welcome? The arms of the tree were open to the northward, which was why Robley had envisioned them welcoming back his boys, come home from the fight. But his boys would not come home. So who was the tree to welcome?

"Damn that thing . . ." Robley said. He was breathing hard. He could not endure the sight of it, the great billow of green leaves, the limbs like spread arms. There was nothing, and no one, whom he would welcome now. Just the opposite. His boys had left the sanctuary of Paine Plantation and now they were dead. It was up to him, Robley Paine, to keep the rest of the world at bay. The tree was no longer a reflection of Robley's heart.

He walked quickly back up the lawn, calling for the overseer. "Mr. Holling! Mr. Holling! Holling!" He stamped up the lawn, stopped twenty feet in front of the hateful tree.

"Holling!"

Four minutes later, Holling came from around the house, walking fast. He was a stout, greasy man with dirty clothes and ugly habits, and Robley did not like him. But he was of that breed who became overseers on plantations and excelled at the work. Robley had never met a good overseer who was also a decent human being. The two traits did not naturally coexist in a man.

Holling approached fast, laboring for breath. "You called, Mr. Paine?" he asked, stopping short, and Robley could see the man's visible reaction to his employer's appearance. "Sir?"

"I'm going to do some cutting on this tree," Paine said, nodding toward the oak. "I need ten of the field hands with axes and saws, boys who can climb. I need ladders and a team to drag the brush away."

Holling's eyes shifted from Paine to the oak and back again. "Cutting . . . on the tree . . . sir?"

"Yes, damn you."

"Ah . . . the niggers is all out in the fields, Mr. Paine, gettin' in the cotton."

"Damn the . . . goddamned cotton, Holling, let it rot! I don't give a tinker's damn about cotton. Get the hands and get them now!"

"Yassuh!" said Holling, who knew when to shut up and act. He turned and ran off.

Why did he not go to war? Paine thought. *Why did that mean bastard live while my boys did not?*

Overseers were too valuable to send off to fight. The meanest, vilest, most violent of men, but they were needed in the South to keep the Negroes in line and could not be spared to march off and fight the Yankees. So the best of the South had to go in their place.

After some time, Holling returned leading a dozen field hands, who carried among them tall ladders and axes and saws, and the last man was leading a two-horse team in traces. Robley could see the black men looking around, could see the apprehension in their faces. Their daily routine did not vary much. Any change was cause for concern.

"Listen here, you all," Robley addressed his slaves. "I mean to greatly alter the look of this tree. We'll start at the top. Who here is the best climber?"

The men shuffled their feet, looked at the ground, shot questioning glances at one another. Paine felt the frustration boiling up and he tried to hold it back.

"Very well. Billy, I have seen you shoot up an apple tree like a squirrel. You go to the top branches. Someone give Billy a saw. Set that ladder against the tree, that'll get you to the lower branches. We are starting at the top, taking the branches clean off."

Twenty minutes of instructing, bullying, pointing, twenty minutes of ignoring Holling, who kept muttering and rolling his eyes until Paine threatened to dismiss him, to order him to the recruiter's office, and finally the tree was alive with men, hacking and sawing at the branches.

Billy was as nimble as Paine had remembered, clambering up as high as the branches would bear, going after one and another with a bucksaw until the branches, with their great bursts of green, were raining down around the base of the oak, where those men still on the ground carted them off.

In short order the tree grew thinner and thinner, and Robley could see through the branches in a way that he normally could only in winter. Soon the upper branches were gone, and then the lower branches, too thick for the bucksaws, so the men went after them with axes, chopping them off and chopping the trunk as well.

The task went quickly, with so many men being driven by Holling, now anxious to please. The sun moved to the west and the towering oak was rendered shorter and shorter, like a sugar loaf, sliced off again and again until there was only the wide base left.

The virtual rain of greenery slowed as the men reached the lowest of the branches, as big around as trees in their own right, and they hacked at them and the wood chips flew like dull sparks in the last of the sun. Finally, with the sun down and the light fading fast, the trunk was cut for the last time. With flailing axes the Negroes hacked it through, thirty feet from the base, ten feet above the only remaining branches, those two that had formed the welcoming arms, now bare and spindly things, stripped of their leaves and smaller branches.

"I want a fire, right here." Robley pointed to the ground twenty feet in front of the tree. "A big damned fire." The Negroes' work was done, but he still had to labor on, and he would need light for his task.

Holling dispatched men to gather up firewood, and soon there was a great bonfire burning, leaping ten feet in the air, the red-and-orange light dancing off the thing that the oak had become, thirty feet of massive trunk and two great arms reaching out into the dark.

"Good," Robley said, his eyes never leaving the tree. "You all can turn in now. Leave the tools."

The slaves murmured something as they tramped off wearily to their tiny shacks, and Holling disappeared as well. For a long time Robley stared at the tree, trying to see what was beneath the bark, the thing that was in there that he was trying to let free.

At last he picked up an ax, held it over his shoulder, and climbed the ladder up the trunk to a place six feet above where the branches reached out from the body. He steadied himself, brought the ax back, and swung at the tree, felt the sharp blade bite. He jerked it free, brought it back again, swung once more.

For an hour and a half he stood on the ladder, hacking away, and when he was done he had cut a great horizontal gash in the trunk, a slice a foot wide in the living oak. He looked at it, grunted, climbed down from the ladder.

His arms and legs ached, he felt weariness clawing at him, but he pressed on, because he had to have this thing done by dawn. There could not be another day without his dire warning, his Colossus of Rhodes there to frighten off the Northern hordes. He picked up a lantern, lit the candle from the massive bonfire, tramped around the side of the house and across the open area to the barn.

He opened the big door and stamped down the length of the barn. In their stables, the horses shifted nervously, made quiet whinnying sounds. They were not accustomed to visitors at that hour.

Paine stopped at a storeroom at the far end, pulled the door open. Along with various tools and equipment waiting repair were can after can of paint, paint for the plantation house and the stalls, for the carriages, for all the myriad things that required it. Robley held the lantern up, snatched up the cans he needed, stuck a few paintbrushes into the waistband of his pants, carried the whole lot back to the oak.

Again he stood before the tree like an artist before his canvas, looking it up and down, wanting not to impose his will on the thing but rather to reveal that which was already there. Then, with paint cans dangling from a short length of rope, he climbed the ladder again.

Bright red splashed into the notch he had cut, and white for teeth around the edge. No whites for eyes, but rather red—this was an angry god. Robley moved from the top of the stunted trunk to the base, slathering it with paint, until at last it was not a tree at all, but a hideous gargoyle, a pagan edifice, a frightening vision of death that would attend any who tried to cross the Yazoo River and pollute the perfection of the Paine home.

Horror, remain at bay, it cried. *Stay on the northern shore, do not visit my home!*

Finished at last, Robley Paine stood before his creation. In the dancing firelight it was a horrible thing to behold, but that was as it was supposed to be. He would fight horror with horror. And before he knew it, he was lying before the tree, fast asleep.

The chill of the predawn mist woke him. He shuddered with the cold, stretched aching limbs, pushed himself to a sitting position. He felt the great weight of anguish on him, but he could not recall, for an instant, what the anguish was for. And then it came back.

He looked up at the oak, at what he had done. The low-lying fog swirled around the thing, making it look like some mythical beast, the red eyes, the gaping red mouth and white teeth, the branches painted with claws dripping blood, the gray coat, an approximation of the Confederate uniform. It was a horror indeed, and Paine nodded his satisfaction.

That will do, that will do, he thought.

But would it? He had slept, and his mind was clear now. It was a good thing he had done with that tree, let the vandals to the north know that there was no welcome there. But would it be enough?

He looked at the river and thought of the great water barriers in history. He was old enough to recall the French Wars, Napoleon's massive army, poised on the edge of the English Channel, ready to swarm over the water and spread its poison throughout England. The water had stopped them.

"No . . ." The water had not stopped them. They could have crossed the water, just as the Yankees could cross the Yazoo River. It was not water that stopped the French. It was Lord St. Vincent, Horatio Nelson. It was England's mighty Channel Fleet.

The realization came to him, a flash, a divine inspiration, and he spoke it out loud.

"I need a ship."

Book Three

ON BLUE WATER AND BROWN

22

CSS *Cape Fear*
Gosport Naval Shipyard
Portsmouth, Virginia
July 25, 1861

Dear Father,

You have no doubt heard by now of our Army's glorious victory at Manassas this weekend past. It gives me great joy, as I am sure it does you and all true Southern gentlemen.

I am pleased to say that my crew and I, with our small tug, were able to act some small part in our present fight for independence. We peppered the enemy very well at Newport News, and even disabled one of their steamers. It was no Trafalgar, to be sure, but I was pleased with what we were able to do with our little boat.

Our casualties were not terribly bad, though any loss of life is to be regretted. And though I would never hold material goods in the same esteem as the lives of my men, I must say that the loss to me in personal effects was quite complete, as a shell burst apparently right in the middle of my cabin. I am able to replace most of what I lost here in Norfolk, but I would ask you to compel M. LeGrande to run up a half-dozen shirts for me, white linen, and ditto pants. I should ask for navy blue, but I have heard of late that the navy will be setting gray as the uniform color for naval officers, which is absurd. Blue is the standard the world over—who ever heard of a navy man in gray? Also, please apply to Mr. Scribner, the cobbler, for a new pair of dress shoes and a pair of boots. He should have the particulars of my size. . . .

Samuel Bowater

To: Mr. William Cornell
42 Water Street
Charleston, North Carolina

Sir:
In April of this year, you hired out a Negro in your possession, name of Billy Jefferson, as coal heaver aboard the Confederate States Ship *Cape Fear*. As chief engineer of the vessel, Billy has been under my supervision. I regret to inform you that, during action with the Yankee navy, Billy was badly burned on his hands, rendering him unfit for duty. As I am sure you have no use for a Negro who is no longer capable of labor, I have enclosed a bank draft for $500 which I think you will agree is a reasonable price for a Negro who can't work. Please fill out a bill of sale and a receipt for the money and send it to me at the address below.

Respectfully,
Hieronymus M. Taylor,
Chief Engineer, CSS *Cape Fear*
Naval Dockyard
Gosport, Virginia

From the Diary of Wendy Atkins:
   I have seen the elephant, as the soldiers say, and it is a horrible, horrible beast. I have been in combat, as sure as any man in the service. Indeed, I would venture that now I have seen worse than many. I was frightened to death by the sights around me, the blood and the carnage. And then soon, I found myself frightened more by my reaction to it, the casual disregard I soon had for death, including my own. I understand now something I had always wondered about: how soldiers and sailors can face such things and not go mad. Or perhaps they do, and I have as well. I don't know.
   Before this cruise I had seen my Two Gentlemen, Samuel and Hierony-

mus, in one light, and now I have seen them, and myself, in another. I believe I will go to Richmond for some time to visit friends. I must get away from here and from my memories for a while and sort them out. I want to be with Samuel and I want to be with Hieronymus and I cannot bear to be with either, so I must leave and see how it falls out.

Office of Ship Maintenance
Gosport Naval Shipyard

Sir:

Per your orders I have completed a thorough inspection of the tug CSS *Cape Fear* and submit the following report:

Hull and Machinery: Despite the severe fire that the vessel received, it appears that no shot struck her between wind and water, and none below the waterline, leaving her hull and machinery in generally good shape.

Superstructure: A majority of the damage done to the vessel appears to have occurred in her superstructure, due no doubt to the enemy's tendency to aim high. A direct hit was made on the forward bulkhead of the deckhouse and the shell apparently exploded within the confines of the galley, resulting in the total destruction of that area, save for the icebox, which is located on the after side of the steel bulkhead which separates the galley from the fidley. (Incidentally, I am told that at the moment the shell hit, the boat's cook, a freedman named St. Laurent, was completely within the icebox, searching for a bottle of heavy cream. Had he not been, he would surely have ended up the consistency of heavy cream himself.) The forward bulkhead and all of the galley's structures and equipment will require repair or replacement. The crew is currently cooking all meals ashore.

An additional shell exploded in the master's cabin right abaft the wheelhouse, destroying the master's cabin and its contents completely and doing significant damage to the wheelhouse, including the total destruction of the chart table and all of the charts, and the destruction of all windows and frames and the collapse of the roof. There is but a small section of the wheelhouse and cabin that may be salvaged.

Conclusion: Despite the ferocious mauling that the *Cape Fear* received at the hands of the Yankees, she emerged with little damage to her hull. The preponderance of the damage was to her superstructure, which is much more easily repaired, and at lesser expense.

It is my estimate that she might be restored to her former condition in a week or less, and at a cost of approximately $300.

Respectfully submitted,
James Meads, Master Carpenter

> To: Flag Officer Forrest
> Flag Officer's Office, Dockyard
> Gosport, Virginia, July 25, 1861

To Whom It May Concern:

Know all ye who read this, that the bearer, Billy Jefferson, a Negro, five foot eight inches tall, of dark complexion with burn scars on both hands, is a free man, made free by Hieronymus Taylor, his rightful owner, as of April 25, 1861, and on my direction is traveling to Canada.

Respectfully,
Hieronymus M. Taylor

From the Journal of Lieutenant Thadeous Harwell:
. . . and then through blood-soaked lashes I opened my eyes to gaze on the noble visage of the Captain. How very concerned he looked! And for me, but a lowly officer! But such is the nobility of the man's heart.

"Nay, lie here, good man, till you have strength enough to stand," quoth he, but I struggled to my feet and with barely strength enough I saluted as crisp as I might and reported myself ready for duty.

23

Went to Miss Sally Tompkins' hospital. There I was rebuked. I deserved it.
Me: "Are there any Carolinians here?"
Miss T: "I never ask where the sick and wounded are from."

—Mary Boykin Chesnut

"Hello, Mississippi."

Jonathan Paine opened his eyes. There was a young black man looking down at him, about his age, a few years older, perhaps. Black hair cut close. A day's growth of beard over a deep mahogany face. He was smiling.

Jonathan fixed the face with his stare for half a minute, a minute. It was not like the other faces, from before, not ghostly and indistinct. It seemed real. So did the bed he was lying on, the room around him.

He had been caught in an undertow of nightmare, swirling images, dreams that were not dreams, jarring motion that made him cry out but would not stop, dark and light shadows, faces moving like phantoms in front of his eyes.

But this was not like that.

"Water . . ." he said. He could barely hear his own voice.

The young man nodded. He reached down and Jonathan could see he wore an apron and the apron was covered with blood. It was an image right from the nightmare, but it was more solid than those ephemeral things had been.

The man lifted Jonathan's head, pressed a glass to his lips. The water was tepid but clean, and Jonathan sipped it, felt the liquid wash over the dry, raw patches in his mouth and throat, cool them and wet them. He drank some more, and then drained the glass.

"More . . ."

They repeated the procedure and then Jonathan let his head fall back, exhausted. He closed his eyes for a moment, but this solidness, this new reality, was too intriguing for him to ignore. He could recall coming to a vague and unconscious understanding that he was dead and in hell. He opened his eyes again. The young man was still there, and that was a relief.

"Where am I . . . ?"

"Richmond. You inna hospital." The young man seemed to find delight in the questions, as if he had been waiting for Jonathan to ask.

Jonathan turned his head, just a bit. He was in some kind of sitting room, a big one, like the sitting room at the Paine plantation, but beyond the molding and the light fixtures and the fireplace, there was nothing else that suggested a private home. All of the chairs, the tables, the book-cases that one might expect were gone, and in their place were beds, per-haps twenty beds in that one room.

There were men in the beds and others bustling around them, and women, too. Men in tattered uniforms, walking on crutches or sitting on the edges of beds. Sunlight streamed in from big windows, filling the place with brilliant light. Far from hell, this place with its white sheets and brilliant sunlight looked more like heaven. But it was not that. In heaven, Jonathan was sure, he would not be in such agony as he was.

"My name's Bobby," the young man offered. "Bobby Pointer. I work for da missus, runs the hospital. I take care a da stables, most times, but now I's helping out here. Nurse, you might say. We gots more wounded boys den we gots horses, now."

Then a woman appeared, beside Bobby, seemed to just float into place. A young woman, not thirty. She had dark hair and wore a white apron, spotted here and there with dark brown stains.

"Is our young man awake, at last?" the woman asked. Her voice was musical. Jonathan could not recall the last time he had heard such a voice.

"Yes, ma'am. Jest opened his eyes."

"Hello, Private. My name is Miss Tompkins. How are you feeling?"

Jonathan tried to nod but could not. He opened his mouth to speak, but there were too many things he wanted to ask, and so he just shook his head.

Miss Tompkins watched his struggle and said nothing. She did not seem impatient or surprised at his inability to speak. After a moment she just smiled again, a lovely smile, patted his arm, and said, "I must go attend to the others, but I'll be back. You are in good hands here, with Bobby." And with that she seemed to float away.

Bobby leaned close, and said in a conspiratorial tone, "She call herself 'Miss,' but da truth is, she 'Captain' Tompkins. Jeff Davis hisself done give her a commission as captain in da army. Imagine dat!"

Jonathan nodded again, still could think of nothing to say.

"You was at da battle at Manassas, you recall?" the young man asked. "You done took a hell of a knock on da head."

Jonathan tried to think. *Battle at Manassas* . . . Yes, he could recall that, but just images. Not like the fleeting nightmare images, but close. He recalled thirst. He recalled noise. He recalled the horror of bullets whizzing past, men screaming and dying.

"Nathaniel . . ."

"Nathaniel? That your name?"

"No . . ." He paused for a long moment, felt consciousness slipping away, thought he might pass out, but the lightness faded. "He was my brother . . . I'm . . . Jonathan."

"Well, howdy, Jon'tin. We been waiting to see if you gonna live or not. You be one tough sumbitch. . . ."

Jonathan stared at the young man. *Tough son of a bitch?* He felt weak as a baby. "How did I get here?"

"You was at Manassas. Somehow you gots in wid da 33rd Virginia, got shot up awful bad. Near left for dead, but someone seen you was still breathing, so they patched ya up, sent ya here. You been crazy wid da fever for a week or more. No one knowed who you was, on account of you not bein' with you regiment. We jest called you 'Mississippi.' 'Cause dat's what it says on you buttons."

Jonathan swallowed and nodded. He could recall the bullets plucking at his coat, the waves of blue Yankees coming on, up that hill. He felt points of pain all over his body, places where the ache was not general but rather concentrated, as if he was being stabbed repeatedly in the same spots. But of all the aches, one clearly pronounced itself the worst.

"My leg . . . it hurts like hell . . ."

"Which one?"

Jonathan closed his eyes and thought about where the pain was. "Right . . ." he said. He opened his eyes again. Bobby was looking at him, and his expression was part sympathy, part amusement.

"I hates to tell you dis, but you ain't got no right leg."

Jonathan frowned at him. *I just told you it hurts like hell. . . .* He struggled to lift his head and look down at his body, lying on the bed. He was covered with a white sheet, clean and sweet-smelling. At the far end of the bed he saw the point of white cloth made by the toes of his left foot. To the right there was nothing.

He fell back on the pillow, stared up at the ceiling.

"You be surprised," Bobby was saying, "how often dat happens. Fella feels pain in a arm or a leg that ain't even there no more." He was trying to sound cheerful. Jonathan would have strangled him if he had had the strength to lift his arms.

It was coming back now, not a trickle of memory, but a flood tide. He had led Nathaniel to the fight and Nathaniel was dead. He recalled the look in his brother's dying eyes, the death rattle as the life ran out of him on the field. He recalled the note he had written, stuffed in Nathaniel's uniform.

His brother's body would be back home now. Robley would have written their parents, told how Jonathan had persuaded Nathaniel to march off, just like all those other times he had lured his brother into trouble.

He closed his eyes against the grief and the hurt. He was crippled, his leg cut off by some army butcher. His parents and Robley Junior would despise him for what he had done, as well they might, the loathsome creature, to lure a brother to his death.

He felt the bed shift as Bobby stood and walked softly away and left Jonathan to lie there and envy the men left dead on the fields south of the Bull Run.

The Union navy was massing for something. Samuel Bowater had not been wrong in thinking so.

As the shipwrights swarmed over the *Cape Fear*, rebuilding her wheelhouse and galley, replacing panels in the sides of the deckhouse, patching holes and strengthening the bulwarks where the gun breeches made off, reports continued to come downriver of more and more ships gathering at Newport News and Hampton Roads.

As the burned-out wreck of USS *Merrimack* was transformed slowly into the ironclad CSS *Virginia*, *Merrimack*'s old consorts, *the Minnesota*, *Wabash*, *Monticello*, *Pawnee*, and *Harriet Lane*, gathered as if for a reunion off Fortress Monroe. Also in attendance were the chartered steamers *Adelaide* and *George Peabody*, and the tug *Fanny*, all ships of the United States Navy. There were others as well, transports and battered old schooners, whose purpose was not clear.

Little, in fact, was clear, save that the United States Army and Navy were preparing to fall on some part of the Confederate coast.

July turned to August. The *Cape Fear* was returned to service, her superstructure repaired, her master's cabin made better than it had been, with oak paneling, hinged windows, and a compass mounted over the bed. It was even extended by two feet aft, adding significantly to the volume therein. The former cabin had, after all, been no more than a bunk for a tugboat skipper, but now it was the great cabin of an officer of the Confederate States Navy.

August crept by, with its sweltering heat and dripping humidity. During the soft Virginia evenings, when the sun began to incline toward the west, and the *Cape Fear* was tied to the seawall or swinging on her hook, Hieronymus Taylor made his way aft to the fantail, violin under his arm, and sitting on the after rail coaxed lovely soft melodies from his instrument.

Moses Jones would soon drift aft, as if by pure chance, and he would lend his voice to Taylor's music. They reminded Samuel, who would sometimes listen from the roof of the deckhouse, of two dancers in perfect sympathy with one another.

An illiterate coal passer and a poor, barely educated Southern peckerwood, but somehow, to Bowater's amazement, they made music as if they were one person, and even he, who had no tolerance for the dreary sentimentality or the shallow joviality of popular music, found some merit in their performances. As did the other Cape Fears, who gathered every night to listen.

Early in the month the Yankees sent hot-air balloons aloft from the deck of a small steamer, with men in baskets suspended beneath to take a look at the Confederate works at Sewall's Point. It was a novelty that warranted a few days' discussions. And still the Union ships assembled, until they were so much a part of the coastline that neither Bowater nor any others of the Confederates on the shore south of Hampton Roads paid them any mind.

Until the afternoon of August 26, when they left.

It was a Monday. The day before, Bowater had wandered over to the riverfront park with a new canvas and easel. There had been several weeks of inclement weather, which had kept him from his usual painting, and that had made him anxious, a reaction which surprised him. It would not have occurred to him that he was anxious to see Wendy Atkins again, though thoughts of her still haunted him. More curiosity than anything, he told himself, a self-flagellating tendency to stoke his own irritation.

The *Cape Fear* was at the dock at Sewall's Point, just south of Hampton Roads, off-loading ordnance. Despite the big Parrott gun in the bow and the twin howitzers, the tug was once again transporting supplies around the Elizabeth River. Bowater hoped to get into action again, indeed he never thought otherwise, but it would not be shelling the Union fleet. No one thought the United States Navy would be caught napping twice.

"Fleet's getting up steam," a captain of artillery noted as he and Bowater and Taylor watched the Cape Fears swaying a smoothbore thirty-two-pounder off the fantail and onto its waiting carriage.

"Is that a fact?" Here was some interesting news. The sharp edge that Bowater had felt after his fight with the steamer was now growing dull again.

Bowater and Taylor followed the gunner up the wooden steps, past the dusty earthworks, the mounds of dirt piled up to augment the fortification already in place.

They climbed up to the top of the rampart, above the black barrels of the guns that leered out over the water. Before them, spread out like a lake, the blue water of Hampton Roads. A little over three miles to the north, Fortress Monroe. Five miles off and a little north of west was Newport News Point, and between them, like a series of black dashes on the blue water, the massed fleet of the United States.

Bowater pulled his telescope from his pocket, snapped it open, and focused it north. He could pick out the *Wabash* and the *Minnesota*. Plumes of black smoke were crawling up from their stacks. Steam frigates getting underway. The wind was light out of the south. When Samuel Bowater was a young boy, no man-of-war could have left the Chesapeake Bay in those conditions. But the steam engine had changed that, had changed the entire nature of war at sea. Now schedules, and not wind and tide, dictated fleet movements. Now engineers lorded it over captains.

"That's a lot of damned ships." The artilleryman's observation yanked Bowater from his reverie.

"And that don't count the ships still on blockade. Or comin' in from foreign ports," Taylor added.

The three men stood silent for several minutes and looked at the fleet. The profile of one of the big steamers began to change, to foreshorten.

"*Wabash* is underway," Bowater said.

"Where you think they're goin'?" the artilleryman asked.

"Hard to say. Charleston? Cape Fear? New Orleans? They have more choices than ships, to be sure."

"Wherever it is," Taylor said, "some poor Southrons are in for a whole lot of hurt."

Thirty hours later, as the *Cape Fear* picked up her mooring off the dockyard, with the sun just a few hours from setting, they discovered where the fleet was bound, and who was in for the hurt.

"Boat's putting out, sir."

Ruffin Tanner, who had remained with the *Cape Fear*, was lashing the helm, looking out the wheelhouse window, as Bowater wrote in the log, *4:43—Done with engine.*

Samuel turned and stepped across the wheelhouse and looked where Tanner pointed. A longboat pulling for them. Odd. He picked up the field glasses that he kept near the wheel, fixed the boat in the lenses. Flag Officer Forrest in the stern sheets. Odder still.

"Mr. Harwell!" The luff looked up from the foredeck. "It appears that Flag Officer Forrest is coming aboard. Please arrange for some kind of side party," he said, and Harwell, who absolutely lived for such pomp, saluted and hurried off.

Five minutes later, Forrest stepped aboard to a credible display involving rifles and cutlasses and Eustis Babcock's bosun's pipe. Forrest exchanged salutes with the officers and Bowater led him up to the wheelhouse.

"They did a good job here, damned good," Forrest said, looking around the rebuilt bridge and cabin and nodding his head. "They do good work, when they do work. Now see here, Bowater. Just got word. That damned Union fleet's anchored at Hatteras Inlet. Got a chart?"

"Yes, sir." Bowater pulled the chart of the coast from Cape Lookout to Cape Henry, unrolled it, and placed weights on the corners.

"There." Forrest put a meaty finger down on the narrow Hatteras Island. "All those ships, you saw them. They're going to blow hell out of the forts. We have two forts there, Hatteras and Clark. Gibraltar they ain't."

"Yes, sir. I've been there. Delivered ordnance to them twice now."

"Yes, yes. 'Course you have. Good. Because you're going to do it again. We've got to try and reinforce them. They don't have above four hundred men, against all those abolition kangaroos Welles sent down there. Commodore Barron will be going down with *Winslow* soon as he can get underway. You'll report to him. Get your ship alongside and get all the ordnance you can take."

"And we are to leave?"

"Immediately, Captain. Immediately. As I hear it the Yankees are already knocking the stuffing out of those forts."

"Aye, sir." Bowater stepped over to the engine-room bell, gave a single jingle. *Stand by.* He waited to hear Hieronymus Taylor cursing from two decks down.

Twenty minutes later, they were tied up alongside the dockyard. With the fires freshly banked it took no time to get head up steam again. It took longer for Bowater to explain to a fuming Chief Taylor why his engine, which he had put happily to bed, was being called on once more. At last, when he seemed sure that Bowater understood the great favor being rendered, Taylor stooped to spread the fires in the boiler.

Goddamned engineers. . . .

The ordnance workers were ready for them: a wagonful of shells and fuses, powder and round shot, whatever could be spared for the beleaguered forts on Hatteras.

With the sun an hour from setting, they cast off and headed downriver, to where the wide Elizabeth grew more and more narrow and channeled at last into the Great Dismal Swamp Canal, a thirty-five-mile cut through the wild Great Dismal Swamp.

The canal was mostly straight, and not terribly wide, only one hundred feet or so in most places. The vegetation grew right up to the banks, tall stands of cyprus trees lining the canal so that, in the gathering dusk, one had the sense of steaming down a city street, with tall buildings to port and starboard.

Samuel Bowater stood just outside the door of the wheelhouse, peering into the deep shadows that fell over the water. They were steaming at half ahead, the fastest that he dared go down that dark river.

"Come left, just a bit there . . ." he called into the wheelhouse, and Tanner repeated, "Left, just a bit. . . ."

"Good . . . steady as she goes." Bowater did not know how long they could keep this up, how dark would be too dark to steam down the canal. The sun was gone, and just the last tenacious threads of light were hanging in the west.

"A little right now . . ." And then the *Cape Fear* eased to a stop. Not a jarring crash, like hitting a rock, just a gentle cessation of movement, hardly noticeable, really, the feel of a slow-moving steamer running up on the mud.

Bowater reached up and gave the engine-room bell two jingles, stop. He looked forward, as far as he could, down the waterway, which was not far. The cyprus trees and the swamp grass seemed to melt into the water, so that he could not tell where one began and the other left off.

He grabbed the bell again, rang three jingles: done with engine.

All hands were called at eight bells in the night watch, four o'clock in the morning. In the predawn dark they ate and went to quarters.

Down in the engine room a grousing Hieronymus Taylor, bleary-eyed and rumpled, ordered Moses Jones to spread the fire while he stripped down, stumbled behind the condenser, and washed away some of the sleep and the film of grime and sweat under the warm spray of the engine room's now functioning shower bath. He toweled off, dressed, lit a cigar, and was feeling something near content when the wheelhouse rang down one jingle, stand by, followed two minutes later by three bells and a jingle, full astern.

Taylor nodded to himself as he shifted the reversing lever and twisted the throttle open. *Patrician put her in the mud . . . thought so. . . .*

Samuel Bowater leaned over the rail of the deckhouse. The water of the Dismal Swamp Canal, dyed brown by the tannin from the ubiquitous trees, was churning into a white froth, boiling up from the turns of the *Cape Fear's* big prop. He looked up at the tree line, slipping ahead, as if the trees were marching on without them, but in fact it was the *Cape Fear* moving, backing out of her mud berth. He let out a quiet sigh of relief. It would have delighted Hieronymus Taylor to no end if they had had to use a steam winch to pull her off. The chief would have made simply giving the order a nightmare of humiliation.

They backed into the canal, and Bowater rang half ahead, then twenty minutes later, full ahead. It was warm and still behind the bulwark of cyprus trees, and the *Cape Fear* plowed her furrow south, and with each mile Bowater felt more and more anxious to get his cargo of ordnance to the forts before they were overrun by the Yankees.

They broke out of the Great Dismal Swamp before noon, steamed past Elizabeth City and down the Pasquotank River and into the wide-open water of Albemarle Sound, like a great saltwater lake. They chugged across the sound and past Roanoke Island and turned south toward Hatteras. To the east, the low, sandy dunes of the barrier islands. From the wheelhouse Samuel could catch glimpses of the Atlantic, stretching away to the horizon, beyond the barren yellow strips of land.

"Sir?" Thadeous Harwell stood forward of the wheelhouse, peering south with the big telescope. "Sir, perhaps you should see this."

Bowater took the glass, pointed it in the indicated direction, sweeping along the line of low sand dunes and swatches of stunted trees, only just visible from the wheelhouse. He saw the dark vertical line that was the Cape Hatteras light. And then, south of that, he stopped.

It looked like a fog bank, or a low-lying cloud, but Samuel knew it could not be those things. It was smoke from artillery, the cumulative output of the guns of the United States fleet, billowing up high in the air, a dull gray cloud rising as high as the lighthouse itself.

"Dear God . . ." Bowater muttered. It took a frightening number of big guns to make a cloud like that. He wondered if they were too late. It did not seem possible the Confederates could stand up to such pounding.

For the rest of the morning and afternoon they plowed their way south.

The *Cape Fear* was moving as fast as she could, a bit more than five knots. Samuel Bowater, graduate of the Navy School, understood displacement and theoretical hull speed, was familiar with William Froude's latest Wave Line Theory, but that did not stop him from hating it all, and wishing a little more speed from the deep-draft tug.

They were still miles away when they heard the cannon fire, a deep rumble, very like thunder, but continuous, absolutely unrelenting. Soon they could see the spray of dirt and sand as the shells exploded on the low forts and the island, the infrequent jets of water as the Yankee ordnance overshot its targets and dropped into Pamlico Sound, on the landward side of Hatteras Island.

It was late in the afternoon when Bowater conned the *Cape Fear* into the shallow harbor, more an indentation in the beach, behind Hatteras Island. The screams of shells through the air, the constant explosions on the fort and the beach around, blotted out any other sound; the *Cape Fear*'s engines, the anchor chain running out, the wind, which was brisk, everything. It was as if the fort was under a rain cloud, an isolated cloud that poured its deluge down on that spot alone. Hardly a shot fell that did not kick up a spray of earth from the ramparts. The gunfire from the fleet was deadly accurate.

Bowater picked up the field glasses, focused them on Fort Hatteras. The dirt was flying in tall brown spouts with each explosion of the Yankee ordnance, flying skyward like surf hitting a rocky shore. He could see no movement from the fort, save for the flying earth and the Confederate flag, standing straight in the stiff wind.

He shifted his gaze to the north, three-quarters of a mile. Fort Clark seemed to be spared the Yankees' attention. He could see no explosions there, no rain of shells.

"Oh, damn . . ." It was not clear at first. He had to take a longer look. But then he saw it was not the Confederate flag flying on the flagpole, it was the Stars and Stripes.

Too late for you . . .

He swung the field glasses south again, looked past the beleaguered Fort Hatteras, over the low sandy island on which it stood, to the broad Atlantic, stretching away beyond.

The Union fleet was at anchor, the massive men-of-war nearly swallowed up in their own gun smoke, bright flashes stabbing through the gray cloud, as they poured their lethal shot on the poor mud walls of Fort Hatteras.

Bowater watched, mesmerized. All those ships. It was a terrible, terrible thing. He could recall the pride he once felt, looking upon those very ships, some of the most powerful in the world, enjoying the awe that their potential power could inspire. What could he do against them with his own tiny man-of-war, though she was nearly as fine as any that the Confederate States Navy could boast?

"Mr. Harwell, you may cast off the Parrott gun and try a ranging shot at the Yankee fleet," he said. Harwell acknowledged the order, ran forward, nearly collided with Hieronymus Taylor coming up the ladder from the deck below.

"Good afternoon, Captain," he said and paused to bite the end off a new cigar, spit the torn bit over the side, and light the noxious thing. He looked up, and for a long moment he just stared out at the Union fleet and the hail of iron they were hurling at the Confederate fort.

"Oh, Lordy . . ." he said at last.

"Behold, Chief Taylor," Bowater said. "This, I believe, is why the Yankees do not lie awake nights for fear of the Confederate States Navy."

24

[E]very effort that nautical skill, invention and courage can put forth must be made to oppose the enemy's descent of the river, and at every hazard.

—Stephen R. Mallory

*I*t was not difficult, Robley Paine discovered, for a man of means to get what he wanted, the increasing constrictions of war notwithstanding. Because the one thing people wanted more than anything was hard currency, gold, and that Robley Paine had.

Robley Paine had never been one for bank accounts, drafts, scrips, ephemeral bits of paper. He had all those things, of course. The world was too complicated for one to do business without them. But Paine's primary concern, his *raison d'être*, had been his boys' legacy, and he would not trust that to preprinted forms and bankers' promises. He would see, before all else, that his boys were set, that the Paine plantation and the Paine fortune would be there for them.

He was not alone in that, of course. It was the dream of every planter in the South. But the wealth of most other men was measured in land and slaves. What cash they had was paper currency issued by banks, or now by the Confederate States, which was already showing signs of devaluation, though the government had been issuing the notes for less than a year.

Robley Paine, however, kept a good deal of his wealth in gold, solid gold, bullion and coin.

Gold was a real thing, something one could hold in one's hand, currency traded the world over and not subject to the machinations of government and finance, inflation, devaluation, the crash of the stock market. The worth of gold would not fluctuate with the fortunes of armies in the field.

Robley had been building his gold reserve for years, had resisted increasing his land- and slaveholdings to make certain the money was there for his boys. Nothing on earth would have induced him to spend it. Let the fiscal world crumble around him, let King Cotton lose his throne, Robley Paine's boys would be sitting on a small pile of gold, that precious metal that had always been and would always be considered wealth.

But now his boys were gone, his reason for keeping that wealth blown away by Yankee invaders, and there was no reason in the world for him to hang on to it. Quite the opposite. Now he had real purpose in the spending of it.

He took passage to Vicksburg, the town draped like a blanket over high hills looking down on the twisting Mississippi below, walked along the river, stepping fast, his cane clicking on the stone quays and the wooden docks. His ancient wound ached until he was limping as if freshly shot, but it did not slow him in his search for a vessel.

He did not find one in Vicksburg, had not really thought he would. From there he took passage south, down to the great port city of New Orleans, a place he knew well, a place where he was known and where he knew people who could help him, a place where he knew he would find what he needed, every article. It was all to be had at New Orleans.

Robley was welcomed into the offices of Mr. Daniel Lessard, his shipping agent, with a greeting befitting an old friend, one who had been a steady source of income for many years. Lessard met him with hand extended and a smile that faded a bit as he looked on Paine's face. "Robley, this is a surprise. . . ." Lessard led Paine into his office, seated him in front of the big desk. "Are you well, sir? If you will forgive an impertinent question?"

"I have had a loss," Paine said, in a tone that brought the discussion to a close. He fidgeted, adjusted the pistol he wore under his frock coat, a .44-caliber Starr Model 1858 Army revolver he had purchased a few years back. Most of the gold he had with him was in the hotel safe, but he carried a significant amount on his person, and he would protect himself. "I am interested in purchasing a riverboat. Do you know of any that might be suitable?"

"I know of many that are for sale," Lessard said. Daniel Lessard was a wealthy man, and he had become such by knowing and establishing a relationship with everyone on the waterfront, from the meanest grifters to the most powerful merchants. "It would depend on what it must be suitable for."

"River defense," Paine said, and Lessard smiled, chuckled, then stopped as he realized that Robley Paine was not joking.

" 'River defense'?" Are you thinking of going into privateering?"

"No, I am thinking of stopping the goddamned Yankees from overrunning our home, that is what I am thinking of," Paine said, feeling the words slip out, himself unable to contain them. He was not able to keep the menace from his voice. Lessard was visibly taken aback.

Oh, damn, oh, damn, Robley, get ahold of yourself.... He could not always distinguish between the dialogue in his head and the words coming out of his mouth. "Forgive me, we are all under a great strain now, with the war . . ."

"Never think on it, sir!" Lessard waved his hand. "I know of several vessels might answer. There is *Star of the Delta*. About three hundred tons, hundred and fifty feet long, around thirty on the beam. Side-wheeler. She does not draw above seven feet. Two high-pressure, noncondensing engines, two boilers, all her machinery just recently gone over, in excellent condition."

"She is for me, if she is what you say, sir," Robley said. He scratched at his face, at the coarse growth of beard, wondered when he had last shaved. No bother. "When might we see her?"

"Now, I should think," Lessard said brightly. He had some interest in this vessel, Robley could tell. The old Robley Paine would have been more cagey, would have discovered Lessard's interest, driven a hard bargain. But now he was too pressed to argue or haggle.

"Show her to me."

The *Star of the Delta* was tied up bow first not two blocks from Lessard's office. She had the look of a vessel which had not moved in some time, but for all that she was in tolerably good order. Paine climbed up to her hurricane deck, stuck his head in the wheelhouse, ran his fingers over the wheel. He climbed down into the engine room with Lessard carrying a lantern to light the way. It cast wild shadows over the masses of piping and hulking bits of iron machinery. Paine looked at it, nodded, realized that he knew nothing whatsoever about ships and engines and such.

At last they returned to the deck above, stood on the fantail, looking out over the wide brown river. "She looks the thing, as far as I can tell," Paine said. He looked Lessard in the eyes, and for the first time since he had resolved to defend the rivers of his home, he felt vulnerable, like a child, out of his depth. "I confess, sir, I am ignorant of these things. I look to you, as a friend, to advise me. Is this the vessel that I need? Is she in decent shape?"

Lessard put his hand on Paine's shoulder, gave him a half-smile, a reassuring look. "*Star of the Delta* is a fine vessel, strong and well cared for. She will certainly serve you well."

For a long time Robley held his old friend's eyes. Then he said, "Thank you. This is a trying time for me, but you have helped me along. And now I must look into the next thing, the harder thing by far, and that is arming her."

"Arming her? What sort of armament did you have in mind?"

Robley shook his head. "I don't know. A shell gun, forward? Smoothbores? At close range the smoothbores have the advantage, you know, with their higher muzzle velocity. But I do not know what I will be able to acquire. Or how, to be honest."

"Well, sir . . ." Lessard said. "This is New Orleans. For a price, my friend, all things are to be had here. . . ."

It was ten days before the *Star of the Delta* could get underway. She bore a new name then, *Yazoo River*. Changing the name had been the only simple part of her transformation.

There were two significant differences between the *Star of the Delta* and the *Yazoo River*. One was the addition of a four-foot iron ram on her bow, a foot below her waterline. It fit snugly around the cutwater and protruded forward like an iron shelf, a foot thick. Heavy bolts went clean through the ram and the *Yazoo River*'s cant frames and held the weapon securely in place.

The second addition was a letter of marque and reprisal, making the *Yazoo River* an official privateer. Robley had tramped through one office after another, filled in government forms, slipped bribes to greasy officials. It was the way of things in New Orleans. He had always understood it and accepted it. But it was harder now. His country was at war, and wicked people were making profit by obstructing the efficient prosecution of that war. It was insufferable, but Paine clenched his teeth, handed over the gold, tolerated it because he had to.

It was a formality, the letter of marque, as far as Robley was concerned, a bow to the legitimate authorities. Privateers captured prizes. Robley Paine was not interested in capturing anything. He intended only wholesale destruction, and he did not need a license for that.

The *Yazoo River* was a cotton-clad. Her armor, piled high on the foredeck and around the wheelhouse and the side decks, consisted of tightly compressed bales of cotton. They might help against small arms fire, Robley imagined, might make the men at the guns a bit more bold with the absurd belief that they were protected by the bales, but they would do no more than that.

Paine had actually purchased the cotton bales to pile on the decks, and that could not fail to amuse him. His fortune was based on growing and selling cotton; he had never purchased it in his life. Fortunately, it was not expensive, with the Union blockade already resulting in surpluses of the crop piling up in warehouses and docks.

Ten days of feverish work, of fighting with shipyard workers and recruiting sailors and engine-room crew, of getting his hands dirty working on the ship and kowtowing to corrupt officials, and spending gold at an extraordinary rate, buying coal and engine parts and food and charts and oil and shovels and slice bars and dockage. All things were to be had in New Orleans, and everyone had his hand out.

Ten days, and finally they cast off from the dock and Mr. Kinney, whom Paine had engaged as pilot, backed the *Yazoo River* out of her berth and into the Father of Waters. He spun the wheel once, rang up the engine room for half ahead, spun the wheel some more. Robley listened to the sounds of the big paddle wheels stop, a moment's quiet, then the clank and splash and creak as they reversed direction.

"How does she feel, Mr. Kinney?" Paine asked. He was nominally captain, but he made no pretensions of knowing anything about boats. He left that aspect to Mr. Kinney and Brown, the engineer, both of whom treated Paine with a veiled contempt, and neither of whom Paine particularly liked. Paine did not think a fit Southern man had any business not being in the armed service. The very fact that Kinney and Brown were available made them suspicious in his mind.

"She's fine, so far." Kinney chewed thoughtfully at the plug of tobacco in his mouth, spit a stream into a spittoon, wiped a brown streak from his thick beard with the back of his sleeve. "Don't know how long them goddamned engines'll go, 'fore they blow all to hell, but so far she ain't bad."

Paine nodded, looked past the piles of cotton on the bow, at the brown water moving past. For all of his concerns about the ship and her crew—most of them were foreign, a surly and uninspired lot—he felt buoyed to be underway. If nothing else happened, nothing at all, he had a ship with a ram and he could end his life plowing it into the side of a Yankee man-of-war and have that to take to his grave, to tell his boys in heaven that he had done that much at least for them.

They steamed south from New Orleans, through the low delta country, the wild marshy places where the big river began to make its slow segue into the sea. The sun moved toward the horizon, but Kinney, for all of his objectionable qualities—and they were many—knew the river, and day or night, it made no difference.

It was well past dark, with the moon coming up, a thin gold sliver, when

Paine began to worry. "We've not missed it?" It seemed as if they had been underway for some time, but Robley had never been that far down the river before.

"We ain't missed it," Kinney said. "Misser Lessard said the long pier north of St. Philip. We ain't missed it."

Daniel Lessard had helped with every step. He arranged the dockyard, located Kinney and Brown, put Robley in contact with the foundry that cast the ram. He had put Paine in the way of heavy guns. All that was needed now was to pick them up.

Another fifteen minutes and Paine could see lights on the high bank to the north, where the river made a dogleg turn, and Kinney rang up slow ahead. "There it is," he said, nodding his head toward the dark window, but Robley could see nothing, so he simply nodded.

Kinney spun the big wheel, rang full astern, spun the wheel again, rang stop. He leaned out of the wheelhouse, called, "Git them goddamned dock lines ashore, you hear?" to someone below, and then with a bump the *Yazoo River* was there.

Where, Paine was not sure.

Kinney turned to Paine, working the tobacco in his jaw. "Here we are, Misser Paine. Long pier north of Fort St. Philip. Whatever business you got here, I ain't got no part of it, hear? You go ashore, do what you want. Me, I stay here."

Paine glared at the man, unsure of what he was implying. They were here to complete a transaction set up by Lessard, and Paine could not imagine there was anything illegitimate about it. So he said nothing, stepped out of the wheelhouse and over the gangplank the crew had set over the side.

It was dark where they had landed, and Paine had to wonder how Kinney had found the place, never mind bringing the *Yazoo River* alongside. He could hear the sound of a million insects carried on the humid air, along with the saline smell of brackish water, the swamp smell of decay.

Thirty feet away, a lantern unshuttered, the light spilling on the hard-packed ground and the sturdy wooden pier on which Robley stood. From behind the lantern, a voice that carried nothing but accusation said, "Who's there?"

"Robley Paine."

"Who sent you?"

"Mr. Daniel Lessard, of New Orleans."

Quiet for a moment, then, "Come on over here."

Robley stepped forward, trying to see the man who spoke, but he was holding the lantern in such a way that no light fell on him. Then, when

Robley was no more than ten feet away, the man raised the lantern, let the light reveal him. A stout man, stout in the way of men who did physical labor, several inches shorter than Paine. He wore a Confederate uniform that did not fit him well, hugging his midriff too tight. The butt of a pistol showed from his holster. Another man stood a few feet behind him, a rifle conspicuous in his hands.

"Who are you?" Paine asked. It occurred to him that Lessard had never told him whom he was to meet.

"You don't ask no question. You got money?"

"Perhaps . . ." Paine said. He was not too happy with the way this was playing out. "Do you have guns?" This greasy fellow, more of the overseer type than the soldier, did not seem to be a man in a position to be selling guns. How would a soldier get cannons to sell?

"Come on," the man said, led Robley back down the pier. At the far end, half on the road, half on the pier, stood a heavy wagon, and behind it another, the sorry-looking draft animals standing patient in the traces.

Paine followed the soldier around to the back of the wagon. The man looked at his partner, gave him a nod of the head, and the other man leaned his rifle against the wheel and climbed into the wagon. He pulled back a piece of heavy, stained canvas. Underneath, the gleaming barrel of a ten-inch Dahlgren.

"New-cast, fully rifled. Come right out of the dockyard at Norfolk," the man said, as if he was the proprietor of a store. Paine looked at the barrel, awestruck by the potential power of the thing.

"Lessard didn't say nothin' about carriages," the man said. "Carriages you got to get on your own. See here." The man led Paine to the second wagon, and once again his partner jumped in the back, pulled the cover off two six-pound smoothbores, just as Lessard had promised. Paine shook his head in wonder.

"Where did these come from?" he asked.

The greasy man exchanged a smile with his partner. "Oh, we know people. Railroad people. Things gets diverted, you understand." He was grinning.

Paine squinted at the man. The light from the lantern, held at his waist, threw deep shadows over his face, making him look even more evil. "You stole these . . ." Paine said at last. "This is Confederate property, and you stole it and now you are reselling it."

"You watch what you say, hear?" the man said. "Stole it? I'm a Confederate soldier, and you calling me a thief. . . ."

Robley Paine felt a deep loathing in his gut. *Confederate soldier?* His boys had been Confederate soldiers, not this pig. His boys were dead, killed for the Confederacy, and this filth was profiteering from the cause, the cause for which his boys died.

"See here," the greasy man said in a more conciliatory tone, "the Confederate Army gots no idea who needs what or where. We gonna lose the war, waiting for them politicians in Richmond to figure where supplies should be. So you think of me as like a private supply officer. It's my business to see gentlemen like you gets what they need to fight proper."

Paine's hand moved for his gun, a practiced move; the muscles of his arm and hand had not lost the motion from his army days, even after all those years. His palm hit the butt, his fingers wrapped around the grip, found the trigger as he pulled the weapon free, his eyes on the startled face of the greasy man who was flailing for his own weapon.

The Starr came up, right in the man's face, hammer back. The gun banged out and Robley let his arm absorb the strong, satisfying kickback. He turned, found the second man in the light of the fallen lantern, and from four feet away put a bullet neatly through his forehead.

Robley Paine looked down at the man at his feet, flung back, one arm stretched behind his head, the other still reaching for his holstered pistol.

A private supply officer. . . . "I disagree, sir," he said.

25

On Tuesday afternoon, the 27th of August, about 4 o'clock, I discovered a large fleet in sight off Hatteras. . . . On the morning of the 28th, between 8 and 9 o'clock, a heavy fire was opened from the steamers Minnesota, Wabash, Susquehanna, *and other war vessels . . . Being a fire of shells only, it might well be spoken of as a flood of shells.*

—Report of Colonel William F. Martin, 7th Regiment Infantry,
North Carolina Volunteers

The Cape Fears fired five shells from the ten-pound Parrott rifle, at maximum elevation, before they decided with absolute certainty that they could not reach the anchored Yankee fleet. Their gunfire did, however, attract the Yankees' notice, and soon shells were falling all around them, sending plumes of water as high as the boat deck as they dropped in Pamlico Sound.

Hieronymus Taylor clumped up the ladder to the wheelhouse. He was in shirtsleeves, the wet patches of sweat radiating out from under his arms and under the straps of his braces, turning his otherwise brilliant white shirt gray. In his mouth, the ubiquitous cigar. He paused, squinting around, the corners of his eyes crinkled with amusement.

Samuel Bowater, in the middle of issuing his orders to Lieutenant Harwell, paused, turned his head, as the spray from a shell, landing no more than thirty feet away, lashed across himself and the lieutenant and Taylor.

"Damn," Taylor said.

"They are getting the range on us, I perceive," Bowater said, changing the course of his orders. "Once I am away, please shift the anchorage, say, one hundred yards north. That should put us out of most of their line of sight. No need to expose ourselves to fire if we cannot return it."

"Aye, aye, sir."

"We'll keep steam up, then, Cap'n?" Taylor asked.

"I think so, Chief."

"Pity the fort can't shift one hundred yards off," Taylor said.

Fort Hatteras did not seem to be returning fire. Bowater wondered if the garrison was out of ammunition, or if the fleet was out of range. With a small garrison and an enemy pounding them mercilessly, it did not seem a very hopeful situation.

"See that there?" Taylor said, nodding south, and Bowater turned and looked.

"What?"

"Ocracoke Island. That's where Lieutenant Maynard come and ambushed Blackbeard the pirate. Cut his head right off, hung it from the bowsprit. Another case of them damned Yankees comin down here and givin grief to a good Southern boy, just lookin for his fun."

"Hmm. I'm not certain your history is entirely correct there, Chief Taylor."

"No, I . . ." A shell whistled by, passing close, and plunged into the sound right astern of *Cape Fear*. "No, I'm sure it happened right there."

"I mean about Maynard being a Yankee. Or Blackbeard being a Southerner, for that matter."

"You sure? Blackbeard spent a power of time in the South. Spent some time in Charleston, I do recall. Where you're from. Hell, he may be your great-great-granddaddy. They say he had fourteen wives."

"He most certainly . . ." Another shell came in, screaming down on the starboard side, exploding inches above the water, and Bowater's comment was drowned in the rat-tat-tat of shell fragments hitting the *Cape Fear*'s side and shrieking past their heads.

"Sir?" Ordinary Seaman Dick Merrow was standing on the wheelhouse roof, scanning around with the big telescope.

"Yes?" Bowater said, happy for a distraction from the silly conversation into which Taylor had drawn him.

"Small side-wheeler coming down sound . . . I reckon she's about three miles off."

"Let me see." Merrow handed the glass down and Bowater focused it in the direction the sailor pointed. He could see the side-wheeler, smoke belching from her stack, could see the dot of white under her bow as she drove hard. From her masthead flew a flag, and though it was blowing straight aft, it appeared to be the broad pennant of a commodore, which made Bowater smile despite himself.

"This would be Barron in *Winslow*," he said to Harwell. "Let us hope he comes with some plan for salvation."

The *Cape Fear*'s boat was lowered and Bowater climbed down to the stern sheets, with Eustis Babcock as bow man and Tanner at stroke oar. They pulled for the beach, ground up on the barrier island, splashed out, and pulled the boat up on the sand.

Bowater tramped up the beach, stopped, and looked around. Extraordinary. Shells were falling in a nonstop hail, exploding on the ramparts, within the fort, on the beach around the fort. With the sun heading toward the west, the fort and the sprays of dirt from the exploding shells were washed in an orange light. The noise was constant—the scream of the shells, the blast of exploding ordnance. And then every so often, by coincidence, there would be no firing, just silence, which was strangest of all. But it never lasted above ten seconds, and then the next shell, and the next, was hurled at the fort.

Bowater led his crew up the sloping shore. A young army lieutenant—he introduced himself as Lieutenant Evans—let them in through the thick oak door set in a rough wooden frame embedded in earthen walls. The Cape Fears huddled under the parapet with the rest of the garrison, while the lieutenant led Bowater up to the ramparts.

The Yankees were hitting the fort hard. With a relatively calm sea, and anchored ships firing on a fixed target, it was not too difficult for the invaders to hone their aim until nearly every one of their shells found its mark.

Bowater walked through the storm of iron, amazed at the amount of ordnance dropping on the fort, amazed that he had not yet been blown away. He moved with a strange calm, as if he was encased in ice.

He was not afraid, despite the shelling, despite the fact that any rational person would be terrified, cowering under whatever might offer some protection. It was a phenomenon he had experienced before. It was what they called bravery under fire, but he knew it had nothing to do with bravery. It was more a trick that the mind played on itself, a turning off of the machinery of fear, in the face of insupportable terror.

When he thought of it, he imagined a Stephenson link and reversing lever, the long iron bar that shifted an engine from forward to reverse. But in his mind the link shifted from fear to fight. The real courage, Bowater knew, was in getting yourself to the place where your mind could shut off.

Bowater mused on these things as he followed Lieutenant Evans up the rough wooden stairs, past craters of brown dirt where the shells had landed, past guns that stared silent and impotent out at the Union fleet.

Fort Hatteras was no marvel of engineering. It was mostly wood-frame, dirt-filled walls, the work of slaves who had been ferried out to the low island to throw up some defense against the inevitable arrival of the Yankees. Albemarle Sound was the gateway to the rivers that ran deep into Confederate country, and Pamlico Sound served as a base for privateers to race out and snatch up Yankee prizes as they labored around Cape Hatteras. Hatteras Inlet was too important for the Yankees to leave alone.

"Colonel?" Lieutenant Evans stopped and addressed an officer, sitting on the top of a small barrel and slumped against the earthen wall of the fort, one arm resting on the top of the parapet. "Colonel Martin, this is . . ."

"Captain Samuel Bowater, Confederate States Navy, sir, at your service."

Martin looked from the lieutenant to Bowater, his head turning slowly from one to the other, as if it was a great weight that needed to build momentum. His eyes looked sunken and his face pale. Colonel Martin was very tired.

"Captain," he said and made to stand, but Bowater said, "Please, sir, don't stand on my account," and Martin, without protest, remained seated.

"It has not been a good day for us, Captain," Martin said, staring over the low wall at the Union ships. "The firing has gone on like this since daybreak. We were forced to abandon Fort Clark this afternoon. No ammunition for the guns, Union troops landing on the beach . . . spiked the guns as best we could. Had to use nails, didn't even have proper spikes. Got most of the boys over here, but we still didn't have enough to man the guns proper."

Bowater nodded. It was a hopeless situation that Martin found himself in, and he had done what he could.

"Shelling's slackened," Lieutenant Evans noted.

Bowater and Martin looked around, as if they could see the absence of shells. The lieutenant was right. The artillery was coming in sporadically now, shells exploding once a minute, perhaps, or less, the fall of shot tapering off like the rain at the end of a quick-moving squall.

"It's getting a bit dark for naval gunnery," Bowater noted. The fleet was getting underway; some of the ships had already moved out to sea, where they could spend the night away from the beach and the guns of Hatteras.

"Well, it is some relief to see the Yankee navy is not immune to the laws of nature," Martin said. "They are damn near immune to everything else. Hardly a shell has missed, and nothing we could do but take cover and endure it. I don't know what more we can do."

Bowater nodded and looked out at the anchored fleet, the big men-of-war washed in the evening light. They mounted nine-, ten-, and eleven-inch guns that could easily hurl shells from a distance that the fort's eclectic artillery could never match. If they so chose, they could batter Fort Hatteras until it was indistinguishable from the sand dunes on which it sat. Samuel felt a bit of Martin's despair play over him.

Damn, he thought, *I am too damned late.* . . . And then he corrected that notion. The moment that the Union navy sailed for Hatteras, it was too damned late.

"Sir," said Bowater, "I do believe Commodore Barron, who is in command of naval forces here in the sound, is underway and will arrive in an hour or so. Perhaps he has news of reinforcement."

Martin seemed to brighten at that, just a bit. "Perhaps. Lieutenant Evans, please send word to the commodore that I would like a conference with him, at the earliest possible convenience."

"Yes sir," the lieutenant said, and he saluted and hurried off.

The shelling tapered away and then stopped as the evening settled down on the ocean and the tortured sands of Hatteras Island. Bowater sat on the parapet, looked out over the water, at his old navy, looked down the length of Hatteras Island, his old flag now flying over Fort Clark. The few stands of trees on the island looked like black patches on gray as the day faded to night, and lights like low-lying stars began to appear on the distant ships. Colonel Martin slept where he sat, his breathing sometimes rhythmic, sometimes labored.

It was full dark when Commodore Barron arrived, tramping up the wooden steps, led by Lieutenant Evans, who brought a lantern with him, and trailed by three other men, who turned out to be Colonel Bradford, colonel of artillery and engineers and chief of ordnance of North Carolina, and Lieutenants Murdaugh and Sharp, C.S. Navy.

Barron was a trim and energetic man, with thick white hair swept back over his head. Bowater guessed him to be in his sixties. They had crossed paths on a few occasions during their time in the old navy. He knew that Barron had entered the United States Navy on the first day of the year 1812, had been aboard the *Brandywine* when she conveyed General Lafayette to France in 1825.

"Commodore Barron," Martin was saying, and it seemed a great effort for him to speak. "Our fort is armed with naval guns, as you can see, and my men are strangers to such ordnance, and I am played out, sir, I will freely admit it. Allow me to formally request that you take command here, Commodore, and do what you can."

Barron made some grunting noise, looked up at the string of lights on the water where the fleet lay at anchor. He could refuse. He was a naval commander; forts were not his affair. He would put himself in the way of no glory by accepting responsibility for an effort that was certainly bound for failure. But for all that, Barron said, "I will accept command, sir, and do what I am able."

Colonel Martin's relief was evident, and he said nothing as Barron began to issue orders. "Captain Bowater, what have you brought down with you?"

"We have powder in barrels, sir, shell for the Columbiad and for the other guns, fuses, round shot, and some cartridges. We have not yet landed any of it, not knowing the state of things here."

Barron looked around the fort, which, with the moon now rising, was all dark shadows and deep blue light. He pointed to the gun that looked out over Pamlico Sound. "No point in leaving that there. Yankees aren't going to pass through the inlet till they've beaten us into the sand. We'll shift that gun around so it can do us some good. Bowater, detail some of your men to get the ordnance you brought ashore, and whoever is left, get them on shifting that gun. Lieutenant Murdaugh, Sharp, same for you. We'll take whatever men your ships can spare. We'll fill out the gun crews with navy men. We have to make every effort, be ready for them when they open up on us at first light."

Bowater returned to the *Cape Fear*, issued his orders, led his detail back to the fort. They joined with the others in the onerous task of creating a new gun emplacement and shifting tons of guns and carriages so that every available weapon was bearing on the Yankee fleet.

Barron was relentless. He drove the men hard and expected as much from the officers, and he got it. Sweating in the cool night, grunting, shouting, cussing, they hauled the big gun from its former position, used levers and block and tackle, staging and brute force to wrestle it to the newly created artillery platforms, one hundred feet away.

Two hours before dawn the men were stood down, allowed to sleep on the dirt parapets around the guns to which they were assigned. They dropped as if they had been drugged, and were not easily stirred when the first streaks of light appeared over the ocean, and the bells of the Yankee fleet rang out, two bells in the morning watch, 5:00 a.m.

They stood, cussed, staggered about, scratched and stretched. They gulped what passed for coffee, ate the porridge served out from the big cast-iron pot.

The men were still eating when signal flags broke out at the masthead of the flagship *Minnesota* and Barron, watching through a long telescope, announced, "That's 'Prepare to engage and follow my motions.' "

Bowater nodded. He was standing thirty feet away at the thirty-two-pounder smoothbore that he and the Cape Fears were manning.

Prepare to engage. . . . It seemed there must be something they should do to prepare the fort for the coming onslaught. But there was nothing. Every gun that would bear was manned, loaded, run out. There was nothing that they could do now but wait.

Ruffin Tanner sat on the dirt parapet, looked out over the water, and Bowater looked at his face in profile, the morning light falling on him. "Tanner?"

The sailor turned. "Yessah?"

"Have we met before?"

"Yessah. I was the one steerin' the boat when we fought that Yankee side-wheeler," he said, but seeing that Bowater was not in a joking mood added, "And I think I seen you once, up to the dockyard in New York, oh, five years back. But we didn't talk, sir."

Bowater nodded. "I suppose not," he said, but still there was something about Tanner's face, some vague recognition, almost like that fleeting sensation of having experienced a place before, but more solid than that, more real.

The morning was quiet, just the sound of the surf on the beach and the scream of the sea birds, and soon the distant clank of chain coming aboard, as steam windlasses hauled up the Yankee fleet's anchors.

It took the Union fleet an hour to get underway, and another hour to close with the fort. It was eight o'clock, the day already hot under the brilliant sun, when *Susquehanna*, leading the big ships, opened up. The shell whistled through the air with a sound that, once heard, was perfectly familiar. It landed on the beach, one hundred feet away, exploded in a spray of sand.

"Here they come, boys!" Commodore Barron shouted from where he stood on the parapet. "Get ready to fire on my word."

Bowater watched the ships, felt the sweat on his palms, the crackling of electricity in his fingers, the jerky, excited motion in his limbs, the churning in his stomach. They were under fire now, and he wanted nothing more than to run and duck under the parapet. It was grit time, and all he could do was to stand there and fight it until his mind was merciful enough to shut down that instinct for self-preservation.

Another shot from *Susquehanna*, and then *Wabash*, both shells falling short as the Union gunners worked to get their range again. And still Barron stood unmoving on the parapet and did not give the order to return fire, as certain as was Samuel that Hatteras's guns would not reach.

One by one the big ships paraded past, then backed their engines and dropped anchor. Together they made a movable fortress with seventy big guns bearing on the fort, against the three guns with which the fort could fire back.

Soon they were all firing, all the Yankee guns, the rain of shells coming in again, the burst of dirt and sand marching closer and closer to Fort Hatteras as the gunners adjusted aim from their stable platforms.

"Let 'em have it, boys!" Barron shouted and hopped down from the parapet as the Confederate gunners cheered. Bowater felt exuberant as he leaned over the barrel of his gun and sighted down its length; he felt charged and ready and all trace of fear was gone now. He yelled with the others, despite himself, yelled to let off the tension like a relief valve on a boiler.

He stepped back, pulled the lock cord taut. No need to adjust the lay of the gun; they had been fiddling with it obsessively for half an hour, waiting for the order to fire. The old thirty-two-pounder was aimed square at the high black side of the steam frigate *Wabash*, once the command of Samuel Barron. Bowater stepped back and jerked the cord, and the gun blasted off with a deafening roar, flung itself back against the breeching.

Bowater kept his eyes on *Wabash*, hoping to see splinters fly, but instead he saw a spout of water where his shot fell three hundred feet short.

"Another pound of power in the charge, Tanner," he instructed, as he stepped over to the breech, twisted the elevation screw to raise the muzzle another few inches. He looked at the screw. Not much travel left. That had better do.

"Look, sir!" Tanner pointed over the parapet and Bowater followed his arm. *Cumberland* was underway, standing into the line of battle under a reefed fore course, topsails and topgallants, with no ugly plume of smoke belching out amidships. She was the only pure sailing vessel there, on either side.

Bowater shook his head. "Lovely." But she was an anachronism, a ship from another time, from Lafayette's age, and not the present. One had only to look at the Union fleet and the manner in which they moved onshore and off, oblivious to the state of wind and tide, to see that the days of the sailing ship were over, rail though the likes of Samuel Bowater might. He watched the stately, silent progress of the sailing man-of-war and felt a soft kind of a sadness come over him.

And then the first of the Union shells to find the parapet exploded, shook the earthworks on which Bowater stood, pelted him with dirt, and romantic notions fled.

"Run out!" he shouted, and the heavy gun was hauled up to the wall, Johnny St. Laurent and Nat St. Clair, landsmen Francis Pinette, Harper

Rawson, and Bayard Quayle, Ordinary Seaman Dick Merrow, Cape Fears all, hauling on the gun tackles.

Bowater leaned over the barrel, called for the handspike until the gun was pointed again at *Wabash*'s midships, stood back, and fired. And once again, a spout of water for their efforts.

Boom, boom, the shells were coming in regular now, marching up the beach, landing on the parapets and the grounds contained within the fort. Bowater guessed that for every Union shell that dropped short, six hit the fort. He heard another gun, from the north, and when he looked in that direction he could see that Fort Clark was opening up on them as well, their own guns now loaded with Yankee shells and turned on them.

Oh, dear God. . . .

A shell hit near enough that the flying dirt stung him in the face, made him flinch, but his men did not hesitate in their swabbing, loading, running out. Bowater twisted the elevation screw until it would turn no more. The gun was pointed as high as it would go, the barrel stuffed with all the powder it would bear.

Run out, aim, fire. A white spout of water, in perfect line with *Wabash*. Two hundred more feet and they would have smashed the heavy ball right through her side. But there was no physical way to coax another two hundred feet from the gun.

"Cease fire! Cease fire!" Barron shouted, the exasperation as clear as the words, and the sound in the fort of men working guns died away, and the only sound left, and it filled the air, was the whistle of shells, the explosion of shells, the flying earth, and the screams of the men whose luck had run out.

Samuel turned toward Number 8 gun, mounted on a naval carriage alongside his own. It was commanded by Lieutenant Murdaugh of the *Winslow*. Bowater met Murdaugh's eye, and the lieutenant frowned in dismay, shook his head, and Bowater nodded his agreement.

And then Murdaugh and the gun and the men around it and the parapet seemed to be ripped apart in a blast of dirt and noise and brilliant light and screaming fragments of metal. Bowater saw the sky and the earthen wall spin past him, heard men screaming and metal screaming and a ringing in his ears like the note of a huge bell, sustained for an impossibly long time.

He hit the dirt with a jarring blow that knocked the wind from him, and for a second all he could do was thrash around, gasping, wide-eyed, thoughtless of anything but getting air into his lungs.

And then he caught his breath, pulled a deep lungful of air into his chest. He felt a burning pain in his leg and arm and shoulder, isolated points of hurt amid the general ache. He could hardly hear through the ringing in his head, and what he could hear was more and more shells dropping on the fort, exploding around him, a percussion section gone mad, and, under that sound, the men shouting and running were like the orchestra's other instruments, fighting to be heard.

He pushed himself up on his arms, struggled to achieve a sitting position. Strong hands grabbed his shoulders, and he looked up to see Tanner and St. Laurent easing him up. They leaned him against the wall, and Tanner pulled roughly at the buttons of his coat. Bowater was too shaken to speak.

He looked over Tanner's head. Number 8 gun was pointing skyward at a crazy angle, its carriage smashed. The bloody, distorted corpse of one of the gun crew lay sprawled over the rough boards of the gun platform. Lieutenant Murdaugh, with whom Bowater had just a second before been silently commiserating, was leaning against the gun, his right arm a horrible, bloody, mangled wreck. White bone jutted out from the torn fabric of his sleeve and the arm lay on his lap at an unnatural angle, and Murdaugh, silent, just stared, as if he was unsure of what he was looking at.

"This ain't too bad, sir, I don't reckon," Tanner said, looking at the bleeding gash in Bowater's arm and shoulder. Bowater turned his head, looked at the blood and the shredded shirt. One of the best shirts to be had in all Charleston, and now it was a rag.

Samuel swallowed, summoned the energy to speak. "Leg . . ." he said and Tanner looked down.

"Oh, damn," the sailor said. He pulled his knife, slit the pants. A pool of blood spilled out from the pant leg. The wound swam in front of Bowater's eyes. He was reminded of fresh butchered meat. He closed his eyes, leaned his head back, breathed hard. He gritted his teeth as Tanner's hands, rough but sure, lifted his thigh and passed bandages around the deep laceration.

Through the din of the shells and the ringing in his ear he heard Barron's voice, ever in command, issuing unequivocal orders. He opened his eyes. Lieutenant Murdaugh was lying on his back and men were attending to his shattered arm, and more men were swarming around the other injured gunners. There were men enough to tend to the wounded, with the Union fleet beyond the range of the guns and the gun crews idle.

"Sharp, get Murdaugh back to the *Winslow*, get Dr. Greenhow to attend to him." Barron turned to Bowater, standing over him, and Bowater had the impression of a stern father looking down on his young son. "Captain Bowater, how are you?"

"I'll live, sir, I should think." Some of the sense which the shell had knocked from his head was coming back, the reality of the fort and the shelling and the silent Confederate guns resolving again.

"Good. Get your men to bear you back to your ship. Get steam up and get the hell out of here."

"Get . . . out?"

"Yes, Captain, get out. Another hour and I'm going to surrender the fort. No reason to lose your ship as well."

Bowater nodded. Of course. Barron was not making a bad choice. There was no choice at all.

26

We came with the Moses family . . . with a wounded soldier they were taking care of. They averred we had fifteen thousand such as he (i.e., wounded, sick, and sore) in Virginia.

—Mary Boykin Chesnut

*J*onathan Paine spent two weeks washing back and forth in a tide of grief and agony, guilt and shame. His dreams were filled with battle and grim death and Nathaniel and Robley, his days filled with an all but unbearable agony in a leg that was no longer there.

Captain Sally Tompkins ministered to him, fed him, saw that he was comfortable, as she did for all the boys in her growing hospital. Bobby, assigned to that room, tended to Jonathan every day. During the clearheaded times, Bobby was someone with whom to speak, when Jonathan felt like speaking, and during the other times Bobby was a ghost, just another ghost that haunted Jonathan's fevered sleep.

Two weeks, and then the fevers passed and the pain subsided into something that could be endured, even while awake, and Jonathan's mind cleared to the point where it began to formulate questions.

"Hey, Bobby . . ."

Bobby was washing and dressing the stump of Jonathan's leg, which terminated just above where his knee had once been. That morning the doctor had been by, had sniffed the stump, said something about "laudable pus," which was apparently a good sign. Jonathan did not understand how the doctor or Bobby or anyone could stand to look at the hideous thing.

"Yeah?"

"What all happened, anyway?"

Bobby paused, looked up from the stump. "What happened wid what?"

"The Battle of Manassas. What happened? We win?"

Bobby smiled and shook his head. "You serious?"

"Yeah."

"You don't know?"

"No."

"Well, damn! I'd say you gots to be the last person in all these Confederate States don't know that! Yeah, we won. We whipped them Yankees good, whipped 'em like dogs."

Jonathan nodded. This was good news. His last image of the battle, the waves of blue-clad soldiers coming up the hill, had not been an encouraging one. He realized that he had, for all that time, harbored a vague idea that the Confederate Army had been badly beaten, though he had never given it any real thought. The pain, and the memory of how he had led Nathaniel to his death, had occupied all of his conscious mind.

"So is that it, then?"

"What?"

"The war. Is the war over?"

"War over?" Bobby seemed more incredulous than before. "No, da war ain't over. What'd give you a notion like that?"

"Before . . . folks used to say that one big battle would settle the thing."

"Well, folks was wrong. It ain't over. Them Yankees ran like rabbits, sure, clear back to Washington, D.C. And now they safe up there and folks reckon it's jest a matter of time afore they come south and we gots to do it all again. That's if the Southern boys don't march north and whip 'em good and for all before dey gets the chance."

Jonathan nodded. "You know . . ." he said, and for the first time his mind wound its way back to the days before Manassas, ". . . we used to think there would just be the one battle. We used to be scared to death we'd miss it, have nothing to tell. I recall how we used to say if only we could lose an arm or a leg or such, go home with an empty sleeve to show the girls . . ."

"Well," Bobby said brightly, "now you surely can do that."

"Sure enough."

Go home. . . . The words burned and tore like the bullets that had grazed and lacerated him. *Go home . . .* He had no home now. His parents would never wish to see him again, after the horrible thing he had done. And even if they did welcome him back, out of Christian charity, he could not face them. He could not face Robley, who would come home a hero and would, for the rest of his life, hold Jonathan in smoldering contempt for disobeying his orders and getting their brother killed.

So what was there for him? He had no money, beyond the family fortune, which was lost to him now. He had no skills, no way to earn a living, even if he was not a cripple. A beggar on the streets, one of these broken, wretched creatures such as he had seen by the docks in New Orleans, that was all that was left to him. He felt the tears well up. Paine Plantation and all its goodness gone, like being denied heaven. He was lost among strangers who, when he first came to them, did not even know his name.

That thought sent his mind wandering down another road. If no one in the 33rd Virginia knew who he was, then no word of his fate would have been sent to his parents.

No doubt Robley would have written, told them about how he had led Nathaniel off to the fighting. He hoped someone had found the note he had stuffed in Nathaniel's jacket and honored the request. He hoped Nathaniel's body was at peace in his native Mississippi soil, in the family plot surrounded by the iron fence, overlooking the Yazoo River.

But they would not know what had become of the third Paine boy.

Most likely they do not care. . . .

Still, he had to send word. Loathe him or not, his parents should know what had become of their youngest son.

"Bobby?" Bobby was putting the last wraps of a fresh bandage on Jonathan's stump.

"Yeah?"

"Is there someone here can write a letter for me? I don't think my arm's up to the task, yet."

"Sure enough," Bobby said. He eased the stump of Jonathan's leg back down on the bed, pulled the sheet over him. He walked off and came back ten minutes later leading one of the white nurses, whose name was Douglas, and carrying a pencil and a few sheets of white paper and a Bible for a desk.

"All right, go on ahead," Douglas said, settling back onto the stool by the bed.

"Very well . . ." Jonathan was surprised Douglas had his letters. He had never struck Jonathan as the brightest of fellows. "Dear Mother and Father . . . By now you will have heard of what became of . . ."

"Hold on there, hold on, partner . . . I'm a little out of practice here." Douglas's pencil moved with deliberate strokes. ". . . 'and Father' . . . all right, what all's next?"

"By now you will have heard . . ." Jonathan continued on, slowly pronouncing each word, as if he was talking to someone just learning English. Douglas's lack of skill was no great handicap; there was not much Jonathan had to say to his parents in any event.

When he was done, Douglas handed the letter to Jonathan and Jonathan held it up and read it.

Deer Mother and Father,

By now yo will have heerd from Robley and he will have told yo the sirkemstanses . . .

Jonathan wished that Douglas's pride had allowed him to ask for the spelling of some words.

. . . sirkemstanses of Natanyals deth. All I can say is I am sufering as yo are, and alweys will. I am woonded but am likly to liv. I jest thot it my duty to tell yo that.

Your son,

Jonontan

Jonathan nodded his head. "Thank you, Douglas, that is fine. If you could fold it and seal it and perhaps you can help me address it, that should do. There's money for postage in . . . my knapsack. Bobby, is my knapsack here?"

"Yessuh. It's under you bed, along with what's left of yer uniform and such."

"Is that a fact? Can you help me sit up?"

Bobby gave Jonathan his hand, helped pull him up to a sitting position, stuffed pillows behind his back. The bright room whirled around Jonathan's head and the dream state washed over him and he thought he would pass out. He closed his eyes, sat very still, and soon it passed and slowly he opened his eyes again.

Bobby was standing beside him. "You all right, Missuh Jon'tin?" In his hands, Jonathan's knapsack, a battered square canvas bag coated with rubberized paint, which was glossy black when it was new, but now was dusty and muted and cracked.

"Yes, yes . . . may I see that?"

"Sure t'ing." Bobby handed the sack to Jonathan, and Jonathan took it as if it was an ancient relic, which it was, to some degree. A relic of a life now gone.

He fumbled with the buckles and managed to get them undone and flipped the flap open. The contents were just as he had last seen them, more than a month before, though it seemed much longer than that. His toothbrush, his hairbrush, deck of cards, extra shirt. His copy of *The Soldier's Guide: A Complete Manual and Drill Book*, with which he would sneak off to a private place and study, more intently than he had ever studied a lesson as a boy. He never wanted the others to see him at it, to think that he lacked any confidence in his soldiering ability.

He shook his head as he thought of it. *What did any of us know of soldiering? Why did I think anyone would believe I knew any more than they did? Why did I care?*

There was the Bible his mother had put in his knapsack without his knowledge, as she had in Nathaniel and Robley's as well. He picked it up, ran his fingers over the embossed gold cross on the black leather cover. He flipped the book open. The delicate pages fluttered by, stopped at a piece of paper inserted between them.

Jonathan pulled the paper out and unfolded it, unsure what it was. He read the words.

Dear Mother,

I am sorry that I have not written more, as I know I should, but they drill us here, night and day, and with guard duty and inspections and such it is hard to find a minute. We are still at Camp Walker, waiting for something to happen. We are all well but many here have the measles. Robley thinks that

It ended there. Jonathan recalled now. He had finally sat down to write it when a fellow from Company C had told him that a cockfight was about to commence at the south end of the camp. He had tucked his mother's letter away, put off writing to his mother to watch a couple of damned chickens killing each other.

Why not? There was plenty of time to write. That was how he had felt. Plenty of time. He was just a boy, and so were his brothers. They had their whole lives.

He leaned his head back on the pillow and felt the warm tears roll down his cheek, and a moment later he heard Bobby walking softly away.

27

If I have erred in all this matter, it is an error of judgment; the whole affair came upon me so suddenly that no time was left for reflection, but called for immediate action and decision.

—Captain John Pope, USS *Richmond*, to Flag Officer William W. McKean,
Commanding Gulf Blockading Squadron

*I*t was October, but it was sweltering in the captain's sleeping cabin of the U.S. steam sloop *Richmond*, and Captain John Pope could not sleep.

He lay on top of his blankets, still wearing shirt and pants, but with buttons undone. He considered getting undressed, could think of no logical reason why he should not, but he made no effort to do so. He felt too vulnerable undressed, too unready. In that place, the Mississippi River, the Head of the Passes, within the boundaries of the Confederacy, he felt vulnerable enough even in full uniform. He did not need to compound his disquiet.

He sat up with a frustrated sigh, swung his legs over the edge of his bunk. From beyond the great cabin he could hear the sound of shovels in coal, the tramp of men carrying coal bags up the gangways, the muted thump of the schooner tied alongside. The watch on deck was taking on coal, though, from the sound of it, with no great enthusiasm.

Pope ran his hands through his muttonchop whiskers, over his bald head, and down the fringe of hair that encircled his head like the grass skirts the South Sea Islanders were supposed to wear. Overhead the ship's bell rang, *clang-clang, clang-clang, clang-clang, clang*. Three-thirty a.m. He sighed again and stood, pushed open the door of the sleeping cabin and stepped into the wide expanse of the great cabin.

It was cooler there, by several degrees. The few lanterns burning cast a warm light on the polished oak paneling. The sundry brass handles and knobs and hinges glowed dull. A lovely place, fine as any drawing room in any mansion in New York or Philadelphia, if not quite so large. But it was big enough for any reasonable man, and Honest John Pope was certainly that.

He grabbed his trousers, which were slipping down his legs, pulled them up, fastened the buttons, and then buttoned his shirt. He considered pulling on his coat and hat but could not bear the thought. *Seven bells in the night watch, no need to be so damned formal*, he thought. He wished his steward was awake so he could snap at him. It was a sickly climate in the Mississippi Delta, and it made him irritable.

He mounted the ladder that ran from the great cabin directly up to the quarterdeck above and stepped through the scuttle and into the black night. He closed the scuttle door and stood motionless for some time, letting his eyes adjust. The great cabin had been dimly lit, but even that was enough light to render him quite blind on deck.

Damned dark tonight. . . .

The wind was out of the north and blowing a steady five knots or more. It wrapped itself around Pope's heavy, sweating frame, gave him a chill, raised goose flesh on his arms, but it felt good. Over the sound of the shovels and the rattle of coal spilling down the chutes and into the bunkers, Pope could hear the swamp sounds, the thousands of frogs and insects and Lord knew what else, chirping away at their nightly choir.

He advanced to the rail, which he could just barely see, and only because the inboard bulwark was painted white, and leaned against it, staring out into the night. The wind carried on it the brackish smell of the river and the smell of rotting vegetation and smoke from some far-off place. He looked east to west but could see nothing beyond blackness from the shore.

The Head of the Passes, the two-mile-wide convergence of the channels leading in and out of the Mississippi. New Orleans was second only to New York in the amount of shipping that flowed through. Or it had been, anyway, before the Rebels set about destroying themselves. It was staggering, the amount of river traffic that had crossed that spot of water on which the *Richmond* was anchored.

But now, with the blockade having brought waterborne commerce to a halt, on that black, moonless, hazy night they might as well have been riding at anchor halfway between the earth and the moon, for all the activity that Pope could see. It was unsettling, that wild, foreign delta all around, harboring snakes and alligators and diseases unknown to a Northern man like Captain John Pope.

"Lieutenant . . ." Pope made his way forward, to where he could see the outline of Lieutenant James Whitfield, silhouetted against the tiny bit of light thrown off by the lanterns on the schooner and down in the hold. Suddenly Pope did not care to be alone on his own quarterdeck.

"Captain?" Whitfield turned, and his voice sounded a bit startled, and Pope wondered if the swamp and the darkness were unnerving the luff the way they were him. "Is everything all right, sir?"

"Fine, fine. Can't sleep. This damned heat down here. Man isn't born to the climate, he can hardly tolerate it."

"Yes, sir. And it's not even the heat so much as the humidity."

"You're right, Lieutenant. I hadn't even considered that."

Pope looked forward, down the length of the deck, which was just becoming dimly visible as his eyes adjusted to the dark. The *Richmond* was a big ship, 225 feet long, forty-two and a half feet on the beam, displacing 2,700 tons. A sister ship to *Hartford*, and heavily armed. She drew over seventeen feet aft, which made her less than ideal for river work, but Pope was not going to complain. He had worked hard, had spent many years in the navy, to rise to command of such a ship.

And *Richmond*, at least, was a steamer, her twin screws driven by two horizontal condensing engines, sixty-two-inch cylinders, each with a thirty-four-inch stroke. The other ships of his squadron, the *Preble* and the *Vincennes*, were entirely sail-driven, making them considerably less adequate for river work.

The thought of the other ships under his command made Pope lift his eyes from his own deck and the line of big, black nine-inch smoothbore Dahlgrens like sleeping bears at their gunports, and look outboard again.

Off their port side and downriver was the sloop *Vincennes*. Pope could see the dull loom of a lantern on her deck. She was one hundred feet shorter than *Richmond* and less than a third of the bigger ship's tonnage, but with her four eight-inch guns and fourteen thirty-two-pounders, she was still a powerful man-of-war. Certainly more ship than the Rebels could muster.

Pope turned, looked forward, past the *Richmond*'s starboard bow, though in the dark he could hardly see even the black shrouds angling up the *Richmond*'s masts. He moved his head a bit, to make sure his vision was not blocked by the rigging. One hundred and fifty yards upriver he could see a single pinprick of light, a lantern on the deck of the sailing sloop

Preble. Just the one light, and the enveloping darkness, and the sound of frogs and insects and the lap of water around the hull.

"Well . . ." Pope began, then stopped. He had heard a noise. A shout? He cocked his head.

Then another shout, loud, an order being issued, but he could not make it out. The furious beat of a drum, feet pounding on the deck. Pope looked around, trying to find the source, but he saw only Lieutenant Whitfield, who met him with eyes wide.

The sound was muted, far off, but insistent, something happening.

"The *Preble!*" Whitfield shouted, pointed forward. A red light was moving aloft with awkward jerks as it was hoisted to the peak of the gaff.

"They're beating to quarters!" Pope shouted. He looked around his own ship, unsure what to do. The night had the quality of an anxious dream. What was happening aboard *Preble?* Pope felt the first inkling of panic creep over him. He had once considered posting picket boats up-river—why had he not?

"Beat to quarters, sir?" Whitfield asked, and he sounded no more composed than Pope felt.

"Yes, yes, Luff, beat to quarters!"

"Beat to quarters!" Whitfield shouted, and suddenly the deck was alive with racing men, men pouring up from the hatches, running to the big, sleeping guns, casting off breeching, men racing to their battle stations even before the startled drummer was able to find his sticks.

"Port side, Lieutenant! A steamer, port side!" a voice shouted up from the waist, and Whitfield and Pope both rushed across the quarterdeck, hit the rail, peered outboard and forward.

The night seemed to be exploding around them, from dead still to wild bedlam. Pope turned to a midshipman who had appeared beside him. "Pass the word to light off the boilers! I want steam up, now!"

"Aye, aye, sir!"

"Sir!" Whitfield pointed out into the dark. A white, undulating wave, the bow wake of a vessel, closing fast, and above it, great roiling clouds of black smoke, visible even against the night's sky. But between them, no vessel that Pope could see.

"What the hell . . ." Pope muttered, then shouted, "Gunners, run out!" and the air was filled with the rumble of twenty big guns hauled bodily up to the bulwark, and then, again from the waist, a voice shouted, "It's the ram! It's the ram!" and Pope sucked in his breath and stood frozen on his spot of deck.

The ram! Reports of this terrible machine had been floating down from New Orleans for months, so many and so differing that Pope had ceased giving them any credence.

The ironclad ram!

"She's gonna hit!" came another voice from forward. Pope leaned over the rail. The white bow wave was frothing wildly, the smoke coming thick from the stack, rolling down over the quarterdeck, and with it the peculiar puffing sound of a high-pressure engine. He could see her hull now, unlike anything he had ever seen floating and built by man. A round black hump, a whale back, a stack like a column standing straight up.

"Dear God . . ."

And then the ram hit, drove itself into the *Richmond*'s side, making the ship shudder as if from a hammer blow. The fasts holding the coal schooner parted with the impact, bang, bang, like a series of rifle shots, and the schooner pulled from the *Richmond*'s side, swirled away downstream.

They could hear the working of the ram's engines, a terrible screeching and banging. As if something terrible was happening within the iron turtle.

Lieutenant Whitfield turned to another midshipman. "Find the carpenter, tell him to check the damage, report back!"

"Port side!" Pope shouted. "Fire!" Wildly, in ragged order, the Dahlgrens blasted away, throwing great long arms of red-and-yellow flame into the dark delta night. Pope saw part of the ram's stack blown away, but there was no chance of hitting the low-lying vessel itself.

The gun crews fell to reloading, and Pope did not stop them. His eyes were glued to the ram, the horrible ram, backing away, slipping down the side, coming aft, coming for him. It gleamed in the light of the muzzle flashes and battle lanterns, a terrible black monster, and Pope felt frozen to the deck, unable to move. He could not take his eyes from the beast.

"Sir?" Whitfield shouted, and Pope finally looked away, shook his head. He felt sick to his stomach, utterly unable to think. They were surrounded here, wrapped up by the wicked delta and all its horrors, caught in Rebel territory, and under attack.

Room! He needed room! Sea room! "Slip the cable!" Pope shouted. "Get a red lantern aloft!" His hand reached for the grip of his sword, where it rested during times of such crisis, but his sword was not there, and he recalled that he was in shirtsleeves.

Damn . . . He thought of dashing below, but could not leave the deck. He had the sensation that the *Richmond* was listing to port. *Has that damned ram sunk us?* he wondered, and the panic began to creep in like the imaginary water rising in the hold.

"Sir?" Pope's steward appeared in front of him, holding his coat and hat and sword and pistol. Without a word Pope slipped his arms into the sleeves of the coat, fastened the buttons, put his cap on his head, allowed the steward to buckle the sword around his waist. He experienced a new sense of calm as he donned the uniform and felt the weight of the weapon hanging from the belt.

"Sir?" Whitfield was in front of him. "It appears that *Vincennes* has slipped her cables. I see her getting her fore topsail set."

"Very good." From the foredeck came a great rumbling sound as *Richmond*'s own anchor chain was let go, rattling through the hawsepipe, making the entire ship vibrate as the chain disappeared into the brackish water of the delta.

Pope whirled around suddenly, remembering the ram. She was a few hundred yards away, downstream, lurking, waiting her chance, it would seem, a black shape on the near-black water. Pope fastened his eyes on the iron hump as the river lapped around the thing, and he loathed it, loathed it more than any thing or any person he had ever encountered.

Then the noise of the running chain ended, and then a final splash as the bitter end hit the river, and then nothing.

"Slow ahead!" Pope shouted, and the master, stationed by the helm, rang up slow ahead and Pope hoped there was steam enough to move the vessel against the stream. He could see the smoke coming in puffs from the tall stack amidships. The firemen were probably throwing oil or resin or whatever on the coal to get it to light off fast. He could feel the turn of the screws, the *Richmond* inching ahead.

"Keep firing on that damned ram, Mr. Whitfield!" Pope shouted, and the port battery began to blast away again in a frenetic, frantic way, like a blinded man lashing out with his fists.

From upriver, more heavy guns, as *Preble* joined in, the round shot from her port-side thirty-two-pounders churning up the river. They were making a deadly crossfire over the ram, iron and flame hurling out over the water, but Pope could not tell if they were having any effect whatsoever.

He could sense the *Richmond* turning, her head swinging downriver. He looked forward, saw the *Preble*, now on the port bow, now on the starboard as the *Richmond* slewed around.

He turned to the helmsman, a curse on his lips, but the man at the wheel was turning it hard, trying to correct. "She don't answer, Captain!" the helmsman shouted, bracing for the old man's wrath.

Not enough steam! The boilers did not have enough steam pressure to give the ship headway, and the rudder would not bite. The *Richmond* was out of control, turning sideways to the current, helpless, with the ram out there in the night.

"Goddamn it!" Pope shouted out loud. It was chaos and he could not make it slow down. Everything seemed to be exploding at once; he could not think.

"There goes the ram, sir!" Whitfield shouted, and Pope's heart leaped, thinking the terrible thing was coming for them again, but it was not. Pope followed the luff's pointed finger. The ram was steaming upriver, making for *Preble*'s port bow, away from the *Richmond* and the *Vincennes*, which was already standing into South West Pass.

"Damnation . . ." It did not appear as if *Preble* had slipped her cable. "Get underway, damn it!" Pope shouted, uselessly.

From the back of the turtle, a light sputtered, a tiny yellow light, and a second later a red rocket arched up and away, making a bold slash of color against the night sky.

"What in hell is that for?" Pope wondered out loud.

"Sir." The carpenter was in front of him now, saluting. "Ram stove in three planks, sir, about two feet below the waterline. Hole's about five inches, I'd say. Pumps can keep up, sir, till I've plugged it some."

"Very good. Carry on." At last, some good news, and Pope felt reason to hope that he might pull this off, that his career might not be destroyed by the attack of the infernal machine.

"Sir, look here!" It was Whitfield again. Pope was coming to loathe the sound of his voice. The luff was looking upriver. Three bright spots of light, low down on the water; they looked like three evenly spaced bonfires.

What the hell now? Pope snatched up his telescope, fixed one of the bright spots in the lens. Flames leaped and danced across his vision, illuminating the water around the raft on which the fire burned.

"Fire raft! Dear God, they are sending fire rafts!" Pope shouted. They were sending fire rafts and he was broadside to the current, out of control, with barely the steam pressure to turn the screws. And suddenly, where there had been optimism, there was now the vision of his squadron engulfed in flames.

Robley Paine stood in the wheelhouse of the *Yazoo River*, watched the fireworks on the water. The ship trembled underfoot as the twin paddle wheels turned slowly astern, holding the riverboat in place against the current.

First to attack, per the plan, had been the ram, the *Manassas*. Formerly the towboat *Enoch Train*, she was now an ironclad, her topsides a rounded hump of half-submerged narrow iron plate, about 150 feet long, thirty feet wide. On her bow was mounted a pointed iron ram, and from her rounded foredeck a sixty-four-pound Dahlgren peered forward.

She was an amazing engine of war, and the more Robley looked on her, the more he wanted such a thing for himself. The Union navy would not be beaten by ships of equal size. The Confederacy was unable to build ships of equal size. The Yankees must be defeated by technological advances, such as the *Manassas*, the first ironclad built in the Western Hemisphere.

Spread out over the river, upstream of the Yankees, was the Confederate fleet. The flagship was the 830-ton steam sloop *McRae*, armed with a sixty-four-pounder mounted on a pivot, four eight-inch Columbiads, and a rifled twenty-four-pounder. With her navy crew and complement of Confederate States Marines, she was run with an efficiency that made Robley despair for the sloppy, disinterested civilian mercenaries he was forced to ship.

The rest of the fleet: the five-hundred-ton side-wheel steamer *Calhoun*, with one twenty-four-pounder and two eighteen-pounder Dahlgren guns; the steamer *Ivy*, just a bit smaller than *Calhoun*, with one eight-inch rifle; the steamers *Jackson* and *Tuscarora*; and the cutter *Pickens*, with an eight-inch Columbiad and four twenty-four-pound carronades. An odd hodgepodge of former merchant ships and assorted guns, but it was the waterborne defense of the southern Mississippi. Between the five of them they did not carry the firepower of even the *Richmond* alone. But they had surprise, and they had the ram, and those seemed to be working well.

One of the Yankee ships was blazing away, and Paine guessed it was the *Richmond* and that the ram had done her business.

Then another ship, closer to the Confederate fleet, began to fire the guns of her broadside. The two ships were lashing out. There was a desperate, panicked quality to their firing. Robley nodded his head as he watched the fusillade. *Good, good.* . . . At last, something was being done. The filthy invaders who had murdered his sons were paying for it now.

Mr. Kinney, the pilot, was showing no sign of approval. He had in fact been muttering curses under his breath for some time. But now, as the second ship opened fire, he became more vocal.

"I signed on here to pilot a boat, I did not sign on to get my damn ass blown off. Didn't say nothing about no goddamned battle with no Yankee fleet."

"You signed aboard a river defense ship, I made no secret about it," Paine said, never taking his eyes from the action downriver. It was the most cathartic thing he had experienced since the death of his boys. He could not wait to fling himself into the fight, to fly at the head of the serpent, guns blazing.

They called the serpent "Scott's Anaconda." The overarching plan of Union General-in-Chief Winfield Scott—wrap a blockade of ships around the coastline of the Confederate States, drive down the Ohio and

Mississippi rivers, from the United States to the Gulf, until the coils of the thing completely encircled the new Southern nation, and then squeeze.

They laughed at this "Anaconda Plan," North and South. But Robley Paine was not so sure, and he was not laughing.

"River defense ain't the same as attacking no damned men-of-war," Kinney pointed out, though what he thought river defense was Robley could not guess.

Paine turned at last from the window, regarded the pilot in the dim light of the binnacle. Kinney's jaw was working furiously at a plug of tobacco. The light glinted on a line of spittle on his beard. He met Paine's eyes with defiance.

"Are you a coward, sir?" Paine asked. "Or merely a Union sympathizer?"

"I ain't none of them, you son of a bitch, and don't say it again. But I'm a civilian, hear? I ain't no navy man, and neither are you."

"I can't disagree. You certainly are not 'no navy man.' But tonight you had best play the part. You have been well paid to do so."

Paine turned back to watch the fight on the river, but Kinney troubled him. They all did, all the white trash he had collected aboard the *Yazoo River*. His initial concern was right, he was sure of it now. Any able-bodied Southern man worth a damn was already in the army or navy, or working at some job vital to the war effort. And everyone else was a shirker, a coward, a craven dog.

The serpent haunted him. It haunted his days, kept him thrashing in a cold sweat at night. He thought of little else. The money he doled out every day for food and coal and wages and maintenance made no impression on him. The letter from his attorney in Yazoo City, telling him in the gentlest terms of the death of his wife, Katherine, failed to move him beyond a certain sadness, and even a bit of envy, at the way her agony was over, while his continued on.

It would be his turn soon. The promise of eternity with his Katherine and his boys was the only point of hope left to him. He would die battling the serpent.

A rocket shot up into the sky, a long streak of red coming right up from the midst of the Union ships.

"There's *Manassas*'s signal!" Robley said, with an excitement unmatched in the *Yazoo River*'s wheelhouse. Thirty yards away, right ahead of the *Yazoo River*'s bow, the nearest fire raft sputtered and flickered as the combustible material heaped on board was lit off. The flames took hold at last, creeping along the edge of the oil-soaked logs and bales of cotton, then climbed up the heap, engulfed the raft—a fifty-foot-long derelict river barge—throwing brilliant light out one hundred feet in every direction. Robley could see the light of the flames dancing on the *Yazoo River*'s bow and the bales of cotton stacked around her deck as armor.

There were three rafts, strung out across the river and attached to one another by a long chain. Controlling the string of rafts at one end was the towboat *Tuscarora* and at the other end the *Watson*.

"Them tugs ain't never gonna keep them rafts under control," Kinney said with a subtle, gloating tone. Paine did not reply.

"Slow ahead, Mr. Kinney. We'll keep just behind the string of rafts."

Kinney hesitated, just long enough to show he followed orders under duress, then reached up and rang the bell. A moment later the big paddle wheels stopped, then slowly started up again, forward this time, barely pushing the *Yazoo River* ahead, while Kinney let the current do the rest.

Paine could see the few lights onshore slipping by, could see the out-of-control Yankee ships lit up in the light of the fire raft, and he felt satisfied. It had all gone exactly to plan, and his only disappointment—and it was a small one—was that the *Richmond* was not now heeling over and sinking fast from the injury doled out by the ram.

"Rafts are out of control," Kinney observed, then stuffed a wad of tobacco in his mouth, ripped off a chunk. The towboats had apparently cast the fire rafts off, and now the current had them, swirling them around, pushing them toward the bank.

Damn . . . Paine thought, but Kinney was right. The unwieldy things were too much for the towboats to control, and the river current could not be relied upon to sweep them down on the fleet.

"Keep her going ahead, Mr. Kinney," Paine said, watching the chaotic flight of the Union ships down South West Pass. They were still blazing away with their great guns, the shells whistling around, the fire rafts and the broadsides lighting the river and the dark night in a macabre, bellicose show.

"You want to steam into *that*?" Kinney asked.

"Keep her going ahead, Mr. Kinney," Robley said again. He rested his hand on the butt of the .44 Starr. He would drive the *Yazoo River* into battle even if he had to fight his own people to do it.

28

*I immediately commenced an investigation for the purpose of learning all the cir-
cumstances of the affair [Pope's retreat], and am sorry to be obliged to say that
the more I hear and learn of the facts the more disgraceful does it appear.*

—Flag Officer William W. McKean, Commanding Gulf Blockading Squadron,
to Hon. Gideon Welles, Secretary of the Navy

The current was sweeping the USS *Richmond* sideways down the
South West Pass, and there was nothing Captain John Pope could do.

They were in a world of warm, humid blackness. The only lights visible beyond the confines of the sloop were the taffrail lights of *Vincennes*
and *Preble*, downriver from *Richmond*, and the three great fire rafts above,
massive trunks of flame, sweeping down on her, no more than two hundred yards away. There was nothing Captain Pope could do but hope the
Richmond drifted faster than the rafts.

He tapped his fingers on the cap rail for as long as he could stand it,
then turned to the master, said, "Port your helm and come full ahead."

"Port your helm!" the master shouted.

"Port your helm!" the helmsman replied and spun the wheel over.
"Helm's aport!"

The master rang the engine-room bell, and Pope could picture the
engineer down among his pipes and boilers and shafts, cursing at the
captain, who once again rang for steam he did not have. But there was
only the jingle of the bell in reply, the low vibration underfoot as the
throttle was opened and the propeller began to churn water.

They stood fixed in place on the quarterdeck, waiting to see what the big ship would do. The screw made a gurgling sound as it roiled the water under the counter, but it did no good. They did not have the steam to turn the ship's bow upriver. The Father of Waters swept them along through the night.

Pope began to compose his report. *The* Vincennes *and the* Preble *proceeded downriver, while I maintained a position broadside to the enemy in order to cover their retreat . . .*

No, no, no . . . who in hell would believe that? They'll ask the pilot for a report, he'll say we could not get our head around. . . .

"Captain?" The pilot, Wilcox, stepped up, one hand on the rail, looking out into the dark.

"Yes?" Pope said. His voice sounded guilty in his own ears.

"We're getting mighty close to the right-hand shore. I'm afraid we'll be aground directly."

"I've tried to get her head around but it won't answer."

"Perhaps if we go astern on the engines we can work off?"

"Perhaps. Ring full astern."

The bell was rung, the engine room jingled in response, and moments later came the jerky, screeching, clanging, hissing noise of two big steam engines turning in reverse, engines that were anything but reliable, particularly in reversing.

The fire rafts, drifting fast downstream, threw the occasional cast of light over the shoreline, illuminating the scrubby trees and dense marsh grass. The engines protested. All eyes on the *Richmond*'s quarterdeck were fixed on the shore, what they could see of the shore, in the fire rafts' light. The minutes ground by and the big ship swept downstream and the engines turned with the cacophony of something going terribly wrong, until, foot by foot, they succeeded in pulling the *Richmond* backward into midstream.

"Perhaps we have steam enough now to turn her head upstream?" Pope asked hopefully, but Wilcox shook his head.

"We don't have room here to turn, sir," he said. "We'll have to wait until we are down by Pilot Town. Should be room enough there."

For a moment Pope said nothing. *Continue on like this?* They were floating sideways down South West Pass, with fire rafts in pursuit and enemy gunboats behind them. There was an unsettled, nightmare quality to the whole thing. But what could he do?

"Very well, Mr. Wilcox, we'll try again at Pilot Town."

Robley Paine looked at his watch. Five twenty-three a.m. An hour and forty minutes after the initial attack. The ram and the fire rafts had scared hell out of the Yankee fleet, sent them skedaddling, but they did not seem to have done more than that.

The rafts had grounded on the western bank and were now burning themselves out. The ram had limped off after her initial attack. Lieutenant Warley, who had command of her, was no coward, Robley knew that, so Robley had to imagine that she was disabled in some way. The engines, he knew, were hardly reliable.

But that was fine. They had done their work, the *Manassas* and the fire rafts. Now was the moment for the gunboats to plunge ahead, to blast holes in the fleeing Yankees, to make sure the Anaconda understood it was not the only dangerous beast in those waters.

"First light," Paine observed. In the east, a band of gray was glowing dull near the horizon. Robley could see the bow of the *Yazoo River* and the bulwark of cotton bales bathed in the dull, blue-gray dawn. Beyond that, the Confederate fleet and the Mississippi River were still lost in gloom.

Kinney grunted, said nothing.

They had been waiting. In the dark, it was hard to know what was happening downriver. The fire rafts cast their wide circles of light, which reflected on the black hulls of the panicked Yankee ships. The mosquito fleet was able to follow behind the rafts, keep an eye on the enemy, until at last the fire rafts grounded out and the Yankees were swallowed up by the darkness down South West Pass.

The head of South West Pass loomed like a cave, and they dared not enter, because there was no way to know what was in there. Perhaps nothing. Perhaps the Yankees had fled clear to the Gulf. Or perhaps the Confederates would meet up with three heavy men-of-war, anchored, spring lines rigged, heavy broadsides waiting for the gunboats.

That possibility gave Robley Paine no pause. He would have gladly steamed ahead, attacked whatever he found, thrown himself and his ship at the Yankees, offered all up to the memory of his sons.

But Hollins was not so inclined, and Hollins was in command, so they waited. Paine stepped out of the wheelhouse, paced the hurricane deck, glanced up now and again. It was growing light fast. He could see the shapes of the other vessels of the squadron, to the east and west of him, shadowy vessels with plumes of dark smoke coming from their stacks. He could see the far banks of the river now, dark against the lighter sky.

He could not see the Yankee fleet. They were gone, driven from the Head of the Passes.

The sight of that empty water, where just two hours before a powerful enemy squadron had anchored, spread joy through Robley Paine like the light of the rising sun.

And then, hard on the heels of that good feeling, fear.

Hollins would never give up the fight as won? he thought.

He looked up at the *Calhoun*, Hollins's flagship, wondering how he might determine the flag officer's intentions. He saw a belch of black smoke pour from her stack, saw the water churn white as her side wheels began to turn and the five-hundred-ton steamer began to inch ahead, the eighteen-pounder rifle on her bow pointing the way, like the nose of a hunting dog on its quarry's scent.

Paine stepped eagerly back into the wheelhouse. "Half ahead, Mr. Kinney," he said. He had been puttering about the river long enough that he was beginning to feel comfortable in his role of captain. "Keep pace with the flagship."

Kinney grunted. *"Flagship . . ."* he muttered in a derisive tone, and it did sound a bit foolish, said that way, but Robley did not care. They were plunging ahead, down South West Pass, chasing after the fleeing enemy, and that was all he needed to know.

Kinney rang the requisite bells, and down in the engine room Mr. Brown jingled back. The *Yazoo River* seemed to come awake. The big stern wheels began to turn and the bobbing, erratic motion of a ship stopped in the stream—underway but not making way, in the parlance of the mariners—changed into the steady rhythm of a ship steaming ahead.

Paine looked east and west. The others, the *McRae*, the *Ivy*, the *Tuscarora*, the *Calhoun*, and the *Jackson*, they were all gathering way, heading downriver in line abreast. Here was the bold advance, the waterborne cavalry charge. The fleet looked to Robley like a line of mounted knights, rolling forward.

And on this charge cried "God for Henry, England, and St. George!" Robley Paine was not happy—happiness was a thing from his past—but he was at least satisfied.

They eased their throttles open, Commodore Hollins's squadron, and churned the brown water white and under parallel trails of black smoke steamed the fifteen miles down the South West Pass to the sea.

Kinney fidgeted, chewed hard, spit on the deck and the sides of the spittoon. "Don't know what in hell y'all think you'll do, if you come on them Yankees . . ." he muttered, and Paine was not sure if he was looking for an answer, but he gave it to him anyway.

"We will go to battle with them, Mr. Kinney. We will fire on them and endeavor to do as much damage as we can."

" 'Fire on them . . .' " Kinney muttered. Paine did not answer again.

The fleet was capable of eight knots over the ground, with the boost they got from the current, and the marshy shore seemed to fly past. The sun broke the horizon and turned the sky a light, hazy blue. Two columns of smoke rose from stacks somewhere down the South West Pass, and the Confederate fleet was closing fast.

"Come left, you stupid son of a bitch," Kinney growled at the helmsman, who turned the big wheel a few spokes. The pilot was becoming visibly more nervous with each mile made good and turning his fear into abuse.

"Steady, Mr. Kinney," Robley said, hand resting on the butt of the Starr. "Don't lose your nerve yet. The iron has not yet begun to fly."

" 'Iron fly . . .' Ain't what I goddamned signed on for! How many time I got to tell you? You never said nothing about fighting no Yankees."

"Mr. Kinney . . ." Robley pulled the Starr from his holster, spun the cylinder to see that each chamber was loaded. "Please be assured that you have much more to fear from me than you do from the Yankees."

Kinney looked from the pistol to Robley's face. He turned, stared out the window at the water under the bow. " 'More to fear from me . . .' Crazy son of a bitch . . ." he said, lower this time, low enough so as not to invite response, which Robley did not provide.

South West Pass was all but straight, a boulevard of water through the delta, and soon the Yankees were in sight, clustered around the bar, one ship on the Gulf side and two still inland of the muddy shallows. The largest of them, the steamer, was pouring smoke, which made a sharp angle as it roiled from her stack and blew away to the south. The ships were motionless, as far as Robley could tell, the steamer broadside to the river, the smaller one with her stern pointed right at the Confederate fleet.

Robley picked up his field glasses, swept the ships on the bar. "They are aground," he said. "I do believe they are aground." It was too much to hope for. The enemy stranded in the mud, right under his bow gun.

He stepped from the wheelhouse and forward, to the edge of the hurricane deck. Below him, the gun crew sat on the deck, leaning against the cotton wall, or stood gazing forward at the distant Yankee ships.

"Gun crew!" Paine called, and the men looked up. "The Yankees are aground! Load and run out!"

The men went through the drill, silent and fast, just as they had done so many times dockside in New Orleans.

"Fire!" Paine shouted out, much louder than necessary. The gunner pulled the lanyard and the ten-inch Dahlgren fired with its great throaty roar, flung itself back against the breeching. Paine could see the shell make a black streak in the light blue sky as it sailed toward the Yankees, shrieked through the rigging, and plunged into the water beyond the bar.

"Lower! Lower! You're firing right over their damned heads!"

On either side of the *Yazoo River* the other gunboats were opening up, firing their heterogeneous collection of artillery, an eighteen-pounder

Dahlgren, an eight-inch rifle, an eight-inch Columbiad; they all fired as fast as they could, pouring shot and shells into the stranded Yankees, hitting back in a way that the Confederate Navy had yet to do, after seven months of war.

The *Yazoo River's* bow gun fired again, but Robley could not see where the shot fell.

And then the Yankees replied, the big steamer, firing her broadside guns at the mosquito fleet. The muzzle flashes looked dull and insignificant in the sunlight. A series of water spouts shot up from the river, two hundred yards short.

"Kinney," Paine called, stamping back into the wheelhouse. "Slow ahead. We'll creep up to point-blank range."

"Son of a bitch! We ain't in range of them Yankees here. We should stay here."

"If we 'ain't' in range, then we should get closer. But see here, I don't need you just to ring a bell. I can ring the bell myself, and that will save me the cost of paying you your wages." Robley reached for the bell cord, but Kinney was there, moving across the wheelhouse with two quick steps, snatching the cord practically from Robley's hand.

"All right, all right, goddamn it . . . slow ahead!"

Robley nodded, left the wheelhouse, took his place on the front edge of the hurricane deck, where his view of the enemy and his own gun crew was unimpeded.

He looked right and left. The line of pugnacious gunboats blasting away, from the 830-ton, bark-rigged side-wheel steamer *McRae* to the fast river tug *Jackson*, made his heart sing. Fighting back, that was the thing. Was there anything more terrifying then sitting idly by, while the serpent wrapped itself around his new nation?

The turn of the *Yazoo River's* stern wheels began to slow, the creaking note lowering in pitch, and the boat's forward motion was checked. Paine whirled around, caught Kinney's eye, and Kinney looked quickly away.

Paine crashed the wheelhouse door open as he burst in. "I give the goddamned orders! I say when to go, and when to stop, is that clear, Mr. Kinney?"

"I reckoned it was time to stop. We getting damned close to being in range of them Yankees." The shot from the steamer's smoothbores was beginning to fall just a hundred yards or so beyond the bow, and some even falling around the boat.

"Slow ahead, Mr. Kinney," he said, soft, and once again Kinney reached for the bell cord and tugged.

I will have to shoot that coward before we are through here . . . Robley thought. He held Kinney fixed with his eyes until he felt the stern wheels begin to turn again, felt the *Yazoo River*'s momentum build. She was out ahead of the others now, but that was where Robley wished to be.

Then, from deep below them, from somewhere near the bottom of the ship, a terrible wrenching sound of metal. Something snapped with a sharp report. The starboard paddle wheel stopped instantly, as if the hand of God had been laid on it, and the boat began to slew.

"Meet her, meet her!" Robley said to the helmsman. They had gone through this drill before. The helmsman spun the wheel, compensating for the off-center thrust of the single paddle wheel.

"Well, shit, reckon that's it," Kinney said with a hopeful tone.

"We have two engines, Mr. Kinney, and we have lost only one."

"You don't mean to keep on here?"

"Slow ahead, Mr. Kinney. I shall signal you when to stop."

Paine walked out onto the hurricane deck. *Am I mad?* he wondered. He knew it was a terrible risk he was taking, driving the *Yazoo River* forward until she was within range of the Yankee's guns. He could not muster even the slightest concern for his own welfare, or for that of his ship and men, which he considered no more than an extension of his own will.

Madness!

But can I be mad, if I understand that what I am doing is madness?

The bow gun fired again, and he traced the trajectory right to the big steamer's hull. They were not above five hundred yards away, easy for their big rifle, and well within range of the Yankee's broadsides.

The round shot was falling all around them now, kicking up spray that fell on the *Yazoo River*'s deck, but the gun crew was performing well, loading and firing, seemingly as oblivious to the shot as was Robley. He was proud of his crew. Were it not for Kinney, all would be perfect.

From the Yankee ship, a muzzle flash, a foreshortened black streak, and Robley watched as it slashed toward them, screaming by his ear, leaving a jagged hole in the wheelhouse astern. He was standing in the hail of iron, leaning into it, as if it was a cool rain at the end of a hot, humid summer day. He was revived by the gunfire, refreshed by the proximity of death.

You sulfurous and mind-tempting flames, vault couriers of oak-cleaving thunderbolts, singe my white head!

A Yankee ball came in on a flat trajectory, plowed down the hurricane-deck rail on the port side, snapping off the stanchions like a scythe through wheat.

Now what are the chances of that? Robley wondered as he looked at the unusual site, the twisted metal posts and rails, hanging at odd angles.

He turned to the wheelhouse, held up his hand for Kinney to ring slow astern, which would hold them on that spot in the river.

From the Yankees came a new note, a sharper crack, not like the flat, dull boom of the smoothbores. Robley brought his field glasses up to his eyes. The smaller ship, the one run bow first on the mud, had moved two guns aft and run them out of the after gunports. These were not smoothbores but rifles, Robley could tell by the higher pitch of their report.

As he watched through the binoculars, the port gun fired, the crack of the gun and the scream of the shell whirling past coming one on top of another. Exploding shells. This was dangerous stuff, much more so than the round shot. Robley felt exhilarated.

The air was filled with the sound of battle, a continuous rolling fire from the Rebels and the Yankees, the buzz of round shot passing close, the scream of the rifle shells, the occasional crash of shot hitting the *Yazoo River*, taking off bits of the superstructure, chipping away at the wheelhouse. And under it all, the hiss and puff and clank of the single engine, driving the single paddle wheel slow astern. And then it stopped.

Paine was aware first of the change in sound, some part of the tapestry of battle noise gone. And then the *Yazoo River* began to turn, to drift downstream, spinning broadside to the Yankee fleet, the current sweeping her into the deadly broadsides.

What . . . what . . . Robley was not sure what to do. They had never lost both engines. They had never been under fire.

Kinney appeared on the deck below, running forward with the awkward run of a short, stocky man. "Let the anchor go! Let the anchor go!" he shouted as he ran. Someone let fly the ring stopper and the anchor plunged down into the water and the chain raced out after it.

From the hurricane deck, Robley watched the action take place but did not know what to say. He turned and looked at the wheelhouse, but there were no answers there. *How in hell did Kinney get down there so fast? Why didn't he just call down from the wheelhouse?*

The chain ran its length and stopped. The anchor grabbed hold and the *Yazoo River* spun around, bow upstream, hanging at the end of the chain, the Yankee shot falling all around and passing over her deckhouse to fall in the water beyond.

Now what in hell? Robley was at a loss. Robley, who was starting to feel his oats as ship's captain, realized he had no idea of what to do.

Boots on the ladder and Kinney appeared on the hurricane deck, and behind him, Brown, the engineer, filthy, sweat-soaked, face streaked with coal dust, eyes red, watery, and utterly disingenuous.

"What is it, Brown?" Robley demanded.

"Lost the rod on the starboard engine. Now it's a bearing on the port crankshaft. It's a fucking mess."

Robley shifted his gaze to Kinney, who met his eyes with defiance. "You best signal one of them towboats to come over here, give us a tow upriver. Fight's over, Cap'n."

For a long moment no one moved, no one spoke. Paine, Kinney, and Brown, they stood facing one another.

Paine broke the silence. "I know you two." He pointed to Kinney, put his finger right in the pilot's face. "You are cock"—he moved his finger to Brown— "and you are bull, and you are both goddamned liars. Go get that engine going."

"I done told you, the bearing . . ."

"Don't you lie to me, you son of a whore!" Robley could feel his control slipping, the emotional dam he had built up to keep the rage contained crumbling. If it collapsed he did not know what would happen, and he was afraid. The dam was the thing that stopped him from simply roaming the streets and shooting down every son of a bitch who did not deserve to breathe, but still did, while his boys did not.

Brown took a step back. He looked frightened, frightened of what he saw in Robley's eyes. "Cap'n, I ain't . . ."

Kinney's hand came out of his coat, a five-inch double-barrel Remington derringer in his meaty palm. "You're a goddamned lunatic, Paine, and all your money don't change that. Keep yer hand away from that pistol."

Robley reached across his chest, put his hand on the butt of the Starr.

"I said keep yer hand away from that pistol," Kinney repeated, his voice rising in pitch. Paine pulled the heavy weapon loose, swung it up.

"Put the goddamned gun down!" Kinney screamed, but Kinney had made a big mistake, because he was a coward, and cared for nothing but his own skin, and was as terrified of hanging for murder as he was of being killed by Yankees, while Robley Paine did not care a whit about any of it.

Robley pointed the Starr at Kinney's trembling hand and just when Kinney realized he had better shoot, because Paine was beyond being threatened, Paine pulled the trigger. The Starr roared, and the .44 bullet hit the derringer with a sharp pinging sound, blew the gun and three of Kinney's fingers clean off the hurricane deck.

Robley swung the smoking barrel around so that it was pointing right in Brown's face, not six inches from the tip of his nose. "Slow ahead, Mr. Brown," he said, just loud enough to be heard over Kinney's shrieks of pain and terror and the rumble of the big guns.

Six minutes later, with the shells and round shot still falling like hail around them, the *Yazoo River*'s port paddle wheel began its slow revolutions, the anchor chain was brought in, and the battered gunboat crept back to her place in the line of battle.

Captain Pope stamped the deck, slammed his fist down on the taffrail in frustration. They were taking fire from the Rebels, and none of the *Richmond*'s guns had the range to hit back. The dammed gunboats were too far away, save for the one stern-wheeler that had come so aggravatingly close. They had watched her slew around and come to anchor, and for a happy moment thought they had shot out her engines or paddle wheel. But fifteen minutes later she was underway again.

He felt like an idiot. He did not think this would reflect well on him.

He turned to the signal quartermaster. "Make a signal to the ships beyond the bar—'Get underway.' "

" 'Get underway,' aye, aye, sir," he said and turned to the bag of signal flags at his feet.

Damn, damn, damn . . . Pope thought. *We have to do something. What?*

The signal flag snapped up the halyard, fluttered there for five minutes, and then came down again. The scream of the Rebel shells, the boom of the port-side Dahlgrens, continued unabated, the smoke hanging thick on the deck before swirling away south.

"Sir?" Whitfield was crossing the deck, a worried look on his face.

Now what?

"Yes, Luff?"

"Captain Handy's coming aboard, sir," he reported with a puzzled tone. "He has his men with him."

"His . . . men? You mean his crew?"

"It would seem so, sir."

"What, has he . . . has he abandoned his ship?"

"Ahhh . . ." Whitfield hesitated, but happily for the executive officer Captain Handy himself appeared through the gangway. He was wearing his dark blue frock coat and cap. Around his waist was wrapped the *Vincennes*'s battle ensign, great folds of red, white, and blue cloth.

"What the devil . . . ?" Pope said as Handy climbed the quarterdeck ladder, stopped, and saluted.

"I am here, sir," Handy reported, his voice near shouting to be heard over the din of the *Richmond*'s guns and the Rebel artillery.

"I can see you are here, Captain," Pope replied, shouting and sputtering. "What the devil are you doing here?"

"Your signal, sir. I am obeying your signal."

"What signal?"

Handy, looking suddenly unsure, glanced around. "Your signal you just ran up. 'Abandon ship.' "

"I didn't signal 'Abandon ship.' I signaled for the vessel beyond the bar to get underway."

"Oh. Well, sir, my signal quartermaster saw the signal flag, blue, white, blue, as did I. We interpreted that as signal number one, 'Abandon ship.' "

"Sir, I do not know what you saw, or thought you saw, but I most certainly did not signal for you to abandon ship!"

"I am sorry, sir," Handy shouted. "But I most certainly . . ."

Pope shook his head, cut him off in mid-argument. "Captain, I will not debate this point with you! Get your men and get back to your ship and defend it from the enemy in a manner such as is expected of you."

Handy shut his mouth, straightened a bit, held Pope's eyes, but made no effort to move. "The thing of it is, sir, before we abandoned her, so the Rebels would not take possession, sir, we set slow match to the power magazine."

Pope's mouth fell open of its own accord. "You . . . what?"

"Slow match, sir. The Rebels . . . she's going to blow any minute, sir."

For two hours, the mosquito fleet pounded the Yankees, and then they were done. Ammunition all but gone, coal bunkers running low, crews near the point of exhaustion, they put up their helms and stoked their fires to provide steam for their tired engines to stem the flood of South West Pass, steaming upriver to New Orleans.

Robley Paine sat on the stool in the *Yazoo River*'s wheelhouse, holding the Starr cradled in his lap. Five feet in front on him, sobbing and cursing, Captain Kinney piloted the boat north. Paine was confident that Kinney would do a proper job, because Kinney was aware that the next bullet would part his skull, the moment the *Yazoo River* touched bottom. It seemed a wonderful motivator.

Paine did not like the sound of the single engine. It was growing noticeably louder, crashing and clanging. But he had confidence that Brown would keep her turning as long as she was physically able to turn. The motivational techniques he used on the pilot seemed to work even better with the engineer.

Robley Paine felt satisfied. It had been a good expedition. It could have been better, could have been much better—they could have sunk or taken or crippled one of the Yankees—but still it had been good.

It was his first experience with naval warfare, and he had learned a great deal. It would take weeks, he knew, to sort out and codify all the lessons from those twenty hours. But two of them stood out, big and bold, like headlines in a newspaper, two things he required to wage proper war.

He needed a crew of proper navy men.

He needed an ironclad.

The *Vincennes* did not blow up. A quarter gunner, who had been ordered to light the slow match, a man with more sense than the captain, understood that blowing the ship to kingdom come in the face of the mosquito fleet was absurd. He followed orders, lit the fuse, then cut the burning end off and threw it overboard.

He did not, however, tell anyone. For two hours Pope and Handy and the combined crew of two ships stood anxiously waiting for the massive shock of the sloop's powder magazine to blow. When at last it was clear that the ship was not going to explode, Pope ordered the Vincenneses back aboard.

For the next ten hours they worked to get the ships off the mud and over the bar to open water, where they belonged. They set kedge anchors and heaved, they passed towlines to the small screw steamer *Water Witch*, and she pulled until she all but buried her stern, but it did no good. Aboard the *Vincennes* they started the water and pumped it over, threw round shot and spare anchors and finally the great guns into the river, but still they remained fast in the mud.

When darkness came they stood down. Pope sat on a quarterdeck hatch combing, his coat unbuttoned, his fringe of hair sticking out at odd angles. The deck seemed to pull at him with a force greater than gravity.

He heard shoes on the quarterdeck ladder and looked up. The midshipman of the watch approached tentatively, which further annoyed Pope.

"What is it?" the captain snapped.

"Boat from *Vincennes*, sir, brought this note." He held out a folded letter as if he was feeding a dangerous animal. Pope snatched it away, unfolded it, angled the paper so the light from the lantern behind him fell on the words.

> SIR: We are aground. We have only two guns that will bear in the direction of the enemy. Shall I remain on board after the moon goes down, with my crippled ship and worn-out men? Will you send me word what countersign my boats shall use if we pass near your ship?
>
> While we have moonlight, would it not be better to leave the ship? Shall I burn her when I leave her?
> Respectfully,
>
> Robert Handy

Good God! That son of a bitch is more eager to destroy his ship then the damned Rebels are!

"Is *Vincennes*'s boat still alongside?"

"Aye, sir. Waiting your reply, sir."

"Go fetch my steward. Tell him I need paper and pen."

Four minutes later the steward came hurrying aft, the midshipman leading the way. No one was slacking off in the old man's presence tonight.

Pope stood and wanted to groan but would not in front of his subordinates. He smoothed the paper out on the wide quarterdeck cap rail and the midshipman snatched down the lantern and held it up for the captain, maintaining a discreet distance. Pope dipped the pen and wrote:

> SIR: You say your ship is aground. It will be your duty to defend your ship up to the last moment, and not to fire her, except it be to prevent her from falling into the hands of the enemy.

He paused in his writing, looked at the note. He knew the words he wished to use in the second paragraph, but he could not write them. It was not fitting for an officer and a gentleman to write the sort of thing he was thinking. Instead, he continued in a more even tone.

> I do not think the enemy will be down tonight, but in case they do, fight them to the last.
>
> You have boats enough to save all your men. I do not approve of your leaving your ship until every effort to defend her from falling into their hands is made.
>
> Respectfully, your obedient servant,
>
> John Pope

He folded the note, handed it to the midshipman, said, "That is for Captain Handy."

The midshipman saluted, hurried away. Pope stepped across the deck, looked out over the dark water at the glowing lanterns on *Vincennes*'s deck.

. . . *Crippled ship and worn-out men . . . Shall I burn her when I leave her? Good God. . . .*

"The damned Rebels have the grit and the will to come down and attack us in paddle wheelers and towboats armored in cotton," Pope said out loud, certain that no one was near, "and that idiot Handy wants to abandon and burn a ship more powerful than the whole Rebel fleet because he is tired and stuck in the mud!"

Pope shook his head. *Dear God . . . here is why this damned war will not be over anytime soon.*

29

[A]fter twenty rounds from the Fort the ammunition became exhausted and the entire garrison, under the command of Capt. Barron, late of the United States Navy, surrendered, and were made prisoners by Butler and his vandals. . . .

—*Richmond Whig*, August 31, 1861

*S*amuel Bowater stared at the face in the mirror over the wash-basin in the master's cabin of the CSS *Cape Fear*. Thinner, more tired, lines more prominent. His facial hair shot through with considerably more gray. But overall, not too bad.

Da, da-da, da-da-da-da-daaa . . .

He smoothed his mustache and goatee and hummed the strains of Wolfgang Amadeus Mozart's Quintet in C Major. In two hours' time, he would be sitting in the cramped, drafty, not excessively clean the-ater, a block from the waterfront in Elizabeth City, a theater generally relegated to minstrel and burlesque shows, and enjoying an uncertain performance of the work as interpreted by the Norfolk and Elizabeth City Quintet.

Da, da-da, da-da-da-da-daaa . . .

Samuel did not expect great things from the Norfolk and Elizabeth City Quintet. If they could come at all close to the sound he heard in his head, he would be content.

Those reservations aside, he was eager for the performance. It had been a long, long time since he had enjoyed real music. He was so starved for the genuine article that he would catch himself turning his ear to his cabin window, actively listening to Hieronymus Taylor's violin, Moses Jones's singing. He found himself tapping his foot to the tune of "Maryland, My Maryland," waving an imaginary baton to coax out the strains of "The Leaving of Liverpool."

They were very good, Taylor and Jones, Bowater had to admit. Such a waste of talent. What a fine Don Giovanni Moses could make. With some work, Taylor could be a first violin. First violin for the Norfolk and Elizabeth City Quintet, certainly.

A blast of wind hit the *Cape Fear*, whistled around her superstructure, made her dock fasts groan. It was mid-November, cold and bleak. Hard on one's optimism, with the gales coming in off the Atlantic, churning Albemarle Sound into steep chop, gray water capped with marching rows of white horses, cold, driving rain.

They were dockside at Elizabeth City, just in from a week's patrol of the sound, running supplies down from Norfolk to the 3rd Georgia, dug in on Roanoke Island, taking long shots at the Yankees in Pamlico Sound. Uninspiring, miserable business, but Samuel was glad to be back at it. There had been moments enough during the past two months when he thought he might never step foot on shipboard again.

It was more than two months before, on August 29th, that Fort Hatteras was surrendered to the Yankees. The ten-inch shell from *Wabash* that had destroyed the fort's Number 8 gun carriage, killed one of the gun crew, shattered Lieutenant Murdaugh's arm, and knocked Flag Lieutenant Sharp galley west had nearly done for Samuel Bowater as well. He was tossed into a sea of hurt. He lost a lot of blood.

He had, besides the wounds to thigh and shoulder and arm, three broken ribs, a fractured humerus, and a mild concussion. He could not remember most of what had happened that morning at Fort Hatteras, even less of the trip back to Norfolk. He recalled some sort of shouting match between Hieronymus Taylor and the lockkeeper at the Great Dismal Swamp Canal locks, but little else.

The first sensation that he felt, once the doctor had backed off the laudanum a bit, was anxiety.

The *Cape Fear*, he was told, had been sent back to Albemarle Sound to join with the little fleet defending Roanoke Island. Roanoke sat square in the middle of the single passage between Pamlico and Albemarle Sound. It was the key to Albemarle Sound and so the key to control of the rivers that wound their way into North Carolina—the Roanoke, the Chowan, and the Pasquotank, as well as the inland passage between Elizabeth City and Norfolk.

It was inconceivable that the Yankees would not push up Pamlico

Sound, fast and in force, and capitalize on their victory at Hatteras Inlet. Indeed, it was no more than half a victory if they did not.

While Samuel had no doubts about Lieutenant Harwell's enthusiasm, he was deeply concerned about the luff's ability to command the ship in his absence. Every day Bowater asked for the news from North Carolina. And every day the news was the same. The Yankees were in possession of the inlet, the Confederates held Roanoke Island, and they all seemed content to stay where they were.

Finally he stopped asking, and contented himself with the newspapers.

Jacob, whom he had kept to aid him during his convalescence, was dispatched daily for the *Richmond Examiner* or the *Whig*, in which Bowater read, "Whose fault it may be, that the little garrison at Hatteras was so poorly provided with ammunition, we leave the proper authorities to enquire. We take it for granted that the marauders will not be permitted to stay long where they are."

Bowater smiled. *If you had stood in that rain of shells, sir, you might not take that so much for granted.*

When he could find it, Jacob also picked up the *New York Post* or *Tribune*. Samuel read the gloating headlines:

THE WAR ON THE COAST
GOOD NEWS FROM BUTLER'S FLEET
FORT HATTERAS BOMBARDED
SURRENDER OF THE REBELS
CAPTAIN BARRON AND 300 MEN TAKEN
THE TRAITORS OUT OF POWDER

He read about the panic and dismay that had seized the South in the wake of Hatteras, the first successful Union invasion of the Confederacy. From the highs of Manassas to this new low.

In Washington and points north, just the opposite reaction. Elation, renewed hope. Samuel wondered if anyone on either side still had any sense of proportion. To compare the successful shelling of an undermanned and poorly built fort by a vastly superior enemy to what the Confederate Army had done at Manassas was simply absurd. If the people of the South—or the North—allowed themselves to play at such emotional tug-of-war, they were all in for a sorry time.

Back in early September, Samuel had been confined to bed, weak, arm hurting like hell, drifting in and out of sleep. He was tossing in feverish dreams when he heard a soft voice call. "Captain Bowater?" The voice incorporated itself into his dream, a woman calling from far off, and he was running to her, but he could not seem to move, for all his flailing legs.

"Captain Bowater?" His eyes fluttered open. He looked Wendy Atkins straight in the face and could not place her.

"Captain . . . ? It's Wendy Atkins. . . ."

"Wendy Atkins . . ." Samuel said the name as the memory came back with the sound of her voice. It had been two months at least since he had seen her. He tried to picture her by the riverfront park, in paint-spattered clothing. She had annoyed him to no end, he recalled, but with all he had been through he could not recall why.

"What are you doing here?" It was all Bowater could think to say.

"I am volunteering as a nurse," she said. "Oh, I know, the height of scandal, a female nurse." She sat on the edge of his bed, leaned down, and spoke in a conspiratorial whisper. "They think we women will become too aroused, working among the men. I tell you, after all the blood and wounds and pus and worse I have seen, I am in danger of never being aroused again!"

Bowater smiled, smiled at what he understood he would have considered shockingly forward half a year before. But not now. He felt bits of his old propriety flaking off, like paint from an unprimed canvas.

"And how do you happen to be here, Captain?"

Bowater told her, in the barest terms, of Hatteras and the awful shelling, and she listened and she nodded and she did not say any of the stupid things—"Oh my . . . how dreadful . . . surely you were afraid"—that most people who had not been under fire said. Instead she just listened, which was just what Samuel Bowater wanted, though not even he himself knew it.

By midmonth, Samuel's strength was coming back, and he made a point of walking up and down the whitewashed, airy halls of the naval hospital, to the limits of his endurance. On these jaunts Wendy accompanied him, lent an arm when necessary, and sometimes they talked and sometimes they did not and it was fine either way.

The broken arm still hurt, but he could move it now, and rather than remain in bed he often sat by the big windows that looked down over the water, or strolled around the hospital grounds. Then one afternoon Wendy appeared, carrying canvas and easel and paints, all quite new.

"Are you going to paint?" Bowater asked. "I would love to watch you, if you would not mind."

"No, these are for you," Wendy said, and there was hesitancy, uncertainty, in her voice.

Insouciance . . . that is it . . . Bowater thought. He had tried to pin it down, the thing he had so disliked about Wendy Atkins. Insouciance. That was the word. An arrogant boldness.

But the insouciance was gone now, and in its place a kind of calm understanding, a maturity he would not have thought could be gained in a few months. Something had happened, and now he could hardly recall the Wendy who had so annoyed him. Nor could he entirely recall the Samuel Bowater who had been so annoyed.

"Very well, then." Bowater sighed, set the canvas up. He looked at the paints and the brushes. Something frightened him, and he did not know if it was an inability to get what was in his heart on canvas, or fear that it would all pour out, that he would make it all appear before him, and have to look on it again.

September turned to October and the cheerless days of autumn, with the cold wind tearing brown leaves from the trees, swirling them down the cobbled streets of Norfolk. Bowater, for all the pleasure he was now taking in Wendy's company—they walked together, set up their easels, painted side by side, working away for hours in companionable silence—was desperate now to get back to the *Cape Fear*. He extended his walks beyond the confines of the hospital, strolling along the waterfront, looking longingly out over the river, assessing the shipping that plowed the gray water under gray skies.

Wendy urged him not to overtax his strength, and he did not, mostly, but he pushed himself to the brink.

In mid-October he sent word that he would be rejoining the *Cape Fear*, that he would take passage to Elizabeth City and meet her there. On that very day he read with some amusement how a band of *ad hoc* Confederate gunboats had chased the mighty *Richmond* and two other men-of-war from the Head of the Passes below New Orleans. Employed an ironclad ram, first such vessel built on the American continent. The CSN stealing a march on the Yankees.

Rams . . . That ancient weapon of Athens and Rome, made obsolete with the ascendancy of sail over the oar. Now with the rise of steam, the oldest of naval weapons was voguish once more.

He read of the first of the Yankee ironclad gunboats, the *Carondelet*, sliding down the ways. He hoped she was as unreliable as this *Manassas* appeared to be.

At last the doctors pronounced him fit to leave. With great enthusiasm he packed his few belongings, dressed in the new uniform he had ordered, his third, the second of cursed gray cloth. Tailored to the same measurements as the last, but he found it hung loose on him, was ill-fitting. He ignored that, ignored the aches he still suffered, the short-windedness.

He would have ignored a missing limb to get out of the hospital and back to his command.

He said goodbye to Wendy, and it was an awkward thing, with a part of him wanting to embrace her, even kiss her, the other part quite unsure of how it was with them. In the end he gave her a hug, she gave him a sisterly peck on the cheek.

"We are in Elizabeth City quite often," he said to her, a veiled suggestion.

"I could take the train down . . ." she said.

Bowater took passage aboard the *Raleigh*, which was transporting supplies from Norfolk to Roanoke Island. He could see the *Cape Fear,* tied to the dock, a half mile away, as they steamed down the Pasquotank River, leaving the Great Dismal Swamp Canal astern.

Samuel Bowater felt a charge he had not expected, a delight at seeing his little command, as he looked her over through a pair of field glasses. She looked good. Trim, tidy, her paint freshened, the brass howitzers on the afterdeck glowing dull under the overcast skies.

"She look good, Massa Samuel," Jacob said.

"Here, have a closer look." He handed Jacob the field glasses. "Are you eager to get back to her?"

"Oh, yassuh. Hospital ain't no place for no navy men like us, suh."

The *Raleigh*'s skipper brought his boat neatly alongside the *Cape Fear.* Bowater stepped aboard his own vessel to the kind of formal greeting he would have expected Lieutenant Harwell to organize. There were bosun's calls and a sergeant's guard with rifles and lines of men at attention. It was all very stirring, but Bowater did not really notice.

It was the smell that struck him at first. The smell of the *Cape Fear*. Before, he would not have said there was such a thing, a distinct odor to his ship. But now, coming back aboard after a month and a half absence, he realized there was. Paint and coal smoke and tar and the unique smell of Johnny St. Laurent's galley—oh, how he had missed St. Laurent's cooking! They all melded together to give the boat a unique and distinct ambiance. Bowater breathed deep, happy to have that in his lungs again.

He stepped down the lines of men, drawn up to greet him. There was a genuine warmth in their welcome. Bowater was touched, and not a little surprised.

"Tanner." He stopped in front of the seaman, dressed out in his best uniform. Tanner, and some others, Bowater noticed, had embroidered "Cape Fear" on the silk bands around their caps. "I don't recall much of what happened that morning at Fort Hatteras, but I do have some memory of your tending to me. Thank you."

Tanner shrugged, hemmed, looked genuinely uncomfortable. "Whatever I could do, sir . . ." he managed to get out before Bowater released him from his discomfort, offered him a hand to shake, moved on down the line.

Hieronymus Taylor and his small engineering department were drawn up at the end of the line. Burgess, Moses Jones, Joshua Beauchamps, Nat St. Clair, and two new faces Samuel did not recognize, black men, one a big, burly fellow, the other more slight, around Bowater's height.

"Welcome back, Cap'n," Taylor said, hand outstretched. Samuel took the offered hand and shook. Taylor's clothing, his frock coat and shirt and pants, were perfectly clean, with a crispness that far exceeded even Lieutenant Harwell's. Bowater looked down the line. It was true of all of the black gang; their clothes were as clean as if they sent them out. *How do they do that?*

"Cap'n," Taylor was saying, "these here are two new members of the engineering division, hired on by permission of Lieutenant Harwell. This big fellow is Lafayette Jefferson—how's that for a patriotic name—and the little fellow is Tommy. Jest Tommy, he says. I took 'em on as coal passers."

And not just their clothes. There was a generally scrubbed appearance about their persons—none of the coal smudges and sweat stains and matted hair Bowater associated with the engine room, as if they had access to a bathtub, or a shower bath. *How do they do that?*

"Ahh," Bowater continued, "is that not an excessive number of coal passers, for one boiler?"

"Well, suh, I'm bringing ol' Moses along as fireman, see? I think he's ready for a step up in the world."

"Very well." Samuel's head was swimming. He wanted desperately to sit.

"You will forgive me, Chief . . ." he said, and making his goodbyes he headed off to the privacy of his cabin, with Jacob close behind.

Da, da-da, da-da-da-da-daaa . . . He'd been back two and a half months. His strength had returned. With the rolling deck underfoot, the ladders to negotiate two dozen times a day, and Johnny St. Laurent's cooking, he was soon nearly back to his former self.

The first week in November brought no relief to the monotony of patrolling Albemarle Sound, the *Cape Fear* now one of the mosquito fleet under the command of Flag Officer William Lynch.

From the south, reports arrived of the Union capture of Port Royal, South Carolina. Big Federal men-of-war pounding the little Confederate forts to dirt—it was a virtual reenactment of Hatteras Inlet on a somewhat larger scale. But on Albemarle Sound, there was little happening. Except a concert by the Norfolk and Elizabeth City Symphony Orchestra, and it was taking on an importance all out of proportion with its promise.

Bowater finished dressing, let Jacob help him on with his coat, pulled his cap over his eyes, and stepped out into the cold. There was the distinct smell of winter in the air, carried on the lashing wind. The *Cape Fear* thumped against her fenders, rocked hard in the short waves piling up around her hull, a lot of motion for a vessel tied to the dock. Bowater stepped down the ladder and ducked behind the deckhouse, catching a lee from the wind.

He tramped down the side deck, opened the engine-room door. The blast of heat was welcome now. He looked down the fidley. Burgess was hunched over the workbench. At the sound of the door opening he looked up.

"Chief Taylor down there, Burgess?"

"Naw. 'E's inna gaal-lay, Cap'n," Burgess said.

Bowater nodded. *What the hell did he say?* It was not worth asking him to repeat it. "Thank you, Burgess."

Down the side deck came the scrape of a violin, the first pass of the bow before tuning the instrument. The note had come from forward—they must be staging their evening concert in the warmth of the galley.

Samuel hurried along, stepped into the galley, the smell of baking bread and a simmering cheese sauce like a warm blanket. Most of the Cape Fears were seated around the place, Taylor and Moses on stools at the forward end. It was a very congenial affair, and it made Samuel sad, that such a thing could go on and he, as captain, could have no part of it.

Not that he wished to, with their crude folk ditties and dreary sentimentality.

"Cap'n, come to join us, sir?" Taylor lowered his violin from his chin and called out.

"No, Chief, I fear not. I . . . ah . . . I'm off, just now, and I wanted to tell you we'll be underway at first light, so we'll need steam up then."

"Never fear, Cap'n, the engineering division stands ever ready. Got them boys to clean the grates and the fireboxes, blew the boiler down, topped off the feed-water tanks . . . they don't get no music unless the engine room's up to snuff."

"Very good. Well, then . . ."

"Where you off to, Cap'n, if you don't mind my askin? Y'all are dressed to the nines, I mean, and it ain't often we poor navy men have a chance for such formality."

"Oh, well . . . as it happens I am off to a concert. Mozart. What they might term 'classical music.'"

"Mozart . . . his music kinda like that Bach fella's?"

"Yes, sort of. In a broad sense. You should take in some classical music, Chief Taylor. With your interest in the violin you might find it instructive."

"Well, that's damned kind of you, Cap'n." Taylor stood, set his violin back in the box. "Sorry, boys, no fiddlin tonight. I'm goin to hear 'classic music' with the Cap'n!"

"Oh, well . . ." Bowater began, over a chorus of disapproval from the men. "It's just that I don't know what to expect from this quintet. Sort of a local, amateur thing. I'd hate to subject you to something that turned out to be awful."

"Ah, it'll be all right," Taylor said, closing and latching the violin case. "Reckon if I started with the best I wouldn't have nowhere to go." He straightened, looked around the galley. "Seems a shame, though. These boys were sure looking forward to their music tonight."

"I should think so, Chief. I don't think it would be fair for you to deprive them."

"Not fair at all. All right, boys. Get your shore-goin rigs on. We all goin to listen to classical music."

"Oh . . ."

"And Cap'n, what about the darkies?"

"Well, there is generally a place in the balcony for servants to sit."

"Well, that's fine. Servants, coal passers, it don't make no difference. Go on, boys, git your shore-goin rigs on."

The galley cleared out as the men went to make their preparations for a run ashore. Hieronymus Taylor began to pull his overcoat on, and stopped. "Cap'n, I'm sorry. It just occurred to me, might be you didn't intend for all the men to come to this here shindy of yours."

"No, no, Chief, that's quite all right. I am always happy for the chance to introduce people to the beauty of fine music," Samuel said, and he knew that if he was a better man he would have meant it.

30

Every day regiments march by. [Richmond] is crowded with soldiers. These new ones are running in, fairly. They fear the war will be over before they get a sight of the fun.

—Mary Boykin Chesnut

They fitted Jonathan Paine with a prosthetic leg. They made him stand while they did it, made him endure their happy banter about his being as good as new, about how the girls were all swooning for a young soldier with an empty pant leg in his uniform. Jonathan said nothing.

They fitted the thing, took measurements, discussed adjustments. They left and came back another day and made him stand again and strapped it on. Bobby stood beside him—he might have been a tree trunk—and Bobby did not make clever jokes.

They gave him crutches and made him hobble about on the thing and his stump hurt like hell. He could hardly bear to look down and see his own damaged body. The act of standing made the room swirl around him in brilliant lit windows and white sheets and rows of beds and he thought he might fall down, but Bobby was there.

Finally they declared the thing done, set it beside his bed, and went away, and Jonathan got back in his bed and did not look at it again. It was a hateful thing.

Bobby came by to clean and dress his stump. He unwrapped the bandages, looked over the truncated limb as if he was evaluating horse flesh.

"Mmm, my. This don't need no cleanin'. This here looks good and healed-up to me."

"You let me know when they start giving medical degrees to darkies. Then I'll be happy to let you treat me." The November wind made the windows rattle, and the sound chilled Jonathan right through.

Bobby smiled, sat down, uninvited, on a stool beside Jonathan's bed. "Don't need no fancy school to tell some things."

Jonathan rolled his head over, looked into Bobby's dark eyes. The black man was the only regular thing in his life. "That a fact? So what can you tell me, Dr. Sambo?"

"I kin tell you you bin layin in dat bed for a long damned time. Lot longer den it take for one shot-off leg to mend up."

"That a fact?"

"Yassuh. Seen plenty a boys come and go, in da time you been layin here. Boys hurt wus den you."

Jonathan rolled his head back, looked up at the ceiling. He knew every crack, every fleck of chipped paint. It was the landscape of the last part of his life.

Bobby was telling him a true thing. He had seen them too, the young men so grievously injured, seen them come and go while he remained, staring at the ceiling.

"Those other boys, they must have someplace to go," Jonathan said.

"I tell you true . . ." Bobby said. He leaned closer and his voice was nearly a whisper. "You best find someplace too. I done heard the doctor talkin to Cap'n Tompkins yesserday. He say dere ain't no reason you should still be here. He say da provosts, dey makin everyone in town give a bed to a hurt man, ain't no room for one ain't hurt."

Jonathan closed his eyes. Of course, this would happen. He had known all along that it would, someday. He could not stay in that bed for the rest of his life, unless somehow his life were to end that day. But that did not seem likely. The only two things he could hope for—to remain fixed in that bed, or to die there—and neither one a possibility.

He was terrified. More frightened than he had been leaving his home for the uncertainties of war. More frightened than he had been looking down that hill—he now knew it was called "Henry House Hill"—into the swirl of battle, or standing in front of the charging Yankees, bullets plucking at his clothing. None of it was half so frightening to him as the prospect of standing up, tucking the crutches under his arms, hobbling out that door.

"You got no idea what kind of hurt I'm going through," Jonathan said, and Bobby said, soft, "You think a nigger don't know nuttin 'bout hurt?

You think a boy sold away from his mammy, five years old, don't know nuttin 'bout feelin sorry fo hisself? Missuh Jon'tin, you gots to go home."

He was quiet for a long moment. He could feel Bobby's presence beside him. Finally he spoke. It was just a whisper. "I can't."

Bobby replied, and his voice seemed to come from some place beyond the room, "You gots to. An I'se goin to help." Then he stood and walked away.

With that exchange, everything, for Jonathan, changed. Where before there had been deadness, nothing, there was now terror. Where there had been no thought of the future, there was now obsession with it. And from that obsession, no clear idea emerged of where to go, what to do. Jonathan felt sick to his stomach. His missing leg ached.

Where will I go? He had no money, no home. *Certainly the army will give me something? Don't they owe me wages, at least?*

He thought of Robley. Where was he? In camp, no doubt. Jonathan did not follow the military situation, could not bear to think on it. But it was not possible for anyone in possession of his hearing to know nothing of what was going on. It was discussed constantly, and in all quarters. So Jonathan knew that the combined armies of Beauregard and Johnston were still encamped in and around Manassas, that they had done little since the Great Battle.

In October, Jonathan heard there had been some fighting at a place called Ball's Bluff and the Yankees had been licked again, but he did not know if the 18th Mississippi had been part of that. Beyond that, nothing.

I could go to Robley.... His brother tried to be the strict disciplinarian. Sometimes Jonathan thought Robley tried to fill in where their father was deficient, in that regard. But he was not unkind. Far from it. He could go to Robley, beg his brother's forgiveness, ask for money enough that he could set up somewhere. Get a job. Surely there were things a one-legged man could do? Clerk, bookkeeper. He wrote a good, fair hand, had a head for numbers.

The whole thing overwhelmed him, made him sick with fear.

He thought of Robley, the last time he had seen him. How very angry he was. And Jonathan knew it was not just his and Nathaniel's defiance that angered him. It was that Jonathan and Nathaniel were going into the fight, and he was not, and he wanted to, as much as his brothers, but his sense of duty would not allow him to walk away from Hamer's Rifles.

Jonathan heard, subsequently, somewhere, that those troops at McLean's Ford had in fact got into the show, late in the day. *So Robley got what he wanted in the end. And if I had stayed put, made Nathaniel stay put, we would have been together and got into the fight just the same....*

And that led to another thought. *How do I know that Robley's all right?*

Jonathan sat up on his elbows, waited for the spinning in his head to stop. "Hey, Bobby . . ."

Bobby, across the room, looked up. He set down the bandages he was rolling, ambled over. He moved fast even while looking as if he was not.

"Yassuh?"

"Is there a way that a fella can find out if someone was killed or wounded in the Battle of Manassas?"

Bobby rubbed his chin. "I do believe they gots lists of all the boys was killed or hurt, down ta da Mechanics' Institute. It's where dey gots da War Department, 'cross from de capitol."

Jonathan lay back again, nodded his head. He had to do it. Stand up, walk out the door, go and see if Robley Junior was still alive, or dead or wounded all this time. He had just compounded the terror. "Will you help me get there?"

"Sure enough," Bobby said with tempered enthusiasm. He went off to get permission to leave, then came back, helped Jonathan sit up, swung his remaining leg over the edge of the bed. Every movement caused his head to whirl, so long had he remained supine.

Bobby helped him strap on the hateful prosthetic, supported him and helped him on with his pants, a cast-off pair of uniform trousers.

Bobby sat him down again and while he fought for equilibrium the black man pulled his shirtsleeves over his arms, buttoned the shirt down the front. He pulled Jonathan's shell jacket out from under the bed, shook it out.

"Let me see that," Jonathan said. Bobby handed it to him.

Jonathan held the jacket in both of his hands. He examined the gray cloth, the brass buttons with "Mississippi" stamped on their faces. They had called him "Mississippi" before they knew his name, because of those buttons.

He stuck his finger through one of the bullet holes. The jacket was riddled with them, as if moths had been at it, and stained with dark patches of blood that had failed to come out, even with the washing Bobby had given the thing.

Jonathan shook his head. All those bullets. How had he lived through it? Why?

"Here, let me help you on wid dis," Bobby said, gently taking the coat from Jonathan's hands, as if he did not want Jonathan to further contemplate his melancholy.

"Miss Tompkins, she say we kin take da buckboard. It ain't too far, but I don't hardly credit you wid da strength to walk to da carriage house."

Jonathan pulled on the jacket, buttoned the brass buttons. It was like stepping into a past life, experiencing something from another place and time. Something that seemed utterly alien to the conscious mind but still completely familiar.

Bobby held out a hand and Jonathan took it and allowed Bobby to pull him to a standing position. Bobby stepped beside him and Jonathan put an arm around his shoulder and they stood there while Jonathan's head settled down.

"I'm all right, I'm all right," he said at last. "Crutches . . ."

Bobby tentatively let him go, stepped away to grab Jonathan's crutches. Jonathan tested his weight on the stump, tried to get a feel for his balance. Not too bad. His shell jacket, cut to fit snug, now hung like a sack coat.

"Here you are, Missuh Jon'tin," Bobby said, handing Jonathan the crutches. Jonathan tucked the armrests under his arms, set the tips on the floor, eased his weight onto them. Took a step, then another. "Good, good . . ." he gasped. "Good . . . show me the way, Bobby."

They walked, slowly, out of the big room, into a foyer of sorts. Miss Tompkins's was an elegant house, at least as well appointed as the Paine plantation house, if not quite as big. Now it was entirely given over to the wounded.

Bobby led Jonathan across the carpeted floor—worn and dirty now with the traffic coming and going—and opened the big front door.

Jonathan hesitated. He was breathing hard, in part from the exertion, in part from the panic that seized him. He had not been outside in months, had never really intended to go outside again. It was not a conscious thought—if he had thought about it at all he would have realized that it was absurd—it was just a feeling, understood, never expressed.

But there was the outside, right through the door. A front porch, the roof of which was supported by columns, a Confederate flag flogging in the breeze. Stairs down to the walk, a white picket fence around a narrow yard, sidewalk, cobbled street, people walking by, carriages, the whole world carrying on, waging war, and it did not know or care about Jonathan Paine and what he suffered.

Jonathan breathed deep, hobbled on, out the door. Bobby closed it behind him, helped him down the stairs and around the back of the white clapboard house to where the carriage house stood. In the open area in front of the carriage house stood the buckboard and two black, restless horses in traces. Their breath made gray clouds around their muzzles on that cold day.

Jonathan stopped and leaned on his crutches while Bobby arranged a crate for him to step up on and onto the buckboard's seat. He gulped breath, felt his limbs trembling from the effort of getting out to the carriage house. His stump throbbed and he was covered in sweat, despite the cold wind that whipped around the courtyard, tumbling leaves and torn papers.

Bobby helped him up onto the buckboard's seat, and with great relief Jonathan sat.

"You don't have ta do dis, Missuh Jon'tin," Bobby said. "You let me know what you wants to find out, I kin go find it out."

"No," Jonathan said, gasping the word. "No. I have to do it." He did not know why. Some kind of penance. Perhaps he would not be satisfied with an answer he did not see himself. Whatever the reason, he had to go.

Bobby flicked the reins, made a clicking noise with his tongue, and the horses stepped out. The buckboard seat bounced and swayed on its springs and Jonathan held on, tried not to think about throwing up.

Richmond was crowded, packed with people, the roads crammed with vehicles. It reminded Jonathan of the docks in New Orleans, that kind of traffic, that kind of bustle. There was nothing else to which he could compare it, he had never seen anything like it.

There were soldiers everywhere, companies and regiments marching past, loitering around, waiting, just as Jonathan remembered, the eternal waiting of military life. Gray-clad privates and privates clad in whatever their home states provided, or whatever they wore off the farm, officers on horses with gold braid swirling around gray sleeves and running wild over the tops and sides of kepis, gold rope twined around slouch hats. Like schools of various species of fish, they moved through the streets.

There were wounded men as well. Men with legs missing, arms missing, men with bandannas tied over their faces to hide whatever horror was left behind when the iron had done its work. In his total self-absorption Jonathan had come to believe that he was somehow unique. Despite the wounded men around him in the hospital, men who had also lost legs, or arms, or their lives, Jonathan had come to believe that he was the worst off, that he had suffered in a way that no one else had.

He sat silent, hanging on as the buckboard jounced, looked around, realized that he had been very wrong in thinking that. He saw a soldier, legs gone, bandanna over one blinded eye, leaning against a building, begging with tin cup extended. *I am not so hard off as that fellow*, Jonathan thought. *When I join him in begging, then I'll feel sorry for myself.* The sight of the man, the thought of himself there on that street corner, rattled him. He wiped the sweat from his forehead with the tattered sleeve of his jacket.

Bobby drove the buckboard with aplomb and a hint of aggression, and soon the big capitol building, with its massive columns at the top of wide granite stairs, loomed up in front, and Jonathan was glad because just riding in that swaying seat was taxing his strength to its limits.

They turned right at the capitol, skirted the small park called Capitol Square, pulled up in front of an uninspired four-story brick building set in a block of buildings that fronted 9th Street. Bobby swung the buckboard in against the curb with a deft tug and flick of the reins, swapped curses with another black man who was angling his ice wagon for that spot.

"We here. Let me help you down."

Bobby climbed out, walked around the heads of the horses, and lifted his arms up to Jonathan, and Jonathan allowed himself to be lifted down like a toddler from a high seat. There was a time, he knew, when he would have been ashamed of that, but he was too tired, too hurt, too afraid to care.

They worked their way through the crowd on the sidewalk, like crossing a fast-moving stream, and into the lobby of the Mechanics' Institute. It was bedlam there, with civilians and soldiers rushing about, and each with an attitude of utmost importance. For a moment Jonathan just stood, leaning on his crutches, feeling the sweat move under his shirt, and stared. After the months of peace in the makeshift hospital it was all very overwhelming.

"Why don't you sit, I'll find out where we gots to go," Bobby suggested, but Jonathan shook his head.

"No. Let's press on."

They forced their way through the crowds, Bobby trying to fend the hurrying crowds away from Jonathan. But he was a black man, and he could be only so pushy, and more than once he had to grab Jonathan before Jonathan was knocked to the marble floor.

They came at last to the Office of Records, which seemed a likely place to start, so they opened the wood door with its opaque window and stepped in. Jonathan crossed to the high counter, leaned his crutches against it, put his weight on his elbows. His forehead felt as if it was burning up. He shivered from a chill, looked around for an open window. His hands were slick with sweat on the polished wood counter.

"What can I do for you?" The clerk came to them at last, harried, but not unfriendly.

"I need . . . I would like to see a list of the men killed or wounded at the Battle of Manassas."

The clerk nodded. "That's the easiest request I got all day. You want it by state, by army, by battalion, how?"

"Regiment. Eighteenth Mississippi. Do you have that?"

"Surely do."

The clerk left them, crossed to the back of the room, rummaged through a pile of papers, thumbing though various folders. Jonathan felt sick. He was breathing hard. Everything in the room seemed to have a sharp edge to it. He looked over at Bobby, and he could see the worry in the black man's eyes. Jonathan was terribly afraid.

At last the clerk found what he was looking for, came back across the room. His movements seemed unreal, slowed down, like a dream. Jonathan imagined this was what it was like those final moments marching up to the gallows, the slow, dreamlike unreality of the thing.

The clerk laid the sheet of paper on the desk, slid it over to Jonathan. "Eighteenth Mississippi. There you are."

Jonathan reached out with a sweating, trembling hand. He tried to lift the paper but could not seem to do it, so he slid it closer, ran his eyes down the list.

Paine, Jonathan, Private, Company D.

Paine, Nathaniel, Private, Company D.

He stopped when he came to the name *Paine, Robley, Jr., Lieutenant, Company D.* He stared at the name, forced his eyes to focus. What was he looking at? He could not recall what the list was supposed to be.

His eyes shifted right, to the next column, the words that lined up with the names of the Paine boys. *Missing. Missing. Killed in Action.*

His breath was raspy, loud in his own ears. His eyes would no longer hold their focus on the list.

"What is it?" Bobby asked.

Jonathan looked up at him, his worried eyes, his hands poised, ready to reach out and save him from hitting the floor. "Bobby . . ." he managed. "I got to go home . . ." and then he felt the strength run out of him like water through a sieve.

31

*SIR: In answer to your letter of 9th instant, asking what is necessary to be sup-
plied . . . twenty surf boats for landing troops, of a build, except being a little
more flat-bottomed, to correspond with those used at Vera Cruz during the Mexican war.*

—Flag Officer S. H. Stringham to Gustavus V. Fox

*I*t was an odd sort of concert. Samuel Bowater did not find the
Norfolk and Elizabeth City Quintet bad, at least not intolerably so. The
first violin knew his business, working through the tragic melody of the
Quintet in G Minor, the joyous notes of the Quintet in C Major. He
played well for the most part, doing no worse than briefly mutilating the
tempo in the second movement and making a hash of a particularly difficult few measures in the third. But overall, not too bad.

Arriving at the hall was worse. It was a terribly improper thing from the
outset, inviting Wendy Atkins to accompany him for the evening, with no
escort, no chaperon, a young woman all but living by herself. The Samuel
Bowater of half a year before would not have considered it.

But now, after the fighting, after the hospital, with the well-established
order of things crumbling around him, now, somehow, it did not seem so
intolerable. And so he had written to her. And she had accepted. But he
had had no intention of displaying his newfound want of morals in front
of the men.

Wendy was waiting for him outside as he made his way along the walk,
a trail of seamen behind like the tail of a comet. "Miss Atkins, may I present Hieronymus Taylor, my chief engineer," Bowater said, and Wendy

held out her hand to shake and Taylor shook and Bowater was certain he saw something pass between them.

"I think perhaps we have met," Taylor said. "Didn't you use to paint them pictures in the park, like the cap'n here?"

"Yes, yes I did . . ." Wendy said.

So that is it . . . Bowater thought, and made himself be satisfied with that explanation.

In the concert hall, Hieronymus Taylor sat on one side of him, grinning a wide grin, Wendy on the other. Every once in a while Samuel would meet Taylor's eyes and the chief would smile and nod approvingly. Taylor beat the time on his leg, doing so with greater and greater enthusiasm as the concert progressed, to Bowater's greater and greater annoyance. But Taylor did not stop, save for the moment when the first violin went astray, tempo-wise, and then Taylor just chuckled, waited for the violinist to get back on track.

For the others, it was a mixed experience. Bowater was aware of the shift in mood among the sailors, from anticipation of something new to an uncomfortable realization that a quintet was just a gang of five stiffs like the old man, playing music with no words, and that was as good as it was going to get. There would be no minstrel show, no one in blackface imitating Negroes and singing "Camptown Races" or "Old Folks at Home," no olio with its crude jests, no burlesque with scantily clad women capering around the stage. Just a bunch of stiffs, sawing away.

Some of the hands tried to remain respectfully alert. Some squirmed, shifted, glanced at the door. Some fell asleep, and Bowater was thankful for that, except for when Jimmy Ogden began to snore and Ruffin Tanner hit him a bit too hard, and he shouted as he jerked awake.

No, it was not the finest musical experience that Samuel Bowater had ever enjoyed, neither the best musicians nor the best audience. He was supremely annoyed to have to divide his attention between Wendy and his cretinous crew.

When it was over the Cape Fears walked *en masse* back to the docks, with coats wrapped tight around them against the buffeting November wind, as Bowater walked Wendy to the boardinghouse at which she was lodging to have their private farewell.

They stood on the porch, catching a bit of a lee from the house, stood for a long time, not moving or speaking. A part of Samuel's mind raged against the impropriety of it all, a part wanted to sweep her away, to use the war as his excuse for throwing all of his well-worn propriety overboard. At last he reached out for her, took her in his arms, hugged her, and she hugged him. A real hug, and not a brotherly one. He looked in her eyes. "I have missed you."

"I have missed you. You'll send word?"

"I will." He kissed her, and she kissed him back. They said nothing more, and she pulled herself from his arms.

Bowater caught up with his men at last on the dock, and Bayard Quayle, who was on sentry duty, did no more than peek out from where he was huddled in the engine-room door to see who it was boarding the vessel. The men each thanked Bowater for the experience and disappeared forward.

"Well, damn me, that was somethin," Taylor said as he and Bowater walked forward.

"Did you enjoy it, Chief?"

"I surely did, Cap'n. I always figured that Mozart and such was too highfalutin for a simple country fiddler like me, but now I see there ain't so much to it. And all together, with them . . . whatta ya call 'em, the bigger ones?"

"Violas? Cello?"

"Yeah. Why, it sounds like a choir of angels!"

"I'll admit the first violin was not the best I have heard. But the music itself is very complicated. It sounds simple, well played, but that is deceptive."

"Aw, I don't know," Taylor said. "Hmmm, hmm, hm, hm . . ." The chief began to hum the first violin's part with surprising recall. "Reckon I could scratch that out."

"You remember that part?"

"Oh, hell, yes. I got a great head for remembering little ditties and such. I hear a tune, I got it"—Taylor snapped his fingers in the air—"like that."

"Yes, well . . ." It was irritating that Taylor should think remembering and reproducing a "little ditty" by Mozart was the same as hearing and then playing some campfire song. "I fear it is a bit more than that, you know. Well, good night, Chief."

Taylor pulled a cigar from his pocket, clamped it in his teeth. "Good night, Cap'n. We'll have a full head of steam by sunup."

"Very good, Chief." Bowater walked to the forward end of the deckhouse, climbed the ladder to the boat deck. He stepped though the wheelhouse and into his cabin. The steam pipes that ran along the deck filled the cabin with glorious warmth, like stepping into a lover's embrace.

Jacob was asleep below, and Bowater had given him permission to remain asleep and he was glad that he did. He wanted to be alone. He was in an irritable mood. His night ashore had been ruined, and all his telling himself that he was glad to introduce his men to such finer things as classical music was not enough to make him believe it.

Hieronymus Taylor . . . son of a bitch white trash peckerwood . . . The chief never failed to irritate him, and then it irritated him further that he let Taylor irritate him, until he had irritation built upon irritation.

It was irritating that Taylor was so damned good at his work. Taylor had a sense for engines that was profound, almost mystical. Every steamer on which Bowater sailed had always had a myriad of problems with the engines. But nothing beyond the most minor of difficulties ever seemed to take place aboard the *Cape Fear*. Bowater had watched Taylor once fix the small steam engine that drove the steering gear—an engine that had squealed its way to what seemed an untimely death—with just a twist of a wrench and a feather touch of a screwdriver. It was like a laying on of hands. It was spooky.

Samuel unbuttoned his coat and hung it on a hanger, smoothed it out, hung the hanger on a rod. He pulled his braces off his shoulders and took off his shirt and hung it up with equal care.

From the galley below he heard a screeching sound, like straining metal or a cat in great pain. He stopped, cocked his ear, frowned.

The sound again, but less discordant, and he realized it was Taylor's violin. He was tuning his violin in the galley below.

Is he intending to play at this damned time of night?

Bowater stood in that spot and listened and did not know what to do. He wanted to tell Taylor to quit it, that he did not care to hear his caterwauling when he was going to bed, that he did not care to hear the damned "Bonnie Blue Flag" at that hour, or any. But he did not want Taylor to know he had irritated him.

Then the screeching stopped and there came up through the deck a series of notes that were not "Dixie" or "Roll the Old Chariot Along" but rather Mozart. Mozart's Quintet in G Minor.

Bowater got down on his hands and knees, held his ear an inch above the deck. Taylor was playing the piece flawlessly, remembering note for note what he had heard two hours before. He went through the first movement, the notes rising and falling with the very passion the old master had infused into them. He did not miss a one. He made the first violin of the Norfolk and Elizabeth City Quintet sound like a hack in a minstrel show.

For ten minutes Bowater remained in his supplicant position, listening to the music coming up through the deck, nodding his head to the rhythm, mouthing the melody as it floated through the deck. He listened to Taylor breeze effortlessly over sections of which, he recalled, the first violin had made a hash. He listened to the chief engineer's beautiful interpretation of that classic work.

Devil take that peckerwood son of a bitch . . . Bowater thought, despite himself. Now he was more annoyed than ever.

Hieronymus Taylor sat on Johnny St. Laurent's stool, in the warmth of the galley, eyes closed, and let his fingers dance over the neck of his violin, let the music flow from his head, down his arm, up the bow, to be coaxed at last out of the body of the instrument.

He hummed softly as he played the Quintet in G Minor. He had not heard it for two years at least before that night, was not sure he could execute it perfectly, but his fingers and his bowing arm knew what to do, once he stopped thinking and just let them go.

The first violin of the Norfolk and Elizabeth City Quintet had not been so very bad, though he had no genuine feel for the music. Still, Taylor could sense Bowater tightening every time the poor bastard made a hash of it. From the corner of his eye he saw the captain shake his head in disgust with each minor imperfection.

Goddamned blueblood, stick-up-his-ass patrician son of a bitch . . . Taylor thought.

Wendy Atkins . . . son of a bitch . . . he thought.

He heard the music go awry as his concentration drifted, and he refocused on Mozart. *Not one damned thing good enough for that bastard* . . . Bowater made him feel insignificant, a poor relation, the hired man who lives in the barn. It irritated him and it irritated him that he allowed it to irritate him.

He crept up on the section where the first violin had made a mess of the tempo. He stood, climbed up on an apple crate so that his instrument would be as close to the sole of the captain's cabin as it could get, played the part with a perfection of timing, as loud as he could.

He heard the galley door open, felt a blast of cold wind sweep away the steam heat. He looked over, expected to see a furious Samuel Bowater. Instead, he saw Ruffin Tanner, framed in the door, lit by the soft light of the single lantern burning in the galley. Tanner stepped in, shut the door behind him, leaned with folded arms against the door.

Taylor looked away, closed his eyes, finished the movement, but the mood was broken with Tanner there, and he felt a bit foolish, having been caught standing on top of the crate.

He bowed the last note, opened his eyes, let the bow fall to his side, and took the violin from his chin. He turned and regarded the sailor, who was patiently waiting for him to finish. He found Tanner gruff, often un-pleasant, highly competent at his job. Tanner was the kind of man he liked, a kindred irascible bastard.

"That there," Taylor said, hopping down from his crate, "is what you call 'classical music.' "

"That a fact? Reckon I'd call it a lot of goddamned noise for seven bells in the evenin watch."

"Would you, now?" Tanner's attitude was something different for the sailor. Aggressive. He wondered if he was going to have to whop Tanner's ass. Wondered if he could. It would be a good fight.

"Well, lucky for you, you done broke the mood, you know what I mean?" Taylor laid the violin and bow in the case. "You done broke my creative spell." He snapped the case shut, set the instrument well out of the way on the galley counter. Turned, faced Tanner, arms folded the way the sailor's were. "I don't much appreciate that."

"No? Well, I don't much appreciate bein kept awake by some white trash peckerwood standin on an apple crate like some kinda dumb ass."

" 'Dumb ass,' you say?" Taylor let his arms drop to his sides, shook them out. Didn't know what was up Tanner's behind, but he reckoned it was time to beat it out of him. "You want to do somethin about this prob-lem of yours?"

Tanner nodded. He unbuttoned the top few buttons of his heavy over-coat, reached a hand in. Taylor braced for what would come out of there—a knife, a blackjack, a gun.

But it was a bottle, a flask-style bottle more than half full of a liquid that looked very much like whiskey. "Long as your goddamned fiddle's put away, guess I can give you something, might bring back that 'creative spirit' you s'all fired worried about."

Tanner pulled the cork from the bottle, took a deep pull, wiped the neck on his coat, and handed it to Taylor. Taylor tipped the bottle back. Whiskey. Quite good whiskey, in fact. "Yup. Yup. I hear that ol' muse sing-in again."

He handed the bottle back, and Tanner stepped across the galley, rus-tled up two glasses, half-filled each with the liquor. Handed one to Taylor.

"Tanner, you got a goddamned funny way of sayin you'd like to have a drink with a man."

"That ain't what I want to say. I want to say, you too damned hard on the cap'n."

" 'Hard on the cap'n? Are you jokin?"

"No, I ain't. And you know it. Ride over him every chance you got. I don't know what the hell you was doin up on that crate, but I bet it ain't no coincidence you was right under the old man's cabin."

Taylor took a sip of his whiskey, hoped he was not flushing red, or at least that Tanner would not see it in the muted light. "This here the master's division gettin all uppity about what us engine-room niggers is doin? Y'all think we should keep to our place? Don't try to come into the big house, like?"

"Ain't about that. I don't give a damn about that. Some of my best friends is black gang. Do what you want to the luff. It's just Cap'n Bowater. I don't appreciate the grief you give him."

"And why are you so concerned about good Cap'n Bowater?"

" 'Cause he saved my life, oncet. Man don't forget that."

Taylor took a drink, pulled out the remainder of his cigar, sparked it to life. He needed a moment to consider this. Bowater did not seem the life-saving kind to him.

After a long silence, Taylor said, "All right, Tanner. Reckon you best tell it."

Tanner looked at Taylor, and for a moment seemed to consider whether or not he would. "You got another one of them cigars?" he asked at last.

Taylor frowned, but he reached in his pocket, withdrew his penultimate cigar, handed it over. Waited patiently while Tanner bit off the end, then handed him his own smoldering cigar to use as a light.

"It was in the Mex War," Tanner said at last. "In '46. At Veracruz. I wasn't in the navy but five years or so. Thought I knew it all, 'course, but I didn't know shit. Anyway, we was bringing ammunition ashore for a navy battery they was setting up south of the city there. Had these big, flat barges, crazy sons of bitches. Couldn't hardly control 'em, even when the weather was good. They'd get four or five of 'em on a hawser, get one of them little paddle-wheel schooners to bring up to the beach.

"So there's Ensign Bowater, fresh from the Navy School, looks clean and proper, like a little sailor doll you'd buy for your daughter. He's in command of this little paddle wheeler 'cause her proper captain's assigned to the battery ashore. They figured that was the real work, let the green-horn take the barges back and forth.

"We're bringin our barges on and off the beach, ain't no thing. Made the last run of the day, sun's goin down. We got about five miles to steam back to the fleet. They was anchored around that island the Mex call Sacrificios.

"Halfway there, and one of them Mex northers come rippin through. You ever experience anythin like that?"

Taylor nodded. "I know about them northers."

Tanner nodded as well. "Then you know, they come right outta nowhere, come tearin down like a bull gone mad. Right in the middle of that big bay, and a norther come down on us, just as it was getting dark. First ya feel that blast of cold air, then the wind starts fillin in. Next thing we know we takin green water over the sides, fillin faster than we can bail. Seas gettin bigger and bigger, and mind, them barges warn't nothin in a seaway in the gentlest of times. Rain's comin down, lightnin flashin around, and ol' Ensign Bowater jest drivin that little schooner for all she's worth, right for the fleet.

"But a mile from the fleet and I start thinkin, 'Damn, we may live through this after all.' Then, sure as hell, the hawser parts, right at our bow. We was the last barge in the line, see? So away we go, twirlin around downwind, jest like a leaf in a damn stream. Last I seen of the schooner and Ensign Bowater, he's jest steamin along still. I don't reckon he even knew we was gone. And I jest shake my head, don't even bother to cuss him out, on account of I didn't reckon we could expect much more, and him a boy right outta school.

"For about an hour we bailed like hell and some prayed and some was cussin and finally we hit the surf, due south of where we lost the tow. It was full night by then—dark comes quick when you got one of them northers—and we didn't know we was on the beach till the barge grounds out. Two good hits and it breaks all to hell and all us sailors on board, there was about twenty of us, we all in the water.

" 'Bout fifteen of us managed to get ashore, the rest drowned, or was beat to death by the surf. Some of us managed to snatch up rifles and even some cartridge boxes and we kept 'em dry, and that was a good thing. See, the Americans was nearly surrounding Veracruz, but surrounding the Americans was all these gangs of Mex irregular cavalry, and guerrillas and any damn Mex got his hands on a gun and reckoned he'd kill and rob him an American soldier.

"So we didn't know what in hell we was going to do, but we set up some kinda defense, there on the beach, ready to fight off whatever Mex comes at us. Didn't take too damned long, either. We'd drifted way south of the American lines, right in Mex territory, and them guerrillas come on, just like sharks. Didn't know they was there till we hear rifles and one of our boys jest falls dead.

"You got to understand, it was dark as hell. Couldn't see a thing. And most of our powder was wet, and us sailor boys, we ain't so good at loading and firing in the rain, not like them infantry sumbitches. We figured we was done for, and it was only a matter of time. I seen that first one go down, and I figured that was it. Never reckoned to get it on no damned Mexican beach.

"Then, right out of nowhere, we hear a steam engine! Steam engine, there on that beach, and we don't know what the hell it was. Then there's a flash of lightning, and there's the paddle-wheel schooner, with them barges still behind, but they're empty now, and backing down into the surf. I never thought no one would come for us. Twenty sailors? On a night like that? Didn't reckon anyone would think it was worth it. Then I reckoned someone musta relieved Bowater of his command, 'cause I sure as hell didn't think that toy sailor'd do it on his own."

Taylor took a last gulp of whiskey, refilled his glass and Tanner's. "And?"

"And I was wrong. Once Bowater realized our barge was gone, he called for volunteers amongst the other barge crews to go after us. Happy to say they all volunteered. Then Bowater, he jest let the paddle wheeler drift downwind and current, reckoned he'd fetch up where we did. Damned stupid thing to do, but he didn't know no better. Then he sees our gunfire. Drops anchor, backs the paddle wheeler down on the beach until the last of them barges is right in the surf. He had 'em tied together, see, to form sort of a bridge. All we had to do was climb over 'em."

"So that's how he saved your sorry ass?"

"Nope. Problem was, those Mex had us under fire. We tried to go back across the beach, they would have come out and slaughtered us. So after a while, Bowater figures this out. Next thing we know, here he comes, leadin the barge crews, with whatever weapons they got, climbin over them barges and into the surf, and right up to where we was hidin. The Mex is firin at us, and we firin at the Mex and some of those poor bastards is getting shot down. But we held 'em. All night, in the damned rain and the wind, we held 'em off.

"First light we starts movin toward the barges. We had half a dozen of the fellows was United States Marines, and they was the only ones knew how to cover a retreat, like. So they organized the thing, and we backed off down the beach, got on them barges, and all the while we can see the Mex gettin closer, firin the whole time, and we's nearly out of ammunition.

" 'Course, as cap'n of the steamer, Bowater's duty is to get on board her, get her ready to get underway."

"That what he done?"

"Nope. He wouldn't get off that damned beach until all of us was. Stupid bastard, and I told him so, but he wouldn't go. Me and him, we was the last ones off that beach. See here . . ." Tanner bent over, pulled up his right pant leg. The lantern light shone on the smooth, hard skin of a scar that wrapped itself halfway around his calf.

"That was a Mex bullet I took just as we was gettin in the barge. Warn't nothin would kill me, but I sure as hell wouldn't have got off that beach if Bowater wasn't there to help. None of us would. He never asked for permission to do what he done, just done it."

Taylor nodded. "Very impressive. It must have been a tearful reunion, you two, up there at Norfolk, all huggin and carryin on about old times. Be enough to make a body puke."

Tanner shook his head. "Bowater don't remember me, and that's how I keep it. I seen him on and off, over the years. Then when I seen him in Norfolk, and fightin for the South, then I said, 'Wherever that sumbitch is goin, that's where I want to go.' That's when I finagled my way on board, here."

"All right. So Bowater saved your flea-bitten hide oncet. That's got nothin to do with me."

"No, it don't. All's I'm sayin is this. You think Cap'n Bowater's a fancy, upper-crust sumbitch, got a broomstick up his ass, and I ain't saying he don't. But the man's got grit, you hear? Kinda grit it took to come get us off that beach, that ain't somethin a man loses. It's somethin you born with. You seen him go after the fleet back there at Hampton Roads, seen him march right through them shells at Fort Hatteras. You may not like him, but he's a man deserves respect. That's all I gots to say."

Taylor was silent, chewed on his cigar. "All right. You done said it."

Tanner picked up the whiskey bottle, examined it, drained the last vestiges of whiskey. "Good night, Chief," he said.

"Good night."

Tanner opened the galley door. The wind whipped in, made the hanging pots clang against each other like bells on a buoy. Then he stepped out, closed the door, and it was quiet again.

Taylor remained sitting, looking at the door. Tanner was a good man. He had respect for a man like Tanner.

Well, goddamn . . . he thought. *This sure as hell complicates things.*

32

―――――

. . . I care not what they say of me there so long as it is evident here that I am
trying my best to get ready to strike the enemies of my country and of mankind.
That I will hit them hard when ready, if possible, I promise you.

—Lieutenant Isaac N. Brown, C.S. Navy

or the second time in his life, Jonathan Paine woke up to find himself staring up at Bobby's face. He shifted his eyes. The ceiling behind Bobby was not the ceiling of the sitting room at Miss Tompkins's. Jonathan remained still, looked back at Bobby.

"Where am I?" he asked in a soft voice. He was afraid.

"You in de Mechanics' Institute. You done fainted."

"How long have I been out?"

"Not more'n five minutes."

Jonathan nodded. *Five minutes?* It felt as if he had been unconscious for hours. He could feel the sweat on his forehead. He felt disconnected, as if he was viewing the world through field glasses. "I think the fever's back," he whispered.

"Sure enough. We gonna git you back to Miss Tompkins, jest as soon as we can."

"I need to write. To my father . . ."

"Oh, you gots a father now? Lord, don't the army provide a power o' things! This mornin you didn't have no father at all."

There was a bustle in the room and Jonathan opened his eyes and two men laid a litter on the floor beside him. They picked him up, feet and shoulders, and shifted him onto the litter and lifted him up. His head spun around. His breath was coming shallow and fast. They carried him out of the War Department building, laid him on the back of the buckboard at Bobby's instruction.

The fever took hold on the jostling, bumping, agonizing ride back, and it did not relinquish its grip for two more days. And when Jonathan finally kicked his way up from the delirium and the sweats and the nightmare images, Bobby was there, and once again the black man was the only real thing in his world.

The fever broke at last, and Bobby helped him sit up in bed and he said, "Missuh Jon'tin, you wants to write to you daddy?"

Jonathan nodded.

He wanted to write. He had to. He had no remaining brother. He was it, the last of the Paine boys, and his parents would have no idea what had happened there at the Bull Run River. He had to tell them, in his own way. It was no longer a matter of wanting to go home. He had to. Now.

Bobby went away, returned with paper and pen and the Bible on which to write.

Dear Mother and Father,

When I wrote before, I was not aware of the tragic death of Robley Junior at the Battle of Manassas. As you grieve for the loss of your sons, so I too grieve for the loss of my brothers.

My last letter, written from this place, must have been something of a mystery to you. I will not relate the particulars here of the great sacrifice that Nathaniel and Robley Junior made on the field of battle, but rather will tell you all that I know when we are once again together. I am at Miss Sally Tompkins's on Main St. in Richmond, Virginia. I am wounded with the loss of a leg but have recovered, and long for nothing more than to return home. If you will have me, I beg you send some money to this place, enough for me to pay my passage home. Until then, I will dream every day of being reunited with you, my loving parents, and will remain

Your obedient, humble son,
Jonathan

Jonathan folded the latter, sealed and addressed it, handed it to Bobby. "I don' know what you wrote, Missuh Jon'tin, but it sure seems to a done you a power a good!"

"I wrote to my daddy. Reckon you never thought to hear me say this, but it looks like I'm going home."

Bobby smiled and Jonathan smiled. *Home.* The word did not mock him now. It sounded in his ear the way the word was supposed to sound, evoked those things that home should mean. He felt something he had not felt since that first bullet slammed into Nathaniel, sent him spinning down to the ground. He did not know at first what it was. It was only later that he realized. It was hope.

Bobby took the letter, carried it to the post office, paid for the postage. For three weeks the letter made its tortured way south, by rail, by steamboat, by coach, until at last the postmaster at Yazoo City plucked it from a pile on a big oak table, read the address, and shook his head. He carried it over to the pigeonhole marked 26, which was Paine's box, and with some difficulty made a space in the mail already accumulated there and stuffed the letter in.

And there it remained. Because Robley Paine was not around to retrieve his mail, and would not have retrieved it anyway, even if he had been there. Because Robley Paine did not believe that there was any person from whom he wished to hear. Robley Paine had given up on this world, abandoned everything except his fight against the Yankees and his hope of heaven, and there was nothing that could come through the mail that he might care about.

At the very moment that the postmaster was forcing Jonathan Paine's letter in among the demands from creditors, the letters to Katherine Paine from sundry relations, the reports from agents in New Orleans and England, Robley Paine, Sr., was tapping his fingers with frustration on the top of the big wooden wheel of the *Yazoo River*.

After shelling Pope's ships, they had returned to New Orleans, heroes all. Kinney, his hand bound in a bloody rag, conned the boat up to the wharf at the foot of Beinville Street. The deckhands made the vessel off to the pilings and bollards, Engineer Brown shut the engines down, and then they all deserted, *en masse*, the entire crew, marching off the battered stern-wheeler into the cheering crowd and were never heard from again.

Frenzy time. Robley was all over the docks, looking for more men, more guns, more munitions, another chance to drive the *Yazoo River* into combat.

He found nothing. Kinney and Brown were well known along the waterfront, knew everyone, knew everyone who knew everyone. They spread the word about Robley, and it wasn't good. Madman. Lunatic.

Kinney might even have brought Paine up on charges for blowing his fingers off, had he not been guilty of what could be construed as mutiny. As it stood, he was lauded as a great and wounded veteran of what the *New Orleans Daily True Delta* was calling "a complete success, and perhaps the most brilliant and remarkable naval exploit on record." So Kinney contented himself with modest acceptance of the praise due him, and silence regarding the particulars.

Robley Paine came in for his share of the praise, but he wanted none of it. He wanted nothing but a competent crew to man his vessel and help him drive it into harm's way, and that was the one thing he could not find.

He appeared one morning at the offices of Daniel Lessard, was greeted with a certain deference there, a reception almost like fear.

When the clerk hurried off to alert Lessard, Robley glanced at himself in a decorative mirror. Not an encouraging sight. He had not shaved in a week, could not recall the last time he had eaten. His eyes stared out from dark hollows, the stubble on his cheeks was drawn in tight where his face was pinched. His clothes were dirty and stained and torn in places. Over it all he wore a cape. He no longer bothered to hide the Starr hanging from his belt.

I have got to clean myself up . . . got to do something. . . . But for all of the wild energy he directed at manning and outfitting his ship, he could not manage even the slightest interest in himself.

"Robley, sir, come in, come in, it has been far too long!" Lessard's voice was smooth as river stones but he could not hide the quick, appraising glance up and down, the uneasy smile he hoped would look genuine.

"Good day, Daniel." Robley let Lessard lead him into his office, shut the door, which Robley did not recall him doing before. He gestured for Robley to sit and sat himself behind his desk.

"Your fame has spread, sir. Your bold action at the Head of the Passes, and your attack on the Union ships down below Pilot Town . . . they have made you quite famous."

"Humph. It was a start, a weak effort. Damned Hollins did us no favors, claiming to have sunk one of the Yankees. Should have. Didn't." Hollins, on seeing the Yankees abandoning one of their ships, had assumed her sunk, and reported her so. It detracted from their accomplishment when it was ultimately discovered that the ship was not sunk at all.

"Still, it was a singular victory. The papers . . ."

"See here, Daniel . . . I'm not blind. Or deaf. I know what's being said. 'Paine's mad . . . trying to kill himself . . .' "

Lessard raised his hands to protest, but Robley cut him off. "Don't deny it . . . I know it's true. You think I'm mad as well, I can see it in your damned eyes. And you know what? I don't give a goddamn. Hell, maybe

I am mad. Got reason enough. But I can't get anyone to ship with me. Damn engine is broken down again, I can't get an engineer on, I can't engage a pilot. I'm stuck here. Got an armed ship and can't get in the fight and all the while the damned snake, squeezing tighter, squeezing . . ."

"Well, Robley, it is not you. It's the war. All the available men are off with the army or the navy. Everyone is scrambling to find . . ."

"Here's what I need. I don't want to get men to fight the ship. Never find 'em. Need navy men. I see that. What I want now is an engineer to get the engines working, a pilot and crew to get the ship up to Yazoo City."

Robley's voice took on a plaintive tone, and he tried to fight it but he could not. He felt so lost there in New Orleans, surrounded by cowards and thieves. Yazoo City was becoming his personal El Dorado, a fabled city, his quest—to reach it. If he could get to Yazoo City, free from the corruption of New Orleans, then he could regroup and fight in earnest.

"That's all I want. To get to Yazoo City. No fighting. Just help me get to Yazoo City, where folks know me, and I'll get my men and fit my ship out there. I'll pay in specie. Gold."

Lessard leaned back and pressed his fingers together and his expression was very different. "Robley . . . that, I think, I can arrange."

The engineer showed up at nine-thirty the next morning, and he was no Chief Brown. Clean and groomed, well-spoken, he had an air of competence and professionalism that made Robley furious. The good men were available to take gold for keeping out of harm's way, it seemed. But Robley said nothing, because the goal was Yazoo City, and he did not wish to compromise that.

Two weeks and fifteen hundred dollars later the *Yazoo River*'s engines sounded better than Robley had thought they could sound.

Lessard sent deckhands, good Southern boys, competent, hardworking, not the foreign trash swept up along the docks. Lessard sent a pilot who did not stink of stale whiskey, a pilot who was courteous and professional and did as he was ordered and explained patiently when he was ordered to do something he could not.

And so, a week before the end of the year 1861, the year in which Robley Paine had witnessed the end of his life, and begun suffering the horrible torment of continuing to live nonetheless, the stern-wheeler privateer *Yazoo River* cast off from the docks of New Orleans and headed up three hundred winding miles of river to Yazoo City.

Victory or death. Victory and death. He would begin that journey there.

*　　*　　*

Eight hundred miles away, buffeted by the gales that shrieked in off the Atlantic, the CSS *Cape Fear* butted her plumb bow into the steep chop, sent spray flying up over the wheelhouse, where Samuel Bowater stood, one hand on the rail that ran around the bulkhead just below the windows, as a succession of seamen struggled with the wheel and cursed.

They watched the enemy at Fort Hatteras, brought supplies to the troops on Roanoke Island. They towed wrecks into Croatan Sound, the passage between Roanoke Island and the mainland, entryway to Albemarle Sound, and sank them. They struggled to drive pilings into the muddy channel bottom to stop the enemy's passing. They watched sickness cut the crew down by a third, working in the freezing rain and the cutting wind. They waited for the Yankees.

Christmas came, and the *Cape Fear* was tied up dockside at Elizabeth City. Samuel Bowater gave Johnny St. Laurent money from his own pocket to buy a special dinner for the crew, and Hieronymus Taylor did as well, though neither knew the other had, and as a result Johnny had more money than he could spend in a Confederacy beginning to feel the pinch of the blockade.

He prepared a meal—mock turtle soup and fried whiting, Fowl à la Béchamel and Oyster Patties for an entrée, with Stewed Rump of Beef à la Jardinière as a second course and Charlotte aux Pommes and Apricot Tart made with dried fruit for dessert—that was not just the best that Samuel had ever enjoyed aboard a naval vessel, but among the half-dozen best he had ever eaten.

They ate in the forecastle, the single biggest space on board, which still would not have been big enough if a third of the Cape Fears had not been in hospital at Norfolk. The place was scrubbed out fastidiously, and both Negroes and officers were invited, and it was a fine time.

Bowater stayed after, lent his tenor to the songs that Taylor and Jones performed, the words of which he involuntarily knew by heart. Taylor gave him the opening movement of Mozart's Quartet in C Major, which, at another time, Bowater would have perceived as an elbow in the ribs, but on that night seemed more a peace offering, and Bowater chose to take it as such. The men endured the classical interlude without complaint.

New Year's followed, and Johnny had money enough left over to stage another grand feast, and once again the festivities were loud and companionable. This despite the howling wind, the spitting snow, the funereal weather. This despite the fact that the Yankees possessed Pamlico Sound and Port Royal, despite the launch of Yankee ironclads on the

Ohio River and the buildup of McClellan's troops in Washington and the apparent inactivity of Johnston.

Despite all of the setbacks that the Confederacy had experienced, there was still the fact that the main armies had met but once, and that once was a Confederate victory, and on that night of December 31, 1861, the men of the *Cape Fear*, like all men and women of the Confederate States, had every reason to hope and to believe that their glorious cause would be carried on to victory with the next campaigning season.

And so the Cape Fears ate and drank and toasted one another and went to bed and prepared to carry on their dreary patrol.

Which they did, at first light the next morning. And then, twelve days later, the Yankees came.

33

Here is the great thoroughfare from Albemarle Sound and its tributaries, and if the enemy obtain lodgments, or succeed in passing here, he will cut off a very rich country from Norfolk market.

—Flag Officer William F. Lynch to Stephen R. Mallory

*R*oanoke Island: the tollgate between Pamlico Sound, now in Yankee hands, and the Confederate waters of Albemarle Sound.

Eight big rivers emptied into Albemarle Sound, the North, West, Pasquotank, Perquimans, Little, Chowan, Roanoke, and Alligator, as well as four canals. Two railways had their terminus there. Albemarle Sound was the back door to Norfolk, and with the Yankees guarding the front door, it was the only way in. Possession of Roanoke Island meant, ultimately, possession of Norfolk, Portsmouth, the naval yard, and virtually all the commerce coming into North Carolina.

Roanoke Island was important, and the Yankees knew it, so they sent over one hundred ships, armed vessels and transports, carrying seventeen thousand men, to take it back.

The Confederates knew it too, but they allowed only one thousand men, two hundred of whom were sick, and the seven vessels of Lynch's mosquito fleet to oppose them.

January 20, 1862. The wind was singing around the wheelhouse and Samuel Bowater could feel the *Cape Fear* jerk at her anchor chain as Jacob woke him. He looked out the window. The sky was dull, lead-colored, the waves whipped into a froth. The weather had not been agreeable in some time. It promised to get worse.

Bowater dressed quickly, stepped out into the wheelhouse. Jacob brought coffee. Harwell was there.

"Good morning, Lieutenant."

"Morning, sir."

"Engine room?"

"Steam's up, ready to get underway."

"Coal?"

"Starboard bunker half full, port bunker three-quarters. Fresh water topped off. Chief Taylor reports the problem with the web bearings is fixed. He says the grates are clean as of now, but said . . . the . . . ahh . . . poor-quality anthracite coal produces a lot of clinker."

Bowater nodded. He could just imagine the way the chief had really phrased it. Taylor took a special pleasure in shocking Harwell because Harwell was so very shockable.

The wheelhouse door opened, and the blast of wet air filled the wheelhouse with noise and cold. Tanner stepped through, shut the door. He was wearing a greatcoat, wrapped tight around him, a tarpaulin hat. "*Sea Bird*'s signaling 'Get underway,' sir."

"Very good. Mr. Harwell, let us get the anchor up."

Harwell saluted, disappeared, and Bowater stepped up beside the wheel and looked out the window. Most of the mosquito fleet was visible to him, riding at their anchors. They were in Croatan Sound, the passage between Roanoke Island and the North Carolina shore, roughly three and a half miles wide. The fleet was clustered off Pork Point on Roanoke Island.

Bowater's eyes moved to the *Sea Bird*, flagship of Commodore Lynch. She was a side-wheel steamer, a former passenger boat, now mounting a thirty-two-pounder smoothbore and a thirty-pounder Parrott. Black smoke peeked out of her funnel, only to be whipped away in the wind. The signal flag, "Get underway," stood out straight and flat in the wind, as if it was painted on a board.

Raleigh had steam up as well. She was a tug, like *Cape Fear*, but smaller, built for canal work. She sported a thirty-two-pounder forward.

The other vessels in the fleet did not have steam up. Bowater could see CSS *Curlew*, 260 tons, an iron side-wheel steamer, the most substantial vessel of the fleet. There were also the *Ellis*, *Appomattox*, and *Beaufort*. Each was a tug. Each mounted a single thirty-two-pounder.

Anchored astern of *Cape Fear* was *Fanny*, the iron-hulled screw steamer taken from the Yankees a few months earlier, and the former tug, now

CSN gunboat *Forrest*. That was it. The mosquito fleet. The ships that stood between the Yankees and Albemarle Sound.

From forward came the clank of chain coming in, and Seth Williams came in from the wind and blowing spray, took the beckets off the wheel, stood ready.

Clang . . . clang . . . clang . . . Bowater looked out the window. Harwell, bundled up in oilskins and sou'wester, waved his arm in a chopping motion. *Up and down*, the anchor right under the bow. Bowater rang slow ahead. The *Cape Fear* began to drift, her anchor free, windborne. The prop caught the water, drove her ahead, Williams met her with the wheel. Underway. To starboard, *Sea Bird* was butting the chop, steaming ahead, and *Raleigh* as well.

Those two, *Seabird* and *Raleigh*, had gone down sound the day before, scouted out the Yankees. Their report was not encouraging. Dozens, literally dozens, of ships coming in over the bar to Pamlico Sound. Gunboats, troop transports, supply ships. They were struggling with the breakers over the bar, but one by one they were managing to get their vessels over.

No one of the mosquito fleet doubted they would, because the officers of the mosquito fleet were all former officers of the United States Navy, and deep in their divided hearts they believed their old service capable of anything.

So the Confederate Navy would be the Spartans, and Croaton Sound their Thermopylae.

Bowater stepped out of the wheelhouse, out of the envelope of steam heat, into the brunt of the wind. It pulled at his sou'wester, tugged at his oilskins, found every tiny imperfection in the covering.

The *Cape Fear* rolled with the uncomfortable corkscrew of a following sea, but Bowater hardly noticed. He stared ahead, watched his beloved bow parting the seas, thought about what they would do next. Sink pilings like mad. Bring more ammunition to Roanoke Island. Try to augment the crews of the mosquito fleet. Drill. Wait for the Yankee tidal wave to wash them away.

And that was what they did. For eighteen days they prepared for the coming of the enemy. And then, on the 7th of February, the preparations were over, because the Yankee fleet was underway.

Thirty gunboats and schooners, the hammerhead, led in the van. Their job was to pound away at the Confederate defense, to beat a hole in it, though which the troops, seventeen thousand troops, would pour.

The mosquito fleet was drawn up, line abreast. They were above the northern pile line, near the north end of Croatan Sound, bow guns pointed downriver. They were anchored, with steam up.

To the east, Roanoke Island. Sandy, covered with low, coarse bushes, dune grass lying down in the wind. Like all of the barrier islands, it looked like no place a person would wish to live.

Fort Bartow, on the shore of Roanoke Island, guarded the pile line. Bartow was a sand-and-turf construction mounting six long thirty-two-pounders. To the west, on the North Carolina mainland, Fort Forrest, with twenty-two-pounders.

Fog sat like cotton batting on the water. At nine it thinned, lifted, swirled away, and behind it, a watery sunlight, visibility clear down to Pamlico Sound.

Two divisions of Yankee gunboats steamed north.

Bowater stood on the boat deck, at the rail, looked out over the water. He wore only his gray frock coat and cap. No oilskins, no sou'wester. It was the nicest day, weatherwise, they had enjoyed in a month.

He put the field glasses to his eyes. The masts of the Yankee steamers looked like winter-bare trees; the smoke from their stacks rolled away to the west.

Heavy footsteps on the ladder. Chief Taylor appeared. He was wearing a frock coat as well, clean and pressed. Pants quite devoid of stains or smears of coal dust. He had shaved.

Bowater looked over at him and failed to hide his surprise.

"Ain't every day a man gets to fight in a gen-u-ine fleet action, Cap'n."

"No, indeed. And it would seem our Yankee admiral is moved by the same spirit." Bowater handed Taylor the field glasses and Taylor took them, put them up to his eyes, scanned the approaching enemy.

"It's a ways off," Bowater continued, "and I'm not as current on the U.S. Navy flags as I once was, but I do believe he is flying the signal 'Our country expects every man to do his duty.' "

Taylor held the glasses to his eyes, chuckled. "Now ain't that original?" He watched the fleet for a moment, then added, "It does appear they are forming in two divisions."

The Yankee fleet, thirty or so gunboats, was coming on in two clusters. Vessels in the southernmost division were towing troop transports. They peeled off, headed east, made for the sandy beach at Ashby Harbor, four miles down the sound. The advance division of Yankees steamed up sound, made right for the fleet and Fort Bartow. They would keep the Confederate forts and the Confederate ships under fire, see that the Yankee troop transports were unmolested.

"Reckon I've seen enough of this here tactical situation, Cap'n. I believe I will retire to the comfort of my engine room."

"Very well, Chief." Taylor turned, disappeared down the ladder and aft.

Bowater was alone on the boat deck. He tapped his fingers on the rail, fought the nausea in his gut. Wondered if the other captains, if Lynch and Parker, Hunter and Cooke, felt the same. Probably. Waiting, waiting, it was always the worst. Let the iron start flying, let that linkage in the mind switch from fear to fight.

Four bells, they rang out from the mosquito fleet, a discordant clanging under a thin overcast sky, and the first gun went off. From a mile down Croatan Sound, from the Union gunboats arranged in a long line abreast, dark squares on the water, wheelboxes bulging at their sides, thin, truncated masts pointing up, swaying in the swell, came the sharp bang of a rifled gun. The smoke jetted from the bow of a big side-wheeler, middle of the attacking division. The shell screamed by, not too close to the *Cape Fear*, plunged into the water a quarter mile beyond the mosquito fleet.

The battle had begun.

Bowater turned his field glasses on the *Sea Bird*. The gun crew was swarming around her thirty-pounder Parrott forward, running her out, twisting the elevation screw. From the flagstaff on top of her wheelhouse, the signal flag snapped out: "Engage the enemy."

"Mr. Harwell! When you are ready!"

Harwell grinned, waved, turned to his gun. He twisted the elevation screw, fiddled with the traverse, calling for the men with handspikes to nudge it here or there. He stepped back, jerked the lanyard. The gun went off with a satisfying jar that shook the vessel under Bowater's feet. He felt himself go calm, as if the smell of spent powder carried with it some powerful drug. He saw the shot fall three hundred yards short of the Yankee fleet.

"You are short, Mr. Harwell!" Bowater cried.

"Aye, sir!"

Harwell fiddled with the elevation screw. Not much thread left—the gun was pointed nearly as high as it would point.

Oh, hell and damnation . . . Bowater thought. *And once more, the guns won't reach.* . . .

The gunfire rippled along the line of Yankee gunboats, blasting gray smoke from the big rifled guns in their bows, sending the shells screaming overhead, plunging around the Confederate fleet. Iron shrieked by, tore up the railing on the starboard side of the boat deck. A shell hit the boat in its davits, turned it into a cloud of white-painted splinters that flew high in the air and then fluttered like autumn leaves onto the boat deck, the main deck, the fantail, the water.

Seven converted tugs and paddle wheelers in the mosquito fleet. Short of ammunition, short of men. They rode at their anchors, fired back as fast as they could, but their shells would not reach the Yankees. It was Fort Hatteras all over again. They could do little but endure the pounding.

And they were not getting the worst of it. The second division of Yankee gunboats turned their attention on Fort Bartow, a larger and closer target. They positioned themselves in such a way that only three of Bartow's guns would bear on them, and from that place they opened up. At times the fort seemed to be nothing more than a cloud of smoke and flying sand and dust kicked up by the exploding shells. But through it all, the stab of muzzle flash, as the garrison fought on.

Bowater paced, pounded his fist on his thigh, muttered curses. "Mr. Harwell! Hold your fire!" He was sick of wasted effort, wasted shells.

Then, through the din and scream, he heard the sound of anchor chain coming in. He looked to the left. *Sea Bird* was winning her anchor. A new flag was going aloft: "Close with the enemy."

"At last!" Bowater leaned over the rail. "Mr. Harwell, let us get the anchor in. We are closing with the enemy!"

"Aye, sir!"

The anchor came aboard, the *Cape Fear* was underway. Bowater swung her north, let the other vessels find their place, came in astern of *Curlew* as the mosquito fleet threaded its way through the obstructions that they themselves had set.

They closed with the Yankees. Half a mile away, nearly point-blank range, and both fleets opened up. But the Yankees had more than twice the guns, and the Yankees, it seemed, had all the ammunition they could want.

The shells came through the smoke. They ricocheted off the water, plucked sections of bulwark and cabin away, whistled and screamed through the air. The Parrott banged out, once every few minutes, whenever Harwell had his shot. The mosquito fleet kept up the fire, the Yankees returned it, three for one. The world was reduced to a haze of powder smoke, the blast of artillery, explosion of shells, the howl of flying metal, weird-sounding through numbed ears.

Eight bells, noon, one bell, two bells in the afternoon watch, and the firing did not subside, and Bowater did not know how any of them were still alive in the midst of it, still moving, ships still floating under them.

He paced back and forth. He stood in the wheelhouse, gave directions to the helmsman, rang the engine room when needed. No maneuvering, though, not really. Nothing fancy. The days of weather gauge and raking shots and fleets tacking in succession were gone, the brilliance of a John Paul Jones or Horatio Nelson part of another time, when wind was the chief tactical consideration.

Finesse and seamanship were no longer part of the equation. Two clusters of gunboats, slugging each other, hitting hard, pounding away until someone dropped. They were not fencers, they were brutes with clubs, flailing at one another. It was exactly the kind of fight that the mosquito fleet could not afford. But the only other option was to run, and that was no option at all.

Tanner bounded up the ladder. "Mr. Harwell's compliments, sir, and he has four shells left."

Bowater nodded. *Then what?* The howitzers were worthless at that range. *Get closer?* The Yankee rifled guns would tear them apart if they tried.

The gunfire was like a rainstorm, it would swell to great intensity, dozens of guns firing at once, a wall of noise, then taper off to a gun or two, clear and conspicuous in the quiet, then swell again.

It fell off now, two guns from the Yankees, a gun from the *Ellis*. Forward and below, Harwell fired the Parrott.

Three shells . . . Bowater thought.

Half a mile off, a Yankee gunboat stood bow on to the *Cape Fear*. Bowater saw the plume of gray smoke, the yellow muzzle flash. He heard the scream of the shell and at the same instant the crash of wood, the tremor through his feet, as the round smashed its way into the *Cape Fear's* deckhouse. He half turned, half spun with the shock of explosion as the shell went off. The boat deck abaft the wheelhouse blew apart, like a volcano erupting out of the guts of his ship.

This is it, this is it . . . Bowater thought, and he could only marvel that they had stood in line of battle for as long as they had before taking that fatal shell.

Four shells . . . Taylor thought. He had been counting, through no conscious effort. It was just the way his mind was. He could not keep himself from processing numbers. So he knew how many shells there were, and he subtracted one each time he felt the bone-jarring crash of the Parrott gun going off, delivering a concussion to the tug that she was never designed to endure.

Wonder what the Hero of Veracruz will do now?

It had been a dull battle thus far, his first and likely only fleet action and he had spent most of it standing there with his thumb up his ass. Underway briefly, then just turns to maintain position. A little ahead, a little astern. Finally he turned the throttle and reversing bar over to Burgess.

"How we doin' there, Moses?" he shouted.

Moses tossed a shovelful of coal into the firebox, straightened, looked at the steam gauge. "Twenty pound, boss! Nice and steady."

"Tommy! What's the coal look like in them bunkers?"

"Black, boss, black as my black ass!"

"Shaddup, smart aleck. How much coal's in there?"

"Little less den half, port side. A quarter, starboard."

Taylor nodded, chewed his unlit cigar. That was not good. The coal was their only armor, the only substantial thing between them and a shell right in the boiler.

Hieronymus Taylor had to make a conscious effort not to think about what would happen if the boiler exploded. He had seen men scalded, some bad, but never one scalded to death. He could barely imagine what it would be like to stand in the way of a full blast of steam. He saw images of skin falling off, eyes seared out, bloody pulped bodies writhing on the deck plates. If he thought too long about it he knew he would run screaming from the engine room, so he pushed the images from his mind.

He ducked under the piping, stepped aft to where the twenty-inch-wide piston maintained its slow, rhythmic stroke in the big iron cylinder. *Psssst, thump, psssst, thump, psssst, thump,* steam and metal keeping their perfect beat. He reached down to the crankshaft, touched his fingertips to smooth bearing. He examined the color of the oil that stuck there. Black. The shaft was running hot, but Taylor knew from experience that it always ran a bit hot, and he was not concerned. He threaded his way out of the engine maze, into the ten feet of open space between engine and boiler.

The *Cape Fear* vibrated, rumbled with the sound of the Parrott going off. *Three shells* . . .

And then there was a crashing sound overhead and Taylor looked up and a shell blew apart in the fidley, fifteen feet overhead. The boat deck— the roof over the engine room, two decks up—was torn apart and the air was filled with the explosion and the higher-pitched noise of shrapnel streaming past, smashing into the engine, the boiler, the steam pipes, pinging and ricocheting off metal.

Dull afternoon light streamed in, lit up the cloud of coal dust and steam and black smoke from someplace. Tommy was shrieking, lying on the deck plates, but the rest of the black gang stood frozen and Taylor stood frozen and all he could think was that the boiler was about to blow and there was not one damned second left to get their dead asses topside.

34

As [the enemy's] force was overwhelming, we commenced the action at long range, but as our shells fell short, whilst his burst over and around us, we were eventually compelled to lessen the distance.

—Flag Officer William F. Lynch to Stephen R. Mallory

The boiler did not blow, the panic passed, and Taylor shouted, "Moses! The boiler hit?"

He could not see the black man. A shell fragment had ripped a hole in the stack, three feet above the boiler. Black smoke came roiling out, filling the engine room. If the boat deck that formed the roof of the fidley had not been blown out they would have been completely blind, and quickly overcome.

The main steam pipe was fractured and a plume of steam was shooting out, whistling like a banshee's moan as it poured its white cloud into the engine room, right between Taylor and Jones. It made an impassable barrier of invisible steam and scalding hot-water vapor the width of the ship.

"Boiler near knocked clean off her mounts, but she holding!" Jones shouted.

"Tommy, what the hell's wrong?" No answer, just screaming. "What the hell's wrong with Tommy?"

"He got hit. Inna leg!"

Taylor tried to see through the geyser of steam. "Can't ya help him, for God's sake?"

"Boss, I'se holdin dis boiler up wid a slice bar! I let go, da whole damn t'ing gonna go!"

Goddamn it . . .

Steam was hissing out of the fractured pipe in a great white cloud. Taylor could feel the hot, condensed water on his face, like a thousand biting gnats. If the pipe burst, they were dead in the water. If the boiler blew, they were just dead.

"All right, all right . . ." Taylor inched toward the steam, ducked under the pipe, squeezed between the side of the coal bunker and the jet of hot vapor. He looked over his head at the pipe, hanging precariously. *Don't break, don't break, don't break . . .* He eased himself under and then he was on the other side of the steam.

Moses Jones was standing beside the boiler. One of the mounts was shot through, and he had shoved a slice bar under, levered the boiler up. The muscles stood out proud on his arms, sweat was dripping off his face. He couldn't hold it much longer.

Tommy was screaming, thrashing on the deck plates. Taylor could see a jagged piece of metal sticking out of his leg, another in his stomach.

"Jefferson!" Taylor shouted. He could not see the other coal passer. "Jefferson!" Taylor ran past the boiler, looked down the side of the big metal tube. Jefferson's body was tossed forward, sprawled out on the deck plates. One hand was on the firebox. Taylor could smell the burning flesh. Where Jefferson's head was, he could not tell.

Goddamn it! Just when I get these sons of bitches trained up. . . . He raced back, said, "You'll have to wait your turn, Tommy." If the boiler blew, then two shrapnel wounds would be the least of his problems. Taylor grabbed on to the slice bar, took up the pressure. "I got it! I got it!"

With a groan Moses let go and Taylor took the full weight, and he could not imagine how the coal passer had held it that long. *Son of a bitch . . .* "Burgess! Burgess!"

The Scotsman was there, ducking under the fractured pipe, and in his hand a jack. He ducked low, shoved the jack under the boiler, twisted the screw. Taylor felt the weight coming off the bar, off his arm muscles, and he breathed deep in relief.

All right . . . all right . . . The sound of the battle was louder now, with the roof of the engine room blown off, and it was rattling him. He heard the anchor chain rumbling through the hawsepipe. Drifting toward the Yankees. Bowater had dropped the hook. *All right . . . think . . .*

"Chief! Chief!"

What the hell . . .

"What!"

It was Tanner, looking down through the great hole that was the boat deck. "Captain needs a report, Chief! Will you be able to get steam up again?"

Steam? Got steam coming out our ass. Good thing that whore's son didn't ring the bell, I'd wring his fucking neck....

Think . . . think . . .

"Tell Bowater, turns on the screw in ten minutes!"

"Ten minutes, aye!"

Taylor looked around. The engine room was dark, a hellish place of choking black smoke and deadly steam. The main steam line was cut through and the return water was leaking as well, and steam was jetting out where a shell fragment had taken a steam pressure gauge clean off. There was hissing back by the engine, but Taylor could not see what was causing that.

It was all secondary to the main steam line. If the steam continued to jet out of the fracture rather than make its way to the cylinder, then the *Cape Fear* was going nowhere.

"Moses, rig up that fire hose and charge the line. Burgess, get me a mess of them croker sacks up by the ash hoist."

"Wadda 'ell's a croker sack?"

"Croker sack, croker sack, you know, them burlap bags up there!"

Burgess nodded, disappeared into the smoke. Taylor skirted the jet of steam, worked his way to the starboard side, the workbench. Steam and smoke swirled around, the smell of condensing water vapor mixed with the output of the firebox. The cloud twisted and swirled and sucked out of the hole in the boat deck above. Dull light from the sky overhead filtered down through the haze. The battle sounded loud, shells flying, bursting, big guns going off. Tommy was whimpering now.

Taylor bumped into the workbench before he saw it, reached out with his hand. The steam from the main steam line was hitting the bench square, but after flying the full width of the ship it had cooled enough that he could reach into it, quick.

His hand darted like a snake, fell on a wrench, pulled it back. The metal was hot and wet. He lashed out again. His hand hit the empty bench, he felt around, one second, two seconds, the steam was starting to hurt. His hand touched heavy leather gloves, and he snatched them and pulled them from the jet.

He pulled the gloves on. They were hot and wet too. He knelt down, reached back into the steam, felt around in the storage bins under the bench. Through the thick leather he felt fishplates—one for the return water pipe, another for the auxiliary steam, and finally one the diameter of the main steam pipe. He pulled it out, worked his way back to the port side.

Moses appeared like a phantom in the smoke. He held the fire hose. Water gushed out. The pump was driven by auxiliary steam—not affected by the fractured main steam line. He directed the nozzle at the bilge.

Burgess was there with the croker sacks. "Wrap them around my arms, tight," Taylor instructed.

"Lemme do this," Burgess protested, but Taylor shook his head and Burgess knew there was no time to argue. He wrapped the croker sacks around Taylor's arms, tied them in place with lengths of spun yarn.

Taylor turned to Moses Jones. "You keep that goddamned water on me while I'm near the steam. You know the drill."

"Yes, boss."

Taylor took the fishplate in hand. It looked like a short piece of pipe, cut in two lengthwise, with flanges on the edges. In cross section they looked like a flattened Greek Ω. The two halves of the fishplate would go over the break in the main steam pipe. They would be secured together by bolts that fitted through holes in the flanges. A simple five-minute fix if you didn't have to do it in a smoke-filled engine room with a jet of live steam in your face.

Taylor unscrewed the bolts and separated the two halves of the fishplate. He approached the hissing jet of steam and Moses turned the fire hose on him, soaking him down, keeping a constant stream of brackish water on him to prevent his being scalded by the steam.

Taylor blinked hard. The smoke burned his eyes and made it hard to see. The white plume that formed ten inches from the pipe was the water vapor, steam condensing in the air. That was not the problem. The actual steam coming out of the pipe was clear, invisible. It was that steam, which he could not see, that could turn him into a scalded horror, begging to die.

He reached up and clapped the fishplate over the main steam pipe, near the leak, inserted the bolts, threaded the nuts. It was clumsy work with the heavy gloves. Twice he dropped nuts, wasted six minutes finding them in the smoke.

His eyes burned and his throat burned and he felt faint for want of water, and from breathing smoke. The blast from the fire hose made it hard to stand, and sometimes his balance would shift and the water from the hose would knock him toward the hissing steam and he would have to fight to keep from being pushed into it.

And all the time he was braced for the pipe to break clean through, to hit him square with a blast of pure, invisible steam.

At last the fishplate was on, set loose, and Taylor slid it down the pipe toward the break. It moved easy, covered half the fracture. The note of the steam went up in pitch as the hole through which it passed was cut in half. Taylor pushed. It would go no farther.

Damn . . . He turned around. There was Burgess with a big hammer, holding it out to him. Taylor took the hammer, tapped it on the flange, tapped harder and harder still. He wound up, swung hard, and it occurred to him, midswing, that he could break the steam pipe that way, cripple them for good, put himself in the way of a faceful of steam.

Too late to check the swing; the hammer struck with a clang like a broken bell. The fishplate shifted six inches aft and the fracture was covered. The note went up again, the steam now squeezing out from behind the plate. Steam was a beast, it had to be contained, it fought to get loose, through any tiny place it could find. It was a malleable beast—no hole was too small. It was a deadly beast if you got too close.

Taylor reached up with the wrench, clapped it on the nuts, began to work them around. He could feel the steam—pure, invisible steam—on the leather gloves, and soon he had to jerk his hand away. Turn, turn, pull his hands away, working the wrench with the blast of water from the fire hose playing over his shoulders, his back, his head.

It took twenty minutes, all told, but finally it was over, the beast was back in the pipe. Taylor ran his leather-clad hand over the fishplate. He could feel no jet of steam, could see no white plume where the steam was condensing.

"That should hold us till the next time," he announced. He stepped away from the pipe, and Moses directed the fire hose back to the bilge. The smoke was lifting up through the boat deck. Visibility in the engine room was better now.

"Good job," Taylor said. He was burned, his eyes and throat raw. He was faint with the heat and he was soaked clean through.

"Burgess, you take over here. See what you can do about patching the stack. I have to go report to the old man. Moses, let's get her up to about fifteen pounds and see how she takes it."

Taylor found the ladder up to the deck above, climbed it. He stopped, looked back. "Yeah, and see if you can do somethin' for Tommy, too." He took the last rungs, stepped out onto the side deck. He had not realized how choked the engine room was until he pulled in a lungful of fresh air. It was the most wonderful thing in the world. He blinked in the light of the dull overcast, stumbled forward along the deck.

The Yankee fleet was half a mile away, muzzle flashes blinking like fireflies. The water around the *Cape Fear* and the rest of the mosquito fleet was torn up with the falling shells, and the Confederates were returning fire at a desultory rate. *Three shells* . . . Taylor remembered; that was all the *Cape Fear* had left. The others could not be doing much better.

He climbed up the ladder at the forward end of the deckhouse, stepped onto the boat deck. Bowater was standing there, his hand resting on the remains of a mangled rail, looking out over the fight as if he was watching a sporting event, one in which he had little interest.

Cool son of a bitch . . . Taylor thought. Bowater looked at him, his right eyebrow shot up.

"Chief, are we taking on water?"

"No, no, had the fire hose turned on me. No fire, no leak. Main steam line took a hard one when that shell exploded, fractured but didn't break. Got a fishplate on it. It'll hold for now. We should be able to get underway in a couple of minutes."

Bowater nodded. "Good, good. Any casualties?"

"Washington got his head took clean off. Tommy's cut up some, but I was a little busy to see how bad."

"Merrow!" Bowater called out to the deckhand standing by. "Get St. Laurent and the two of you get down to the engine room, see what you can do for Tommy."

"Aye!"

"How's the fight goin, Cap'n?"

"It is going the way one might have predicted. Actually, not so bad. We've lost *Curlew*." Bowater pointed toward the swampy shoreline that formed the west side of Croatan Sound. The side-wheeler was hard aground, listing to starboard. "Shell went right through her, either came out the bottom or buckled her plate. She just barely made it to shore before she sank."

The boat deck began to tremble underfoot with the familiar throb of the engine, turning slow. "Reckon we have steam up, Cap'n."

"Good. Mr. Harwell!" Harwell, who had been nursing his last remaining shells, looked up from the foredeck. "Weigh anchor, please!"

Taylor and Bowater stood at the forward edge of the boat deck, watched the battle raging all around them.

"There goes *Forrest*," Taylor observed. The screw tug, which had been standing in line abreast with her companions, was now drifting back, spinning around slowly in the weak tidal flow. They watched her drift away. There were a hundred things that could have put her out, from a thrown prop to a cracked bearing to a shell in her boiler that scalded half her crew to death.

A splash at her bow and her anchor was down. The tug straightened, stopped her drift, but she was out of the fight. Two down. Nearly a third of the fleet knocked out.

They banged away for another hour and a half. Harwell shot off the last rounds, and then they were spectators, like watching a play, like sitting through hours of *Hamlet*, fully aware that the Prince of Denmark has no hope to live past the curtain.

Five o'clock and the light was fading fast and the Union ships retired. Fort Bartow was a near wreck, the mosquito fleet battered. Coal was running low, there was not above a dozen shells left among all the Confederate fleet.

With the winter night coming on fast, they stripped *Curlew* of anything worth having. *Sea Bird* took *Forrest*, her propeller disabled, in tow, and the little ships steamed north, forty miles to Elizabeth City.

It was a black night, and the ships had no lights showing, because they did not know what the Union fleet was about. Bowater paced the wheelhouse, peered out into the dark, gave orders to the helmsman, the engine room. Nervous work.

And so it was with a lovely sensation of relief that the first gray light of dawn showed the fleet in relatively good order, steaming line ahead, and the mouth of the Pasquotank River opening up before them.

They anchored up at Elizabeth City, hauled the *Forrest* up on the ways. They could hear gunfire from Roanoke Island, artillery and small-arms fire. It was a horrible thing to hear, but there was nothing they could do. The Yankees were ashore; it was a land fight now. And even if it was not, they had no ammunition, and they were finding there was none to be had at Elizabeth City.

Lynch sent Hunter to Norfolk to retrieve ammunition. He appointed William Parker to organize the town's defenses. Parker organized the local militia to man the pathetic fort at Cobb's Point, pressed an old schooner into service as a makeshift battery.

Around noon the firing at Roanoke Island slackened and then stopped, like a dying man taking his last breath, and everyone in the mosquito fleet knew that the Yankee machine had rolled over the Southern defenses. Bowater could not shake the feeling that they had not done enough, but in his most honest, most private analysis, he could not imagine what more they could have done.

The Yankees' next step would be Elizabeth City and the mosquito fleet, the last ember of resistance. The men on Roanoke Island had stood and fought to the last, until they were absolutely overrun. Now it was the navy's turn.

They waited through the next day, sent boats down sound to reconnoiter the Yankees, preparing to get underway. That night the captains met. They agreed to fight until the ammunition was gone, then try to escape.

Failing that, they would run their vessels ashore, burn them, destroy the signal books, save their men. The fleet was arranged in line abreast, bows pointing downriver. They divided up what ammunition they had.

It was 3:00 a.m. when Samuel Bowater returned to the *Cape Fear*, staggered into his cabin, fell facedown on his bunk. He did not take off his coat or his shoes, or his sword or pistol. Even in sleep he was careful not to put his shoes on the bed.

Jacob roused him before dawn. He staggered into the wheelhouse. It was bitter cold. The steam pipes were popping and crackling as Hieronymus Taylor got up a head of steam in the boiler and the first wafts of hot vapor blew through.

Men moved about the deck like clumsy shadows, clearing for action, ready to greet the dawn at quarters, as men-of-war in times of conflict had done for a century or more. They cleared away the bow gun and the howitzers, loaded and ran them out, then retreated to the warmth of the galley, with the old man's permission, to wait for what would happen next. They huddled against the bulkheads, scarfing toasted bread with cheese, sun-dried-tomato-and-chive omelettes, and deviled partridge, cold.

Bowater ate his omelette standing in the wheelhouse, and though his concentration was taken up with the gathering dawn, the slow revelation of the mosquito fleet at anchor, the riverbanks on either hand, he could not help but notice the extraordinary lightness of the eggs, the perfect blend of savory cheese and sharp chive, the subtlety of the tomatoes that St. Laurent had dried himself. Samuel had seen them, months before, spread out on racks on the boat deck, had nearly ordered them struck below. They were very unseamanlike and disorderly. But he held his tongue, guessing he would be glad for it. And he was.

More and more of the river revealed itself: tangled shoreline, rippled gray water, stubby oak and pine along the shores. And downriver, rising above a western bend, columns of dark smoke, bending in the offshore breeze. The Union squadron, underway.

Harwell appeared for orders. "Luff, I imagine they will employ their former tactics, steam in circles around the fort, pound it to rubble. I hope those militiamen will stand up to it."

"I hope so, sir. They may be militia, but they are Southern militia, and I would warrant them for standing as tall as any abolitionist regular."

"Let us hope you are right. Now please assemble the gun crews and have them stand ready. We'll wait for what presents itself."

"Aye, sir," Harwell said, saluted, hurried off.

Such enthusiasm, such patriotism . . . Bowater thought. *Is Harwell a naive romantic, or am I a cynical, unsentimental cad? Or is it both?*

Samuel Bowater watched the young luff get the men to quarters. He was giving them some words of encouragement, he could tell.

Morituri te salutamus, Bowater thought.

Lieutenant Thadeous Harwell stood behind the breech of the big Parrott gun, hands clasped behind his back, looking down river.

Gladly do I lay down this life for my beloved Southern home, and only regret that I shall not live to fight on. . . .

No . . .

Happy am I to lay down my life for my . . . *for this, my beloved Southern* . . . *beloved Confederacy. . . .*

There, that has more of a classical sound. . . .

Happy am I to lay down my life for this, my beloved Confederacy, and only regret that I shall not live to fight on. . . .

Good.

He ran it over, again and again, in his head. Said it out loud, but softly, like a prayer, so no one would hear. The trick with dying words, he imagined, was to commit them to memory so well that one could not forget them when the time came. He could not imagine what must go through a man's mind at the time. Probably a lot. If he wanted to go out with some noble words on his lips, he had best be ready.

"Happy am I . . ."

By eight-thirty the Union fleet was in sight. The ships came steaming around the bend, trailing their black plumes of smoke. Through field glasses Bowater could see the churning white water around their bows. They were coming on fast, fourteen Yankee gunboats stretched across the river, a waterborne cavalry charge. The Confederates were as ready as they were going to get.

Waiting, waiting . . . Once again. Bowater could feel his stomach twisting like a fish on a hook. He regretted the second helping of omelette.

Wait for it, wait for it . . . Bowater found himself thinking, over and over. Just a handful of minutes and the Union fleet would be under the fort's guns, and it would be a three-way exchange of fire—Union fleet, mosquito fleet, Fort Cobb. Roanoke once more.

Line ahead now, they came up with Fort Cobb and the fort opened up on them, the thirty-two-pounders blasting away with their flat, echoing report, kicking up spouts in the river. The Union ships returned fire, rifled shells and spherical case shot. One by one they blasted the fort as they passed.

Bowater waited, waited for the lead Yankee to turn, to start the big circling maneuver that would take the ships by the fort again and again until they had reduced it to nothing. Just as they had done at Hatteras. Just as they had done at Roanoke Island. So fixed was this idea in his mind that nearly the entire enemy fleet was past the fort, and was coming on, before he realized they were not going to do it again.

They were bypassing the fort, giving it one good shot and then ignoring it, giving it the attention it deserved, which was very little. It was the mosquito fleet they wanted, and they were coming straight on, full-speed, right for their quarry. It would be ship to ship this time. It would be Trafalgar in miniature, not Roanoke Island. It would be the Yankees' advantage, three to one.

35

[T]he desertion of [Elizabeth City] situated near the head of the Dismal Swamp Canal, would have been unseemly and discouraging, more particularly as I had urged the inhabitants to defend it to the last extremity.

—Flag Officer William F. Lynch to Stephen R. Mallory

"That stern-wheeler, there . . ." Bowater stood in the wheel-house, pointed to the onrushing Yankee, three hundred yards downriver. "Right for him. We'll go in shooting."

"Aye, sir." Tanner at the wheel looked grim. Bowater grabbed the engine-room bell, gave three bells, full ahead.

Sons of bitches . . . It made Bowater mad, in a way he had not been mad before. The arrogance of the damned Yankees, bypass the fort, sweep forward as if they were brushing aside an annoyance. It was the entire Yankee way of thinking; brush aside anything that was in their way, any tradition, any sacred right, anything that prevented their building more factories, more railroads, unleashing more mechanical horror on the world.

Suddenly this fight seemed personal. Suddenly Captain Samuel Bowater, detached and professional navy man, a man who followed orders, felt himself a wild-eyed patriot.

He stepped out of the wheelhouse, went forward. "Mr. Harwell, we are going for that stern-wheeler that seems to be coming for us. Let's shoot him in the nose as we approach!"

Harwell waved, turned back to his gun. Bowater could feel the deck vibrate as Taylor poured on the steam. Bowater heard the water boiling under the counter, felt the tug build speed and momentum as the river-banks slipped past. She was not a quarter horse, she was a knight's charger—heavy, slow, strong as could be.

They closed fast, bow to bow. The Yankee fired; Bowater felt the wind of the shell as it passed. Harwell fired, took the Yankee's fore topmast clean off. He spun the elevation screw, lowered the aim. He was not used to firing so close.

The Yankees were charging down on the mosquito fleet, coming on line abreast now, picking their targets. Two of the enemy were falling on *Ellis*, and she was turning, firing, backing, trying to keep from their grasp. Bowater could see Yankee troops on the ships' decks—they must have augmented their navy crews, while the Confederates were desperate for anyone who could stand.

One hundred yards separated the Yankee from the *Cape Fear*. Harwell fired again, blew the upper third off the Yankee's stack. Smoke poured out in an ugly, disorganized cloud.

But now the Yankee turned, presented her broadside, three big guns, the bulk of her armament. Bowater grabbed the rail hard, clenched his teeth, waited for what would come.

Boom, boom, boom, the big guns opened up right in their face. Bowa-ter felt the deck shudder, saw a plume of splinters burst right in front of him, as a shell hit the deckhouse and kept on going. Another whipped the head off the rammer at the bow gun, neat as an executioner's ax, tossed his body back onto the foredeck as the shell continued down the side deck. Bowater heard it hit the port howitzer, a terrible clanging, a shattering of wooden carriage, a pause, and then the screaming of the men who were in the way.

"Captain! Captain!" Tanner shouted from the wheelhouse. His course was right for the Yankee, steaming to hit her amidships.

"Steady as she goes!" Would the *Cape Fear* take the impact? Who knew? This was her last fight in any instance, that much was clear.

Fifty yards, forty yards. "Mr. Harwell, get your men away from the bow!"

Harwell shouted, waved, led his men aft, back toward the deckhouse.

Thirty yards. Bowater could see Yankees scrambling now. The broad-side guns were running out again. Too late. Smoke pumping from the broken stack, the side wheels gathered speed, as the Yankee gunboat tried to get out of the path of the suicide Rebel.

Twenty yards. The Yankee's side wheels churned, kicked water; the Yankee inched forward, tried to turn bow on. Bowater felt some bit of sanity return. It was not time to die, not yet.

"Tanner, take her side wheel out! Glancing blow!"

Tanner nodded, looked relieved. He spun the wheel to starboard, angled in, swung it to port. The *Cape Fear* was moving fast, carrying a lot of momentum. The ships were side to side, passing on opposite courses. The *Cape Fear*'s bow struck the wheelbox, blew it apart with the impact, went right on through, spraying paddles, twisting paddle-wheel arms, as the side wheel destroyed itself against the Rebel.

They powered past. Bowater watched running Yankees, shouting Yankees, angry Yankees, so close he could see their faces. Small arms banged away. Bowater could hear the thud of bullets hitting woodwork. The Cape Fears fired back.

On the Yankee's boat deck, a lone figure, an officer, leaning on the rail. Lieutenant S. P. Quackenbush. Bowater knew him well, had spent long hours on watch with him, in past years. Quackenbush doffed his cap and Bowater doffed his as they passed, as if the entire scene was not bizarre enough.

The Yankee's forward gun went off, right into the *Cape Fear*'s deckhouse, the muzzle not ten feet from the bulkhead. The proximity saved them; the shell just made a hole and kept on going.

"Come left, come left!" Bowater shouted, and Tanner spun the wheel and Bowater looked out over the wild melee on the river. *Sea Bird* was sinking fast, rammed by a Yankee gunboat. *Ellis* was side by side with a Yankee and they were going at it, hand to hand, but the Yankees carried marines on board, and they outnumbered the Rebels four to one.

The smoke lay like morning fog on the river, the gunfire was nearly continuous, the gunboats moved in and out of the clouds from their own guns. Boats whirled, steamed ahead, fired, slewed around in the wild dance on the water.

Bowater stood in the wheelhouse door. "Make for *Ellis*—let us see if we can come to her aid." *Full ahead.* They were still going full ahead. He looked at *Ellis*. He did not think they would reach her in time.

Ellis's crew was being pressed by boarders from two sides. Cutlasses flashed, small arms fired. Hand-to-hand naval combat. It was something from another era, like this entire wild ship-on-ship fleet action.

The *Cape Fear* staggered, as if shoved from behind, slewed sideways, and the aft end seemed to explode. Bowater turned to see splinters and bits of rail and wood flying as high as the deckhouse.

"Steady as she goes!" he shouted to Tanner, then ran aft, skirted the huge hole that had been the boat deck, stopped at the after rail. *Quackenbush!* His ship was disabled but his guns would still bear, and he was firing, had hit the *Cape Fear* square on the stern. The lovely rounded fantail was gone. The vessel ended three feet shorter in a jagged, gaping profusion of broken frames and shattered planks. But it was well above the waterline, and would not stop them.

Quackenbush! There was a sense of betrayal. Before, Bowater had fought anonymous ships, captains who might as well have been foreign enemies. But Quackenbush? They had laughed together. They had traded bottles of wine, for the love of God, and Quackenbush had displayed a surprisingly refined palate!

Both howitzers were knocked out, the guns on the deck, the carriages in half a dozen pieces. Three dead men lay scattered about, as if they had fallen exhausted, except that they were each missing one or more limbs. The rest of the gun crews were gone, forward, Bowater supposed.

Bowater pushed himself off the rail, ran forward again. Another shot, broad on the starboard beam; the deckhouse shook. Bowater stumbled, fell forward, broke his fall with his hands. He used the momentum to scramble back to his feet.

A Yankee gunboat had broken through the bank of smoke, was steaming down on them, a dark cloud roiling up from her stack. A screw steamer, no vulnerable side wheels. A cable length away, coming right at them with malicious intent.

Bowater ran back to the wheelhouse. "Come right, come right!" Tanner spun the wheel. *Ellis* would have to look after herself. Bowater glanced back at the tug. Too late in any event.

It was a jousting match once again, the *Cape Fear* and the Yankee, bow to bow and coming straight on.

Bowater stepped to the front of the boat deck. "Mr. Harwell, you see your target!"

"Aye, sir! I only have two more shells, sir!"

Bowater nodded. *Two more shells. Howitzers gone.* The only weapons left were the men and the *Cape Fear* herself.

"Use them now! We'll ram and board her!"

"Aye, aye, sir!"

Madness! The fight was lost, it was a suicide run, take one of the bastards down with you. Pointless, but Bowater could think of no other option. Run for Norfolk? He could not do that.

"Merrow, run down to the engine room. Tell Chief Taylor I want the throttles open wide, and then all hands out of the engine room. Tell him to arm his black gang with pistols and cutlasses."

Merrow repeated the basics of the order, hurried off. One hundred yards; the Yankee fired again, missed. Harwell fired and missed as well. Fifty percent of the *Cape Fear*'s ammunition plunged uselessly into the river.

Samuel Bowater watched the water boiling under the Yankee's bow, the plume of smoke from the stack, the determined, deadly, relentless onrush of the enemy, and for the first time since the first shot at Fort Sumter, he looked on the enemy and hated him.

Chief Taylor prowled. He looked at steam gauges. Creeping past twenty-five pounds, the boiler was pushing out maximum steam. He examined the fishplate, peered into the firebox. There was clinker on the grates, glass that formed from the melting sand in the coal, and it was impeding the draft of the fire. He frowned. They should wing the fire over to the other side of the firebox, break that clinker out of there. But now was not the time.

He prowled back to the engine, ran his eyes over piping, watched the motion of thrusting and rotating parts. All was well.

He was not so sure that was the case topside. They had taken a shell in the transom; he could see places where daylight shone through the hull. The deckhouse was so punched through there was more hole than bulkhead. They had been going full ahead, weaving, turning. That could not be good.

He lit his cigar, puffed it to life. He looked at the coal bunkers. Coal bunkers, by definition, were not always full of coal. Sometimes, such as now, they were only a quarter full. That made them, by Taylor's lights, a piss-poor choice for the protection of a fighting vessel. Who ever heard of armoring that might or might not be there during a fight?

They were a quarter full now. That meant that for most of the vessel's side, there was only a single layer of inch-and-a-half white oak planks over live oak frames standing between rifled ordnance fired at point-blank range and the ship's boiler.

Don't think about that, can't think about that. . . .

The *Cape Fear* heeled into a turn. Taylor staggered, his hand reached out, automatically fell on a nonhot surface to steady himself. Burgess dumped coal on the deck plates. Moses shoveled, flung it in the fire. Jefferson dead, Tommy laid up, they were short-handed.

A voice called down the fidley. Taylor looked up. Merrow standing in the door. He had not even noticed the door opening, so much of the sides, bulkheads, and roof were gone.

"Chief Taylor! Chief Taylor! Captain says open the throttle up and then all hands out of the engine room! Arm yourselves with pistols and cutlasses!"

Pistols and cutlasses? It sounded like a pirate melodrama. He wondered if such an order had been heard on those waters since Maynard came after his hero, Blackbeard.

"You heard him!" Taylor shouted. "Everyone out! Cap'n wants to play rough!" The throttle was already wide open, no need to touch it.

Moses and Burgess looked at him, reluctant. Leaving their engine room for the last time.

"Come on, you damned weepy, sentimental old ladies, get the hell out of here!"

A shell hit the deckhouse, crashed through, took out the after bulkhead, exploded on exit, ripping apart the frames, the knees. With a wrenching, cracking sound half the boat deck sagged down into the fidley, and what was keeping it from collapsing into the engine room Taylor could not tell.

The destruction energized Burgess and Jones. They flung shovels and slice bars aside, leaped for the ladder, scurried up.

Burgess reached the top, paused, looked back, Moses one step below, Taylor a step below him. One last look at their fiefdom, and as they looked the starboard coal bunker exploded in a spray of planking and frames and anthracite coal. The engine room rang with the sound of metal striking metal, of red-hot ballistic shards of steel shell slamming into the boiler.

"Son of a . . . !" Taylor managed to get out. Burgess leaped through the door and Moses leaped after him. Taylor took the steps, flew up the steps, leaped headlong out of the engine-room door as if diving in the water, hit the deck, rolled, scrambled.

Behind him, the door blew clean out of its frame, flew twenty feet outboard, pushed by a great white cloud of condensed steam that blasted the window out of the sides of the engine room and shot like a geyser through the gaping hole in the boat deck.

Metal clanged on metal, the air was consumed with a great whooshing sound, the muffled sound of an explosion below as the boiler blew apart. Taylor tried to make himself as small as he could, lying prone on the deck, pressed against the deckhouse, arms over his head. He waited until the whooshing and the clanging were gone and then he looked up.

There was an odd quiet now. The *Cape Fear* did not vibrate, the engine did not thump. Dead in the water. Probably filling fast.

He scrambled to his feet. "Burgess, Jones, y'all still alive?"

They nodded, so Taylor reckoned they were. "All right, git yerselves some weapons. Cutlass, whatever y'all want. I'll go see the cap'n."

He staggered forward, rounded the remains of the deckhouse. A Yankee steamer was bearing down, fifty yards away, the son of a bitch that put a shell in their boiler, no doubt.

Taylor grabbed on to the ladder, pulled himself up. The angle was not right, the *Cape Fear* was listing. Must have blown a hole in the bottom.

He came out on the boat deck. Bowater was there, sword in one hand, his engraved .36 Navy Colt in the other. He looked surprised.

"Chief! You're alive!"

"If you care to call it that."

"I saw that cloud of steam, I thought y'all were done for."

"Almost. Next time, I reckon. Shell right in the boiler. I think we are sinkin."

"We are no doubt sinking. And soon we'll be fighting these bastards here." He nodded to the Yankee gunboat, coming on fast.

"Might you have a weapon of some sort handy?" Taylor asked. Tanner stepped out of the wheelhouse, the useless wheel abandoned. He held out a cutlass and a rough sea service pistol. "Here, Chief," he said. Taylor took the weapons. He glanced at Bowater and Tanner, the easy way they held their weapons, as familiar as a wrench was in Taylor's hands. He felt awkward, like an amateur. He had not spent the past decades in the naval service, handling such things.

Damned navy, stupid damned navy . . .

The Yankee was twenty yards away, throttling down, marines and sailors on her bow, ready to board. "Let's go meet our guests," Bowater said and led them down the ladder to the foredeck, where Harwell had his men assembled, ready to repel.

Ten yards and the Yankees opened up with small arms, rifles and pistols, and the Rebels huddled behind the bulwark and the silent Parrott and fired back. The gunnel of the Yankee gunboat was ten feet or more above the *Cape Fear;* it was like firing up at the top of a castle wall.

The Yankee came dead in the water, bumped against the *Cape Fear,* and suddenly there were shouting, cursing blue-clad men leaping down from the deck above, landing on the *Cape Fear's* foredeck, men climbing down the Yankee's side, finding footholds in hawse pipe and wale, falling on the *Cape Fear,* wielding swords and pistols.

Wild! Taylor lifted his pistol, held in his left hand, shot a U.S. marine, five feet away. A bullet grazed his arm. A sailor was aiming a pistol at him, so close he could touch him. Their eyes met. Taylor swung his cutlass, knocked the gun aside just as it discharged and blasted its .38-caliber round into the deck. The sailor tried to raise the gun again but Taylor stepped into him, slammed him in the face with the hand guard of the cutlass, and he dropped.

The chief looked around. The fighting was hand-to-hand all over the deck. There was Bowater, firing, parrying, lunging, right in the thick of it. Taylor felt that weird fighting energy he knew so well, not from combat, but from more waterfront tavern brawls then he could ever recall.

He saw a gun aimed at Bowater, ten feet away, saw the finger squeeze the trigger, the trigger deflect, and he raised his cutlass and chopped down. He felt the blade hit bone, the gun go off, the man scream.

He felt a punch in the shoulder, as if someone had hit him hard, but there was no one there. It spun him half around. He clapped a hand over the spot; it came away red.

Taylor staggered, almost fell. *Just my shoulder . . .* he thought, did not know why that should affect his balance. And then he realized—it was the *Cape Fear*. She had lurched, rolled. She was going down.

Lieutenant Thadeous Harwell, for the first time in his charmed life, led his men forward into the face of a boarding enemy. Such heroics were supposed to have gone out with John Paul Jones, with Decatur and Collingwood. They were not part of modern naval warfare. But now he was given the chance to do it—ancient, noble warfare in modern times.

They were marines, but Harwell was not afraid. He shouted as he ran, waved his sword to urge the men on, though it was only twenty feet. He came sword to sword with a graybeard, an old salt, felt bad for the old man. A lifetime at sea, and Harwell, young, strong, quick, turned his blade aside, thrust, ran the sword into the man's belly.

He pulled it free, did not watch the man fall. A marine aimed his pistol, fired. The ball burned a trail through his side, but Harwell raised his pistol, shot left-handed, knocked the man down.

Bowater was there, heroic Bowater. Harwell wished he could achieve the captain's quiet stoicism, that lofty air. Sometimes he felt like Bowater's puppy, wondered if Bowater felt the same.

Another cutlass-wielding sailor, climbing over the Parrott. Harwell met him, blade to blade. He tried to raise the pistol but the sailor did not give him the opening to do so. Their weapons rang against one another, and Harwell felt the shivers down his arm. This one was good.

Harwell pressed the attack, tried to throw him off. The sailor took a step back, came up against the Parrott. Trapped, fending off Harwell's blade. The opening would come. One stroke, two strokes.

Harwell was flung forward. He thought he had been shoved. He fell, off balance, past the surprised sailor with whom he had been fighting, down to the deck. He hit the hard yellow pine planks, came to a stop. Tried to move but could not.

He opened his eyes. He was looking at the front wheel of the Parrott's gun carriage. He was jammed up there in the bow and he could not seem to move. He could feel nothing but dull warmth from his waist down, and he was confused.

Get back . . . in . . . the fight . . . The words ran though his head, but somehow he knew he would not be able to do so. He felt a warm, sticking something on his cheek.

Dear God . . . I have been hit! He tried to cry out but he could not make a sound. He had had dreams like that, where he was trying to shout but could not. This was the same thing. Was it a dream?

Then the pain came, a wave of agony shooting out along legs, arms, head, and he knew it was not a dream. He did not know what was wrong, but he knew that this was it. He was going to die. Frightening and comforting all at once. The pain was so very great, he saw death as a warm blanket pulled over him.

There was terrific excitement on the deck. Men were shouting, guns going off, but not as many. He thought that the deck was at an odd angle, but he was not sure. The Parrott lurched a bit, slid toward him. The pain swelled, eased off, swelled again. He felt cold.

Suddenly he was moving. The gun-carriage wheel disappeared and the world seemed to whirl around. He looked up. Gray sky, smoke. He did not know what was happening.

A face blotted out the sky. Captain Samuel Bowater. The captain had lifted him up, was cradling him. Harwell tried to smile, was not sure if he had managed it.

"We fought them off, Lieutenant!" Bowater said, loud. "Thanks to you, we fought them off!"

Then Harwell remembered. The words! The final words! And here, of all men on earth he would wish to say them to, here was Captain Samuel Bowater, whom he loved so dearly.

Harwell made to speak, and then a panic rushed over him. He could not recall! All that practice, and now the moment, and he could not recall. He wanted to weep.

The edges of his vision were growing dull, and he felt a lightness to his body, and then suddenly in a great rush they were there, the words he had labored over. Joy spread over him like the heat in front of a blazing fire, and he spoke and he could hear his voice was clear and loud and strong.

"Happy am I to lay down my life for this, my beloved Confederacy, and only regret that I shall not live to fight on. . . ."

Bowater was nodding. He had heard the words, understood the sentiment. Of course, such a noble spirit would understand. The world seemed to be growing brighter. Brilliant light seemed to be streaming from around the captain, and soon the captain was lost in the light and then it was all light and then nothing.

*   *   *

Samuel Bowater held the dead lieutenant in his arms and he felt tears roll down his cheeks, surprising and bitter. The poor bastard had been shot right in the back, spine severed, lungs torn up, artery blown apart.

He had lied to Harwell, but he did not feel bad about that. They had not beaten the Yankees back. They had fought to a standstill, fought until the *Cape Fear* lurched hard, began a death roll, and the Yankees fled from the sinking tug, climbed back aboard their gunboat. Some of the Cape Fears had followed them, preferring prison to death in the river. The rest remained, grabbed on to things that would float.

He had told Harwell they had won because that was what the lieutenant, with his wild, romantic notion of war—a notion that was not dimmed by real and bloody combat—would have wanted in his dying ears.

Harwell had smiled. He had tried to say something, it was unintelligible, a mumble of half-formed words, and then he died. He died with the smile on his lips. Bowater could not take his eyes from the smile.

The *Cape Fear* rolled again, and Bowater nearly fell over. He looked back. The after end, right up to the middle of the deckhouse, was underwater; debris and dead men were swirling around in the stream.

A hand fell on his shoulder. He looked up. Taylor was there, bleeding from three places, cigar in his teeth, violin case under his arm. "We got to go, Cap'n," he said.

"Go where?"

"Dunno. Find some damned thing will float."

"I'm taking Harwell."

"All right. I'll help."

Taylor grabbed Harwell's feet, Bowater grabbed his shoulders, and they lifted and Taylor grunted and cursed and Bowater guessed that the wounds hurt more than he would let on.

Tanner was there, helping with the weight. They half-walked, half-slid down the deck to the water. No one spoke, no one had any idea of what they would do when the boat sank under them.

Then around the shattered deckhouse, moving fast, churning the water, came the CSS *Appomattox*. Lieutenant Simms in the wheelhouse pointed, reached up, and rang the engine-room bell. The *Appomattox* slowed, settled into her wake, stopped beside the sinking *Cape Fear*. Men on her fantail, anxious faces, grabbed hold of the Cape Fears, pulled them over the tug's low bulwark. Men on the *Cape Fear* handed wounded over, scrambled over after them.

The Yankee gunboat fired, too high, the shell screamed past. Taylor and Bowater handed the body of Lieutenant Harwell over. "Go on, Chief," Bowater said, and Taylor scrambled onto the tug.

Bowater turned to Tanner. "Go . . ." he said and stopped. This had played out before—him, Tanner, enemy guns, the last men to leave. "Well, I'll be damned."

"You remember."

Bowater shook his head. It was too much. Think on it later. "Go on, Tanner, I won't argue this time."

Tanner nodded, climbed over the bulwark. Bowater took one last look around. The breeching on the Parrott gave way and the big gun slid down the deck, slammed into the front of the deckhouse. Bowater wanted to weep. He turned, climbed on board the *Appomattox*, felt the deck shake as Simms ordered up all the steam they had.

Bowater stood on the fantail, watched the *Cape Fear*, his first command, slip away. She went down fast, the river lapping over her, her deckhouse, her foredeck, her boat deck. Last of all he saw the wheelhouse, his wheelhouse, a place that he had come to love as much as any place he had known, go under with a roil of bubbles, and then she was gone.

He stared at the spot, but it was soon far astern, with the *Appomattox* running upriver to the Dismal Swamp Canal. Bowater surveyed the scene of the battle. Steamers everywhere, Union ships weaving in and out, but the fight was over. *Sea Bird* was all but sunk. *Ellis* was in Yankee hands, *Black Warrior* on fire, *Fanny* run aground and blown up, the *Forrest* set on fire on the ways.

Bowater forced himself to climb up to the wheelhouse, where Lieutenant Simms was looking upriver, giving helm commands.

"Lieutenant," Bowater said, "on behalf of myself and my men I thank you for your brave and timely arrival."

Simms smiled, nodded. "Wish I could have been there before you took that damned Yankee shell. My bow gun got knocked out, only had the howitzer, which was of little value."

Bowater looked back. The steamers were receding in the distance, the fight left astern. "Nothing you could have done . . ." he said at last. "Nothing to be done."

They continued on upriver in silence, and soon the locks of the Great Dismal Swamp Canal were ahead, gaping open like welcoming arms. Bowater glanced down at the deck of the *Appomattox*.

"You've taken this boat though the locks before?" he asked.

"No. Reckoned this was as good a time as any to give it a try."

Bowater nodded. "You think she'll fit in the lock?"

Simms frowned, shrugged. "I don't know."

The river narrowed, the lock gates lay open. Simms rang the engine room. Half ahead. He rang again. Slow ahead. They approached the locks going two knots at most. Simms scanned the opening, looked at the *Appomattox*. Bowater did the same. Twenty feet away. Bowater had opened his mouth to say he did not think they would make it when Simms said, "It'll be tight, but I think we'll fit."

The helmsman gave the wheel a subtle turn. The bow eased into the lock gates, the granite sides of the lock slid past. The *Appomattox* lurched to a stop, the men in the wheelhouse stumbled to keep their footing. Bowater looked down the side. The tug was jammed halfway into the lock, stuck fast.

Book Four

THE FIGHT ON WESTERN WATER

36

𝔑𝔢𝔴 𝔜𝔬𝔯𝔨 𝔇𝔞𝔦𝔩𝔶 𝔗𝔯𝔦𝔟𝔲𝔫𝔢,
Thursday, February 13, 1862:

BURNSIDE'S EXPEDITION
ITS FIRST TERRIBLE BLOW
CAPTURE OF ROANOKE
DIRECT NEWS FROM THE ENEMY
Rebel Fleet Completely Destroyed
THE PANIC AMONG THE PEOPLE
ELIZABETH CITY ABANDONED
THE TOWN DESTROYED BY FIRE
GOV. WISE NOT IN THE FIGHT
Only 50 Rebels Escaped from the Island
2,500 TROOPS TAKEN PRISONERS
O. JENNINGS WISE WOUNDED
A Major and 300 Privates Killed
OVER ONE THOUSAND WOUNDED
WILD STORIES OF UNION LOSSES
REPORTED LOSS ON OUR SIDE

Fortress Monroe, Feb. 11, via Baltimore, Feb. 12.

By a flag of truce today we learn the complete success of the Burnside Expedition at Roanoke Island.

The Island was taken possession of, and Commodore Lynch's fleet completely destroyed.

Elizabeth City was attacked on Sunday, and evacuated by the inhabitants. The City was previously burned, but whether by our shells or the inhabitants is not certain.

All the gunboats but one were taken, and that escaped up a creek and was probably also destroyed.

There appears to be no bright side of the story for the Rebels.

Stephen Mallory, Esq.
Department of the Navy
Richmond, Virginia

Sir:

I am a private citizen with great dedication to our noble cause. In my effort to aid in throwing off the yoke of tyranny, I have, at my own expense and endeavor, purchased and fitted out a private ironclad man-of-war. I have been able to make some use of the vessel, participating in the attack on the Union fleet at the Head of the Passes and the subsequent shelling at the bar, an action of which you have no doubt heard. My vessel is the *Yazoo River*, though, being a private man-of-war and not an official naval vessel, she received less attention than the efforts of my valiant crew warranted.

The *Yazoo River* currently sails under a letter of marque and reprisal, not because I entertain hopes of reaping some profit from her (I look for no pecuniary gains whatsoever) but rather that she might carry the war to sea with some degree of legitimacy. I would gladly risk myself, my ship, and my men to the last measure for the good of the cause, but I would not give the Yankee barbarians excuse to hang my men as pirates.

I find, to my dismay, that the people available for employment on private men-of-war are not what one might wish, generally foreigners, weaklings, and cowards, as any true Southern man is already in the service, be it the army or navy, or employed at some indispensable trade. For all of the effort and money I have poured into my ship, I find I cannot make decent use of her for want of good men. It has become clear to me that this fine ship must be manned by men of the Confederate States Navy, for only such men as have voluntarily and selflessly joined in the fight can be counted upon to act with zeal, dash, and bravery when the hard and dangerous work is to be done.

This is the reason I appeal to you. For the good of our cause, I would like to offer my ship to the Confederate States Navy, at no cost to the service. She is an ironclad, side-wheeler, three hundred tons, 147 feet length overall. She has two boilers and two noncondensing engines with eighteen-inch cylinders, all in good repair. She currently mounts a ten-inch Dahlgren forward and two six-pound smoothbores aft, which are of limited use. I would be grateful if the navy was able to supply more and better ordnance.

I say I will give the *Yazoo River* to the navy at no cost, and that is true, but I would make one demand. It is no longer possible for me to sit idly by while others fight the Northern vandals. Since I have some knowledge of the waters here, I would insist that I be retained aboard in the capacity of pilot, so that I might aid in my way in the great fight. I do not require pay for that service, but do insist upon an official appointment to serve in that capacity.

I look forward to your reply, and remain,

Your obedient servant,
Robley Paine

Norfolk, Virginia, February 12, 1862

Dear Mrs. Jefferson,

My name is Hieronymus Taylor and I am the Chief Engineer aboard the ship CSN *Cape Fear,* aboard which your son Lafayette volunteered. I regret to inform you that Lafayette was killed during the fight at Roanoke Island on February 7.

Lafayette was a good boy and a hard worker, very much liked by his shipmates. He stood his post bravely to the end and he is sore missed.

I know that money can never make up such a grievous loss, but perhaps it might help some to make up for the support a lost son might have provided. I have enclosed one hundred dollars for you in Lafayette's memory, and I hope it is pleasing to him as he looks down from heaven on our suffering here on earth, now that he is in the hands of Jesus and his suffering is at an end.

I am very sorry for your loss, and remain, Your obedient, humble servant,

Hieronymus Taylor

Mrs. Ada Jefferson
Wilmington Street
Elizabeth City, North Carolina

From the report of Captain Samuel Bowater, CSN:

Norfolk, Virginia, February 12, 1862

. . . and upon realizing the *Cape Fear* was in a sinking condition, the enemy returned to their own vessel, at which time those men remaining aboard the *Cape Fear* made preparations to abandon ship. Gallantly, Lt. Simms brought his vessel *Appomattox* alongside, despite the great danger of enemy fire at close range, and took off the surviving crew of the *Cape Fear* and the wounded, as well as the body of Lt. Harwell.

I will not attempt to explain Lt. Simms's decision to make for the canal, except to say that it is a decision I myself would have made, given the fact that the Confederate fleet was lost and there would have been no purpose served in fighting on, and the only result would have been the loss of the last ship and crew. It is unfortunate that the *Appomattox* proved to be two inches too wide to fit in the lock and Lt. Simms was forced to burn the vessel there. I cannot speak too highly of the gallantry of this officer, and the debt owed to him by the men of the *Cape Fear*.

Of the men of the *Cape Fear*, they all performed well and to my full satisfaction, but I would like to single a few out for special commendation. First Assistant Engineer Hieronymus Taylor stood his post despite the grave danger of enemy shells hitting the boiler, and when called upon joined in the hand-to-hand fighting and displayed calm and leadership in that capacity. Seaman First Class Ruffin Tanner was ubiquitous during the fight, serving as helmsman, repelling boarders, and aiding the wounded off the ship. He was the last man, besides myself, to leave the sinking vessel.

In particular I would like to praise Lt. Thadeous Harwell, who manned the bow gun and was foremost when the fighting became hand-to-hand. He was a brave and gallant officer, displaying the finest qualities of the Southern officer and gentleman, and he was tragically killed in the final moments of the fight. He will be missed.

In all, the *Cape Fear* suffered one coal passer, four seamen, and one officer, Lt. Harwell, dead, and seven wounded, one of whom it is thought will not survive his wounds.

After the forced abandonment of the *Appomattox*, my crew showed a laudatory desire to remain together. As a unit we traveled to Norfolk, and now take lodging at the naval shipyard. If it is necessary, for the need of the service, that we should be split up, then we are of course perfectly agreeable to that. But I would suggest that, since we are, as a crew, now well trained and used to working with one another, we might better serve if transferred as a whole to another vessel, if such a one is available. I await your pleasure in this matter, and have the honor to be,

Samuel Bowater
Lieutenant, Confederate States Navy

Hon. S. R. Mallory,
Secretary of the Navy, Richmond

Instructions from the Secretary of the Navy to Flag Officer Farragut, U.S. Navy, regarding the operations of the West Gulf Blockading

Navy Department, January 20, 1862

SIR: When the *Hartford* is in all respects ready for sea, you will proceed to the Gulf of Mexico with all practicable dispatch and communicate with Flag Officer W. W. McKean, who is directed by the enclosed dispatch to transfer to you the command of the Western Gulf Blockading Squadron.

[T]here will be attached to your squadron a fleet of bomb vessels, and armed steamers enough to manage them, all under command of Commander D. D. Porter, who will be directed to report to you. As fast as these vessels are got ready they will be sent to Key West to await the arrival of all, and the commanding officers, who will be permitted to organize and practice with them at that port.

When these formidable mortars arrive, and you are completely ready, you will collect such vessels as can be spared from the blockade and proceed up the Mississippi River and reduce the defenses which guard the approaches to New Orleans, when you will appear off that city and take possession of it under the guns of your squadron, and hoist the American flag thereon, keeping possession until troops can be sent to you.

As you have expressed yourself satisfied with the force given to you, and as many more powerful vessels will be added before you can commence operations, the Department and the country will require of you success.

Destroy the armed barriers which these deluded people have raised up against the power of the United States Government, and shoot down those who war against the Union, but cultivate with cordiality the first returning reason which is sure to follow your success.

Very respectfully, etc.
Gideon Welles

Flag Officer D. G. Farragut,
Appointed to Command West Gulf Squadron

37

We cannot, either with cotton or with all the agricultural staples of the Confederacy put together, adopt any course that will make cotton and trade stand us as a nation in the stead of a Navy.

—Commander Matthew F. Maury, CSN

A cold front rolled through Yazoo City, foul weather out of the north. Robley Paine pulled the collar of his heavy coat up around his face, felt the scraggly growth of ill-tended beard scrape on the cloth. He squinted into the wind, looked out across the water.

Yazoo City. The *Yazoo River* was tied up at one of the docks that jutted out from the trampled riverfront, a few miles west of the town. At the base of a series of low hills covered with a tangle of scrubby trees, coarse grass, the place where businesses that catered to the river traffic clustered. A few dilapidated machine shops, some carpenters, blacksmiths, boiler shops, they gave service to the great fleet of vessels which, in the days before the birth of the Anaconda, would come upriver to load cotton from Yazoo City's wharfs.

Paine looked upriver. He could see part of the town itself from where he stood on the *Yazoo River*'s hurricane deck, the brick buildings and perfectly parallel roads, the bare trees like skeletal hands. The river looked as if it came to an abrupt stop right at the town's waterfront. In fact it made a hard turn left at Yazoo City, a bend of nearly 170 degrees, as if the river had been rushing right for the town and had deflected off the waterfront, bounced back in the direction from which it came.

It was a dead time. February in Yazoo County had never been a bustle. Too cold for Southern blood to do much, nothing to be done in the cotton fields, no bales piling up on the wharf for transport to the cotton mills of the North, and England.

It was even more dead now. Most of Yazoo County's young men were off to war, commerce quashed by the blockade.

The Anaconda was circling, Robley could feel it, as if it was breathing down his neck. New Orleans would be next. Farragut was in command of the Western Gulf Blockading Squadron. He had big steam frigates. He had mortar scows.

The forts to the north, Fort Henry, now Fort Donelson, on the Tennessee River, fallen to Grant. The Union gunboats would push down the Mississippi River, and Farragut would hit New Orleans, and the head and the tail of the serpent would move toward one another, down the Father of Waters.

Robley Paine shook his head. *Can't think on that, can't think on that. . . .* He let his mind wander down that route and it would dead-end in a brilliant red rage. The Anaconda closing in, and he was sitting on a river gunboat—just the thing that the Confederates needed to hold the snake off—and he could get no help in running the thing. Letter after letter with no response, gold sent out with an utter lack of discretion, but neither patriotism nor greed seemed to move anyone to help him in his quest.

He climbed down from the hurricane deck, down to the side deck and down the brow to the dock. It was a Tuesday morning, but there seemed to be no one around. He unhitched his horse and led it over to a step from which he could mount. His old wound ached too much now to allow him to put a foot in the stirrup and swing himself up.

He rode slowly into town, and as he approached he began to see people, who waved to him, bid him good day. Yazoo City was not the paradise he had dreamed of; there were no mechanics and carpenters and engineers and sailors who swarmed to help him, to fight the Yankee. But neither was it New Orleans, den of iniquity. He was known here. Respected. The people of Yazoo City thought he was mad—he could see that, he was not delusional—but still they treated him with the deference and respect that the name Paine warranted in that county.

He rode down the main street, stopped at the post office, and slid off his horse. With teeth clenched against the pain he climbed the granite steps, pushed the door open.

"Mr. Paine, good day," the postmaster called out.

The first time Robley had shown up there, six weeks before, he had seen the fear in the man's eyes. Robley seemed to inspire fear these days, but he did not care.

The postmaster told him then, coughing, hemming, stammering, that they had run out of room in the box, that he had sent all of the Paines' mail down to Paine Plantation.

Robley did not care about that. That was before he began writing to Secretary Mallory, before he had begun shipping gold for railroad iron and guns and shells, before his real work had commenced. That mail was the detritus of the dead, something that had relevance once, when he was alive, but it meant nothing now, like Katherine's dresses, which, he imagined, still hung in her wardrobe.

He had not returned to Paine Plantation to retrieve the mail, had not gone back to that place at all. He did not think he could bear it. He had steamed past, on his way to Yazoo City, looked at the hideous gargoyle he had made of the old oak, wondered what he had been thinking. Had he thought that was enough? Painting a tree? He did not understand then, as he did now, the sacrifice that needed to be made.

"I've got a letter for you, Mr. Paine," the postmaster said. It took a moment for the words to register. *A letter?* Paine had been coming in every other day for a month and a half, and nothing had arrived for him. He had come to expect that, and the postmaster's words caught him by surprise.

The postmaster held the letter out and Robley took it, stepped away, staring at the envelope. It was addressed to Captain Robley Paine, Yazoo City. In the upper left hand corner, preprinted, it read "Department of the Navy, Richmond, Virginia, Confederate States of America."

For a long moment Robley just stared until his hands were trembling too much for him to read the return address any longer. He tore at the envelope, dropped it, retrieved it, tore it open. He pulled the letter out and unfolded it.

Dear Captain Paine:

I beg you to forgive my long delay in replying to yours of January 16th, but I am certain you can appreciate that matters of the service have me much diverted and in many different directions.

Your offer of the ironclad gunboat *Yazoo River* is a generous and patriotic one, and much in keeping with the grand spirit of the South and the magnanimous spirit of her people. It is a particularly timely offer, as it has become clear to me, by recent events, particularly those on the Tennessee River, that ironclad gunboats will be the deciding factor to winning the war on the Western Rivers, which, in turn, will be integral to winning the war overall.

On behalf of the Confederate States Navy I enthusiastically accept your offer to make the *Yazoo River* a commissioned vessel of the Confederate States Navy, and your offer to act as her pilot, as our experience has shown that skilled pilots are very difficult to come by.

As to the manning of the *Yazoo River*, I am currently reviewing the names and qualifications of those men currently available, but I am in no doubt that the kind of men you seek will be found and transferred to the *Yazoo River* as expediently as possible.

Once again, allow me to commend you on your patriotism and selflessness as displayed by this act. I remain,

Your humble and obedient servant,
S. R. Mallory
Secretary of the Navy, Richmond

Robley read the letter, fast. He was breathing shallowly. He forced himself to breathe normally, read it again, then read it again. Thoughts crowded his head, fought for attention, the emotions swirled like smoke.

Confederate States Naval Vessel *Yazoo River* . . . The words sounded like music in his head. *At last, at last . . .*

Then the darker thoughts clawed their way up. He had exaggerated some in his description of the vessel. He had called her an ironclad. And if he had his way, so she would be. He had written, sent orders, money, to iron foundries throughout the South, had written follow-up letters, had his attorneys write follow-up letters. So far, nothing. Not a scrap of iron had arrived. The *Yazoo River* was still a cotton-clad.

He had overstated his own qualifications as well. Mallory called him "Captain." Naturally, the Secretary would assume an experienced river pilot would merit that title. Not a big problem—he could get around that one. Take a real pilot at gunpoint if he had to, so long as he was aboard when the CSS *Yazoo River* got underway.

He read the letter again. He had to get back to his office in the *Yazoo River*'s wheelhouse. He had to write follow-up letters, find out where his gunboat iron was.

Jonathan Paine pushed open the back door of Miss Sally Tompkins's house, clomped down the back steps. He held a big basket crammed full of filthy sheets and bloody bandages. The wind plucked at the red-and-white strips, pulled them out, set them flapping like banners. Jonathan turned a shoulder into the wind, hurried across the yard, along the path worn down to dirt and fringed with brown grass.

Bobby stood at a cauldron hanging from a tripod over a blazing fire. He agitated the contents with a big stick, like one of Shakespeare's witches.

Othello plays in Macbeth, Paine thought, and the thought made him smile. He stepped quickly across the yard. He was moving well with his prosthetic leg now, walking more like a man with a hurt leg than a man with no leg at all. The limp reminded him of his father. Of the three boys, he had always favored his father's looks the most. Now the effect was even greater.

He moved within the radius of the fire, caught what warmth he could. He and Bobby dumped the bloody bandages into the water and Bobby began stirring again.

For some time they just stood, enjoyed the warmth of the fire and the fresh air outside the stuffiness of the hospital, and said nothing. They were perfectly comfortable in one another's company, could enjoy silent companionship. Jonathan wondered if this could have happened anyplace outside a hospital, where his wound and Bobby's nursing had put black man and white on something like even ground.

"Been two months now," Bobby said at last, never taking his eyes from the boiling water. A few itinerant flakes of snow began to whip around the yard.

"Month and a half. Since the last one."

They were talking about letters home. Jonathan had written three, had been waiting for a reply. When he was healed enough that he could no longer stay on at the hospital as a patient, he stayed on as a helper, assisting Bobby in changing dressings, washing bandages, wrapping the dead. Not so many wounded now, mostly dysentery, ague, camp fever. What wounds there were were more often from accidents than the enemy. He nursed and he waited. He heard no word from his father.

"That like you daddy?" Bobby asked, looking up at last. "He the kind would jest not write?"

Jonathan shook his head. "No. No, that is not like him at all."

Bobby nodded and stirred.

"Could be the mail isn't getting through," Jonathan said. "I can't imagine things are running too well, as far as mail."

"Could be. 'Course, ya sent three letters."

Jonathan nodded. He did not believe that all three letters had failed to arrive. He could not imagine why his father had not written back.

"I have to go back," Jonathan said at last. "I can't wait to hear. I just have to go."

He had not said that out loud before, because it frightened him. His world was closed down to Miss Tompkins's hospital. The one time he left it had nearly killed him—he had been another two weeks in bed. Now the very thought of crossing the line of the white picket fence was terrifying.

He had never said it out loud, because doing so was like an announcement, a commitment, and he had not been ready.

Bobby nodded his head, and they were silent for a moment. "Yassuh. You gots ta go. An if ya likes, well, I'll go wid ya."

Jonathan smiled. "That's right kind of you, Bobby. But it ain't like you can just up and leave."

"Why can't I?"

"Well . . . well, hell, Bobby, you belong to Miss Tompkins, for starters."

"No I don't."

"You don't?"

"No suh. I's a free man."

"You are? How come you never told me?"

"How come you jest reckoned I's a slave?"

Jonathan smiled, shook his head. He had just assumed. He did not know why.

John Scofield sat in his office, elbow on his desk, chin in hand. He stared out the big window that looked out over the outer office. The window made the office seem more a fishbowl than private work space.

Cold air blew in from the outside window, which was opened a crack. Late February in Atlanta, Georgia. Generally not so cold, but a norther was blowing through, and temperatures plummeted.

He could hear conversation drifting up from the yard below, heated conversation, the hottest thing going in Atlanta. Generally, when the Scofield and Markham's Gate City rolling mill was in full production, when the iron was pouring and the rolling mills rolling it out, when plate and bar and railroad iron was being loaded onto flatbeds in the siding, he would never have been able to hear something so quiet as a conversation three stories down. Not even a shouted conversation, as this one was.

But he could hear it now, because nothing was happening, no work being done. Prices were going up all over the Confederacy. Skilled men such as ironworkers were in great demand, and they knew it. The fact that their jobs kept them out of the army did not seem to impress them any more. They wanted higher wages, and just as Scofield came to expect from their ilk, they were not subtle about it.

He shook his head. He sighed. He could not make out all of the words, but he caught a few, mostly *damns* and *y'all gonna be surprised when we . . .* and *you sons of bitches . . .* It did not sound as if it was going well.

The conversation below stopped abruptly. Scofield swiveled around, looked at the door beyond the empty outer office, wondered who would come through. He waited. Finally it opened. Frank Ouellette, haggard, defeated, came in, closed the door behind him with more force than necessary.

He walked into Scofield's office without knocking. He flopped down in a chair. Scofield thought of the Yankees retreating after Manassas. They must have looked like old Frank.

"Well?" Scofield asked.

"They ain't budging. Another ten cents a day, and they ain't too happy with Confederate scrip no more."

Scofield shook his head. The war was less than a year old. If the Confederacy lost, he wondered if it would be due to the Yankees' fighting prowess or the greed of the Southern mechanics and laborers.

"I don't know as we can do that . . ." Scofield said.

Ouellette shrugged. "I told 'em. They think you and Markham, and me, we live like damned kings, think we making money hand over fist here."

The two men were silent for a moment, and then Scofield felt the first stirring of an idea. "I wonder if we might give them some little token, something that will inspire them to get back to work. . . ."

"Such as?"

"Everyone's worried about this here Confederate scrip. How's about if we pay them—even give 'em a bonus—in specie. Gold. Ain't a thing satisfies a greedy man like real gold."

"Sure, but . . ." Ouellette began, paused, saw where Scofield was heading. "That fellow, wrote last month . . ."

"Exactly. Never did count what he sent, but I'm certain they's enough to go around, a couple of times. That should get them all fired up for work."

Ouellette nodded. It had been something of a shock, the day the package arrived. Gold in coins and an order for iron, preferably rolled out into gunboat iron, drilled for six bolts. Some rich lunatic building himself an ironclad.

They marveled, shook their heads, put the gold in the safe, set the order aside. The Confederate Army and Navy were desperate for milled iron. There was no time to fulfill an order for some civilian with big dreams in the naval line. Perhaps in a year or so, but not now.

"You never had any intention of filling that fella's order," Ouellette pointed out. "You just gonna hand out his gold and let him flap in the wind?"

"No, no . . . I can't do that. Wish I could, but I can't." Scofield rummaged through a pile of papers in a basket on his desk, pulled out a letter from near the bottom of the heap. "We'll start handing out gold to our malcontent workers there, and if that induces them to get back to work, then I reckon this . . . Robley Paine . . . gets the gunboat iron he's asking for."

38

[A]bout 1,000 tons [of iron] plating is being manufactured by rolling mills in Atlanta, Ga., for an iron-plated frigate nearly completed at New Orleans.

—Stephen R. Mallory to President Jefferson Davis

They arrived back in Newport, weary, battered, wounded in mind and body. Bowater saw his men safe in barracks at the Gosport Naval Shipyard. Ten-thirty at night, he had finished his reports, oral and written, told his tale to Forrest and the others, been dismissed.

He wandered out of the shipyard, too torn up to sleep, or even to remain in one place. He walked the streets. He knew where he would end up.

He approached the old house quietly. No lights burning. Behind it, within the tended yard, he could see the carriage house. A light shone in the window. Late, but not that late, and Samuel did not care much for convention at that moment.

He hopped the picket fence, landed soft on the grass, crossed to the carriage house. He rapped on the door, realized as he did that he might scare her to death, that she might not answer. But he heard soft footsteps across the floor, and the door opened.

Wendy was there, the light from a candle diffused through her long, dark hair. She was wearing a loose night dress, holding a book. Bowater saw a sudden flash of fear in her face, which softened to recognition, concern.

"Samuel . . . I thought it was my aunt. Dear God, what has happened to you?"

She opened the door wider, stepped aside, and he stepped in, looked around without seeing anything. "I have been in a fight, Wendy . . ." he said.

She put the book down, stepped up to him, wrapped her arms around him. For a long moment they embraced, and then Samuel pushed her gently back. "Do you have a canvas?" he asked. "Might I borrow some paints?"

Wendy nodded, stepped away. She picked up a small canvas, set it on the easel that stood in the corner, offered him her paint set, the one he knew so well.

He shed his frock coat and hat, let them fall on the floor, rolled up his sleeves. He stared at the canvas, let the picture form on the white surface, let his mind create it so that his hands had only to fill in the places where paint had to go. He took up a pencil, slashed a few lines across the surface, general outlines. He dabbed paint on the palette, began to work with a wide brush.

Wendy pulled up a stool and sat beside him and a little back and watched silently as the picture emerged. Samuel was hardly aware of the time passing, minutes, then hours, as the foredeck of the *Cape Fear* grew out of the white field before him, the gray skies and brown water, the sharp points of muzzle flash. And on one edge, dimly seen, Lieutenant Harwell's face in the instant of death.

Samuel felt himself a part of the scene on the canvas as much as he had been a part of the real fight, he felt like a participant in the picture, painting from within the scene. He felt the tears roll down his cheeks as he rendered not the horror of the thing, but the suggestion of that horror, which was more frightening by half.

Three hours, four hours he worked, letting it all come out through his brush. Wendy sat on a small fainting couch, fell asleep with her head on her arm, and Bowater painted on.

At last he stepped back, set the brush down. Wendy came awake, as if she sensed this was the moment. She stood, joined him.

"That's it . . ." she whispered, as if she knew what it was he was trying to render. "That is it exactly."

Bowater looked long and hard at the canvas, and for the first time he felt a mesh, a perfect fit, between what he saw in his head and what he saw created in paint.

He turned away from the painting, hoped he had managed to get what was in his head out and plant it permanently on canvas. He ran his hands around Wendy's waist, pulled her near. He could feel her smooth skin through the thin material of her night dress. She wrapped her arms around his neck, pulled his head down to hers, and kissed him, and he kissed her back, with a desperate urgency.

Wendy cocked her head aside and Samuel ran his lips down her long neck, buried his face in her hair, kissed the soft place behind her ear. She pushed him away, took the top button of his shirt in her fingers, unbuttoned that, and the next and the next, and then eased the shirt over his head. She ran her hands over his chest. They felt cool and small against his skin. He ran a finger down her cheek, down her neck, took up the end of the tie that held her night dress up, tugged it free.

The garment fell open and Wendy shrugged it off, let it fall to the floor. The light of the three candles by which Bowater had been painting played over her white skin, the curves of her thighs and back and hips, and Bowater traced them with his hands. He stepped out of his shoes, let his trousers fall to the floor, led her over to the small bed in the corner.

He lay down with her, half on top, let the feel of her skin against his overwhelm him. She was beautiful, loving, warm. She smelled of violet water and soap. She smelled alive and good and like everything that the fight at Elizabeth City was not, and Samuel tried to envelop himself with her, to become a part of her and let her drive away everything else.

They made love, desperate and slow, consuming one another, and when it was over Samuel was spent in every way he could be, and he slept in a way he had thought he would never sleep again.

The weeks wound past. The Cape Fears lived at the Gosport Naval Shipyard and they waited. Bowater waited with them by day, raced to be with Wendy Atkins when his few duties were done.

They waited for orders. They waited for news from the Western Rivers. They waited for the Yankees to come overland from Albemarle Sound and take the shipyard back. They waited to see if the CSS *Virginia* would roll over like a dead whale, jam in the dry dock, or sink.

February 13, 1862. Float test for the nearly complete ironclad. For no reason other than curiosity, Samuel Bowater and Hieronymus Taylor stood near the edge of the dry dock and watched the water creeping up, lapping over the twenty-two-foot-deep hull of the former United States steam frigate *Merrimack*, now the Confederate States ironclad *Virginia*.

Bowater stared down into the water swirling into the dry dock. He recalled the night he was down there, looking for the bitter end of a burning fuse, the cold water knocking him around. With the *Cape Fear* they had assisted in getting the old wreck up and into the dry dock, had witnessed nearly every inch of her transformation from burned-out hulk to modern war machine.

He ran his eyes over her ugly, boxy shape. *Merrimack* had been no sleek clipper ship, but still she had had some elegance to her. There was nothing lovely about the ironclad. She was all function. But that was all right with Bowater, because he saw no loveliness in war, and he no longer felt that aesthetics had a place aboard the engines of war.

The water came up and up and the shoring dropped away and finally the *Virginia* floated free. Around the dry dock there was a shared sense of tension, like the shared sense of fear prior to combat. No one cheered, no one spoke loud. There was an undercurrent of muttering as several hundred navy men expressed several hundred opinions.

"Well, damn . . ." Taylor said, soft. "She didn't roll over after all. I'll be damned. . . ."

Three days after that, the dry dock was flooded again, the gates opened, and the *Virginia* was christened and floated out into the Elizabeth River.

It was the most solemn christening that Bowater had ever attended. No political speeches, no flags, banners, fireworks, music. It was a quiet, thoughtful christening by professional navy men, who understood the profundity of the moment, who understood the change in their world that the 275-foot iron-skinned monster represented.

They watched in silence as CSS *Virginia* moved slowly out into the stream, pulled by silent warps. It made Bowater wish that no one other than professional navy men ever be allowed to any christening.

Fitting out, provisioning, began in earnest, and an air of anticipation blew through the shipyard, lifting the gloom of winter and past defeats. And so it was with mixed emotions that Samuel Bowater reported to Commander Forrest for orders he guessed would take them away before the iron monster could sally forth.

He was right.

They were on a train the next morning: Bowater, Taylor, Tanner, Seth Williams, Eustis Babcock, Dick Merrow, Harry McNelly, all of the surviving members of the *Cape Fear*'s crew, transferred bodily to a new vessel, rattling along over a thousand miles of mediocre, terrible, and sometimes nonexistent railroad, to a riverport town that only a few of them had ever heard of.

Some of the men had friends, wives, girlfriends on the platform to see them off. Wendy arrived. She had two baskets with bread, cheese, cold roast beef, wine. She gave one to Hieronymus Taylor, who was more than a little surprised to see her there, and to Samuel Bowater, who was surprised she had brought a basket for the chief.

"Hieronymus and I met once, before that night at the concert," she said. "I will tell you the particulars someday. Oh, don't look like that, it was nothing at all."

They held one another. They kissed. Neither cried. Neither thought of the likelihood of that being their last embrace, on a windswept, sooty railroad platform in Norfolk, Virginia.

The former Cape Fears were five days in transition. They walked a total of forty-three miles between different rail lines, past torn-up track, washed-out track. They slept on train seats that shook as if the earth was opening up beneath them, and on the floors of train stations. They ate greasy food bought from vendors on platforms which Samuel Bowater paid for from his own pockct.

They arrived at last on the crowded docks of Memphis. It was February 24. From there they were two days on a stern-wheeler, running south, a considerably more comfortable means of travel.

They docked at Vicksburg in the shadow of the high hills, the Gibraltar of the West. They boarded a smaller steamer, made their way northeast, up the Yazoo River. They steamed into Yazoo City. They looked for an ironclad. They did not see one.

The steamer nosed into the dock, the brow was lowered, the men disembarked. Samuel Bowater looked around. Yazoo City was a moderate-sized town, neat roads, brick buildings that suggested that money flowed through the place.

The wind was out of the north and cold, colder than he would have expected for central Mississippi. He wondered if that was typical. He had no idea what he would do next.

He saw the captain of the steamer, busy in the wheelhouse. "Y'all wait here," he said to the men, climbed back up to the wheelhouse. "Captain?" he said through the open door.

The steamer captain looked up. "Yes, Lieutenant?" Bowater was wearing his best uniform frock coat, in anticipation of coming aboard his next command.

"My men and I have taken passage here to report aboard the ironclad *Yazoo River*. Do you know where she is tied up?"

"Ironclad?" The captain looked confused. And then he chuckled. "Oh, sure. The *Yazoo River*. That's the boat old Robley Paine bought. You seen her when we was steaming by the docks, downriver. Side-wheeler, painted black. That's her."

"You're . . . sure?"

"Sure."

"Ahh . . . but she is not an ironclad."

"No," the steamer captain agreed, "she surely ain't."

Bowater nodded. *You will make contact with one Captain Robley Paine, a civilian, who has undertaken to build the ironclad* Yazoo River *at his own expense. You will engage Captain Paine as pilot of the* Yazoo River. Orders, direct from Stephen Mallory, Secretary of the Navy.

"This Paine, he is a riverboat captain? A pilot?"

"He's a planter, like all the gentlemen lives along the river here. He ain't no pilot, don't know a damned thing about boats, as far as I know."

Bowater nodded. He felt sick.

Down from the wheelhouse, back over the brow to the hard-packed dirt landing where his men stood huddled, braced against the wind. "All right, men. Follow me," Bowater said, led them south along the dirt road the captain had pointed out, the one that would lead to the work docks, the side-wheeler *Yazoo River*.

With each step Bowater's heart sank deeper. The dilapidated machine shops, the boatyards whose buildings were in need of basic carpentry themselves, the tall grass shooting up around discarded engine parts, coils of rotten rope, rusted anchors, all made him depressed and angry.

They marched on, came at last to the dock to which the side-wheeler was tied, and now that he looked at it he saw that indeed she had a name board on her bow and the name board said *Yazoo River*. He had hoped, right up until that moment, that the captain had been mistaken, that the real, gleaming, powerful ironclad was somewhere upriver of them.

Bowater drew the men up at the bottom of the brow and no one said a thing. They hunched their shoulders against the wind and looked. They saw the peeling black paint. They saw the twisted rails and shot-up superstructure, battle damage unrepaired. They saw the bales of cotton piled up on the deck, forming a sort of barricade around the bow and stern where the vessel's three antique guns were mounted.

After a minute of that, Bowater saw a face peer out of the wheelhouse window. The face disappeared, and then a tall, gaunt man in a long coat stepped out onto the hurricane deck, sized them up, disappeared again.

A moment later he stepped out of the deckhouse, having apparently come down an inside ladder. He stood at the top of the brow. He held a shotgun in his hands, a heavy revolver on his belt.

"Ain't this fella heard of Southern hospitality?" Taylor wondered out loud.

"Who are you?" the gaunt man demanded.

"I am Lieutenant Samuel Bowater, Confederate States Navy. I have come to assume command of the ship *Yazoo River*."

The man was silent for a moment, scrutinizing the cluster of sailors. He set the shotgun aside, stepped down the brow, stopped five feet away.

"I'm Robley Paine. Do you know who I am?"

"Yes, I do."

Paine was a frightening sight, not at all what Bowater had envisioned. Bowater had been thinking of a plump, jolly, well-dressed individual who was looking to play at sailors, a Southern version of a Henry Fielding squire. Paine was not that.

Thin in an unhealthy way, eyes sunk deep, peering out from dark circles, darting side to side. There was a nervous, agitated quality to him, and a deadness to his eyes that was unsettling. He had not shaved in some time.

Bowater had an instant dislike for the man, which made his anger at Paine's deception that much greater.

"This is it?" Paine said at last. "This is all the men to crew the boat?"

"This is the boat?" Bowater asked, taking a step forward. "You represented to Secretary Mallory that she was an ironclad. What the hell is this?" It had been a long trip, and Bowater was tired. He was beginning to lose his reserve.

"She will be an ironclad. She is not yet. She is a cotton-clad."

Taylor stepped up, which further irritated Bowater. "She is a what, sir?"

"Cotton-clad. She is not the only one on the river."

" 'Cotton-clad'?" Taylor chuckled. "You mean to say that she is armored with the lightest, softest, most flammable material known to man? I'm not sure that would be my first choice. Iron, I would think . . ."

"The cotton is effective against small-arms fire." Paine turned on Taylor like a snake striking. "We do not wait for everything to be perfection. We fight the Yankee with what we have. Men do. Cowards and weaklings hang back and complain."

An ugly silence. Everyone waited for Taylor to respond, but Taylor just gave out a low whistle, made his eyes go wide, smiled, and wandered off, assessing the *Yazoo River*.

"Be that as it may," Bowater said, "we were led to believe that we were manning an ironclad, and that you were a qualified pilot, and I am not pleased, sir, by what I see." This was not going well at all.

"Nor am I, sir. I have sunk no small part of my fortune into this ship, I have driven her into combat already, and I intend to do so again. I gave her over to the navy because I wished to man her with men who would fight. I will not be happy to find officers and men of the Confederate States Navy who are backward in their willingness to do battle with the enemy."

Bowater stiffened. Paine's insinuations were coming very close to intolerable insult, and it was only the wild intensity with which Paine spoke—as if Paine was not responsible because he had no control over what came out of his mouth—that made Bowater hold his tongue.

Taylor came ambling back, and before Bowater could reply he said, "This here's the *Star of the Delta*, ain't she?"

"Pardon?" Paine said, the word shot out like a bullet.

"This here riverboat, she's the old *Star of the Delta*, ain't she? Used to run N'Orleans to Natchez, regular."

"I believe that is her former name," Paine said.

Taylor shook his head, grinned, stuck an unlit cigar in his mouth. "This jest gets better an better."

Bowater rounded on Paine, ready to give him the full broadside; Paine rounded on Bowater, ready for the same. From up the road came the clomping of hooves on the hard-packed dirt. The men on the landing, as one, turned, looked, happy for some diversion.

A young man on a sorrel mare rode up, reined to a stop. "Mornin, Mr. Paine," he said.

"Morning, Billy."

Billy paused, as if he felt he should say more, but could think of nothing, and the moment became awkward. "Got a telegraph for ya." Billy held out the note. Paine took it from him, unfolded it, read it in silence. Billy rode off.

" 'To Robley Paine,' " Paine read aloud from the paper. " 'From Stationmaster, Jackson, Mississippi. Sir, have received shipment eight hundred tons iron for you, stop. Please retrieve at earliest convenience, stop.' "

Paine looked up at Bowater, and there was a different look in his eye. In another man the look might have been triumph, but not in Paine. Paine seemed too far gone to appear triumphant over anything. "There is your ironclad, Lieutenant. It is on the siding in Jackson. Tomorrow we will go and fetch it."

39

In conversations with the Secretary, I always have been under the impression that, for purposes of coast defense, he conceived that ironclad rams were the best vessels.

—Commander John M. Brooke, CSN

Robley Paine hunted wagons. He mounted his horse, rode the countryside north of Yazoo City, visited plantations he had first visited before he was old enough to walk. He spoke with fellow planters he had known since he was a boy.

They were polite. They kept their distance, did not invite him in. They had no wagons to lend.

Robley explained the situation. He had eight hundred tons of railroad iron, rolled and drilled, and another half ton of nuts and bolts, sitting on a railroad siding in Jackson. He needed wagons to haul it to the Yazoo River, to build his ironclad gunboat, to protect them, all of them, from the filthy hordes of shopkeepers and mechanics sweeping down from the north, and up from the south, closing in. He spoke emphatically and sometimes he caught himself speaking too loud, sometimes shouting.

The planters never took offense, which was the worst of it, as if it was pointless to be offended by the ravings of a madman. They nodded, shook their heads. "Not like I don't know about them damned Yankees, Robley," they would say. "My boy's with Beauregard right now." But they had no wagons, and they thought he was mad. He could see it in their eyes.

He rode all day, plantation to plantation, talked with his oldest friends, who treated him with the wariness with which one treats an unfamiliar dog. He got no wagons.

The next day he dispatched five of Bowater's men with a local boy to lead them back to Paine Plantation to retrieve the three serviceable wagons in the barn. He told them there had been horses once, and there might still be, or perhaps not, he did not know. Robley continued his search, covering the plantations south of town.

There were no wagons to be had.

He found himself rubbing the butt of his Starr as he talked with his reluctant neighbors, found himself imagining how it would be to jerk the gun from his holster, take horses and wagons at gunpoint, frighten some cooperation into his fellow planters.

Once, riding along the empty roads from one house to the next, he thought he had done so. He stopped, tried to recall if he had used his gun on someone.

No . . . he concluded. *No* . . . He had only dreamed of it. It worried him some, that he could not always differentiate.

On the third day, near desperation, Paine hired three teamsters in Yazoo City, all that were to be had. The sailors returned from Paine Plantation with two wagons, eight horses, the worst of what had once been there, but all that was left. Like some pathetic parade they rolled south toward Jackson. Five wagons to move eight hundred tons of gunboat iron over forty miles of mediocre road. It was not a job that would be quickly done.

And all the while, every minute, Robley Paine felt the snake, squeezing, squeezing.

Samuel Bowater was happy to see Paine ride off mornings, felt his stomach fall when Paine returned after sundown. The whole thing—Yazoo City, the *Yazoo River*, the ugly weather, the feeling that he had been shunted off to the end of the earth and left there—it all made his mood bleak and desperate.

But to have Robley Paine watching over him, those sunken, crazy eyes boring into him, to field the inquiries delivered with no inflection, no sense of curiosity or companionship, as if he was a different species from Robley Paine and not worth any empathy, made him edgy and depressed. Robley Paine struck him as a man who, for whatever dark reason, no longer cared in the least for his own life or for anyone else's. And if he had no care for life, then he certainly had no care for more mundane things, such as courtesy or any of the niceties that allowed men to coexist.

Robley Paine was not an easy man to be around, and so, when he left, Bowater was, if not happy, then at least less miserable.

He stood on the hurricane deck, in huddled conversation. The weather had moderated quite a bit, the cold north wind backing and dropping. The sun fought its way through high haze, and the temperature climbed to near fifty degrees.

"Very well . . ." Samuel said. "Mr. Polkey, what do you have to report?"

Artemus Polkey was one of three shipwrights for hire at Yazoo City. Somewhere in his fifties, grizzled, fat, he did not inspire a great deal of confidence. The two missing fingers on his left hand inspired even less. But of the three ship's carpenters, Bowater judged him most competent, based on the necessarily brief interviews he had conducted. And so Artemus Polkey was hired to oversee the refit of the cotton-clad *Yazoo River* into an ironclad.

"Wellll . . ." Polkey drew the word out, worked the plug in his mouth, spit artfully over the side. "Her bottom ain't too bad, an that there's the chief of your concern. Seen a couple o' planks is a bit punky, but ain't nothin I'd worry about. Deck beams, carlings, clamps, it all looks good to me."

Bowater nodded. "Good. So how do we make her an ironclad?"

"Wellll . . ." Polkey spit again. "Reckon we take all the goddamn superstructure off her, jest strip her right down to the gunnels, jest leave the weather deck and a big damn hole where the fidley was. Build us a casement along the whole length where the deckhouse is now. 'Bout eight foot high. Build her out of live oak, say, foot thick on the sides, foot and a half fore and aft bulkheads. Bolt that ol' iron right onto that."

"Can you do that? Do you have the men?"

"Ah, shit . . . ain't talkin but four flat sides, like a cabin. I don't need no shipwrights to do that. Hire house carpenters. Even hire out some darkies, know how to swing a hammer."

"The sides of the casement cannot be vertical. They must be sloped, say at a thirty-five-degree angle."

Polkey chewed some, nodded. "Makes things a bit harder, now, but we can do that." Bowater was beginning to like the man.

"Good. Chief Taylor?"

Taylor wore his battered cap back on his head, his uniform frock coat unbuttoned over a stained and coal-dust-smeared shirt, pants glazed with dirt. Since the sinking of the *Cape Fear* he had not enjoyed the silent insubordination of clean clothing.

"Me and the ol' *Star of the Delta* go way back," he said.

"Did you serve on board her?" Bowater asked.

"No. No. Towed her a bunch, when she was broke down, which was damn near a weekly occurrence."

Bowater frowned. He thought he was over the stab of nausea that followed bad news, but he realized he was not. "What is the condition of her machinery now?"

"Seems someone gone over it recently. Someone who knows his business, I'm pleased to say. Overall it ain't so bad. Burgess and me, we got steam up in both boilers, got turns on both her engines and they held together. Reckon they will for some time more. They's a power of things I could do. You jest let me know how much time I gots to play down there."

That was the question. How much time? If they never found more wagons for hauling iron from Jackson, the ironclad *Yazoo River* would not be underway for the next two years. But how might they haul it faster? How many men would they get to work on rebuilding the ship? Could he recruit from the nearby army units? Would Mallory send more men?

So many variables. Absolutely no way to know how long it would take to do anything. He did not know what move of the Yankees he needed to be ready to counter.

"Six weeks. We must be underway in six weeks," Bowater said decisively. They needed a goal, a definite date, even if it was only one that he made up, right off the top of his head.

Incredible . . .

The word echoed around David Glasgow Farragut's mind.

Incredible . . .

He was not sure to what specifically he might apply the word—there were so many things.

Incredible how swiftly a man's fortunes could change.

Number 38 on the captains' list of the United States Navy after fifty years' service. A Tennessee man who had never blinked in his support of the Union, but who, he assumed, was still considered questionable thanks to his place of birth. Just two and a half months before, he had been festering away on the Navy Retirement Board, dying an interminable death. His nation was consumed by war—the one thing for which he had trained his entire life, boy to man—and he was behind a desk, shuffling papers.

But no more. He looked around the day cabin on his flagship, the USS *Hartford*, 225 feet long, forty-four feet on the beam, 2,900 tons. Solid. Indefatigable. His.

Incredible.

Farragut was sixty years old, his square jaw clean-shaven. The sun that came in through the aft windows glinted off the bands of gold braid that circled his cuffs, winked off the double row of buttons down the front of his dark blue frock coat. His lean, hard body was perfectly complemented by the frock coat. He had been wearing navy blue for forty years. It seemed very odd to him when, on one of those few occasions, he found himself in civilian clothing of a different color.

He read over the report, one of an endless stream of reports he was writing.

USS *Hartford*
Ship Island, March 5, 1862

DEAR SIR: The *Pensacola* arrived here on the 2d, just in time to escape a severe norther, which has now been blowing for nearly six hours. Had she encountered it, God knows when she would have arrived. They represent the engines as perfectly worthless. The engineer is afraid for the lives of his men, and said it would not last an hour longer; that I will test.

He set the report aside. His eyes, which were not terribly strong, were starting to hurt. Reports, orders, requisitions, dispatches, he was sick of it all. He had come to fight the enemy and all he did was sit at his desk. For now.

He looked down at the sundry papers spread over the desk in front of him—newspapers, reports, personal correspondence. Stolen material, all. He felt a flush of guilt. Absurd. This was war.

Warm, briny air wafted through the open window, rustled the paper. A month before he had been in New York City, where bitter, numbing wind funneled in through the Narrows and made the waterfront a frigid misery. His hands, he recalled, had been so numb he was hardly able to hold a pen. But now he was riding at anchor at Ship Island, off the coast of Mississippi, lovely, semitropical, water the color of turquoise. He enjoyed the sun and the warm air. He enjoyed looking out over the ships under his command.

The warm air carried on it the smell of coal smoke. USS *Colorado* had arrived an hour before, was picking her way slowly though the anchorage. She was a big bastard, a forty-gun steam frigate, eight- to ten-inch Dahlgren pivots. She drew nearly twenty-three feet aft. Farragut did not know if he could get her over the bar and into the Mississippi River.

They would be fighting a river war with a blue-water navy, making ships do something they were never intended to do. Foote's fleet, the "Pook Turtles," they were made for this kind of fighting, perfect for the

Western River Theater. But not the *Hartford*, and certainly not the *Colorado*.

The marine at the cabin door announced Henry H. Bell, captain of the fleet, responding to the summons Farragut had issued moments before. Farragut called, "Come!" and Bell stepped sharply across the cabin's deck, stopped at the desk, saluted, crisp and businesslike.

"Captain," Farragut said, returning the salute. He spread his hands, indicating the papers on the desk. "Here is the booty from our raid on the Biloxi post office."

"You should have had them take gold, sir. Laurens de Graffe or Jean Laffite could have made their fortunes with such a raiding party."

Farragut smiled. "There's gold enough here for me. You should see what is in these papers." He picked one up, held up the headline. *Surrender of Nashville!*

"Nashville, sir?" Bell looked taken aback, and then he smiled.

"The Rebels suffered a defeat at Donaldsonville as well. Grant and Foote are sweeping south along the Mississippi. New Orleans is in a panic. The papers speak volumes of discontent. It's all collapsing around them, Henry. When we take New Orleans, I do believe the Southern morale and their will to fight will just melt away."

"Wonderful, sir."

For just over twenty days now, Farragut had been admiral in charge of the Western Gulf Blockading Squadron, chosen by Welles and Lincoln not just because they trusted him to blockade but because they trusted him to fight.

The rumble of an anchor chain, and Farragut and Bell looked out the starboard windows to see *Colorado*'s anchor kick up a spout of water as it plunged into the harbor.

"Captain Alden should have news of Porter, sir," Bell said.

"Yes, he should. I hope it is good." Farragut was already sending ships up the Mississippi, up to the Head of the Passes, up as far as the forts, probing the Rebels, feeling them out. But the first real attack would be David Dixon Porter's. Porter had with him a convoy of old schooners and scows, each mounting a squat thirteen-inch mortar, able to lob heavy exploding shells over the walls of the Confederate fortifications. This mortar fleet would soften Forts Jackson and St. Philip up some before Farragut's big ships blasted their way past.

"If I may, sir . . ." Bell was hedging, wanted to ask a question he was not certain would be well received.

"Yes?"

"If I may, when do you think we will make the push to New Orleans?"

As it happened, Farragut had been thinking along those very lines, and so was well prepared to answer that question. He had been calculating when Porter would arrive, how long it might take to get the big ships over the bar, how much pounding the forts would need.

He planned to head up to the forts himself in a few days in one of the smaller ships, take a firsthand look at what they would be facing.

"Six weeks," Farragut said decisively. "I do believe we will be ready to take New Orleans in six weeks' time."

40

There was neither foundry nor machine shop in the place [Yazoo City]. The ship was in a very incomplete condition. [T]here was not a sufficiency of iron on hand to finish the entire ship.

—Lieutenant George Gift, CSS *Arkansas*

They tore into the *Yazoo River*'s deckhouse with iron bars.

Samuel Bowater stood on the foredeck, watched Artemus Polkey wander back and forth, looking over the deckhouse like a sculptor looking at a block of marble, trying to decide where to make that first, crucial cut.

The sun was just up, the river and the boat were still bathed in blue-gray dawn light, and already Samuel wanted to scream, *It's not a work of art, just tear the damned thing apart!* But he held his tongue.

At last Artemus nodded, patted the planking right around the door to the galley. "Right here," he said. "We'll start takin her down from here." He hefted a four-foot wrecking bar, and with a swiftness and economy of motion which surprised Bowater he slammed the chisel end into the plank and with half a dozen levers of the bar dropped a five-foot section of plank onto the deck.

He nodded again, issued orders to the men milling about, the ship's carpenters Polkey had hired and the Yazoo Rivers who were assigned to him, essentially every man who was not on the iron wagon train.

"Let's rip her up, boys!" Polkey shouted, and the men fell to with a will. The morning was torn apart with the crack of wood, the squeal of protesting nails being wrenched free. The men were sweating in the cool air. Wanton destruction was in their blood.

Bowater wandered down to the dock, watched the progress for a few minutes. He had been wrong about Polkey, and he was glad of it. Artemus Polkey deliberated, chose wisely, but for all his age and girth, he was a hurricane once the decision was made.

Satisfied with the destruction taking place, Bowater walked over to the carpenter's shed which had been transformed into an office for him. He opened the protesting door, stepped on nails and sawdust and wood chips on the floor, sat on the stool in front of the high desk. He looked at the papers, preprinted forms, pen, ink, laid out in front of him, and he sighed.

This was his lot for now, the lot of the ship's captain. Reports, requisitions, requests. Write to Mallory, update him on the state of things, beg for sailors and money, two things the Confederate Navy never had enough of. Write to the local army commander, beg that any sailors or machinists or engineers or carpenters in the ranks be reassigned to him. Best of luck. Write to local bakers and butchers and meat packers for victuals.

He wrote for the bulk of two days, and then the first wagon train arrived, each creaking wagon half filled with gunboat iron, the most that the weary horses could pull. They unloaded the iron, stacked it on the landing, tended the horses. The next morning the wagons left again.

Bowater did the math. At that rate, and assuming none of the wagons broke or horses died, it would take 250 days to transport all the iron to Yazoo City. He tucked that information aside and did not think about it again.

When he had written all he could, and could do no more until he received replies, Samuel took up a wrecking bar and went at the deckhouse. In ten minutes he was sweating. In half an hour his arm muscles were protesting and he had cut his hand. In an hour and a half he had torn his sailor's pullover in three places, cut the other hand, and was walking with a slight limp, but he felt better than he had in a week at least.

He looked with satisfaction at the wreckage on the deck. He had personally torn out a good portion of what had been the first-class passenger cabin, could see daylight where bulkheads had been, where iron casement soon would be.

Well, perhaps not soon.

"Captain Bowater?" He heard a man asking after him, looked up. A fellow on a big black horse, wearing the kind of riding clothes worn by those wealthy enough to afford clothes just for riding, a tall black silk hat on his head, thick silky black mustache under his nose. "Artemus, where might I find Captain Bowater?"

Polkey spit, jerked his thumb at Samuel. Samuel set his wrecking bar down, wiped his hands on the pullover, and stepped down the brow as the man dismounted.

"I am Captain Samuel Bowater." Bowater extended a hand and the man took it, shook. Samuel caught the quick glance up and down, the man's eyes noting the torn and filthy clothes, bloody hands.

"A pleasure, sir. 'Officers will haul with the men,' and all that, eh, just like old Drake?"

Bowater looked down at his clothes. He wondered when he had decided it was all right for him to appear in public, on duty, in such shabby attire. "We do what needs to be done. How may I help you?"

"My name is Theodore Wilson, sir. I own the plantation a mile north of town, five hundred acres of the finest cotton land. In any event, I was in town collecting my mail and the postmaster mentioned there was mail for the ship, so I thought it would be a friendly gesture to carry it down to you."

"Friendly, indeed. Thank you, sir," Bowater said. He waited while Wilson fished the canvas bag out of his saddlebag, waited to see why the man had really come.

Wilson handed the bag to Bowater. It was light and the letters made only a small lump in the bottom. They had not been there long enough for the bulk of the mail to catch up with them.

Wilson ran his eyes over the *Yazoo River*. "Robley Paine was by my place the other day, asking after something. Wagons, I think." Wilson was quiet as he surveyed the boatyard with a half-amused smirk. "I have always had a keen interest in river navigation, Captain. In fact, I own a small screw steamer, often pilot her myself, runs to New Orleans and such." He paused again. "So this here's Robley Paine's boat, is it?"

"No. No, it's not."

"No? I had thought . . ."

"This ship belongs to the Confederate States Navy. Mr. Paine has donated it for his country's use."

"I see . . . There is a story abroad that ol' Robley intends to make her an ironclad."

That was it. Curiosity. Amusement, perhaps. Come down and see what the fools were about, make great conversation over billiards and mint juleps.

"She is being converted to an ironclad this instant. You see the iron plate there." Bowater waved toward the pile, a sad little stack of rail.

"Not much iron for an ironclad vessel."

"That's the first of it. We are moving it from Jackson as fast as we can, but are hampered by a lack of wagons. It seems not all the people hereabouts are as great patriots as Mr. Paine."

That barb made Wilson stiffen, just a bit. "There is no man in Yazoo County, you will find, who is wanting in love for his country, and support for the cause."

"I don't doubt it, sir. Don't mistake me. The men who put their lives in jeopardy for a cause, like my sailors there, or Mr. Paine, are often the ones who grumble the most. After all, didn't our Lord Jesus himself doubt the wisdom of his cause on the night before his death? No sir, I find the staunchest patriots are often those who remain safe by their own hearths."

Wilson's eyes flashed with anger now, but Bowater did not care because he had had his fill of the Wilsons of the world. "You come close to insinuation, sir, and I do not care for it. I have a son fighting in the army, as do most of the men around here."

"Yet when Robley came to you with the simple request for help, just a damned wagon and some manpower, you would deny him? When every bit of stubbornness on your part makes the Yankee—the Yankee who would kill your son—stronger?"

Wilson looked at Bowater for a long moment. "I will forgive your remarks, sir, as you are a stranger here, and do not know the recent history."

Bowater said nothing.

Wilson chewed on a stray hair of his mustache. "Robley Paine's gone mad. Surely you have noticed?"

Of course he had noticed. Curiosity battled with disgust at listening to such gossip. "I am satisfied with Mr. Paine's dedication to the cause. Beyond that I am not interested."

At that Wilson smiled, and Bowater could see he was not fooling the man. "It's not a surprise he's lost his mind, of course. I might have myself, under the circumstances. . . ."

Silence. Stand-off. Finally Bowater surrendered. "What circumstances?"

"Robley had three boys. Fine lads, he doted on them. His entire world. They joined Hamer's Rifles, the company that mustered out of Yazoo County in April of last year. His oldest boy, Robley Junior, made lieutenant. Anyway, they were all killed at Manassas. All three."

Bowater nodded. *Dear God!* That bit of information fit like the last brick in the wall, made sense of everything he had seen Robley Paine to be.

"You impress me, Captain," Wilson continued. "I was afraid that Paine had collected together a cadre of madmen, undertaking some fool thing. I just hope you are not wasting your time here, on some madman's dream."

Bowater straightened. Wilson's approval felt like a dirty thing, like Judas's handful of silver. He saw, in that instant, Robley Paine for what he was, and Theodore Wilson for what he was, and he could not hate Paine, and he could only hate Wilson.

"Mr. Wilson," he said, picking the words carefully, "I have never been deluded about the state of Mr. Paine's mind, not since meeting him. And now that you tell me the cause, I must say, I can hardly find fault or weakness in him for what he has become. But understand this . . . Robley Paine has thrown everything that he is and everything that he has into fighting for the cause for which his sons died. His is the purest, most unadulterated patriotism. He will die like his boys, fighting for his country, fighting for all you men who lie abed while the guns are firing, and I, sir, as an officer of the Confederate States Navy, will be proud to be with him."

Bowater picked up the mail sack. "Thank you for delivering the mail to us. Now if you will forgive me, I have an ironclad that requires building."

He turned, walked back into the office. After a few minutes he heard the jangle of Wilson's horse's tack, heard the clomp of hooves as he rode away.

For a long time Samuel was too angry to move. Angry that he had been saddled with a madman's project. Angry that men such as Wilson, who had the means to make the ironclad *Yazoo River* a real thing, would not. Angry that in this modern time, this age of reason, men could still fight a war in which some sorry bastard could lose his three sons in an afternoon and become the shell that was Robley Paine.

"Son of a bitch . . ." he muttered and dumped the letters out on the desk, shuffled through them, set them in piles. Three for Hieronymus Taylor, that was unusual, a few more for various men in the ship's company, some addresses written with a neat, well-practiced hand, others with the nearly illegible scrawl of the barely literate. Bowater separated them out.

Three letters for him; his father, Wendy, and his sister, Elizabeth. He looked at his letters, considered opening them, stared for a long time at Wendy's name. The anger was still burning in him, and he liked it, did not want to lose the sensation, like the taste of a fine meal in one's mouth, and so he left all news from home aside, even word from Wendy Atkins, and it surprised him that he could. Time for amusements and distractions some other time. He set the rest of the letters aside to distribute to the men at the dinner break.

Richmond, Virginia, felt somber, oppressed. The string of Confederate defeats at Port Royal and Roanoke Island, Fort Henry and Fort Donelson, made it feel like a city under siege, even though the nearest enemy was one hundred miles away—General George "Little Mac" McClellan did not seem inclined to move out of Washington.

Jonathan Paine felt the dull panic. He knew he had to go, and he felt sharp fear. He felt the fear turn into frustration, and then anger, and that was good.

For some weeks after the decision to go home, after Bobby's essential offer to accompany him, Jonathan still did not leave Miss Tompkins's. A seeming epidemic of dysentery swept through the Confederate camp, boys skinny and weak and gray-faced were brought in in regular succession, crowding the already crowded rooms, filling the beds and then the extra beds brought in and then the pallets piled with straw on the floor. They moaned, called out, clawed the clothing of the people who came to help. They got better and went back to their units or they died and were buried outside of Richmond.

It was a nightmare scene, under cold, gray winter skies, and neither Bobby nor Jonathan felt they could leave until it was over. Finally, on the day that three young soldiers were dismissed from the hospital and sent back to their regiment, and not one new patient arrived, Bobby suggested that they go to the Mechanics' Institute and find out what Jonathan needed to do to be officially discharged from the army, and to get a bit of money for his trip home.

Jonathan tasted the panic in his throat, felt the slight tremor in his palms. *This is just damned stupid . . .* he assured himself, but that did nothing to ease his fear. Indeed, if Bobby had not brought the buckboard around, had not helped him on with his coat, led the way out, if Bobby had not in his subtle way forced Jonathan to leave Miss Tompkins's house, Jonathan doubted that he ever would have.

They arrived at the Mechanics' Institute, and it was in every way the bedlam that Jonathan recalled from his previous visit.

Bobby battered a path through the crowd, excusing himself with bowed head and sincere pleas of "Beg pardon, suh," "I'se sorry, suh," "Massah, he gots a leg missin', beg pardon . . ." He had the ability to cover his insolence and pushiness with a veneer of respect, and thus get away with it. It was just what soldiers did, Jonathan realized, what they called "flanking" the officers. Give them just enough respect so they could not call you for insubordination.

They came at last to the Office of Orders and Detail, stood in line until Jonathan's stump began to throb. When finally they came up to the tall oak counter, Jonathan leaned his elbows on it, took as much weight as he could off his legs.

"How may I help you, Private?" the clerk asked.

"I lost a leg at Manassas. I'd like to go home. But I don't believe I have been officially discharged from the army. Also, I'd like what pay is due me."

The clerk looked at him for a long moment, then let out a sigh. "What was your regiment?"

"Company D, 18th Mississippi, but . . ." The clerk turned and left the room before Jonathan could explain the complicated circumstances of his situation.

They waited ten more minutes and then the clerk returned and informed Jonathan Paine that he was dead. Or missing.

"Well, sir, I never was dead, but I was missing for some time, but now I'm here."

"Your discharge will have to come from your commanding officer. We will have to write to him and get him to sign the papers. Without that, you stand the chance of being taken up as a deserter."

"Deserter? My damn leg's been shot off. That isn't proof enough I'm legally discharged?"

"You are not legally discharged, Private, without the letter from your commanding officer. And unless you have one written on your wooden leg, signed and sealed, I suggest you do this proper."

Jonathan stared at the clerk, tried to think of some rejoinder, but he was beat and he knew it and the clerk knew it, too. The clerk reached under the desk, pulled out a preprinted form, lifted his pen from the inkwell and said, "Eighteenth Mississippi, was it?"

41

Thanks to the patriotism of the noble people of Yazoo City, I shall not need the guard that I asked for. The citizens here, though but a handful are at home from the army, will sustain me so long as I shall deserve their support.

—Lieutenant Isaac N. Brown, CSN, to General Daniel Ruggles, C.S. Army

Two days after Wilson's visit, the wagons returned from Jackson with their sorry load of iron. The horses and men looked played out, as if they had been wandering in the wilderness for forty years.

None of them looked as tired as Robley Paine. Bowater physically helped him down from the driver's seat of his wagon, leaned him back against the big wheel, not sure if the man could stand on his own. "We're getting there, Mr. Paine, bit by bit," he said with a concern he had not felt before. Paine looked up sharp. He heard the change in tone.

"It is not enough," Paine said. Exhaustion stripped the words of their bite.

"It will be enough. Let me help you to your bed. You must rest."

Paine nodded, put his arm over Bowater's shoulder, and let himself be led away. They would leave again in the morning. But half a day of rest between trips was not enough, not enough for Paine or the other men or the horses. They could not keep this up.

The iron was unloaded, stacked, the horses tended. That night Bowater lay in his bunk in the makeshift barracks in the old carpenter's shop, stared at the dark. He read and reread Wendy's letter, five pages long. Tales of nursing, conditions in Norfolk. She had a flawless sense for how newsy a letter should be, and how sentimental and how serious and how lighthearted, the ingredients tossed together to form a perfect confection.

He loved it, he loved her, but it was not enough to pull him from his black mood. He fell asleep at last, woke with head pounding, joints aching, as if he had slept tensed on the edge of a cliff.

He woke to the sounds of wagons on packed dirt, the jangling of traces, voices loud in the early morning. He woke thinking that the wagon train was ready to roll out again, that they had organized and prepared while he slept.

He climbed out of bed, wearing only the sailor's slop trousers he had taken to wearing, now that the bulk of his work involved manual labor. He pulled on his pullover, and looking like a hungover Jolly Jack Tar stumbled out of a whorehouse.

There were wagons there, but not the wagon train. These were different wagons, bigger, with fresh teams of draft animals, black men sitting on the driver's seats, long whips held lazily across their laps, waiting. He could see none of his own men abroad. Bowater did not know what was happening, but he realized that whatever it was, it had nothing to do with him.

"Captain!" Theodore Wilson stepped up, and again gave Bowater's clothes a half-amused glance up and down, and if Bowater had not been so groggy he would have been angry with himself for having not worn his frock coat and gray pants.

"Mr. Wilson . . ."

"I have a confession, Captain. When I came down the other day, it was not simply to deliver the mail."

"Really?"

"No, sir. I was curious. Curious to see if this thing, this ironclad, was really a viable enterprise. Not going to back a loser, sir. Never have. But I am impressed by what I see. And in truth, Captain, and I mean this with all humility, when I am impressed, I see to it that others are impressed."

"I am impressed with your due humility."

"Laugh if you will. I can get things done in this county. Behold, sir. Wagons."

Bowater looked out over the wagons. Twenty that he could count, and more coming down the road. Big, sturdy vehicles. Suddenly the *Yazoo River* was a real possibility.

Robley Paine approached, limping but moving fast. "Wilson, what's happening here?"

"Good morning, Robley." Wilson smiled, but the warmth and concern in his voice was a cover, a sham. Beneath it, Bowater could hear only discomfort and fear. "I have spoken with the others, and we have decided we must help you in building your boat."

Robley squinted at him. The old man was not fooled by any of it. Robley Paine, mad as he might be, understood the entire situation in an instant. "Captain Bowater is in charge here, you understand? His orders are final, and neither he nor I give a goddamn how much land you have, or how many darkies or how much money. You understand that, then your help is welcome."

Wilson shifted uncomfortably. "Of course, Robley, of course . . ."

"Good," Robley said, and then, as if forgetting his caveat of a second before, said, "See your men and horses fed. We leave for Jackson in one hour."

It was pandemonium for an hour, with the teamsters and the horses and the shipwrights all getting their breakfast and their coffee and then getting horses and wagons ready, and the first screeching of nails as boards were pried from the side of the *Yazoo River*. And then the wagons rolled off and the noise dropped off to a fraction of what it had been and a sort of peace seemed to settle over the boatyard.

Samuel Bowater found himself in such good spirits that he was able to face the ream of paper needing his attention.

"Cap'n Bowater?" Hieronymus Taylor stuck his head in the door, interrupted beef requisitions.

"Come in, Chief."

Bowater had seen little of Taylor in the past week. The chief and Burgess and Moses had disappeared down into the engine room and mostly remained there, like bats, or some other nocturnal animals. They would appear at mealtimes, and after work, filthy, drenched in their own sweat. They would tear off their clothes and plunge into the Yazoo River, and sometimes some of the others would join them. Beyond that, they were absent, down in their own underworld of steam pipes and boilers and condensers and pumps and cylinders and pistons.

"I do hope you are not here to report some insurmountable problem," Bowater said, wondering if this was the end of his buoyant mood.

"No, no . . . ain't nothin like that. We havin' some problems with the damned valve linkage on the starboard engine. We don't get it squared away, we like to do nothin' but steam in circles."

"It is something you can fix?"

"Oh sure, sure . . . but, well, fact is, I need to head on down to Vicksburg. I know a shop down there, can make me what I need. Ain't a damn thing 'round here, 'cept some country blacksmiths, and what I need's a bit more refined, ya understand? So if it ain't a problem, reckon I'll take the packet on down to Vicksburg."

Bowater nodded. He did not doubt Taylor's veracity, but there was something the chief was not saying. He considered probing deeper, but did not.

He did not like Taylor, but he trusted the man enough now that he would take him on his word. Whatever it was he sought in Vicksburg— reversing gears, a good drunk, a fancy girl—whatever Taylor felt he needed, Bowater was ready to let him have it. He did not ask what it was. He imagined he would find the answer repugnant.

"Very well, Chief. When will you be back?"

"Next Wednesday, reckon. Burgess and Jones gots their jobs, they'll carry on without me."

"Very well. And since you are venturing into civilization, please ask Polkey and Johnny St. Laurent if there is anything they need."

"Aye, sir," Taylor said, with the most respect and relief that Bowater had ever heard from the man, and disappeared.

Samuel turned back to his beef requisition, then set the letter aside. Time to start tearing into the *Yazoo River*. He felt more ready than he had since arriving.

They worked all that day until the sunlight was gone, and the next day, being Sunday, Samuel Bowater gave the men the day off, because he still could and because the men needed a break, and so did he.

He took easel, canvas, and paints and wandered a bit down the riverbank, to a place one hundred yards from the ship. The weather had turned warm with the first appearance of spring, and with his back to the shore Samuel looked up the winding length of the Yazoo River, the bursts of new green on the trees, the dots of color that represented the early spring flowers, the old black paint and fresh-cut wood of the *Yazoo River*. It was lovely. He pulled a pencil from his paint kit, made thin lines across the canvas.

The hours melted away as the canvas was crisscrossed with fine gray lines, the outline of the riverbank and the stands of trees, the sandbars and reeds like underwater obstructions laid down to stop a tiny armada, and far away, the building ironclad. He mixed paint on his palette, dabbed away at the canvas, filling in the lines, making the colors before him reappear on the canvas.

He was happy for a while, lost, and then he heard footsteps behind. He turned and looked. An older couple, around his parents' age, wandering down along the riverbank, looking as if they were out for a stroll. Locals come down to see the ship being built. Sometimes Bowater felt like Noah, with all of the town coming down to watch the madmen building their boat.

He turned back to the painting, which he was liking less and less. He hoped the couple would leave him alone, but he knew they would not. He knew they would approach, look over his shoulder, make some comment that would reveal their absolute ignorance of art.

He made fine green lines where the reeds emerged from the river, heard the sounds of the couple's feet on the gravel behind him.

"Captain Bowater?" the man asked. Bowater put his brush down, turned around.

"I am he. How may I help you?"

"Good day, Captain. It is a pleasure to make your acquaintance. We have followed your actions in the papers with great interest." The man was red faced, with a grand white mustache. He wore a black frock coat, a tall silk hat, walked with a gold-headed cane. His wife wore broad hoops, kept the sun at bay with a silk parasol. The man's voice was soft, dignified, educated.

"Please," the man continued, "allow me to introduce ourselves. My name is Eli Taylor. This is my wife, Veronica."

Taylor . . . ?

Mrs. Taylor gave a curtsy, which Bowater returned with a shallow bow.

"We were hoping, Captain, to see our son," Mrs. Taylor said. "Hieronymus Taylor? We understood he is engineer aboard your ship."

Bowater looked at Veronica Taylor. She must have been a beautiful woman in her youth. She was still a beautiful woman, all poise and dignity. "Forgive me, ma'am, I think perhaps you are mistaken," Bowater said, and even as the words left his mouth he thought, *How many Hieronymus Taylors might there be in the navy?*

"It's no surprise you should think so," Eli Taylor said, and his voice sounded sad. He held up a little photograph, a tintype in a stamped tin oval frame, such as were produced by the thousands all over the country.

"This is our son," the man said, and Bowater took the picture. Staring back at him, in shades of gray, was a younger, cleaner Hieronymus Taylor.

"I apologize," Bowater said. "It's just that . . ."

"We understand, Captain," Eli interrupted him. "Hieronymus can be . . . difficult, at times."

Indeed? Bowater thought.

"He has simply rejected all of his upbringing," Veronica said, with a tone of exasperation mixed with disappointment. "His brothers and sisters are not like that, I can assure you."

"We live in New Orleans and took ship up," Eli prompted. "We heard from friends in the Navy Department that he might be here."

"Yes, yes he is . . . no, I mean, I'm sorry, he is assigned to this ship. But he had to go away for a few days. He had business in Vicksburg."

Eli frowned and Veronica sighed and said, "I knew we should not have written ahead, Eli."

"Yes, dear, perhaps you are right."

"I am so sorry you missed him," Bowater said, and meant it, though he did not know if his disappointment was for the parents or for himself at missing Taylor's discomfiture.

"Yes, well . . ." Eli said, and let the rest die off.

"He should be back by Wednesday."

Eli nodded. "Perhaps it is best we missed him. I fear when he left home there was some . . . trouble. We have not been as close as I might wish."

"I'll tell him you came," Bowater suggested, but Eli shook his head.

"No, no, Captain. If it is all the same, I suppose if Hieronymus does not care to see us, I won't have him think we are thrusting ourselves on him."

It was a very sad scene, and Bowater was looking for something helpful to say when Veronica noticed the painting.

"You are an artist, Captain?"

"Oh, no. I dabble. It passes the time."

Veronica and Eli Taylor took a closer step, scrutinized the canvas.

"It is very good," Veronica said.

"I do believe I see the influence of the Hudson River School, sir. A Charleston man, you must be familiar with the work of Washington Allston?"

"I have seen his painting, yes."

"We have two Allstons in our collection," Veronica Taylor said.

"Your work is reminiscent of Durwood, as well, but not nearly as pretentious. Of course, we have seen only your work in progress. Are you familiar with Fitz Hugh Lane?"

"Why yes, I am . . ." Bowater stammered. "You are well versed in painting, I see."

"Oh, we are great patrons of the arts, sir. Every bit of it."

"All our children were raised to appreciate the finer things, Captain," Veronica said. "Painting, music. Hieronymus has a great gift for music. They were trained in the classics since childhood."

Bowater nodded. He did not know what to say.

"You might say we're overboard on the subject," Eli said. "We named Hieronymus after Hieronymus Bosch, you know, the fifteenth-century Dutch painter."

"Did you indeed?"

"Oh yes. His middle name is Michelangelo."

42

I have spent my life in revolutionary countries and I know the horrors of civil war, and I told the people what I had seen, and what they would experience. They laughed at me and called me "granny" and "croaker."

—David Glasgow Farragut

he mighty USS *Hartford*, mounting twenty nine-inch Dahlgren smoothbores, two twenty-pounder Parrott rifles, one heavy twelve-pounder, and one light twelve-pounder, flagship of the Western Gulf Blockading Squadron, was stuck in the mud.

Farragut stood on the quarterdeck, leaning on the rail, looking across the deck, over the brown, slow-moving water, over at the low, marshy shore three hundred feet away. South West Pass, one of five ways into the Mississippi River.

Black smoke roiled out of the *Hartford*'s stack, drifted off to the west. Beyond the bow, Farragut could see another plume, smaller, just as black. The side-wheeler *Calhoun*, with a towline to *Hartford*'s bow. The two ships, *Calhoun* and *Hartford*, were stoking up their boilers, building up steam enough to drag the deep *Hartford* through the mud. They reminded Farragut of bulls pawing the ground in preparation for the charge.

From the foredeck, over two hundred feet away, the executive officer called back, "Ready, Captain Wainwright!"

Wainwright, captain of USS *Hartford*, waved, called to the quartermaster, "Four bells!"

The quartermaster rang out the bells, and underfoot Farragut could hear the engine room respond, a tremor in the deck as the engines dug in, two horizontal condensing double-piston-rod power plants with thirty-four-inch strokes and cylinders sixty-two inches in diameter. Farragut looked over the side. The river was boiling and the mud was swirling like brown storm clouds.

He felt a slight jerk as the *Calhoun* took up on the towline and pulled. He looked across the deck, lined up one of the mizzen shrouds with a stunted tree on shore. The seconds ticked off, and slowly, slowly, the shroud seemed to draw away from the tree. They were moving.

"I believe it took *Brooklyn* an hour to tow across, sir," Wainwright said. "We might go a bit faster, with *Brooklyn* having dug a trench for us."

"Perhaps." Farragut knew all that, and Wainwright knew he knew it. Saying it was Wainwright's not too subtle way of pleading for patience, patience for a situation over which none of them had control.

Patience. It was something Farragut was running out of as quickly as he was running out of coal. They could not begin to attack New Orleans until Porter's gunboat flotilla arrived, and the last he heard they were in Key West. They could not attack until they took their big ships over the bar, but it was all they could do to get *Hartford* and *Brooklyn* over. How they were going to get *Colorado* over, with her nearly twenty-three-foot depth, he could not imagine.

These ships were not built to fight this war . . . he thought. Most of the ships under his command had been laid down with the thought that they would be fighting the British navy on the high seas. It certainly had not been contemplated that they would be used in an attack on New Orleans.

From the main topmast crosstrees, now the highest point aboard *Hartford*, the lookout called, "Boat approaching! Steaming from the south! Looks like one of our dispatch boats, sir!"

Wainwright turned and looked south, but Farragut did not. With his eyes, he had no hope of seeing the boat until it was almost up with them. Nor was he that curious. He had seen enough dispatch boats in the past month to satisfy him for life.

With creaks and groans and billowing black smoke and the occasional jerk, the *Hartford* drove over the mud. Forty minutes after the *Calhoun* took up the strain, the ship gave a little lurch as she broke free from the last desperate grasp of the river bottom and surged ahead into deep water. Forward, Farragut could see the *Calhoun* sheer off as the towline was dropped.

"All stop!" Wainwright said. "Stand by the anchor!" he shouted down the length of the deck.

The *Hartford* was just settling on her hook when the dispatch boat pulled up alongside.

"Admiral, sir!" the lieutenant in command called up.

"Yes, Lieutenant?" Farragut called down. What news it was that could not wait for the lieutenant to come aboard he did not know, but he could guess.

"Admiral, sir, Commander Porter's compliments, sir, and he reports his arrival at Ship Island with his mortar fleet."

"Excellent!" Farragut replied. He looked upriver. *Brooklyn* was lying to her anchor, head to stream, three hundred yards away. "Lieutenant, steam up to *Brooklyn* and tell Captain Craven, with my compliments, to give his people their dinner and then I will signal to get underway. We'll anchor at Head of the Passes."

The lieutenant repeated the orders, saluted, spoke to someone in his wheel-house that Farragut could not see, and the little steamer chugged on its way.

The Head of the Passes . . . He would plant the Union flag on Louisiana soil, and pray God it would remain.

Let the festivities commence . . .

On May 10, the newspapers in Yazoo City ran banner headlines, and those headlines proclaimed the death of the wooden walls.

Theodore Wilson arrived on his black horse, reined to a stop in a shower of small stones and dirt, leaped off, paper in hand.

"Captain Bowater! Captain Bowater, sir, did you see this?"

He handed Bowater the paper, shifted from foot to foot as Samuel read the article. CSS *Virginia* had sailed two days before. She rammed and sank the USS *Cumberland*, burned the *Congress*, which had run aground. Sent the Yankees into a panic, gave new hope to an emotionally battered Confederacy. It had been a hell of a maiden voyage.

Bowater read the account with the kind of interest only a professional navy man could have. He read the breathless claims of the obsolescence of all wooden vessels and smiled. The *Virginia* was too unseaworthy for the open ocean and of too deep a draft to get up any of the big rivers that emptied into the Chesapeake.

CSS *Virginia* was not the future. She was only a glimpse of it.

But one would not know that looking at the gleam in Theodore Wilson's eyes. "What do you say to that, Captain?"

"Very impressive."

Hieronymus Taylor ambled over. He had returned from Vicksburg, bleary-eyed, with a tear in his frock coat he did not recall getting. Had behaved a bit cagy at first, as if he was feeling Bowater out, but that did not last long.

"What's so impressive, Cap'n?" Taylor asked, took the paper, read the first few paragraphs. "Well, damn. Looks like your ironclad done some good, Cap'n."

" 'Your' ironclad?" Wilson asked.

"Hell, yes," Taylor said, looking up at Wilson. "Whole damn thing was Cap'n Bowater's idea. What the hell you think we was doin in Norfolk so long? Cap'n here suggested it to Mallory, drew up the first plans. Weren't no one thought it would work, but then, sure enough, once them others smell success, hell, they all come around like dogs to a . . . somethin. Anyhow, that's why they sent Cap'n Bowater out here, figured he could do the same to the ol *Yazoo River*."

Taylor folded the paper, handed it to Bowater. "Congratulations, Cap'n," he said, then ambled off.

Bowater turned to Wilson. There was a light in the man's eyes he had not seen before. "None of that is true," Bowater said, but he could see Wilson would not be disabused of his fantasy.

Nor was Wilson a man to fantasize alone. The enthusiasm which he had displayed in organizing the wagons seemed to double up on itself. More wagons arrived, and carpenters, blacksmiths, machinists, laborers, black and white, from plantations all over Yazoo County. They set up their makeshift foundries on the shore, in a semicircle around the now cut-down riverboat. Wilson brought his screw steamer *Abigail Wilson* down and tied her astern of the *Yazoo River*. Her hoisting engine was made to drive several steam drills on shore, and her cabins became housing for the officers of the *Yazoo River*.

Newspaper reports two days later of the battle between *Virginia* and the Yankee ironclad *Monitor* did nothing to cool the ardor. Southern papers shaded the story in such a way as to make it sound like a Confederate victory, but any experienced navy man, reading the bare facts of the thing, could see it was a stalemate.

It was also the first time in the history of naval warfare that two ironclad vessels had battled it out. The future seemed to be arriving at an alarming rate.

Not only did the plantations send help, but the men of the town began to arrive as well, to lend their brawn and in some cases valuable skills to the work. Women came at noon with lunch in baskets. Children gathered up scraps of wood, swept sawdust into piles, scurried for tools.

The train of wagons arrived every third or fourth day, and eager hands pulled the plates of iron off the beds, stacked them carefully on the landing, and soon the once sorry pile was transformed into an impressive mountain of iron. And still it came.

Ironclad fever swept like the plague through Yazoo City. The people had read of the future in the papers, and they wanted a part of it. Suddenly the vision of a madman had become the most effective means of keeping the Yankee at bay. They were like Noah's neighbors, who began to see the wisdom of the thing as the water crept up around their ankles.

All of the *Yazoo River*'s superstructure was gone, and in its place rose a casement, a low deckhouse with angled sides, and a small wheelhouse, no more than a four-foot-high hump on the roof through which captain, pilot, and helmsmen could see. The side wheels, delicate spider structures, were encased in oak two feet thick, a housing with flat, angled sides intended to protect that most vulnerable part of the ship from enemy fire. Paddle wheels were ideal for riverboats. They were not ideal for men-of-war.

The sides and bulkheads of the casement, foot-thick live oak, were pierced for ten guns—two pointing forward, two aft, and three on each broadside. It was optimistic, since they still had only the guns that Robley Paine had purchased for the ship, but Bowater was firing off a continual barrage of letters and he hoped one of them might have an effect.

Hieronymus Taylor tore the engines apart. He checked the cylinder bores and replaced piston rings with new ones he had had turned in Vicksburg. He checked the piston-rod packing and rebuilt and realigned the engines so that they would not tear themselves apart driving the big side wheels.

With block and tackle and crowbars they lifted the paddle wheels off their bearings and checked for wear and pitting and cracks. They checked crosshead bearings and mapped them with lead wire to see where they were worn and scraped them to get the proper clearance. They ground the steam valves and scraped the flues in the boilers.

Two days before they began bolting iron to the casement, the crew arrived. Fifty men, twenty-three of whom were genuine able-bodied sailors, the rest ordinaries, culled from the army and from the coastal defenses and sent to man the newest ironclad. At their head was Lieutenant Asa Quillin, executive officer, quiet, efficient, a thoroughgoing navy man whom Bowater had known briefly on the South American station.

Six weeks after the former Cape Fears had arrived in Yazoo City, a month and a half after Samuel Bowater had been greeted with the possibility that the ironclad *Yazoo River* might be no more than a madman's dream, there were over 150 men working on the ship, six forges set up on the riverbank, a crew of seventy-five experienced seamen, and any number of local men ready to sail aboard the ship in the unskilled berths.

Once, Samuel Bowater recalled, he had told Taylor the *Yazoo River* had to get up steam and leave in six weeks' time. He had made that number up. He would never have guessed then that they would actually be underway just a week later than that.

*   *   *

Richmond was getting nervous, and so was Jonathan Paine. On the 1st of April, General George McClellan had begun loading his vast army on board steamers, bringing them down the Potomac, down the Chesapeake Bay to Fortress Monroe for a push up the Peninsula to Richmond. He would be only fifty miles from the Confederate capital before he encountered his first Southern soldier. Grant and Farragut were moving on the Mississippi, to Jonathan's worried mind closing in on Yazoo City.

It was just a few weeks shy of one year since the moment his body, riddled with bullets, had been flung to the dirt on Henry House Hill. During that time, the long slow climb out of despondency and self-flagellation, the difficult work of regaining interest in his life, Paine Plantation had taken on a mythical quality, an El Dorado, a Canaan, promised but unattainable. It called to him. It frightened him.

The Army of the Confederate States would not give him leave to go there.

Then finally, as the spring flowers were beginning to dot the drab landscape with color, and green leaves filled in the spaces between spindly branches like a painter adding another layer of pigment on a canvas, just when Jonathan Paine was considering going once more to the Office of Orders and Detail, though it was clear from the last three visits that his badgering was not appreciated, a letter arrived.

Bobby brought it into the drawing-room ward, where Jonathan was writing a letter for a corporal of the 4th South Carolina who had broken his arm in a fall from a horse. "Jon'tin, you gots a letter . . ." Bobby said and for a moment Jonathan could only look at him, and down at the letter.

Confederate States Army, Office of Orders and Detail . . . The words were printed in neat block type on the envelope, and Jonathan's name and address handwritten below. He tore it open, his stomach twisting. He knew what it should be, but he still feared it was something else.

He pulled out the paper within, unfolded it. A preprinted form, lifeless save for the intricate decorations featuring eagles and flags and cannons sprawling across the top. The blank spaces were filled in in a hurried, largely illegible hand, but Jonathan Paine could certainly read it well enough to puzzle out his own honorable discharge from the Confederate States Army. There was as well a bank draft for the amount of ten dollars.

Jonathan looked for a long time at the two documents. There was a time when ten dollars would have been meaningless to him; his family spent more than that on sundry amusements on any given month. But now it represented his entire net worth. It was not just money, it was the way out of the desert.

"You still want to come to Paine Plantation with me?" Jonathan looked up at Bobby. "Help me get home?"

"Yassuh."

"Then let us go."

It did not take them long to pack. Jonathan had only his knapsack, the tattered remnants of his uniform with someone else's uniform pants, someone not so fortunate as he, he imagined, in regards to wounds. Everything that Bobby had fit easily into a haversack and a bedroll. They said their goodbyes to Miss Sally Tompkins, the volunteers and patients at her hospital, ambled out into the crowded streets. Jonathan was not afraid. It was springtime.

They purchased tickets to ride the Richmond & Petersburg Railroad out of town. Bobby helped Jonathan aboard the car, making a path with his finely honed ability to knock people aside in a subservient, humble way. He set Jonathan down on a seat, set his haversack beside him, said, "All right, then, Missuh Jon'tin, you gonna be jest fine here. I's gonna go to da car where da colored folks ride."

"Very well, Bobby. Remember, we get off at Petersburg, at the junction with the Weldon & Petersburg Railroad."

"Oh, I remembers, Missuh Jon'tin," Bobby said, and with a smile he disappeared into the crowd.

It was a scene they played out many times over the next ten days, as they made their way laboriously south, then west. The trip would have been a simple matter, except Tennessee was in large part in Union hands.

So they went south on the North Carolina Railroad, the Wilmington & Manchester Railroad, the South Carolina Railroad, rattling up over the Appalachian Mountains before falling back down to Atlanta, Georgia, where they changed to the Alabama & Georgia Railroad, which took them through the low, hot, humid country of Alabama, to the old Confederate capital of Montgomery, and from Montgomery, by steamboat and rail, to Jackson, Mississippi. Eleven hundred miles of choking, rattling railcars, of waiting at depots while soldiers, bound for the front, took precedent over wounded soldiers going home, of eating just enough to stave off hunger, and no more, because they had so little money and no idea of how long it needed to last.

During those long hours flopped on benches in deserted depots or standing off to one side while men jostled for the cars, Jonathan told Bobby about Paine Plantation, about the beautiful lawns rolling down to the water, about the welcoming oak tree, about the summer nights when the fireflies made their own living constellations in the tall grass by the Yazoo River. They talked about all that, but they did not discuss Jonathan's parents, because he had not heard from them and he was afraid.

From Jackson they had just enough money to secure a ride on the coach to Yazoo City, with Jonathan riding inside and Bobby on the box with the Negro driver. They walked from Yazoo City south, following the river.

It was all so familiar, it all fitted into place like the pieces of a puzzle. The smell of the bougainvillea and the pine, warmed in the sun, the river smell, mudbanks and rotting weeds. From the woods that lined the dirt road came the raucous call of the blue jay, the *chickadededede* of the Carolina chickadee. Cardinals flashed red against the dark green. The cooling breeze carried on it woodsmoke and warm, turned earth. It was delightful to Jonathan. It made him afraid.

At last they came to a dirt drive that branched off the road and Jonathan stopped and Bobby stopped and Jonathan said, "Here we are."

"This you home?"

"This is it."

They were quiet for a moment, Bobby letting Jonathan do as he wished, in his time. No bullying now, there was no need. "Very well . . ." Jonathan said at last. "Let's go."

They walked down the drive and soon, from the distance, the edge of the white house peeked through the trees. They walked on, the trees yielding to open space, the house emerging from its hiding place.

The lawn was overgrown; little care had been given to it. He could hear no sound from the house, nothing to indicate it was occupied. He felt his stomach churn, wondered who he would encounter first, if he would encounter anyone at all.

They pushed through the knee-high grass, Jonathan leading the way, circled around the house, giving it a wide berth, as if it was something to be wary of. The edge of the wide porch and the distant river came into view. Jonathan stopped short.

"Dear God . . ."

The limbs of the oak tree had been hacked off, save for the two lowest, which stuck out like skeletal arms. The remaining trunk had been painted, the paint peeling off in big flakes but still visible.

Jonathan limped slowly around the front of the house, eyes on the tree, mouth fixed. From the front he could see that the tree had been cut to look like some sort of monster, a gargoyle or some such. It rose thirty feet off the ground, leered at the river with its hideous mouth, hacked from the living wood and painted. Above the mouth, the painted remnants of eyes glared north. There was no new growth on the truncated limbs. The tree was dead.

"Dear God . . ."

Jonathan looked at Bobby, and Bobby's eyes were wide, as if he had seen the thing that the tree had been painted to represent. "That ain't right, Missuh Jon'tin . . ." Bobby managed to stammer.

Jonathan looked up at the front of the house. Paint was peeling there, too, and the path to the porch was all but overgrown. Just a narrow strip of flattened and trampled weeds indicated that anyone had gone in or out of the house recently. The front door gaped open. There was no one around.

"Come on," Jonathan said. He began walking slowly toward the porch, and after a pause he heard Bobby following behind. He climbed the steps with the now-familiar sound, creak, clomp, creak, clomp, of leather shoe and wooden leg. He crossed the porch slowly, stepped through the door.

The smell hit him first, the familiar smell of the plantation house. It was wood polish and leather and cooking smells and dust. It was a living smell, and it made Jonathan think the house was not a dead place, that there was still life there.

Behind him, he heard Bobby stepping into the foyer. He turned. His friend was looking around, his eyes still wide.

"Welcome to Paine Plantation, Bobby," Jonathan said. "I fear it is not everything I made it out to be."

Bobby nodded. "You gots any notion where da folks is?"

Jonathan shook his head. "Hallo?" he shouted, and his voice bounced around the empty space. "Hallo? Is there anybody here?"

The two men waited. There was no answer. "Come along," Jonathan said, led Bobby deeper into the house, every inch a perfect fit with his memory, every little bit of the place sparking one memory or another. Bobby was absolutely right to think the place haunted.

He led Bobby into his father's study. There was dust on the surfaces, unlike in the foyer or the hall, as if it had not been entered in some time. That did not bode well, not for any hope of his father's being alive. Jonathan could not recall a day going by that Robley Paine, Sr., had not sat in his study.

On the desk was a stack of mail, and Jonathan began sorting through the letters. Letters from agents, creditors, letters to his mother and father, a few to him or his brothers. He found the letters that he had written, unopened, halfway down in the stack. He went through them all. They told him nothing, save that his father had not read his mail in the better part of a year.

He saw a few papers scattered on the floor, stooped with some difficulty and picked them up.

Dear Sir:
  We regret to inform you of the death of Lt. Robley Paine, Jr., Company D, 18th Mississippi Regiment, 3rd Brigade . . .

Jonathan dropped the letter. It was old news. Old news to him, old news, apparently, to his parents.

He crossed the room, picked up two more papers, lying one on top of the other.

Dear Sir:

We regret to inform you that, as of this date, Private Nathaniel Paine, Company D, 18th Mississippi Regiment, 3rd Brigade, and Private Jonathan Paine, ditto, are missing. . . .

He turned the other over, sucked in his breath when he saw it. It was a message from another world, a message written by him in a former incarnation. *Nathaniel James Paine, Company D, 18th Mississippi, 3rd Brigade, son of Robley and Katherine Paine, Yazoo, Mississippi. Please God send me home to be buried in my native earth.*

Jonathan read the words, and as he did he was back on Henry House Hill, the bullets plucking at his garments, the grief pouring from him as his beautiful brother Nathaniel lay dead at his feet.

Robley confirmed dead, Nathaniel confirmed dead. Their father would take it for granted that Jonathan was killed as well, with no word from him, the army calling him missing.

Oh, God, Father, where are you? What have you done? Jonathan wanted to fling himself to the ground, wrap himself in the house, the only familiar thing left to him. He would have fallen then and there, pressed to the floor by his grief, if a noise from beyond the room had not jerked him from his sorrow.

He looked up sharp, and Bobby did, too. There were footsteps in the hall, soft, approaching stealthily. Jonathan had opened his mouth to demand identification when the person in the hall called out, "Who dere? Who dat?"

It was a woman's voice and it sounded very much like Jenny, the old cook. "Jonathan Paine," Jonathan replied.

They heard a sound like a grunt, and then the back door of the room burst open and there stood Jenny, fat and squat, a shotgun in her hands. Their eyes met and Jenny's eyes went wide and her mouth dropped open and the shotgun fell out of her hands and discharged, blowing the leg off a Queen Anne chair.

Jenny clasped her hands to her mouth, began backing away. "Oh, Lord, you's a ghost fo sartin . . ."

"No, no, Jenny . . ." Jonathan took a step toward her, reached out his hand. "It's me, really me . . . I'm alive . . ."

Jenny still shook her head, but she stopped backing away.

"Jenny . . . where is everyone?" Jonathan asked, as soft as he could.

"They's all run, Massa Jon'thin . . . they's all run in-country, on account o' dem Yankees, comin' down de river . . ."

"Yankees?" Jonathan could not imagine the Yankees had penetrated that far into Mississippi.

"Yassuh. I's de only one dat stayed . . ." Her voice trailed off, and she cocked her ear toward the front door. "Oh, Lord, I hears dem now!" she exclaimed, apparently as frightened as she had been of the vision of Jonathan's ghost.

In the silence Jonathan listened, and he heard, far off, the huffing of a steam engine. "Come on," he nodded to Bobby, and the two of them crossed out of the study, down the hall, and onto the porch once again.

Half a mile upriver, and heading down, trailing twin plumes of black smoke from two stacks, a paddle wheeler was brushing the water aside. Jonathan looked for a long time, let the boat get almost abreast of the plantation, before he could figure out what it was he was looking at.

He had seen paddle wheelers all his life, but he had never seen one like this. It rode low in the water, and the superstructure was flat and not ten feet in height, save for a small house on the top and forward, where the wheelhouse would be, though the one on that boat was more the dimensions of a doghouse.

There were three square windows in the side, and two in the front bulkhead. The entire thing, including the wheelbox, seemed to be made up of wide planks painted a dull brown.

"Dear Lord," Bobby asked, speaking softly. "What in da hell is dat?"

Jonathan watched the boat as it steamed past. "It's an ironclad. An ironclad gunboat." Jonathan had read of such things in the papers in Richmond, but had never laid eyes on one.

"Dey Yankees?" Bobby asked, but even as he asked, Jonathan's eyes were resting on the flag, flapping astern from the tall ensign staff. The stars and three broad stripes, red, white, red.

"No," Jonathan said. "It's a Confederate ship." The serpent was close. Men in Yazoo City were sallying forth to beat it back. He had returned just in time.

43

April 15—The enemy brought up his whole fleet. . . . Orders were repeatedly given to Captain Stevenson, of the river fleet, to cause the fire barges to be sent down nightly upon the enemy; but every attempt seemed to prove a perfect abortion. . . .

—Report of Brigadier General Duncan, C.S. Army,
Commanding New Orleans Coast Defenses

The order came from Secretary Mallory.

NAVY DEPARTMENT, C.S.
Richmond, April 15, 1862

Sir:

Work day and night to get the *Yazoo River* ready for action. The preparation of ordnance stores and the drilling of the crew should all progress simultaneously. Not an hour must be lost. Spare neither men nor money. Put the best officers you can get on board the ships, if those we send don't arrive in time. Proceed at the first possible convenience to New Orleans and place yourself and your vessel at the disposal of Commander Mitchell, CSN.

S. R. Mallory
Secretary of the Navy

Lt. Samuel Bowater, CSN
Yazoo City

New Orleans, Bowater thought, as he read the terse order. *So it is to be New Orleans.* . . . There did not seem to be much consensus as to the direction from which the chief threat was coming, north or south. Hollins and his fleet had been sent upriver from New Orleans to meet the Yankee ironclad gunboats, leaving New Orleans with little in the way of naval protection.

Now there seemed to be a shift in policy.

The *Yazoo River* was, happily, a far way toward completion when the telegraph arrived. Hieronymus Taylor had pronounced her engines as fit as they were going to get, and nothing short of running them under load could reveal any further defects. The gunboat iron was bolted in place, so it looked as if the entire upper works were covered with wide wood strips painted dull brown.

The guns and ordnance had arrived the day before Mallory's telegram; three nine-inch shell guns and six thirty-two-pounder smoothbores. That left one gunport empty, and into that went the ten-inch Dahlgren of *Yazoo River's* original battery. The old six-pounder was left on the landing.

They hoisted the guns aboard, set them at their gunports. They finished off the last of the armor, the iron over the wheelboxes. The officers' quarters were no more than a few roughed-in bulkheads, the crew quarters were hammocks slung along the gundeck, but that was how it had to be. Bowater did not think they would have to endure that inconvenience for long.

On the 18th of April they were underway. The crew numbered 153. They included the original Cape Fears, the new men sent by Mallory, and eager volunteers from Yazoo City, men who were not sailors, but who were perfectly capable of hauling on a gun tackle or carrying shot and charge to guns, or heaving coal in the engine room. Artemus Polkey signed on as ship's carpenter. A pilot by the name of William Risley, thickset, heavily bearded, volunteered to take the ship south and to fight her if need be.

There was no place for Robley Paine. He was not a pilot, not even a sailor. His leg had become so lame that he could hardly walk at times, and his health was not good.

Still, when he came to Bowater, and admitted to all of those imperfections, and begged to nonetheless accompany his ship on what they all understood might be her death run, Samuel was much moved. The *Yazoo River* was there because of Robley Paine, and him alone. Bowater knew he could not leave Robley Paine on the beach, force him to watch his ship sail off without him.

They got off the dock under their own power and steamed down the

Yazoo River. Four miles above the Mississippi, one of the main bearings on the starboard engine cracked in two, bringing the engine to a halt with a sound that made every man aboard wince. They limped into Vicksburg on the port engine. Taylor and Burgess worked for seven hours straight, right through the night, and the next morning they were underway again.

From Vicksburg it was 250 miles to the Crescent City. They steamed all day, all night, with both engines wide open, slowing only when they had to shut down the port engine to replace a throttle valve that jammed half-open.

Samuel Bowater looked out the narrow window at the forward end of the wheelhouse. It was not really a window, more a long rectangular opening in the armor plating, but then it was not really a wheelhouse either, but more of a low pilothouse, a four-foot-high ironclad box with sloped sides sitting on top of the casement.

Six feet below the roof of the box, mounted on the gundeck, was a platform that formed the deck of this truncated pilothouse. On that deck was mounted the wheel and the two telegraphs to the engine room. Crowded onto the platform, the lower part of their bodies in the casement, upper half, from the chest up, in the short wheelhouse, stood Bowater, the pilot, Risley, the helmsman, and a midshipman to relay the captain's orders. It was the oddest lash-up Bowater had ever witnessed, but he reckoned it would do.

He moved his head from the port beam forward beyond the bow, to the starboard beam. The great, wide, brown Mississippi lay before them, over a mile wide, and crowded with shipping as they closed with New Orleans. Amazing. He had very little experience with the river, had never been stationed in New Orleans. It took no imagination to see why this was where the lifeblood of the Confederacy flowed.

"How far to New Orleans, Pilot?"

"Fifteen miles. Be another sixty-five downriver to Fort St. Philip, which I reckon is where the fleet is. Ain't no use in stationing at New Orleans. Time the damn Yankees get to New Orleans, it's too damn late to stop them."

Bowater nodded. "Carry on," he said, and stepped the four steps down from their little pilothouse deck to the gundeck below. Four steps, and the heat rose by twenty degrees, from what Bowater guessed to be around eighty to around one hundred. Sweating and shirtless men struggled with the big guns, loading and running out in dumb show, those experienced in naval gunnery instructing those who had never been this close to a cannon.

Bowater walked slowly through the odd twilight of the ironclad. In sixteen years at sea he had been aboard nearly every type of vessel afloat, but he had never seen anything like this. They were in a box, a rectangular box with sloping sides. The rough-cut wood of the deck and the sides and bulkheads was painted white to aid in visibility, and it helped, some, but still the interior of the ironclad was gloomy. A row of lanterns hung along the centerline, despite the brilliant sun that poured in through the open gunports.

Samuel paused and looked along the port battery. If he looked at just that, just that small section of the gundeck, he could almost believe he was on the lower deck of a regular man-of-war. The broadside guns, the gunports, the sloping side like a ship's tumble home, were all familiar things.

It was when he looked forward, when he saw the forward bulkhead, the forward-facing guns at right angles to the broadside, that the illusion was blown away. He was not on a proper man-of-war. He was on an ironclad ram, a newfound engine of war.

Ironclads at sea, armies moving by rail, communicating by telegraph. Rifled cannons, rifled rifles, exploding ordnance. They were all Americans, Yankees and Confederates, like it or not, all children of that particular genius that was America. How apt then that in less than a year of war, Americans fighting Americans, they should alter forever the very nature of warfare.

Bowater stepped forward and was joined by Lieutenant Asa Quillin, stripped down to shirtsleeves, his shirt clinging to him, as wet with perspiration as if he had been doused by a bucket. Together they strode the length of the deck, gave words of encouragement to the men working the guns. Bowater stopped to talk with Ruffin Tanner, whom he had promoted to acting master's mate and given command of the starboard battery.

"How do you fancy being an officer, Mr. Tanner?"

Tanner gave a long, slow chew of the tobacco in his mouth. "Ain't bad."

"How are your gun crews coming along?"

"Good. Gettin better. I don't reckon aiming will be much of an issue."

"No, I think not. Rate of fire, that's what we're looking for."

"That's what you'll get, Cap'n."

The *Yazoo River* steamed through New Orleans, the crowded docks, the sailing vessels, the paddle wheelers, the screw tugs, crisscrossing the river like water bugs. There was wild activity there, frenetic activity.

Hieronymus Taylor came up the steps from the engine room to the gundeck, joined Bowater in the pilothouse. He stoked up his cigar and the smoke was sucked through the narrow windows and out into the evening.

"Home sweet home," Taylor said, smiling as he peered out at the waterfront. "This won't be the first time I got my ass whopped 'round these parts, far from."

"Is it always this busy, Chief?" Bowater asked.

"Yeah . . ." Taylor said, and then, a moment later, "Well, maybe not . . . somethin strange about it, seems like one damned big hurry. What you think, Mr. Pilot?"

"I think everyone with a boat's tryin to get the hell out of town afore the Yankees gets here."

Taylor nodded. "And fools we be, we goin' in the opposite direction."

They passed the city, made the 180-degree bend in the river ten miles south, and then another ninety-degree turn before the Mississippi straightened out for its final run to the Gulf.

They were fifty miles from Forts St. Philip and Jackson when they heard the gunfire.

Bowater thought it was thunder at first, a late-day storm brewed up by the sea and humidity of the Gulf. It seemed too massive to be gunfire. But it rolled on and on, distant and muted and constant, long after thunder would have died away.

"Do you hear that?" He turned to Risley and the pilot nodded.

"Mortar boats."

"Mortar boats?"

"Yeah. Twenty or so. Old schooners, mostly. They towed 'em up, got 'em tied up to the riverbanks. They each have a thirteen-inch mortar on board, dropping them shells right into the forts. They must be murdering them poor bastards garrisoning them places. Idea is to knock the forts out and wreck the chain they got across the river, then Farragut can take his ships right up."

Risley took his eyes from the low gray cloud of smoke, visible now over the low marshy land to the south. "Hell, Captain, don't they tell you nothin?"

Theodore Wilson stood on the dock, looked down the Yazoo River as far as he could see. Behind him rang the noise of packing up a shipyard, a shipyard which had come together out of nothing, had formed like Adam from the dust, a new thing. All of Yazoo County rallying to his, Wilson's, call, and through his influence and leadership they had turned a madman's dream into a reality, into a formidable weapon of war.

Wilson had to admit it, to himself, at least: the past month and a half had been the best time of his life. The energy surrounding the rebirth of the *Yazoo River* as an ironclad had been terrific, like an electrical storm, and him in the middle of it. In the directing of resources, the delegation, the supervising, he had felt like a brigadier general. In the sheer physical work he had found a new devotion to the cause of Southern liberty, more profound than he had thought possible.

When he had first confronted Samuel Bowater, he had thought himself a patriot. Now he could not even recall that person he had been, what that Theodore Wilson had thought and felt.

The *Yazoo River* steamed off for New Orleans, and Wilson felt as if he had, by mistake, left some part of himself aboard, forgotten to retrieve it before the ship sailed, like a coat left draped over a rail or a box of tools. He thought of tomorrow with dread. What was there now, now that the ship had gone without him?

He had considered sailing with her, of course. He had some seamanship, some piloting skills, from running the *Abigail Wilson*. But not enough to pilot a vessel like the *Yazoo River*. He had arranged for Risley to sail as pilot, aware of his own limitations.

So what else could he do? Nothing. He had no military experience, had never even seen a gun fired in anger. Manual labor, haul a gun tackle, run ashes up the ash hoist, that was it. Shovel coal. He would be subservient to Bowater, subservient even to Robley Paine, and that would not do. So he stood on the dock, watched her steam away, supervised the disassembly of the *ad hoc* shipyard.

He heard footsteps behind, a shuffling, limping walk, two people, someone to ask him what they should do next, and he did not know. He was tired of this work. It was anticlimax.

"Mr. Wilson?" The voice was strong, familiar, but he could not place it.

"What?" he said, exasperated, and turned around. His eyes met the face staring at him and he sucked in his breath, felt his heart charge, his limbs jerk with the involuntary reflex of shock and panic, an encounter with the supernatural.

"Dear God . . ." It was nothing supernatural—Wilson realized that in the instant he was sucking in his breath—but just as surprising.

"Jonathan Paine? What in hell are you doing here, boy? We all thought you were dead."

"Nearly was." He lifted up his pant leg, and Wilson looked with horror at the wooden appendage. "Lost that at Manassas. Robley Junior, Nathaniel, they weren't so lucky. Both got killed. I got the idea my daddy thinks I'm dead, too."

Wilson nodded. *God, this sorry son of a bitch looks like hell!*

Skinny as a stray dog, his cheeks sunk, unshaved, in a uniform that was torn and patched. He looked old, twice his twenty or so years. Of all the boys, Jonathan had always favored Robley the most, and now he looked even more like him—the wasted, mad Robley Paine.

Behind him stood a Negro of about Jonathan's age, one Wilson did not recognize, a slave, perhaps, he had picked up along the way.

What am I going to tell him? Wilson wondered, but Jonathan spoke again.

"I been down to Paine Plantation. My mother's dead."

Wilson nodded. "I knew that, son. I'm sorry."

"There's only a few of the servants left. No one knew where my daddy was. Someone thought he was at Yazoo City. Fellow in town told me to look here." Jonathan looked around, as if he still might find his father.

What do I tell him? His father went mad with grief, spent all of his money—all of his boys' money—to build a machine with which to kill himself?

"Your daddy was here. You missed him by two days. He had a dream to build an ironclad gunboat, and damned if he didn't do it. They went down to New Orleans, to fight the Yankees. Folks reckon there'll be a hell of a battle."

Jonathan nodded. There was a strange look in his eyes, not the flash of impetuous youth, not the wild, undisciplined thing that Wilson was used to seeing in the youngest of the Paine boys. "New Orleans . . ." Jonathan looked out at the river, as if he might fling himself in, let the brown water carry him to his father, to the sea.

Wilson looked down at the ground, the few blades of grass shooting up between the gravel, kicked at the loose rocks. He looked up. The old six-pounder from *Yazoo River* was sitting on its carriage near the edge of the landing. Robley Paine's gun. Jonathan's now, he reckoned.

He had opened his mouth to tell Jonathan that, that he was the proud owner of a six-pounder smoothbore—he could think of nothing else to say—when he stopped, and involuntarily he shifted his eyes to the *Abigail Wilson*, still tied to the dock. He ran his eyes over her bow, pictured the sweep of foredeck, then glanced back at the six-pounder.

"You looking to go to New Orleans, then?" Wilson asked.

The gunboat USS *Itasca*, 150 feet long, five hundred tons, steamed up the Mississippi River, farther than any Yankee had come in a year.

Lieutenant C.H.B. Caldwell, commanding the *Itasca*, stood by the big wheel, aft. He had been charged by Admiral Farragut with removing the heavy chain, supported by half a dozen derelict schooners, which the Confederates had stretched across the river. He and his consort, *Pinola*, had labored for hours under the fire of Forts Jackson and St. Philip. They had managed to pull one schooner free. Their mission so far, a failure. Caldwell was not ready to report as much to Farragut, doubted he ever would.

The mortar flotilla was firing a covering fire, trying to distract the Confederate gunners, keep their minds off the two Yankee gunboats moving upriver. Streaks of light arched up high overhead, dropped into the wide area between the walls of Forts St. Philip and Jackson, made great billows of light as they exploded.

The forts were firing too, blasting at the riparian intruders with rifled shells. Exploding ordnance tore up the river, peppered the *Itasca* and *Pinola* with iron, but Caldwell was too angry to care. He steamed through the narrow opening left by the removal of that one schooner. He was playing his last hand.

He turned to the midshipman beside him. "Go down to the engine room, give the chief my compliments, and tell him that when I ring full ahead again, I want every ounce of steam I can have. Tell him to throw pitch, turpentine, whatever on the fires. I need it all."

"Aye, aye, sir!" The mid saluted, ran off.

Two hundred, three hundred, four hundred yards upriver the *Itasca* steamed, until the line of schooners was lost to sight, and visible only in the light of exploding ordnance. The shells dropped all around the gunboat, screamed down the deck, took off the head of the mainmast; it was like steaming into a hornet's nest.

"Port your helm, hard aport!" Caldwell said. Fort St. Philip, which had been right ahead, its walls bristling points of light where the guns were firing at them, was now on the port side, now astern, as the gunboat turned to run with the stream.

Caldwell grabbed the telegraph, swallowed hard, rang full ahead.

The deck vibrated as the engineer stoked the fires up and the prop churned the water and the speed built. The gunboat was moving fast now, with the current, covering the distance that she had just steamed. Against the stars overhead Caldwell could see great quantities of smoke rolling out of the stack, and he wondered what the chief was throwing on down there.

Fort Jackson to starboard was firing madly, but Caldwell could see the schooners now, the chain between them, could see the point he intended to hit, the place where the chain hung lowest between two hulks.

"I'll take this," he said softly to the quartermaster, and the surprised man stepped aside, let the captain take the wheel. Caldwell gave a half turn, brought the helm amidships. He could not risk the possibility of the helmsman misunderstanding his command. They had one try, and one try only. No practice run, no drill.

They were coming on fast to the schooners, one, two, three, and between schooners three and four he pointed the bow of the gunboat. He could feel the engines throbbing below, could hear the sound of the hull pushed as fast as she could go through the water. And then they hit.

The bow of the *Itasca* hit the chain and kept going, up, up, as if she was leaping a wave, and the pounding engines drove the ship on, higher and higher. The gunboat seemed to be crawling out of the water as it lifted up, as it rode up on the chain.

And then it stopped and the throbbing engines could push her no more. She sat there, hung on the chain, and it dawned on Caldwell that they might remain in that position, hung up on the chain under the Confederate guns. The forts would blow them to pieces at first light, a failure on his part much worse than failing to break the raft.

The first tendrils of panic were creeping up his throat when the chain broke under them. The bow of the *Itasca* dropped down, sent the spray flying high over the rails, rocked the vessel with the waves created by her own impact.

The straining engines shoved the gunboat ahead. To port and starboard, the old schooners that had held the chain were now caught in the fast-flowing current. They swept downstream, swinging on the chain, making a gap in the obstruction like barn doors swinging open.

Caldwell smiled and would have shouted if he had not controlled himself. Forward, someone with less control whooped, and more followed suit.

Lieutenant Caldwell looked at the wide gap in the chain, big enough for the flagship, big enough even for the side-wheeler *Mississippi*. He had done his job. Now there was nothing but the forts and the Confederate mosquito fleet between Farragut's big ships and the city of New Orleans.

44

I wish you to understand that the day is at hand when you will be called upon to meet the enemy in the worst form for our profession.

—Admiral David Glasgow Farragut, General Orders to Captains

They worked as hard and as fast as they could: Theodore Wilson, Jonathan Paine, Bobby Pointer, the crew and new volunteers of what "Captain" Wilson was calling the "CSS" *Abigail Wilson*. They removed the towing bitts, rigged up gun tackles, swayed the gun carriage and six-pounder aboard. They procured shot and powder, topped off potable water, brought aboard food and sundry other supplies.

The days ticked by: April 18, 19, 20 . . . The Jonathan Paine of a year before would have been frantic, yelling at everyone to hurry, arguing with Wilson over every new thing he had to have aboard. The Jonathan of a year before would have made an insufferable pain of himself, would no doubt have been thrown off the boat.

The one-legged, sunken-cheeked Jonathan was no less frantic, though he kept it to himself now, and simply worked as hard as he was physically able.

He had picked up the story of his mother's death, his father's life, piece by piece, from dozens of sources, like reconstructing a mosaic from a disorganized heap of tiles. He did not like the picture forming.

The servants remaining at Paine Plantation told him how his father had cut the limbs off the tree, turned it into what it was, for what reason they did not know. He did it at the same time his mother took to her bed, never to rise again. It was at the same time, Jonathan surmised, that they had received word of the death of their sons.

He heard the rest—travel to New Orleans, spending money wildly, the boat, the fight with the Yankees at the Head of the Passes, the return to Yazoo City, the conversion of the ship into an ironclad. None of it, none of it, sounded like the methodical, stable, well-considered father he knew. When the mosaic was put together it revealed a picture of a man who had gone mad with grief, who was flinging himself at the enemy as a form of suicide.

And now, Jonathan knew, the enemy was coming in force at the river defenses below New Orleans. It was a good opportunity to die. Jonathan could not bear the thought of his father's going to his grave without ever knowing the truth, without knowing that the Paine line would live on. So he worked until the stump of his leg throbbed in agony, and then he stuffed cotton between the stump and the wood and worked some more.

They took on coal on the 20th, ready to get underway that afternoon.

"Bobby," Jonathan said. They stood on the landing as the coaling commenced. "If you wish, you are welcome to wait my return at Paine Plantation. You know how to get back there."

"I was figuring on comin wit you, Missuh Jon'tin."

"This is not going to be a fine thing, Bobby. As I understand it, there aren't but a few Southern boats against all the Yankee fleet. I don't know as any of us'll come through this one."

Bobby nodded. "But I do love a boat ride, and I ain't never seen N'Awlins. I gets to do dem tings, I reckon I'm fit to die."

Jonathan smiled, slapped Bobby on the shoulder. "Good," he said. Bobby was part of the journey, part of the entire thing. Jonathan did not like the thought of undertaking the last part, playing the final act, without him.

An hour later they left the dock, steamed out into the stream. They were a day and a half getting to Vicksburg, with "Captain" Wilson putting the *Abigail Wilson* hard into the mud half a dozen times. They tied up at Vicksburg and the captain, in a tacit admission of incompetence, hired a river pilot to take them to New Orleans.

They were underway again just a few hours later, steaming downriver through the night. Wilson was anxious too, Jonathan could see, eager to get into the fight. Driving him, no doubt, was the thought that Robley Paine might die a hero in combat and Wilson himself would never see a shot fired. Whatever it was, Jonathan did not care, as long as they were steaming for New Orleans, and doing so with all dispatch.

*   *   .*

The pounding of the forts by the mortar flotilla downriver had been frightening at first, in its lethal potential. The round thirteen-inch shells fell with uncanny accuracy, exploding as they hit, the Yankees having worked out the elevation, trajectory, charge, and fuses exactly. The shells exploded with a deep, angry-God sound, sent shards of iron screaming. One shell through the roof of the casement, which served as a hurricane deck for the *Yazoo River*, would be the end of them all.

For all the daylight hours and well into the night, the sky was slashed apart with the streak of burning fuses as the thirteen-inch mortars lobbed shell after shell into the forts. Twenty-one mortars all firing together; the sound of individual guns was lost until it was all one big rumble of mortar fire, whistle of shell, explosion of shell. The twilight hours, the night, were lit with the continuous flash of detonations, muted through the pall of smoke from expended power which hung permanently over the water.

The men of the *Yazoo River* could do no more than stand on the hurricane deck, watch the awesome fireworks, and shake their heads at the resources the Yankees were able to array against them. Twenty-one specially equipped ships just to blast two forts? Would they never run out of shells?

Finally, after a few days, when the wonder of it all had worn away, the shelling became simply monotonous, and soon they hardly heard it at all. None of the shells were being lobbed at the fleet, huddled upriver of Fort St. Philip. The Confederate Navy and the River Defense Fleet did not seem to be a great concern to the Yankees.

The storm was building, Hieronymus Taylor could feel it. Like so many times out on the Gulf, when the sky would get blacker and blacker and the water would turn a weird grayish blue and you could feel the change in the atmosphere, feel it on some primal level, and you knew when the sky opened, and the wind began to whistle, and the seas rose, that it was going to be bad.

That was how he felt, early evening, April 23, 1862, sitting on the hurricane deck of the *Yazoo River*, worrying the cigar in his mouth, looking downriver at the desultory fireworks. The bombardment had slowed around noon, for the first time in five days. There were rumors the ships of the Yankee fleet had shifted their anchorages around. Change. It meant something was going to happen. The storm had to break soon. The pressure was too great.

He turned and looked at the boats on the Confederate side. An odd assortment, and none too menacing. Besides the *Yazoo River*, there were the *McRae* and *Jackson*, old wooden steamers, veterans of the river war. There were two vessels from the Louisiana State Navy, the *Governor Moore* and the *General Quitman*, both wooden steamers mounting two guns each. There was part of the *ad hoc* River Defense Fleet, the commander of which, John Stephenson, had such an aversion to taking orders from a naval officer that Commander Mitchell finally decided to just ignore him and his boats.

There was the low, whale-backed ironclad ram *Manassas*, the oddest thing that Taylor had ever seen afloat. But she had proved her worth before, at the Head of the Passes, and Taylor hoped she would again, and perhaps with greater results.

Lastly there was the ironclad *Louisiana*. She was a massive affair, 264 feet long, sixty-two feet wide, with an eclectic collection of sixteen guns. She was potentially the greatest threat to the Union forces, another CSS *Virginia*, let loose among the wooden walls. Unfortunately, her odd combination of paddle wheels and screw propellers was inadequate to maneuver the huge vessel. She was unable to steam under her own power, and even with tugs could not get upriver against the current. She was tied up at the foot of Fort St. Philip, a floating iron battery, no more.

First Assistant Engineer Hieronymus Taylor sat for a long time on the hurricane deck, looking out over the water, thinking. There was much to ponder. The sun sank into the marshes. To the north lay his beloved New Orleans. Would there be Yankees in those narrow, ancient streets in the next week? The next day?

It was near midnight, most of the ship asleep, when he sighed, stood, tossed his cigar overboard. In the evening quiet he heard it hiss in the water. He stepped forward to the small pilothouse. The officers were maintaining watch as if at sea, and Bowater and the pilot Risley were standing on the pilothouse roof, talking in low tones about the river, the current, what they would be up against.

"Evening, Captain," Taylor said, in a neighborly way, looking up at Bowater, standing on the four-foot-high roof.

"Good evening, Chief." Bowater was in shirtsleeves, rolled up, his braces dark against the white shirt. He was smoking a cigar as well, the first time Taylor had ever seen him do so.

"Expecting some excitement tonight, Cap'n?"

"Could be. Could well be."

Taylor nodded. "I think so too. Tonight's the night. I can feel it in my bones." With that he turned and climbed down to the deck, then through the small door into the casement. Only a few lanterns were lit. The guns lurked in the dark, and between them, men sleeping at quarters, like grown bears and their cubs, all hibernating.

Taylor threaded his way through the men, found Acting Master's Mate

Ruffin Tanner lying on his back, mouth open, snoring. He nudged him with his toe, nudged harder until the sailor woke up.

"What the hell . . . ?" Tanner muttered, looked up through half-closed eyes.

"Tanner, you awake?" Taylor asked.

"Am now, you son of a bitch . . ."

"Good. I need ya to get a couple of your sailor boys, launch the starboard boat."

"Starboard . . . why? This on the cap'n's orders?"

"No, it's on my orders, and I would be damned grateful if you would stop arguing and do it."

Tanner climbed to his feet, stretched, looked Taylor over. Then he nodded. "Starboard boat." They understood one another, the sailor and the engineer. Taylor knew he could count on the man.

Taylor opened the hatch to the engine room and climbed down, climbed into the familiar heat and Stygian atmosphere.

"Jones! Where the hell you at? You hidin in the damn coal bunker again?"

Moses Jones, fireman of the watch, stepped out from behind the engine, an oil can in his hand. "I'se here, boss. What da hell you needin now?"

"I need you to round up all the darkies we got in the engineering division. They's you and Tommy, they's William and Noah and Caesar we got up in Yazoo City . . ." The men from Yazoo City were slaves whose owners had hired them out to the navy as coal heavers. Taylor wondered if their masters thought themselves patriots for such sacrifice. "What other darkies we got aboard?"

Moses cocked his head, squinted at him, trying to divine the man's motives. "What you wants ta know for?"

"Will you stop yer damned arguing, you black son of a bitch?"

"They's the two fellas in the steward's division and Johnny St. Laurent."

Johnny St. Laurent. Taylor wondered how he could have forgotten him.

"All right, see here. You round up all them fellas from the engineering division, Tommy and them new hands from Yazoo City, an y'all meet me on the fantail. Just do it," he added to Moses's forming question.

Taylor climbed back up into the casement, made his way aft to the makeshift galley where Johnny St. Laurent slept. He shook the sleeping cook until he got a response.

"Johnny, come with me," Taylor said, and Johnny, who had been with Taylor on many a misadventure, stood and followed without question.

They met on the fantail, Hieronymus Taylor and a cluster of black men in Confederate sailor's garb. On the starboard side, Tanner and two seamen held one of the *Yazoo River*'s boats against the ironclad hull.

"All right, you boys," Taylor began, and then he was interrupted by footsteps in the casement, stepping through the door. Captain Bowater.

"Chief, what are you doing?" Bowater asked. It was not a friendly tone: anger, confusion, but mostly suspicion.

"I'm lettin' the darkies go, Cap'n. They ain't got a dog in this fight."

"You are . . . what?"

"Letting the darkies go. Givin them a boat. Let 'em sail on down to the Yankees. We don't need 'em, don't need no divided loyalties for the fight we got comin."

"What makes you think their loyalties are divided?"

"Well, let's jest see." Taylor turned to the men on the fantail. "Any you men don't want to go over to the Yankees, wants to remain in the Confederate Navy, stay and fight, step on over there."

Taylor pointed to the port rail. There was a long pause. No one moved.

"Who is going to pass coal, Chief?"

"I can pass coal. Burgess can pass coal. Got two white coal passers, don't need so damn many down there anyhow."

Bowater was silent, clearly did not know which way to go on this.

"How 'bout you, Cap'n? You gonna let your boy Jacob go?"

"Jacob's been with me all his life. He certainly would not think of deserting."

"That a fact? Why don't we ask him?"

The two men stared at one another. The moon was rising, and gave just enough light that they could see one another's eyes, but just barely.

"Very well. Tanner, go fetch Jacob," Bowater said.

Silence on the fantail, an ugly silence, like two men holding one another at gunpoint. And then a moment later Tanner and a very confused Jacob climbed out the small door onto the deck.

"Jacob," Bowater said. "Mr. Taylor here wishes to let all of the Negroes go, let them get into the boat there and row down to the Yankees and ostensible freedom. He suggests I allow you to go, so I will.

"The choice is yours. Remain where you are, and stay with me, or step over with those other men"—Bowater pointed to the cluster by the starboard rail—"and go with them to the Yankees. What will it be?"

The silence settled down again, and every eye was on Jacob, and Jacob clearly was not happy about it. His eyes shifted between Bowater and the men at the starboard rail. At last he made some little sound—it might have been a muttered word—and with three quick steps he crossed to the starboard rail and took his place there.

Jacob shook his head. Taylor could see the sorrow in his face, his eyes.

Finally he spoke. "Massah Sam'l, I'se sorry. Really, I'se sorry. But what the hell else you expect me ta do?"

Bowater looked from Jacob to Moses, to Johnny, then to Hieronymus Taylor. Then, without a word, he turned and disappeared through the door into the casement.

"All right, y'all, this here's your chance and you best take it!" Taylor said, loud, and his voice moved the men to action. They climbed down, one after another, into the boat, faces frightened and expectant, all at once.

"Boss." Jones stopped, as Taylor knew and feared he would. "This here, this here's a fine thing you doin'. . ."

"Shut up. Think I wouldn't rather see your black ass stop a shell before mine? Git the hell in the boat, afore I change my stupid mind."

Moses nodded, and to Taylor's irritation smiled and then climbed into the boat and took up an oar.

"Go on, y'all!" Taylor shouted. "Head on downriver, that's where you'll find them Yankees, lead ya to the Promised Land!"

The men at the thwarts dipped their oars and pulled and the boat began to fade into the night.

"Go on!" Taylor shouted. "Go work in one of them damned factories up North, see how damned good ya had it here!"

Then from the dark, from the amorphous white shape which was all he could see of the boat, Moses Jones's voice cut though the dark like a knife. *Oh, Shenandoah, I'm bound to leave you . . .*

Then all of the men in the boat together: *Away, you rolling river . . .*

Then Moses again: *But Shenandoah, I'll never grieve you . . .*

Hieronymus Taylor stood on the fantail and watched until first the boat and then the singing were swallowed up in the dark. He smiled despite himself, shook his head, stepped into the casement, and shut the ironclad door.

Samuel Bowater stood on top of the pilothouse roof, alone, watched the boat pull away downriver. Jones's voice, deep and clear, floated back to them.

Jacob's desertion had moved him in a profound way. He would never have guessed it, was certain, when he agreed to test his conviction, that Jacob would remain by his side. That he had opted instead to leave the Bowaters' service for the uncertainties of freedom in the North shocked Samuel, changed his outlook in a fundamental way.

He toyed with these thoughts, but his mind wandered. His father, his mother, Wendy, Robley Paine, they all stepped up for consideration, vague, half-formed thoughts. He sat on the hurricane deck, leaned back against the pilothouse.

He did not know what time it was when he awoke, nor what woke him. He opened his eyes, looked into the dark. There were footsteps on the hurricane deck. He did not move.

A figure stepped past the pilothouse, stepped to the forward end of the hurricane deck. In the moonlight Bowater recognized the beaten-down frame of Robley Paine.

For a moment Paine did nothing. Then with some difficulty he knelt down on the deck, bowed his head. Clasped his hands. For a long time he remained there, in silent prayer, and Bowater was not sure what to do.

Finally Bowater rose, and his foot scraped on the deck and Paine looked up.

"Ah, Mr. Paine, I did not see you there," Bowater said.

"Quite all right, Captain," Paine said. He stood painfully, stepped over to Bowater. There was something different about his face. The muscles seemed less tense, the edge of madness dulled. "A fine night," he said.

"Lovely . . ." Bowater said, and then, before he knew he had said it, added, "Why did you do this, sir? The ship, all of it?"

Paine looked at him with a look that seemed to peel the buffers of secret thought away. "I don't know. I don't know why I did most of what I did, this past year. I don't even recall a lot of it. I did it for my boys, I suppose. Their memory. My wife was able to let herself die, but I did not have that trick. I guess I did it because I was doomed to live when I did not want to, because the Everlasting has set His canon against self-slaughter."

His voice was stronger, more clear than Samuel had ever heard it. He was quiet for a moment. Then he said, "In any event, here we are. And even if what I did can do nothing for my boys, it can at least help my country, and that is something." He turned to Bowater. "You are the only one who has ever had the grit to ask me that."

Bowater nodded. This man before him was not the mendacious lunatic who had greeted them at the landing at Yazoo City. The transformation of the ship had somehow transformed him as well. Or maybe it was the proximity of eternal rest that revived his mind.

Then, like punctuation to the thought, the guns of Fort St. Philip opened up, two hundred yards away. Instant change, like waking from a dream, the dark and quiet blasted away as gun after gun hurled iron and fire over the water. And lit up by the muzzle flashes of the big guns, the Yankee fleet, moving slowly, line ahead, upriver, through the boom, through the crossfire of the forts.

The lead Yankee ship staggered under the hammer blow from the fort but did not stop, did not even slow. Her sides flashed with gunfire as she hit back, wooden warship against fixed fortification. Fort Jackson began to blast away, and then the next Yankee ship in line, and the next. In less than half a minute a full-scale battle had appeared, right under their bow.

Below, Bowater could hear his officers and petty officers shouting, could hear the tramp of 150 men rushing to battle stations, but he remained, transfixed. He considered sending for Jacob, having him fetch his frock coat and hat, but he rejected the idea. Too hot for that. He wondered at himself. There was a time when he would not have considered going into battle without his proper uniform, despite the heat.

And then he remembered that Jacob was no longer aboard. He wondered about him and Moses and the other Negroes, if they had made it through or were caught up in that.

No, they had had time. They would have made it through.

Robley Paine turned to him, one side of his face lit with flickering orange light. "Our time has come," he said.

"It has indeed," Bowater replied. "It surely has indeed."

45

On the morning of the 25th the enemy's fleet advanced upon the batteries and opened fire, which was returned with spirit by the troops as long as their powder lasted, but with little apparent effect upon the enemy.

—Major General Lovell, C.S. Army, Commanding Defenses of New Orleans

There was no plan, no organized waterborne defense. There were not enough Confederate ships to warrant it, and with the River Defense Fleet doing what it wished to do in any event, it had never seemed worth trying. Sally forth and fight, that had been the only plan. Captain Bowater rang up half ahead, called down to Lieutenant Asa Quillin to slip the stern anchor which held them head downstream.

The noise of the chain running out came rattling through the deck. The bitter end went overboard and the *Yazoo River* twisted in the stream, free of the muddy bottom. The quartermaster, wide-eyed with the shock of being roused from sleep by cannon fire, still trying to button his pants, turned the wheel with one hand, held his pants with the other, brought her on a heading for the battle.

Risley, the pilot, climbed up to the platform beneath the pilothouse. Without a word he took the wheel, let the helmsman get his pants in order. "Heading, Captain?"

Bowater watched the battle for a moment before replying. It was as if the night had exploded, great flashes of red and orange, the concussion of the great guns making the casement of the *Yazoo River* shudder, even half a mile upstream. In just a few moments of fighting the smoke had become thick enough to make some of the gunfire look muted, dull bursts of color in the dark and the gloom.

Quillin appeared in the pilothouse looking for orders.

"You recall, Mr. Risley, Horatio Nelson's words, just before Trafalgar?" Bowater said. " 'No captain can do very wrong if he places his ship along-side that of an enemy.' That must be our strategy tonight, because I think we'll get no instructions from the flag. So let us plunge right in."

"Aye, aye, sir," Risley said. The quartermaster took the helm again. "Find the closest damn Yankee and steer right for her," the pilot instructed.

More footsteps on the platform and Hieronymus Taylor appeared, ubiquitous cigar in mouth, his frock coat open, his hands in his trouser pockets. "Forgive my intrusion," he said. He looked forward, out the slit of a window, at the panorama of violence under their bow. "Ho-ly God . . ."

"What is the report from the engine room?" Bowater asked, irritated. He was irritated about the Negroes, irritated about Taylor's being there in the pilothouse, irritated in general with the man.

"All's well, Cap'n Bowater. Boilers blown down, fires are clean, grates are clean, steam's up."

"You have coal heavers enough?"

"We have coal heavers enough."

Bowater turned back to the fight before him, tried to ignore Taylor. The rest of the mosquito fleet was scrambling, slipping anchors, steaming downriver. Risley ordered a hard turn to starboard to avoid collision with one of the River Defense Fleet. It was helter skelter, with no organized line of battle, and Bowater wondered if there wasn't as much danger of colliding with friend as there was of being run down by their enemies.

"Well, reckon I'll crawl back in my hole," Taylor said, and when Bowater failed to respond, added, "Captain?"

Bowater turned. Taylor wore a strange look on his face. Not contrition, not arrogance, not apology. Something else. A touch of sentiment, perhaps.

"Cap'n Bowater, we have been through quite a bit together, you and me. I got to say it now. You are one cold, patrician son of a bitch, but you got grit. It's been a pleasure."

Taylor extended his hand, and the words and the gesture were so genuine that Bowater was taken aback. He would not have credited the man with such sincerity.

Bowater took the extended hand, enveloped it in his two hands, and shook. "Chief Taylor, you are one insufferable pain in the ass, but you are a hell of an engineer."

Taylor smiled around his cigar. "Cap'n, if you live through this here jaunt, and I don't, I would surely admire it if you could see that put on my headstone."

"It'll be done."

Taylor regarded the men in the pilothouse. He snapped a crisp salute. "*Morituri te salutamus*," he said, then turned, disappeared into the gloom of the ironclad's lower deck.

They had halved the distance in the time that he had spoken with Taylor, the fast-flowing Mississippi River sweeping them down on the enemy. The fight had mounted in its intensity, the smoke and noise and gunfire building on itself. The first of the Yankee ships was just now coming between the forts, blasting away with both broadsides, pushing on upriver.

And the forts were giving it back. Five days of shelling seemed to have made no difference. The big guns were blazing away so that the walls of the forts might have been on fire, so solid was the sheet of muzzle flash.

The smoke rolled over the river, more and more smoke, hanging like an acrid fog, glowing orange. And through that smoke the ships moved, the big, slow-moving Yankee screw steamers, the little ships of the Confederate defenders. Into that hailstorm of iron, Samuel Bowater pushed the *Yazoo River*.

He turned to the midshipman, Mr. Worley, and said, "Go below. Tell the gun captains to fire at any target on which their guns will bear. They are to fire at will."

"Aye, aye, sir!" the mid said, a bit too loud and high-pitched, and he hurried off.

A gunboat was leading the Yankee line, a schooner-rigged screw-driven craft, 150 feet or so in length. "There! Steer for her!" Bowater said, pointing through the slot, and as he did a tugboat appeared out of the gloom, crossing their bow, starboard to port. In the flashing gunfire Bowater could make out the Confederate flag on her stern. He got out no more than the first syllable of a helm command before they struck.

The men in the pilothouse staggered as the two vessels hit, and Quillin shouted, "Damned idiot!"

Bowater looked out the slot. The tug was hung up on their bow and men were rushing along her deck, shouting, waving arms. The gunfire was so continuous now that the whole scene was lit in orange, the tug silhouetted against the flames of Fort Jackson's barrage.

Bowater grabbed the telegraphs, gave a ring, shoved the handles to full ahead. *No time for this horseshit. . . .* The engines responded immediately, the *Yazoo River* surged ahead, pushing itself into the tug. With a snapping and crunching sound, audible over the gunfire, the tug peeled off the

Yazoo River's bow, bumped against her side, disappeared astern, and the ironclad was once again racing toward the fight.

The Yankee gunboat was surrounded, Confederate ships pounding her from all sides, more maneuvering to board. No room for another. "Pilot, do you see that big ship, the one coming up next?" Bowater was shouting now, he could not be heard otherwise over the gunfire.

"Aye!"

"We'll make for her!"

The broadside below opened up, the guns of the ironclad *Yazoo River* firing for the first time in anger. The casement shuddered, the smoke swirled up from the gundeck, sucked out of the slits in the pilothouse. With it, the squeal of carriage wheels on the deck, the rumble of the guns being run out, and another gun, and another. The flames from the muzzles lashed out from the side of his ship, the muzzles themselves hidden from his view over the edge of the casement.

The embattled Yankee gunboat passed down the *Yazoo River's* port side and the next ship in line loomed up, and Bowater sucked in his breath. *It is the* Pensacola! *Dear God, it is my* Pensacola!

Four years he had served as second officer aboard that ship. There was not one inch of her that he did not know, that he had not been personally involved with in some way or another. Four years of his life played out on those decks, and though he would not admit to the sentiment, he had come to love her dearly, as much as any man had ever loved a ship, and that was very much indeed. And there she was and she was trying to kill him.

Forward and below, the *Yazoo River's* guns fired away, point-blank range, nine-inch shells and thirty-two-pound round shot, right into the guts of his old ship. Bowater clenched his fists. *Pensacola* must hit back, and no one knew better than he how hard a punch she could throw.

They were just abreast the *Pensacola's* foremast when the Yankee sloop opened up on them, eleven nine-inch Dahlgrens to a broadside, a forty-two-pound rifle. For an instant there was nothing to be seen through the pilothouse slot but a sheet of flame. A shell glanced off the casement, whirled past with a hysterical scream, but more hit square, made the iron ring out with a deafening clang—like being trapped in a church bell—made the entire vessel shudder and roll.

The *Yazoo River* fired back, even as the last of the *Pensacola's* shells were slamming into her armored sides, but now there was a new sound that cut though the gunfire. Screaming. The wounded.

Bowater looked around for Quillin, but the luff had gone below to supervise the guns. "Mr. Risley, you have the con! Back and fill to keep alongside *Pensacola* . . . the big Yankee there! I'm going below for a moment!"

"Aye, sir!" Risley said. Bowater took the steps at a run, plunged down into the gloom of the gundeck. It was a dark place, even on a sunny day, but in the night, with the smoke of battle, it was like a place from another world. The row of lanterns amidships swayed with the slight rocking of the ironclad in the river and cast their pools of pale light over the scene. Men swarmed around the guns, toiling at their charges—they put Bowater in mind of Roman slaves condemned to the mines.

It was hot in the casement, certainly above one hundred degrees. Samuel felt the sweat stand out on his forehead and back, felt the running perspiration trace cool lines on his skin and sting his eyes. He blinked it away, wiped a shirtsleeve over his face.

The place was filled with smoke and noise, men shouting, guns running out, the wounded screaming. Minié balls pinged like hail against the armored sides, thudded in the deck when they managed to find an open gunport, twanged off the muzzles of the guns. Quillin appeared out of the gloom. "Sir, we have five down, three of them are dead."

"Did shot pierce our armor?"

One of the *Yazoo River*'s guns went off, then another, then the *Pensacola*'s broadside hit again. The casement shuddered and rang, the ironclad staggered under one hammer blow after another. The air was filled with the scream of metal, the sound of shrapnel slamming into the wooden sides.

Bowater could do nothing but stand, arms out, trying not to fall as the deck shuddered under him. There was Harper Rawson in front of him, pulling a swab from the muzzle of his gun, stepping back to give the loader room. He saw Bowater, gave him a half-smile, and then another shell hit the casement outside and Rawson's chest seemed to explode as if a grenade had gone off inside him. He lunged at Bowater, a surprised expression frozen on his face, as something hit Bowater's shoulder and sent him spinning to the deck.

"Sir! Sir!" Quillin was kneeling beside him.

"What the hell . . . ?"

"It's the bolts, sir! The bolts holding the iron plate! The impact of the enemy's shells sends the nuts flying!"

Dear God . . . The nut would have killed him if Rawson's body had not slowed it down. He struggled to sit up, with Quillin's help, put his hand down in a pool of Rawson's warm, slick blood. He struggled to his feet. The men were working like madmen in the gloom, apparently oblivious to the threat from their own vessel. They had their fighting blood up—Bowater recognized it—they would not be frightened by the proximity of death.

"Get some hands to clean this up! Try to keep the blood off the decks! Get the wounded out of the way!"

"Aye, sir!" The hammer blows fell against the *Yazoo River*'s side; the ship staggered under the impact. Iron screamed across the casement, slammed into the wooden framework, but Bowater's fighting blood was up too, and he took no notice as he climbed back up to the pilothouse.

Pensacola was nearly past them now, pushing upriver, working her way across the stream as if she had lost her bearings. "She's too fast, sir, I couldn't keep on her!" Risley shouted, and Bowater nodded. His shoulder hurt like hell but he did not think it was broken. He stared out the slot at the night and the smoke and fires.

Behind *Pensacola* came another of the big ships. A side-wheeler. *Mississippi*, Bowater had no doubt. Not too many like her in the navy anymore, her big paddle wheels so exposed and vulnerable. She was twenty years old, Commodore Perry's flagship when he opened Japan; now she was an anachronism in the age of the screw propeller and the ironclad.

"Here is *Mississippi*!" Bowater shouted, pointing to the bull of a ship charging upstream. "Right for her! We'll ram her if we can!"

"Aye, sir!" shouted Risley, with the first hint of hesitation. But ramming was their only hope. Their pathetic battery could do little against the frigate's thick sides.

Bowater looked at the telegraph. Risley had ordered slow astern to keep the *Yazoo River* where she was. He grabbed the handles, rang the engine room, shoved the indicator to full ahead. Ramming, like the ancient galleys, but with two condensing horizontal side-lever engines to take the place of the poor bastards chained to the benches, working the oars.

Bowater felt the speed build, felt the deck tremble, the *Mississippi* looming ahead. Her paddle wheels dug into the river and her broadside lashed out at the night, but her shot went high. Bowater fixed his eyes on the place abaft her paddle wheels where he would hit.

"Captain!" Risley shouted. "Look at that sumbitch!"

Bowater looked though the slot on the port side. A low hump in the water, the wake washing over her bow, the flash of gunfire glinting off her round, wet sides. The ironclad *Manassas* was steaming for the *Mississippi*, her throttles wide, smoke rolling from her stack.

"Come right! Come right!" Bowater shouted to the helmsman. They were on a collision course, *Yazoo River* and *Manassas*, would hit one another before either hit the Yankee.

The *Yazoo River* sheered off, her bow turning from her intended target, her chance to ram the side-wheeler gone. Bowater watched with some irritation as *Manassas* raced forward. The *Mississippi* was firing wildly, blasting away, like a man frantically slapping at bees, but her guns could not be depressed enough to hit either ironclad.

Hit them, hit them, hit them . . . Bowater thought as he watched the whale-shaped former tug charging the big side-wheeler. He could see it all, in shades of orange and black, the man-of-war pushing hard upstream, the half-submerged ram racing for her side.

And then the *Manassas* struck. The *Mississippi* rolled hard to starboard with the impact, her paddle wheel thrashing as it lifted out of the water. The current swept *Manassas* past; Bowater could see the gaping hole the ironclad had ripped in the big ship's side. The *Mississippi* rolled back on an even keel, a great bear baited by dogs, and as she did she fired her broadside, the flash of her eight-inch guns dancing off *Manassas*'s wet sides.

Bowater felt the deck jerk underfoot as a shell entered one of the *Yazoo River*'s gunports and exploded. The dark gundeck below the pilothouse was filled with brilliant light for just a fraction of a second, the already noisy place filled with the blast of exploding powder, the shriek of flying metal.

Jonathan Paine watched Theodore Wilson as Theodore Wilson watched the battle through the wheelhouse window. The *Abigail Wilson* was making turns for slow astern, holding her place in the river, half a mile upstream from Fort St. Philip.

Wilson said he wanted to think about his strategy. Wilson was afraid, Jonathan Paine knew it.

Wilson did not know that he had less than sixty seconds to either steam ahead or die. Less than sixty seconds to grab on to the bell rope for the engine room and ring up full speed ahead before Jonathan would pull his pistol—a .44 Adams and Deane he had retrieved from Paine Plantation—and shoot him in the head.

Twenty-three, twenty-four, twenty-five . . .

Wilson had been all bluff talk steaming downriver, but his bravado had begun to waver when the sounds of the gunfire mounted, the flash of the ordnance became visible over the low-lying marsh. Now he toyed with the bell rope, twisted it in his fingers, stared downstream.

Twenty-eight, twenty-nine, thirty . . .

It was a mesmerizing sight, the big ships moving through the clouds of smoke, half hidden, lit up orange with the flash of guns, the smaller Confederate vessels thrashing around in a disorganized attack. Jonathan understood the effect that such a scene could have. He recalled looking down the slope of Henry House Hill, watching the chaos of battle, wondering how he could ever plunge into it himself.

But he had done so, and the fear of it was gone, and though he understood Wilson's trepidation, he had little time for it. He did not doubt that his father was there, somewhere in that maelstrom. Nothing would prevent Jonathan's finding him. There was no time to waste. Less than thirty seconds, in fact.

Forty-one, forty-two, forty-three . . .

"The thing of it is, I'm not quite sure what we should do . . ." Wilson broke the uncomfortable silence. "I had hoped to get here in time to meet with the commanding officer, get orders from him. Now . . . ?"

"Time for orders is gone, I reckon," Jonathan said. He did not much care what Wilson decided to do. He figured he would have to shoot him at some point, and hold the pilot and helmsman at gunpoint, in order to use the *Abigail Wilson* to locate Robley Paine. "Looks to me like it's every man for himself, those boats getting in where they can hit the hardest."

Wilson nodded, considered the strategic situation.

Fifty-three, fifty-four, fifty-five . . .

"All right, damn it!" Wilson said with finality. "Let's go!" He rang the bell, three bells, full ahead. He grinned with the relief of having made a decision. Jonathan took his hand from the butt of the .44.

With turns ahead and the swift moving current, the *Abigail Wilson* surged forward, steaming from the anonymity of the dark river into the fire and the light. A quarter mile from that stretch of river where Forts St. Philip and Jackson covered the water with their withering crossfire, where the big Yankee ships were struggling through the smoke, blind, firing away, where the Confederates swarmed like feral dogs, biting, dodging, biting again.

Wilson stepped out of the wheelhouse and Jonathan followed behind. Down below on the foredeck, the men were gathered around the old six-pounder smoothbore.

My gun . . . Jonathan thought with some amusement. Wilson had been careful to tell him that, to ask permission to put it aboard the tug. As if Jonathan Paine could care about such a thing, as if he could ever wish to own, or even see, a cannon.

"Here we go, boys!" Wilson shouted to the gun crew, his voice a little too loud, a little too exuberant.

Bobby was standing back some from the bow, leaning on the rail, keeping out of the way, ready to jump in and help, the way he always was. The flash of gunfire lit his dark skin. Like the others, his face was turned to Wilson, but his eyes shifted, met Jonathan's. Jonathan gave him a little wave and Bobby gave a half-smile and waved back.

The men at the six-pounder cheered, waved their hats. Jonathan knew where they were at, in their heads, knew the blood lust and the apparent insanity that made men willing, even desire, to charge into such a fight. He did not feel it himself. Nor did he feel fear, or anger, or hatred of the Yankees, or much of anything at all, beyond a profound need to look into his father's living eyes, at least one more time.

Then they were there, like steaming into a hurricane, right in the middle of the gunfire. The shells screamed over their low deck and wheelhouse, the smoke embraced them so that everything beyond the *Abigail Wilson*'s bow became dull and indistinct. The fires and the muzzle flashes lit the smoke from within. The guns were deafening.

Dead ahead of them loomed one of the big Yankee ships, a ghost ship in the smoke, and the *Wilson*'s gun crew fired at its dull outline. The six-pounder sounded puny against the backdrop of serious artillery. There was no way to know if they had hit the Yankee, or if they did, whether their shot had done any damage.

A tug emerged from the smoke astern, passed close, the Confederate flag snapping at the ensign staff, a raft of some sort made off to the bow. One hundred feet beyond the *Wilson* and the raft burst into flames, lighting up the tug and the big Yankee for which she was steaming.

Fire raft! Jonathan thought. He had heard of such things. The idea went back to Sir Francis Drake, and further. He watched, fascinated. The tug looked for all the world as if she was on fire, with the mounting flames of the raft sweeping back toward her, and Jonathan figured if she was not, she soon would be.

The Yankee was turning, trying to avoid the threat, but the big ship could not outmaneuver the smaller tug. The flames on the raft cut through the smoke, illuminated the tug and her target.

The fire raft slammed into the Yankee, the impact making the flames leap high, catching the Yankee ship's rigging, sweeping along her painted sides. She was engulfed. Jonathan could not see how she could avoid burning to the waterline.

The tug backed off, leaving the raft against the Union ship's side, turned hard, making her escape. But the flames had not distracted the Yankee gunners. From the ship's side, ten guns opened up, point-blank range, ripping the tug to pieces. The wheelhouse and deckhouse were shattered, the boat slewed around as the helmsman was killed, the steering gear wrecked. She turned a half circle and began to settle fast, water pouring in through some unseen rent aft. She listed to starboard, her bow lifted from the river.

"Helmsman!" Wilson shouted. "Make for the tug there!" He was pointing at the sinking vessel. "We'll see if any of those poor bastards are still alive!"

The *Abigail Wilson* turned north, turned toward the blazing Yankee ship and the thundering fort beyond. The Confederate gunners in the forts had seen the Yankee man-of-war's distress, were concentrating their fire on her, while she was hitting back as hard as she could. Jonathan could see men swarming around the flames, heard the hiss of steam as hoses played on the fire. On her stern he could read the name *Hartford*.

They came up with the sinking tug. Wilson stepped over to the rail, oblivious of the shells whistling past, the occasional minié ball hitting the deck.

"No one alive there," Wilson said and turned his back on the sinking tug. Jonathan looked for himself. The vessel was a wreck, torn apart, sinking fast. There was no sign of life aboard, no one yelling for help. With one broadside the Yankee ship had reduced it to a complete wreck, as if a furious storm had been pounding the hull against a reef for two days.

"That son of a bitch is done for! Let's get downriver!" Wilson shouted. It was not clear to whom he was speaking or to whom he was referring, but the helmsman put the helm over to port and the tug turned, plunging into the fight, the men at the bow firing at anything too big to be a Confederate vessel.

Jonathan Paine could not have imagined a scene such as the one around him. The Battle of Manassas seemed a well-organized, leisurely affair compared to this. It was madness, the dark night lit up only by cannon fire and burning ships, the war elephants of the Yankee fleet pushing upriver. Confederate vessels everywhere, ripping around the water, looking for their chance, or listing from shots below the waterline, or in some cases fleeing upstream. There were Rebel boats surrounded on all sides, blasting away at every point on the compass, Union ships hounded by gunfire on every quarter.

Into that madness the *Abigail Wilson* steamed, engine full ahead, her bow gun barking out as fast as the men could load and fire. Bobby was hauling on one of the train tackles now; three men lay dead or wounded against the bulwark. Minié balls were splintering the wood, a shell took off part of the boat deck as it screamed past.

Jonathan looked up. A big side-wheeler was passing them, firing into the night as it went. Most of the shot was high—perhaps the gunners were concentrating on the forts, perhaps it was the accidental shell that had hit the *Abigail Wilson*. It would take only one well-placed accident to end them.

"There!" Wilson shouted, slapping Jonathan's arm, pointing.

Jonathan followed his arm. There was a boxy-looking ironclad, two hundred yards downstream, just visible through the smoke. She looked to be in some difficulty, did not look as if she was fully under control.

"What?"

"That's her! That's the *Yazoo River!* Your father's ship!"

Jonathan sucked in his breath. After all this long journey, the proximity to his father seemed unreal, and suddenly he was afraid. He looked again at the ironclad. Smoke was coming from her stack, and from the many holes in her stack, and from her gunports it seemed. Jonathan could see the smoke in the bright light that seemed to pour out of her, and stupidly he wondered why they had her lit so bright below, how many lanterns it would take to do that.

The *Abigail Wilson* closed with her, and the shock of coming up with his father's boat passed and with it the dull stupidity that had numbed Jonathan's mind. Of course they were not lighting up the interior of the boat with lanterns. The ironclad's gundeck was on fire.

46

A few moments after the attack commenced, and the enemy succeeded in passing with foreseen ships . . . the battle of New Orleans, as against ships of war, was over.

—Report of Major General Lovell, C.S. Army,
Commanding Defenses of New Orleans

obley Paine opened his eyes to brilliant light and heat, and he thought for one confused moment that he had fallen asleep in the summer sun, on the bank of the Yazoo River, at Paine Plantation.

That thought passed quick, washed away by a wave of pain in his leg, an ache that seemed to encompass his entire left side. He pushed himself off the hard surface on which he was lying, moved by instinct, compelled to get out of the way.

It came into focus—the gun deck of the *Yazoo River*. His ship. It was on fire.

He grabbed on to the wheel of one of the broadside guns, pulled himself to his feet as if climbing a steep cliff. He turned, leaned against the gun. He could no longer ignore the pain in his left side. He made himself look.

He was burned, all along his side, his frock coat and shirt, his trousers charred and in some places burned away, revealing ugly, cooked flesh, black and red and raw, through the holes. He sucked in his breath as the pain came again, worse, somehow, now that he had witnessed the damage.

He had been serving as gun captain, he recalled, of the second gun aft on the port side, in the place of a man who had been decapitated by a flying bit of metal. He remembered reaching down for a cartridge, and nothing else.

Robley turned his attention from his wounds to his ship. The whole forward bulkhead, the two guns pointing forward, and the forwardmost starboard broadside gun were all engulfed in flames. The fire seemed to fill the gundeck, blazing and spreading, lighting up that dark place with a brilliance it had never seen. The white paint was curling, bubbling, dripping from the sides. He could see the dark shapes of bodies, motionless, resting in their crematorium. The casement was filling with smoke and the smell of burning paint and the sweet sickish smell of cooking flesh.

Robley looked around for an officer, a petty officer, someone to take charge. He found Quillin on the starboard side—his head and his shoulders, one arm, and a part of his torso. Where the rest of him was he did not know.

Ruffin Tanner was bleeding from his forehead but keeping his gun crews at their work, seemingly oblivious to the fire. Babcock, the boatswain, came running aft, carrying a bucket, leading a line of men carrying buckets, and they flung the water and sand at the fire, a useless gesture, as far as Robley Paine could see.

Midshipman Worley came racing down the deck, stopped, began to back away.

"Mr. Worley! Mr. Worley!" Robley Paine pushed himself off the gun, limped across the deck, grabbed the young man's arm. Worley flinched, looked up at Paine, his eyes wide, his mouth hanging open.

"Worley, is the captain alive?" Paine shouted. The midshipman shook his head, but from the look of unreasoning panic in his eyes, Paine could not tell if the gesture meant the captain was dead or that Worley thought it incomprehensible that someone should ask such a thing at such a time.

"Is the captain alive, damn you?" Paine shouted again, shook the midshipman, who offered no resistance.

"We're played out . . . we must strike . . ." Worley managed at last.

"Strike? We'll not strike."

Worley seemed to come to his senses, or whatever senses were available to his terrified mind. He jerked his arm from Paine's grip. "We must strike!" he shouted.

Paine grabbed his arm again, leaned close. "Listen to me, Mr. Worley," he said, and spoke as gently as he could and still be heard. "We will fight, and we will die if we must, but we will not strike!"

Worley shook his head again, and Paine could see the boy thought him mad. He twisted free again, turned, and raced aft. Paine could see him in the light that the fire was throwing clear down the length of the deck. He could see him race past the pilothouse deck, even as Captain Bowater was coming down, could see him continue aft, and he had no doubt as to where the boy was headed.

"Damn!" he shouted, limped after him, each step a searing agony. Captain Bowater raced past him, heading forward, did not even notice him, but Paine did not care. Bowater had his job, he had another. He hobbled past the gun crews that worked their big guns as if at drill, oblivious to the flames, the shells pounding against the armor, the nuts whizzing across the casement, the dead and wounded mounting on the deck.

He came to the after end of the casement, where the flames at the forward end were making weird shadows on the overhead and the sides and the deck. The door that led to the fantail gaped open, and Robley Paine stepped through.

If he could have stepped from one planet to another, Paine doubted the change could have been more drastic than stepping through that casement door. The temperature was fifty degrees cooler in the night air. Instead of the tight, crowded deck, the muffled sounds of battle, the brilliant illumination of the burning casement, here it was dark, black, save for the blooms of orange that shone through the heavy smoke.

Here the noise of battle was not muffled by two feet of oak and iron. Here the sound of the gunfire was thunderous and sharp, the kind of sound that was once the exclusive purview of angry gods. This was not the tight, insular world of belowdecks. Here big ships loomed out of the smoke and the night, great broadsides blazing away. Here a dozen Confederate vessels flung themselves at the big ship, firing away, enduring the disproportionate battering.

Clear aft, his outline black against the distant gunfire of the forts and the Union fleet, Worley struggled with the flag halyard. Had he been less panicked, Paine knew, he would have had the flag down and overboard already, and then how could the *Yazoo River* honorably continue to fight, when to all appearances she had surrendered? This could not happen. Paine hobbled on, drew the Starr from his holster.

Worley managed to get the halyard off the cleat, began to pull the flag down, when Paine came up with him, raised the pistol to shoulder height. "Mr. Worley! Mr. Worley!" The midshipman turned, startled, frightened. "Mr. Worley, raise that flag again, or by God I will shoot you like a dog!"

They stood for a moment, facing one another, and then Worley shook his head and continued to haul the flag down. And Paine would have shot him, would have put a bullet through his head and felt not the least twinge, but in that instant when Worley turned and looked at him, with the terror in his eyes, Paine saw in that instant his youngest, Jonathan, four years old, terrified of the thunder in a summer storm, curled on his lap in the study, looking up at him, wide-eyed, yet trusting in the safety of his father's embrace.

Paine took his finger from the trigger, flipped the gun around, took a step toward Worley, and hit him with the butt of the gun, a solid blow, not a lethal blow. Worley went down fast. Paine holstered his gun, hauled the flag up the ensign staff again.

Ping, ping, ping, a sound like hail hitting the casement. Paine turned. He had been looking upriver and north at the Union ships steaming line ahead past them, but this new sound was from the south, and downriver. Paine crossed to the starboard side. Another column of ships was coming up, a line of ships, stately and impregnable. That was what Tanner's gunners were shooting at.

Ping, ping—they were minié balls, striking the iron plate. Then made little sparks like a train's wheels on the tracks as they ricocheted and Robley knew it was time to get back in the casement. He looked at the midshipman at his feet, wondered if the boy was safer inboard or out.

Thud, thud, thud, the bullets began to hit the deck, kicking up little furrows in the wood, and the question was answered. Paine bent over, grabbed Worley under the shoulders, screamed with agony as he tried to lift and drag the motionless young man.

Come on, come on, come on . . . Paine ran the words over and over in his head as he pulled, inch by inch. A bullet clipped Worley's foot and Worley rolled his head, moaned, but did not come to.

Paine lifted and pulled. He felt a bullet pluck at his frock coat, felt another graze his arm. He wondered if this was how it had been for his boys, at the end, the bullets teasing them, like a cat toying with a mouse.

And then a bullet hit, hit him right in the arm, right above the left elbow, shattering bone. He dropped Worley, howled in pain and in outrage. Another bullet seared across his belly, he could feel the line it tore in his flesh. He jerked the Starr out of his holster, leveled it at the ship ranging up alongside, two hundred feet away.

"You bastards!" he shouted, fired the Starr into the night. The minié balls pinged and thudded around him, tore at his clothing. The hammer of the Starr came down on an empty chamber.

What now?

A minié ball hit him in the shoulder, sent him reeling back.

Shove Worley against the bulwark and get inside!

He took a step forward, like walking into a hailstorm. Another bullet hit him in the leg. He crumpled to one knee. A bullet tore into his stomach and he fell over, rolled on his back, looked up at the dull blanket of smoke overhead.

This is it. . . . He had seen men enough with belly wounds in the Mexican War, knew it was over for him. If the Starr had had one round left he would have blown his brains out, but it did not, and Robley knew that God would not allow him so quick an end, not after all the suffering he had inflicted on others over the past year.

That was all right. He would take it, endure it manfully. It was a gift, really, a chance to repent what he had done, to beg the Lord's forgiveness, and in the end he would see his Katherine, his boys. . . .

The world seemed to explode around him, and at first he thought it was his wounds, but then he knew it was not. The Yankee ship was firing on them, firing its great guns, paying the *Yazoo River* back at last for whatever hurt Tanner had managed to inflict.

There was something else as well, some other sound, some other excitement. He turned his head. Another boat was coming alongside. Not a big ship, just a boat, like a tug or some such. Paine watched with a vague interest as it ranged up beside them, hit the *Yazoo River* with a thud that made the ironclad tremble. Someone came up over the side with a rope in his hand, and then another man and another. Yankees attacking? No, the Yankees did not seem willing to bother. Friends, then.

He closed his eyes against a wave of pain, listened to the sounds of men rushing around. He could barely hear, for the pounding of the blood in his head. He felt hands on him, on his face. He opened his eyes. Someone was kneeling over him, a dark shape, familiar somehow.

The big Yankee ship fired again, the light of the muzzle flash illuminating the face of the man looking down at him. Robley gasped, did not know what to think. Twenty years older, hurt, come from the grave, it was his son, Jonathan Paine. His son.

In the engine room: smoke, noise, heat, steam, an edge-of-disaster feel. Full ahead with both engines, fires carefully tended, maximum achievable steam pressure in both boilers. There was no chance the safety valves would blow. Hieronymus Taylor had tied them off, considered them a nuisance in such circumstances.

The boiler-room temperature was 132 degrees. One of the coal heavers had already passed out, had been dragged into the engine room, splashed with water, allowed to lie there. No time to manhandle him up onto the gundeck.

The glass water gauge on the starboard boiler shattered, spewing boiler water, water right on the edge of steam, all over another of the coal passers. He howled, plunged his arm in a bucket full of tepid water, but then manfully picked up his shovel again.

Burgess raced to the gauge, pulled on the chain that shut off the valves above and below it, whipped a screwdriver from his pocket. He danced around the piles of coal on the deck plates, twirling screws, as the coal passers fed the beast, the firemen pulled ashes from below the grate.

Chief Taylor stood by the reversing levers and throttles, looked around. Chaos, controlled insanity. The whole thing pushed as hard and as far as it could be pushed. Under the hiss of steam, the roar of the fires, the clank of pistons and rods and shafts, sounded the leitmotif of war, the hollow, jarring concussion of shells striking the casement above, guns going off, the uncertainty of what was happening beyond those superheated confines, the possibility of a shell coming through the side and through the boilers, scalding them all, killing them instantly, if they were lucky.

Taylor did not like the looks of the starboard feed-water pump, the "doctor." He did not like the way the mounting bolts were working in the starboard engine, did not like the color of the rapeseed oil he lifted off the crankshaft. He was not pleased with the sound emanating from the shaft bearings. Four stay bolts were leaking on the starboard boiler, six to port. There was a lot he did not like, a hundred things within his fiefdom that he feared might let go at any moment. But so far the gauge glass was the worst disaster they had endured.

He glanced up at the telegraph. It was pegged full ahead, had been for the past hour. But full ahead now was not what it had been an hour before. The stack was shot full of holes and not drawing well, the grates were clogging with clinker from the poor-quality coal—no time to clean them now. The fires were not as hot as they could be, steam pressure falling.

Taylor pulled a rag, wiped his forehead and eyes. How much longer until a major catastrophe? How long could they push this hard?

The gundeck hatch opened, and Taylor looked up. "Holy mother . . ." He could see flames leaping around the casement, could see the brilliant light of a full-on fire raging in the tween decks. *How long has that been burning? What the hell else is going on up there?*

Dick Merrow came scampering down the ladder. His face was blackened, holes charred in his clothing. "Chief, Chief, captain says we can't charge the fire hoses! Whole casement's going up!"

Taylor clamped on his cigar, and while Merrow danced around as if the floor plates were red-hot, waiting for an answer, Taylor traced in his mind the entire firefighting system, from auxiliary steam to the water pump to the intake, to the piping to the casement, to the hoses. "All right," he said at last, "tell the old man he'll have water as soon as humanly possible."

Merrow nodded, got some relief from the words, raced up the ladder.

Bang, bang, shells hit the casement above, made Taylor stagger. *Damn . . .* Whatever ship was hitting them now, it was much closer, or throwing heavier metal. The sound of the impact was deep and dull, a visceral sound. The *Yazoo River* staggered as if it had been hit with a fist, pushed sideways through the water. Taylor wondered if a shot toward the waterline would blow its way into the engine room, into the boiler room. Probably.

Fire pump . . . He pulled himself back to the immediate threat. Problem had to be with the fire pump, or the steam line going there. He cursed under his breath. The pump was in the most awkward of positions, aft, behind the port engine, right up against the after bulkhead. He thought of sending Burgess to crawl into that filthy, dark place and fix it, but he could not do it. Too lousy a job to delegate.

"Burgess!" Taylor shouted. Burgess looked up, held up a hand to signal he heard. "I'm going to see to the fire pump!" Taylor pointed aft. "Take over here!" Burgess nodded.

Taylor grabbed up some tools and a lantern. He worked his way around the engine, ducking under the piping, skirting the condenser. Shells slammed into the boat; Taylor staggered, put his hand against the cool, damp metal of the condenser, steadied himself. He inched on, following the steam line that led to the pump. Found the steam gauge—pressure enough to drive the thing. Reckoned the pounding of the shells had knocked something on the pump galley west.

He pushed aft, moving fast. The shells came faster, slamming into the ship, the dull, ugly sound frightening in the sweltering shadows of the engine room. He dropped to his knees, crawled along under the long shafts driving the paddle wheels, the creaking pillow blocks.

Got to damn well move . . . he thought, picturing the fire above, and then he was tossed aside as if he had taken a swift kick in the ribs, slammed into one of the pillow blocks.

The engine room filled with a flash of light; Taylor had a second's image of lightning and deep shadows on the engine and the bulkheads and sides of the engine room. Filling the room: the sound of gushing water, flying metal, the deep sound of an explosion, but muffled, like a bomb going off in a pile of sand. The furious hiss of steam, then dark again, and a hot, fine mist enveloped him, fell on his hands and face, just on the edge of painful.

A shell had hit a boiler. The starboard engine stopped, the noise in the engine room cut in half. Taylor closed his eyes, prayed that everyone had been killed in that instant. And as he prayed, the first horrible, insane shriek of agony rose up from the shadowy place forward of the engine, followed by another, and a third. Taylor clenched his teeth. The sound did not seem human, could not come from a human throat, save for a person in unimaginable agony, the flesh seared from his body.

"Die, damn it, will you die!" he cried out. There were three men shrieking—there was no way to tell which three—the screams in no way resembled human voices, or indeed anything earthly at all.

Taylor hesitated. Go back? Fix the fire pump? He crawled on, dragging his tools and his lantern. He found the fire pump, his hands moving on their own, reaching for tools, twisting, banging, wrenching.

The pump leaped to life—it took its steam from the port boiler—and even as Taylor heard the water sucking up through, pushed up the pipe to the hose above, he could not have told anyone what he had done to fix it. The screams of the dying men filled the engine room, pushed every other thing out of Taylor's head. He was sobbing loud, bawling like a baby, completely consumed by the sound of his men screaming their lives away. He was too aware of the twitching agony he felt in his head to know or care about the pump.

He left the tools, grabbed the lantern, crawled back the way he had come, banging his head, lacerating his hands and arms, oblivious.

Die, please, God, why don't y'all die? He wanted them to stop, he wanted their pain to stop. He crawled on. He did not want to see them.

He skirted around the condenser, stepped into the open space between the engine room and boiler room, blinked away the tears, held the lantern up. The exploding boiler had blasted the other lanterns away—his was the only light below. Its feeble flame glinted on the wet deck, the jagged edges of the shattered boiler, the twisted fire tubes and flues, the insane web of mangled piping.

Screaming, screaming, it was like a physical thing. Taylor could see one of them, off to the side, writhing on the deck, and from the place where the dying man had fallen, right by the reversing levers, he knew it had to be Burgess.

"Oh, God, oh, God, oh, God!!" Taylor sobbed, more frightened, more sick, more desperate than he thought a sane mind could endure. He ran over to his workbench, reached up to the shelf above, laid his hand on his sawed-off shotgun. It was wet with boiler water, the metal warm to the touch. He grabbed up a box of cartridges, a box of percussion caps, shoved them in his pocket.

The hatch overhead opened, a voice shouted, "What's happened here?"—the question hardly cutting through the screams of the scalded men. Taylor tried to put a percussion cap on the nipple of his shotgun. His hands shook and he dropped it, heard it ping on the deck plate, grabbed another. In six tries he managed to get two caps on, one for each barrel, and all the time the screaming, the horrible screaming, more awful than any pain Taylor had ever endured.

He picked up the lantern, crossed the engine room. The glow from the port boiler's firebox threw an orange light on the deck plates and the pile of coal. Taylor moved quick, stopped. Took a step forward. Made himself look down at the man in the pool of light on the deck, who had to be Burgess.

Every bit of exposed flesh had been scalded from Burgess's body, but he had been too far from the boiler to die instantly. Instead, the lantern revealed wet, bloody, pulped flesh, reds and pinks, the hideous form of a man with nothing recognizable as human save for his shape and the frantic, thrashing movements.

Taylor blinked hard, trying to see, and his sobs were nearly as loud now as the shrieking man at his feet. He lifted the shotgun, cocked the hammer.

"Please forgive me, oh, Lord God, please forgive me!" he wailed and pulled the trigger. The gun jolted his shoulder, filled the place with the sharp crack of the gunshot, a good, honest sound. Burgess jerked once, lay still. The screaming was cut by one third.

Taylor grabbed up the lantern, turned toward the boiler. Two bodies, lying still, killed mercifully in the blast. Taylor could not tell who they had been.

He moved around the port boiler, still intact. Two men were tossed up there, one of them, or what was left of him, a coal heaver named Collins they had picked up in Yazoo City. Flayed alive, and still alive; Taylor could see white teeth through the horror that was his face, the dark hole of his mouth as he screamed. Taylor lifted the gun, aimed, closed his eyes, squeezing the tears out, fired the gun.

The blast of the shotgun, then quiet. He swung the lantern around, around to where the third screaming voice had been. One of the men sent by Mallory, Travis something. His pants were shredded, the skin nearly gone, nothing of his leg but half-boiled muscle and skin draping off. He looked at Taylor, his eyes wild, a trapped animal look.

"Don't kill me, Chief! Please, God, don't kill me!"

Taylor looked at the boy. He lowered his gun. "I won't kill you, boy. Gonna hurt like a son of a bitch, getting you outta here, but I won't kill you."

"Chief Taylor! Captain wants to know what's goin on!" The voice from the hatch. Taylor turned, saw Ruffin Tanner drop from the ladder to the deck plates, saw his eyes move around the shattered engine room.

"Lost the starboard boiler, whole black gang's dead, but me and him." Taylor jerked a thumb at Travis. "We need some hands to get that poor bastard out of here."

Tanner nodded. "Fire hose is working, they're getting the fire down some. You need more hands down here?"

Taylor looked around. One boiler, one engine. "How much longer you think we gonna keep up this fight?"

"Not long. We ain't long for it now."

Taylor nodded. "No. You don't want to send any of them poor bastards down here."

Tanner nodded, stuck out his hand. Taylor took it, shook. Tanner disappeared up the ladder.

Taylor looked around. The firebox on the one remaining boiler was gaping open, the fire glowing red. Red meant too cold; it should be white-hot. He grabbed up a shovel, dug it into the pile of coal on the deck plate, heaved it into the boiler.

Coal passer. Twenty-five years ago he had begun his engineering career as a coal passer, the first lesson in years of education, formal and otherwise. Runaway from affluence, lured by a passion for machinery that his parents could not understand. Changed his clothes, changed his accent, been playing the peckerwood so long he did not know how to play any other part.

He dug up another shovelful, tossed it in, spread it around, watched with satisfaction as the fire began to change color. Twenty-five years, coal passer to chief and back to coal passer, and now it would end like this. All right, then. He would die like a man, with a coal shovel in his hand. That would do. He did not want to live anyway, not with the things he had in his head now.

They were really getting pounded this time. One of the big Yankees alongside, Bowater did not know which. *Brooklyn*, perhaps. It did not matter. She was moving slow upriver, giving back double what the *Yazoo River* could deal out.

The fire was raging in the forward end of the casement, Babcock leading his pathetic bucket brigade against it, the fire hose lying limp and useless on the deck. The ironclad shuddered with the impact of shells against her sloped sides, shuddered with the recoil of her own guns as Tanner kept his men at it, despite the fire and the carnage around them.

And there was carnage. Like nothing Bowater had ever seen or imagined. He once thought, having fought in Mexico, that he knew what war was. That memory embarrassed him now. He had had no notion. At Elizabeth City he had had a taste. Now he was having the main course, more bitter than he could have imagined.

Black smoke and the stink of burning paint and burning men roiled out of the blaze, the light from the fire revealed it all; the half-bodies, the sprays of blood, the odd limbs. Men lying as if asleep, save for the fact that their heads were gone. Bowater could not count the dead, the bodies were not intact enough for that, nor could he tell how many were being consumed by the flames. His officers were gone. He had seen what was left of Quillin. He had not seen the second officer or Worley for some time.

He looked at the hose. If the water did not start running soon, they would have to abandon ship. He was not sure how they would do that. Run her aground, he supposed.

Another shell struck, not the casement this time, but low, under his feet, somewhere aft. He turned, and as he did he felt the entire ship shudder, shudder in her guts, heard a muffled blast, and a whoosh and gasp, like the last breath of some giant beast. The hatch to the engine room lifted on its hinges, a great rush of gray steam blowing up in a hot wet blast from below.

Boiler . . . Bowater closed his eyes. A shell had hit a boiler. He could not imagine what horror it had done below. He could not imagine that anyone in the engine room had lived through that.

He heard the note of the engine change, the sound running through the casement drop off as one of the engines faltered and died. He had to get back to the pilothouse, could no longer remain below, directing the firefighting, but all his officers were gone.

"Babcock! Take over here! Do your best—I don't think we'll get fire hoses now. Tanner! Drop down to the engine room, see what's happening, report to me in the pilothouse!"

He had turned to head for the pilothouse when he saw the fire hose jerk and twist, like some animal one had thought dead suddenly springing to life. Water spurted, hissed, then streamed from the end, and Babcock snatched it up, charged the fire like a knight with a lance.

Incredible . . . Bowater thought. *But too late* . . .

He climbed back to the pilothouse. "Starboard engine's gone, Captain," Risley said. "Rudder's hard over, just keeping her going straight."

"Very well." Bowater looked out the slot. The ship that had punished them so greatly was pulling ahead, steaming upriver, past them, and in her wake, another ship, of around the same size and class. USS *Richmond*, Bowater thought, wondered if they had changed her name.

One by one, leisurely, *Richmond*'s broadside opened up, with the precision of a salute, the shells screaming by, clanging on the armor. Smoke and steam from the fire down below rolled into the pilothouse, obscuring everything, setting Bowater and Risley and the helmsman to coughing, gagging. But still the *Yazoo River* fired back, one shot to the enemy's three.

The smoke drifted away, Bowater had a clear view again. The night was on fire, the wild reflections of red and orange, the flames through the smoke, the noise. Noise such as he had never heard. He felt his head swim, felt an unreality come over him. If only it would stop, even for a minute, give him time to think, to organize. If only the noise would stop.

And then, from *Richmond*, amidships, another gun fired, bigger than the others, a deep roar, a giant waking up, angry.

Eighty-pound Dahlgren rifle . . . was all Bowater had a chance to think. *Richmond* carried one, on slides. Eighty-pound Dahlgren rifle.

The shell hit aft, made the *Yazoo River* slew around, exploded with a noise that stunned Bowater. He was thrown forward with the impact, slammed against the side of the pilothouse, bounced back, flailing for a handhold but finding nothing. He fell, down, down, saw the stairs coming up, reached out a hand to stop himself, and then he was tumbling to the deck below, and then, at last, it was quiet.

47

April 27, 1862—New Orleans gone—and with it the Confederacy. Are we not cut in two? The Mississippi ruins us if lost.

—Mary Boykin Chesnut

*B*owater crawled out of the blackness, was dragged out of the blackness, a voice pulling him up by the weight of its authority. Bowater realized, as he kicked toward the surface, that the voice was Hieronymus Taylor's.

His eyes fluttered open. Taylor was bending over him, the light of a fire flickering off his stained, soaked shirt, his unshaved face, his plastered hair.

"Come on, Cap'n, wake up now!" Taylor was saying. A command. Bowater kept his eyes open.

He sat up on an elbow. His head was pounding. He looked around. The fire in the casement was not the blaze it had been, but it was not extinguished either. "How long have I . . ."

"Not above five minutes." It was Tanner who spoke now. Bowater saw him standing behind Taylor.

Why are they here? Bowater shook his head, to clear it, to indicate he did not understand.

"Last shell took out the starboard paddle wheel. We dead in the water, Cap'n," Taylor said.

Bowater struggled to his feet and Taylor helped him and together they climbed up the few steps to the pilothouse. The port side of the pilot-house roof was bent up and back, like a tin can wrenched open. Risley was lying on the deck, wide-eyed and dead. The helmsman was gone, Bowater did not know where. They did not need a helmsman anymore.

He looked to starboard, where the roof had once obscured his view. The round hump of the iron-encased wheelbox was ruined. Where it had stood in its elegant arc there was now a gaping hole with shards of iron and wood jutting out at every angle, the wrecked bits of the paddle wheel, buckets and arms and shaft, tucked inside what was left of the box.

They were adrift, sweeping downriver on the current. Yankee gunboats were passing them by, but the *Yazoo River* was not firing at them, and they were not wasting powder on an obviously dead ship.

Bowater looked aft. The fight was upriver of them now. He could see the smoke, like a fog bank seen from a distance, the glow of fire rafts, gun-fire, the blazing defiance of the forts, and the Union fleet steamed past, as if all the preparations the Confederacy had mounted to defend their great-est seaport were no more than an annoyance, a show with lights and smoke.

He watched for a moment, two, looked at the battle the way he would look at a grand canvas depicting some long-ago sea fight, the Battle of the Saints, or Trafalgar or some such. Because that was what the Battle of New Orleans was to him now. History. He was no longer a part of it, any more than he was a part of the fight against Napoleon's tyranny.

He turned to Taylor. "No engines?"

Taylor shook his head. "Concussion shattered the main steam pipe, port side. No steam, no fire pump."

Bowater nodded. They could not maneuver, they could not fight the fire in the casement. Half the crew were dead or wounded. It was over. The *Yazoo River* was a shooting star which had arced across the dark river in a blaze of violence, burned out on her way to earth.

So how do we get off of her? Bowater wondered. *No power . . .*

And yet he was hearing a steam engine, and not so very far off. He turned and tried to look down the port side, but his view was obscured by the twisted metal of the pilothouse roof. He put his hands on the top of the casement, hoisted himself up so he could look around the edge of the wreckage. To his surprise he saw a tug, very like the *Abigail Wilson*, tied alongside, all the way aft. A voice, sounding very like Theodore Wilson, called, "Ahoy, the *Yazoo River!* Do you need to abandon ship?"

On Bowater's orders they searched the casement, located the wounded, made certain the dead men were truly dead. The *Yazoo River* would serve as a funeral pyre for them, they would go down to their graves with the Confederate flag flying proud on the ensign staff.

Back on the fantail, Bowater was the last to step out of the sweltering, smoke-filled, burning casement. The air was cool and sweet in contrast, the sounds sharper. Someone was holding a lantern, the light falling on the miserable remnants of his command.

On the starboard side, Robley Paine lay on the deck, held in a man's arms. Bowater stepped over, knelt beside him.

"Robley? Robley?" Paine's head lolled over. Blood was running out of his mouth, a thin, dark line down his chin. He smiled a weak smile.

"Captain Bowater . . ." he said.

"We're going to get you off," Bowater said, but Paine shook his head and the man holding him said, "He's bleeding bad. . . ." He choked the words out, was on the edge of sobbing, and the emotion surprised Bowater. He had not believed anyone cared so much for mad Robley Paine. And then he realized he did not know this man.

He looked up sharp, into the face of a young man, but not so young. The face of a veteran, young eyes grown quickly old. He saw a patched army shell jacket, a battered kepi. Bowater squinted.

"I'm Jonathan Paine. I'm his son."

Behind Jonathan Paine, a young black man was squatting, looking down at the old man as well. The situation was so odd, requiring so many questions, Bowater did not bother. He turned back to Paine.

Robley lifted a long, blackened hand, the fingers like the thin branches of a winter tree, and Bowater took it, gentle. "I am the lucky one, Captain . . ." he said, his voice so low Bowater had to lean down to hear over the distant artillery fire. "I have got everything I wanted, and merciful God has brought one of my boys back. Despite all my sins, he has brought my boy back. . . ." He coughed, but he was too weak to cough with authority. "I am the lucky one. I can rest now. But you, Captain, you must fight on and on. . . ."

Bowater gave his hand a little squeeze. "Godspeed, Robley Paine," he whispered. He eased the man's hand to the deck, stood, gave him his last minutes alone with his son.

One by one the men clambered over the tug's low bulwark and spread out along the deck, helping their shipmates over. They moved fast, every man aboard aware of the fire creeping toward the powder magazine. As far as Bowater could tell there was no more than half of the original crew left, perhaps less. He looked for Babcock but did not see him. The old man would go down with the ship.

When the fantail was cleared of healthy men, they began to pass the wounded over, some able to help themselves a bit, some who seemed near death, who no doubt would be dead soon.

Last of all they passed Robley Paine over to the tug, and when he was over the young black man followed, and then Jonathan. Bowater noticed how very much he looked like his father. He limped as well, as had Robley, and needed a hand getting across to the tug.

And then it was Samuel Bowater, Hieronymus Taylor, Ruffin Tanner.

"Guess I don't get my headstone," Taylor said.

"Battle ain't over yet," Tanner said.

"War is not over yet," Bowater said. Together they grabbed on to the tug's bulwark, hoisted themselves over, as the men crowding the side deck made room for them. Fore and aft the lines binding them to the *Yazoo River* were let go. The *Abigail Wilson* turned hard, peeling away from the ironclad, her propeller digging in.

Bowater climbed up into the wheelhouse. Theodore Wilson was there, grim-faced. He seemed to have none of the boy-playing-at-soldiers quality Bowater had associated with him.

"Captain Bowater," Wilson said.

"Captain Wilson," Bowater said without irony.

"Don't rightly know where to go. Can't go upriver, unless we care to be blown out of the water."

"Battle's over. No sense in killing these men. You've done what you could." They were silent for a moment as the tug continued her aimless course downriver. "Have to imagine there's still a blockade at the Head of the Passes. I don't imagine we'll make it to sea," Bowater continued.

Theodore Wilson nodded, and then the wheelhouse was lit up with the brilliant orange light of the *Yazoo River* exploding, followed by the deep rolling boom of the blast, as thunder follows lightning, and the concussion of the shock wave, the sudden heat that engulfed them.

Wilson, Bowater, the pilot, all the men in the wheelhouse spun around, looked upriver, beyond the tug's starboard quarter. A great column of flame was rising up from the ironclad, like Moses's pillar of fire shining forth in the night. The sound kept coming and coming. The great mountain of flame seemed like a solid thing as it hung there in the air.

The *Abigail Wilson* began to pitch and roll, and debris began to rain down around her, splashing in the water, on occasion hitting the deck or the boat deck, flaming bits that were stamped out by the crowds of men on board.

The column of flame collapsed, fell back down onto the shattered remains of the *Yazoo River* and burned there, a blazing patch of fire on the otherwise dark river. The funeral pyre of those brave men, the end of a ship for which so many had struggled, died, and still would die. Those men, that ship, they had fought their lives out, and now it was up to history to decide where in the whole story that struggle fitted.

Bowater watched the dying ship. He guessed that the casement had contained the blast, had funneled the shock wave straight up. That must have been the case, because, incredibly, in the light of the burning vessel, he could see the Confederate flag, still run up the ensign staff, still intact, still waving in the land breeze filling in with the coming dawn.

They steamed downriver to a mile or so above Pilot Town, but with the coming light they could see the Federal ships getting up steam, could see the Stars and Stripes waving over the town, so they turned and steamed upriver again. They tied up at a half-forgotten landing fifteen miles south of Fort Jackson. They buried their dead.

Bowater suggested they burn the *Abigail Wilson*, but Wilson hesitated, demurred, found reasons why that was not the best plan. In the end they left her tied up, hoofed it down the dirt road from the landing to the road running north. They carried the wounded on stretchers improvised from material aboard the tug. They found transportation among the growing convoy of wagons fleeing the coming bluebellies.

In New Orleans they were swept up in the general exodus, the panicked retreat from the city. The wounded were brought to hospital. Half of the remaining men melted away. But Bowater had saved enough money from his cabin, and Wilson had funds enough, and enough gold was found in Robley Paine's coat pocket, to secure transportation for the rest of them. Samuel Bowater led his men north to Yazoo City. He had no other place to go.

And so it was, on a grim 1st of May, 1862, that Samuel Bowater and Hieronymus Taylor and Ruffin Tanner found themselves seated on an old oak log, staring out over the remains of what had once been their shipyard, out at the slow-moving Yazoo River. Telegrams had been dispatched to Mallory, reports, lists of dead, wounded, missing. They waited on orders.

Taylor sparked a cigar to life. Tanner took a long pull from a bottle of whiskey, which he then handed to Taylor, who drank and then handed it to Bowater. Bowater drank, returned to his thoughts of Wendy, handed the bottle back to Tanner.

New Orleans was lost. The Confederate Army had been beaten at Pittsburg Landing, and the Yankees were pushing downriver, closing the gap between the head and tail of the snake. The Eastern Seaboard and the Gulf were blockaded. McClellan was on the Yorktown Peninsula with more than 120,000 men and marching for Richmond. Soon the Gosport naval yard would have to be abandoned. Banks was chasing Jackson in the

Shenandoah Valley with crushing superiority in numbers. McDowell threatened Fredericksburg and Richmond.

The elation that had followed Manassas was gone. In one year the swaggering confidence of the men who had fired on Fort Sumter had been changed to something else. Acceptance of war, a long war. Resignation. Despondency, in some cases.

But not defeat. Never defeat. The fire of resistance burned on, and it was not close to burning itself out.

The bottle came around again. Bowater took a pull, handed it back to Tanner. "Know what Robley Paine said to me? There when we were abandoning the ship?"

The others murmured no.

"He said he was the lucky one. Said he was getting what he wanted. The rest of us, we would have to keep fighting, fight on and on."

The three men were silent.

"That's what he said," said Samuel.

Taylor took the bottle. Lifted it high. "Here's to Robley Paine." He took a drink, handed it to Bowater.

Bowater lifted the bottle. "Here's to getting what you want." He drank, passed it back to Tanner.

Ruffin Tanner lifted the bottle, looked at the reflection of the abandoned shipyard in the glass and dark liquid. "Here's to fighting," he said. "Here's to fighting, on and on."

Wendy Atkins brushed the tears away, gulped a deep breath. Happiness, relief, sadness, loneliness were all mixed together. She sat on the edge of her iron bed, read the letter again.

Postmarked Yazoo City. May 1st. A brief sketch of the Battle of New Orleans, assurance that he, Samuel Bowater, was safe, had come through with just the usual bruises and scrapes. But they had lost, the Union fleet had brushed them aside. They would make a stand elsewhere, Samuel said. Once he received orders.

She felt the tears come again, and now they were all sadness, now that his survival was assured, and the relief that came with that passed into memory. She cried because she read the profound sadness in the words. She cried because the loneliness was palpable and because she knew about loneliness, could take it herself, but could not endure the thought of Samuel, her Samuel, having to suffer so.

Wendy Atkins knew about loneliness. She had known about it all her life. But when Samuel Bowater left for Mississippi, she learned that there was a whole other level of which she had not been aware, like discovering a room in a house which you had not suspected was there.

She put the letter down, took a deep breath. Looked around the little carriage house, now crammed with a year's accumulations. She looked down at the bed and remembered their night together.

Wendy stood and knelt by the bed, ran her hands underneath. At last they fell on what she was looking for and she pulled it out; an oversize carpet bag, empty now. She set it on the bed, opened it, considered what to pack.

It was just growing light when Jonathan Paine rose, sat up in the bed he had occupied since the time he had been taken from the family cradle, deemed old enough for a real bed. He looked around the familiar room. It was all gray-and-blue shadows in the weak light, but he did not need any light at all to know what was there. He was like an old man, visiting the scene of his youth, the shadowy remains of a life he had once had.

He swung his one leg over the edge of the bed. He fastened his prosthetic leg in place, pulled his pants on and his shirt. He did not wear his uniform anymore, the only clothes he had known for more than a year. He did not have to. All of his things were there, just as he had left them. His clothes fit loose now, but they fit.

All his things were there. Only his family was gone.

Jonathan stood, limped across the room and down the stairs. He could hear Jenny moving about in the kitchen. Bobby would be rising soon. He would want to help, but Jonathan did not want his help this time. Later, perhaps, but now it was his task alone.

He stepped quietly out the front door, climbed down the steps. The morning light was spreading, the scraps of fog hanging low over the river and twisting around the clumps of trees on the bank. Jonathan walked around the house, up the slight hill to the family plot. He stood for a long moment, looking at the place where his mother was buried, the fresh-turned earth beside it that marked his father's grave.

Robley had died before the *Abigail Wilson* tied up. Jonathan had seen the body carried back with him. His father had been born and raised on Paine Plantation, had known all his greatest joys on that patch of land. When his body rotted away and mixed again with the soil, it had to be that soil, it could be no other.

At last Jonathan tore his eyes from the twin headstones, walked back down the hill. In the shed he found a big felling ax. He swung it over his shoulder, headed back to the house.

Jonathan hobbled past the porch, up to the old oak, the earthly remains of his beloved tree. He looked it up and down, the horrible thing his father had created there. But not his father, not really. The gargoyle had been cut by a man driven mad by grief, and that man may well have looked like Robley Paine, but it was not him.

Jonathan hefted his ax, let it rest on his shoulder as he adjusted his grip, then brought it back and swung it at the base of the tree. He felt the good, sharp steel bite into the ancient wood. He wiggled it free, brought the ax back, and chopped again, and this time a chip flew.

It would not be easy. It would take a long time. He was alone now, with only Bobby to help him. His family was gone and the Negroes had mostly all run to the Yankees. But still he knew he would not stop until he had cut down this terrible thing that had once been the Paines' precious tree, this nightmare the war had made. Rip the stump out, roots and all.

And then he would plant a new oak. It would not be the same—it could never be the same—but it too would grow tall and strong. He would raise it up from the ground, this new and beautiful and good thing.

Historical Note

How much I owe of the pleasure of my life to these much reviled writers of fiction.

—Mary Boykin Chesnut, February 25, 1861

Glory in the Name is fiction, of course. There never was a Samuel Bowater or Hieronymus Taylor, the ships that they sailed did not exist. The men, however, and their ships are based on real men and vessels of the period. Further, the situations in which they are involved, the battles, the trials, of the Confederate Navy, are all real, and portrayed as accurately as I was able, basing my depictions on copious primary source evidence. Other than Bowater and company, the people and events are described as they were.

Here, then, are a few comments on the action covered in this book.

In early 1861, months before the firing on Fort Sumter, which is generally considered the beginning of the Civil War, the Confederate government began its military organization. Initially, already existing militia units were formed into Southern regiments, their numbers swelled by the thousands of men who rushed to join.

For the Confederate Navy, things were not so simple. Officially established on February 20, 1861, the navy had no ships and little means of obtaining them. Sailors were scarce, since the Southern states had never possessed much of a merchant marine. The only thing that the Confederate Navy had enough of was officers, and that was only because they had so few ships that needed them.

The Confederacy had enough officers, but they did not have a glut of them. Officers of the United States Navy showed a greater reluctance to resign and support their home states than did their brother officers in the United States Army. In the spring of 1861 there were 1,385 active-duty officers in the navy, including the midshipmen at the Naval Academy. Of those, only 375 chose to join the Confederacy, and a third of those were Academy midshipmen. Only twelve of seventy-eight captains joined the South. Clearly there was, as Mary Boykin Chesnut put it, "an awful pull in their divided hearts."

Perhaps the foremost example of that divided heart was Franklin Buchanan, who had entered the navy as a midshipman during the War of 1812. Thinking his home state of Maryland would secede, Buchanan tendered his resignation. Then when Maryland stayed in the Union, "Old Buck" tried to take his resignation back. But it was too late in the eyes of Navy Secretary Gideon Welles.

Buchanan's predicament illustrates the kind of uncertainty that was rampant in the early months of 1861. With five states seceded from the Union within months of his taking office, Abraham Lincoln wanted very much not to make things any worse than they were. That was the thinking behind the administration's handling of the threat to Gosport Naval Shipyard in Portsmouth, which turned into a debacle for the Union.

In April, Virginia, the most influential of the Southern states, was still teetering on the brink of secession. Lincoln and his cabinet were afraid that any little offense might tip the state into the Confederate camp. So, despite clear threats to the naval yard, Lincoln and Gideon Welles did nothing to defend the place, since that, they felt, would be seen as an act of aggression against Virginia. Nor did they send the ships off to the safety of Fortress Monroe or Washington.

To make matters worse, the yard was commanded by the old and uncertain Charles McCauley, and many of the officers under him were Southern men whose real objective was to see the valuable navy yard in Southern hands. The growing tension both inside and outside the yard and the threat of state militia massing in Norfolk finally reached the boiling point on April 20, 1861. Swept by panic, the Union officers decided to scuttle and burn the ships and flee from the shipyard, burning it in their wake. Even this was poorly done. A wealth of ordnance was left intact, and the fires did not do nearly the damage intended. The sailing vessel *Cumberland*, all but obsolete in the age of steam propulsion, was towed to safety, while the *Merrimack* was burned and sunk. A year later, the *Merrimack*, reborn as the Confederate ironclad *Virginia* (and commanded by Franklin Buchanan), would batter the *Cumberland* to death, killing nearly half her crew.

It would be some months after fighting began before the United States Navy could organize itself enough to bring its power to bear. But when the first hammer blow fell, it fell on Hatteras Island in North Carolina.

Hatteras Island is one of the barrier islands that line the southern coasts of the United States like a castle wall. Behind Hatteras Island lies Pamlico Sound, which connects to the north with Albemarle Sound. Apart from being an ideal spot for privateers to lurk and dash out at Union ships rounding Cape Hatteras, the sounds connect to five major rivers which run into the heart of North Carolina and southern Virginia. Strategically, it was a valuable spot, and it was here that the United States Navy chose to bring its overwhelming force to bear for the first time.

Forts Clark and Hatteras were no marvels of construction, and they were weakly defended. In fact, the Confederate government never made any great effort to defend the valuable sounds, perhaps because they recognized from the onset that it would be impossible in light of Federal naval superiority, which it certainly was.

On August 27, 1861, a little more than a month after the First Battle of Bull Run, the United States Navy arrived off Hatteras Inlet. Steaming in an oval pattern, they poured their fire into the forts, while the forts' guns could not even fire far enough to hit back.

In his report to Secretary Mallory, written while he was a prisoner aboard the flagship *Minnesota*, Samuel Barron wrote:

> [T]hey [the Union ships], after some practice, got the exact range of the IX, X, and XI-inch guns, and did not find it necessary to alter their positions, whilst not a shot from our battery reached them with the greatest elevation we could get.

With the situation hopeless, Barron ordered the white flag run up.

It was not until February of the following year that the Union forces followed up their victory at Cape Hatteras with the obvious move on Roanoke Island, which would close off Albemarle Sound and threaten Norfolk from the south. When they did come, they once more came in overwhelming strength, and brushed aside the three thousand Confederate troops and the small mosquito fleet that the Confederate government allocated for defense of the island and sound.

The naval battle at Elizabeth City, a fleet action fought by two fleets of small gunboats, was one of the only such naval fights in the Civil War. Indicative of the changing nature of warfare at sea, it is also one of the few instances of hand-to-hand fighting during naval combat in that war.

In the Gulf of Mexico, Confederates and Federals played at the same game, with the Union navy attempting to further its stranglehold on Southern ports, and the Confederacy resisting with all means available, which, in the largely agricultural South, was not much. Many of the ambitious ironclad projects begun by the Confederate Navy ended up as bonfires on the ways before the ships were ever in the water. Delays were epidemic, with so few facilities in the South able to manufacture the many elements that went into an ironclad vessel.

One ship that did become operational, the first ironclad ever built in the United States, was the *Manassas,* built as a privateer and commandeered for naval service. In the end she proved to be more of a psychological threat than a physical one, and though she did deliver a few good hits, and stove in some planks, she was never able to sink a Union vessel. Nonetheless, she was enough to frighten Captain John Pope into abandoning the Head of the Passes, in one of the most shameful of all Civil War naval episodes, known today as Pope's Run.

Despite that one victory, the small fleet of gunboats and even the two big forts south of New Orleans were not enough to stop Farragut's heavy ships from fighting their way past. Had the ironclad *Louisiana* been operational, she might have tipped the balance in the South's favor, but like so many of the Confederacy's naval efforts, she was hampered by design and manufacturing problems. In the end she was no more than a floating battery, and not a terribly effectual one at that.

Like the fledgling United States Navy during the Revolution, facing the might of the Royal Navy, the Confederate Navy had an impossible task from the onset. Eighty years after the Revolution, the problem was exacerbated by technological advances that made it more difficult to compete with the industrialized North. Benedict Arnold could build a fleet of ships in the woods of New York and take on the British on Lake Champlain, but by the mid-nineteenth century, naval warfare was too sophisticated for that sort of thing. The brave men of the Confederate Navy stood up to the Union juggernaut with whatever they had that would float and mount a gun, but in the end they could do no more than delay the inevitable.

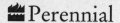 Perennial

Books by James L. Nelson:

GLORY IN THE NAME: *A Novel of the Confederate Navy*
ISBN 0-06-019969-5 (new in hardcover from William Morrow)

At the outbreak of the Civil War, the Confederate Navy consisted of only a meager collection of ships and a handful of men. One of those men is Samuel Bowater. Struggling with the pressures of a first command in a naval service just a few months old, Bowater and the men of Cape Fear place themselves between the Confederate shores and the massive Union Navy.

"A triumph of imagination and good, taut writing." —Bernard Cornwell

THE GUARDSHIP: *Book One of the Brethren of the Coast*
ISBN 0-380-80452-2 (paperback)

With the bounty from his years as a pirate—a life he intends to renounce and keep forever secret—Thomas Marlowe has begun a new life in Virginia and has won the command of *Plymouth Prize*, the colony's decrepit guardship. But now a threat from his illicit past looms on the horizon, and Marlowe must choose between losing all or facing the one man he fears.

"A master both of his period and of the English language." —Patrick O'Brian

THE BLACKBIRDER: *Book Two of the Brethren of the Coast*
ISBN 0-06-000779-6 (paperback)

King James, a former slave and Thomas Marlowe's comrade-in-arms, took over a renegade slave ship, killing the crew in a moment of rage. Forced to bring him to justice, Marlowe sets out in pursuit of the African-turned-pirate. But Marlowe is not James' only threat, as factions aboard the ship vie for control and betrayal stalks him to the shores of Africa. There, in the slave port of Whydah, they will have a final showdown.

"First-rate popular action writing." —*Publishers Weekly*

THE PIRATE ROUND: *Book Three of the Brethren of the Coast*
ISBN 0-06-053926-7 (paperback)

American seafarers have found a new source of wealth: through the Indian Ocean and carrying fabulous treasure to the great Mogul of India. Thomas Marlowe is determined to find a way to the riches of the East and secretly plans to hunt the Mogul's ships. But Marlowe does not know he is sailing into a triangle of hatred and vengeance— a rendezvous with two bitter enemies from his past.

"A rousing swashbuckler." —*Publishers Weekly*

Want to receive notice of author events and new books by James L. Nelson?
Sign up for James L. Nelson's AuthorTracker at www.AuthorTracker.com

---

Available wherever books are sold, or call 1-800-331-3761 to order.